THEIRS IS A HERITAGE BORN OF CENTURIES OF SPLENDOR AND STRIFE, CONQUERORS AND CHAOS . . .

Dolores "Dee" Guadalupe Sorenson—She escaped life in a barrio to become a Los Angeles Superior Court judge. But five hundred years of Mexican history will be harder to shake off, as will the enigmatic man laying claim to her heart.

Beatriz "Bitsy" Martinez—An innocent abroad, Bitsy will soon discover a Mexico few Americans ever see . . . as a prisoner in the steaming jungles of the Yucatán.

Chayo Sedano—She is Mexico's most beloved actress. But behind the glamour and the sultry charm lies a woman descended from a king, a woman who is ruthlessly plotting to change the course of history.

Carlos Gonzalez—Philosopher, poet, priest . . . and Chayo Sedano's chauffeur. Exactly who is this handsome Mexican, and why can't Dee get him out of her mind?

Emperor Maximilian—Only the love of his beautiful native mistress would sustain this reluctant ruler. For his was a reign dogged by treachery and violence, burdened by a queen's insanity, and destined for tragic failure.

Gonzalo Guerrero—Who began it all. A Spanish seaman in the fifteenth century, he survived shipwreck and torture to become a Mayan king. His legacy of blood and treasure traveled down the ages—to explode in modern Mexico.

MAXIMILIAN'S
GARDEN

Nina Vida

BANTAM BOOKS
NEW YORK · TORONTO · LONDON · SYDNEY · AUCKLAND

MAXIMILLIAN'S GARDEN

A Bantam Book / June 1990

ALL RIGHTS RESERVED.

Book design by Terry Karydes

Map designed by GDS/Jeffrey L. Ward

ISBN 0-553-28536-X

Published simultaneously in the United States and Canada

Bantam Books are published by Bantam Books, a division of
Bantam Doubleday Dell Publishing Group, Inc. Its trademark,
consisting of the words "Bantam Books" and the portrayal
of a rooster, is Registered in U.S. Patent and Trademark Office
and in other countries. Marca Registrada. Bantam Books,
666 Fifth Avenue, New York, New York 10103.

PRINTED IN THE UNITED STATES OF AMERICA

KRI   0 9 8 7 6 5 4 3 2 1

To my husband, always at my side

Then felt I like some watcher of the skies
　　When a new planet swims into his ken;
Or like stout Cortez when with eagle eyes
　　He star'd at the Pacific—and all his men
Look'd at each other with a wild surmise—
　　Silent, upon a peak in Darien.

John Keats
"On First Looking into
Chapman's Homer"

CONTENTS

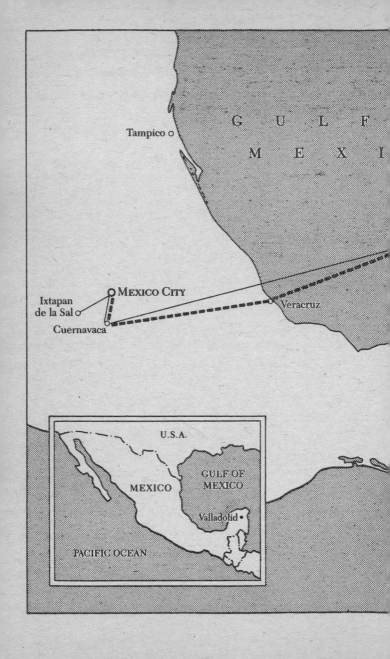

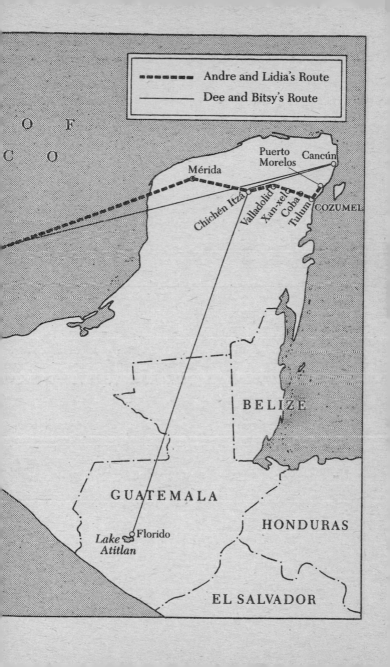

PART I

Dolores

Guadalupe

Sorenson

1

The air in the courtroom was oppressive, sticky with trapped cologne, motionless despite the fan that had been brought in to stir the stale air.

"Are you placing these in evidence, Mr. Blewett?" asked Dee, as District Attorney Blewett handed her the photographs.

"Yes, Your Honor."

"Has Mr. Fineman seen them?" She turned the pictures at various angles trying to make sense out of the body parts.

"Yes, he has, Your Honor."

When the defendant wasn't talking to his attorney, he stared at Dee, watching, she imagined, for the flinch when she looked at pictures of the dead girls or listened to the gruesome testimony of the witnesses.

"Are these two bodies or only one?" she asked.

"Two, Your Honor," Blewett said. "A leg is missing. We found it in a dumpster behind Von's Market on Pico, and if Your Honor needs to see the other picture—"

"That's all right."

"I object to counsel's characterization of the evidence, Your Honor," Leonard Fineman, the defense attorney, said hotly.

Dee turned to the court reporter. "Would you please read the last portion of the record, Miss Holmgren, the part that Mr. Fineman objected to. I seem to have lost my train of thought."

The reporter looked up helplessly. "That was John's portion, Your Honor. He just took it out to dictate. I'm sorry."

"That's all right. I should pay closer attention when you two change places. The court will call a recess for ten minutes."

She tucked the wide sleeves of the judge's robe up inside the gown, then bent over the washbasin and splashed cold water on her cheeks. When she looked up into the mirror, her face, normally the color of coffee and cream, was flushed, as though she had a fever.

The People of the State of California v. *Farley Carrington III*. An unlikely name for an unlikely murderer. Carrington was an investment banker. He owned two Rolls Royces, a house in Trousdale Estates, one in Rancho Mirage. He flew his own Beechcraft Bonanza. His mother was a member of the DAR. He came to court in neat suits, with his thinning brown hair combed flat down on his head. He smiled a lot and looked intelligent. He also picked up prostitutes on Sunset Boulevard, had sex with them, and then left their hacked-to-pieces bodies strewn along the center divider of the Hollywood Freeway.

It was a fine case with which to start her criminal court career. Everyone said so. You can make a name with a case like this, they said.

It had looked like it was going to be a straight trial at first. Pretty clear-cut evidence that Carrington murdered the girls. The purchase of a chain saw in his name. Bits of hair, fragments of bone. Dee had thought she would get it over with fast, but then his attorney had made the insanity plea.

"The defendant pleads not guilty by reason of insanity, Your Honor," Fineman had said. "The defendant also requests that the sanity phase of the trial be heard by Your Honor sitting without a jury."

That had been four months ago. Four months of Fineman trying to convince her that his well-dressed, well-bred client was a lunatic. Four months of Blewett shoving pictures of the dead girls in her face.

Everyone had been right. She was making a name for herself. At least twice a week there was a story in the LA *Times*. Her picture was usually in there, and also some quotes. And then the article about her came out at the beginning of the week.

She could almost hear the assignment editor of the View section of the *Times* saying, "The judge's name is Dolores

Guadalupe Sorenson. Send a woman over to interview her. Oh, the judge is a Chicana, so send Ortega. She'll know all the right questions to ask."

Her desk was piled with exhibits, deposition transcripts, orders to show cause, motions, briefs. She sat down and cleared a space, then poured herself a cup of coffee from the carafe on the credenza behind her desk. When Sidney Schwartz, her court clerk, came in and dumped a box of daily transcript on the floor at her feet, she was leaning back against her chair with her eyes closed.

"Almost time. You feeling all right?"

"Fine." She sat up and shuffled a few papers around while Sid perched on the edge of her desk and pulled *The Racing Form* out of his back pocket. He was in his fifties, a diminutive, rumpled man who favored floral ties and golf sweaters. He had been Dee's clerk since she was appointed to the superior court bench. In the three years they had spent together in Domestic Relations, he had hardly spoken to her. She had supposed his coolness might have stemmed from the fact that she had been appointed to the bench straight out of the district attorney's office, or because she was young, or Hispanic, or a woman, or all four. But when Judge Pelletier had assigned her to the criminal division at the beginning of the year, Sid had asked to come along. Now their relationship was easy and relaxed. They never spoke about why it had changed.

"I think I have a fever," she said.

He glanced up from the paper. "You're not the only one. Everyone's getting their fill of blood and gore today."

"Four months of this case is a strain."

"If it's any consolation, Fineman just told me he's very impressed by your stamina, said he didn't think you had the balls to hear a case like this."

"That's very kind of him."

There was a soft knock at the door, and Sid said, "Should I let 'em in?"

"Why not? We've got time."

"It's hot as hell in there," said Larry Blewett, as he came in and dropped down into a corner of the leather couch. Leonard Fineman, the defense attorney, followed him in and stood near her desk, patting his forehead with a folded handkerchief.

"Sid's already checked with the building engineer," Dee

said. "As long as you're both here, why don't we talk about some housekeeping matters. Sid and the court reporters are complaining that the exhibits aren't properly tagged, and all those boxes of exhibits stacked all along the walls—some of them are duplicates. Perhaps you could each take charge of your own exhibits, weeding out redundancies, identifying them properly. We don't know what's in what box. Besides, it's a fire hazard."

"I'll take care of mine," said Fineman.

"I'll take care of mine after rebuttal," said Blewett.

"Rebuttal?" said Dee. "Are we that close?"

"I have very little more to put on," said Fineman. "I may have surrebuttal when Larry gets through."

"I'll need time to go over the psychiatric reports again," said Dee. "Larry, how much longer for you?"

Blewett shrugged. "A few days. I'm winding up."

"And for final arguments?"

"Figure me for a day and a half," said Fineman.

"The same," Blewett said.

"I think that covers what we needed to talk about, then, gentlemen," Dee said, "unless there's something I haven't—"

"My client's as crazy as a loon, Your Honor," Fineman said.

"He's as sane as I am," Blewett retorted.

Leonard Fineman lifted one eyebrow. "That sane, huh?"

Dee stood up. "Well, I don't want to talk about any of this. You know I can't—it's not the time to—" She put her hand to her head. "Let's take a long lunch. I have to get some fresh air. I've got a terrific headache."

"It's the grossness of the case, Your Honor," Blewett said. "I've got a headache, too."

2

Dee often walked from the courthouse to Olvera Street for lunch. It was a nice walk if you weren't in too much of a hurry. When there wasn't time she would drive over and either have lunch on the patio of La Golondrina or buy some *churros* from the Mexican bakery and stroll the street, eating the sweet rolls and watching the people. Olvera Street was the oldest street in the city. Mexicans had ambled over its dusty stones in the early 1800s when Los Angeles was a sleepy town called Pueblo del Río Nuestra Señora la Reina de Los Ángeles de Porciuncula. LA for short. Olvera Street was the closest Dee had come to Mexico or anything Mexican since her mother died.

The street was ever-changing. In the summer when the tourists jammed the restaurants and bought pottery birds by the thousands, the vendors were jovial as they folded and smoothed the dollar bills. In the winter, when the rains swept and shined the smooth stones of the street and the tourists were afraid of getting wet, the vendors sat bundled in heavy sweaters, and, staring silently and hungry-eyed from within their open kiosks, waited patiently for spring. It was close to Thanksgiving now, and there was movement on the street, a hint of fortunes rising. Brightly colored piñatas hung from poles and rafters and the vendors smiled once again from behind trays laden with freshly rearranged trinkets.

Twelve o'clock, Bitsy had said, but then she was always late.

"There'll be two of us," Dee told the hostess when she stepped beneath the awning of the restaurant's patio. A Japanese tourist was sitting on a donkey near the fountain, a tasseled sombrero on his head, smiling as the photographer snapped his picture. Dee's mother once brought her here to have her picture taken sitting on a donkey.

"That's how I met your father," her mother told her. "I worked for a sidewalk photographer in Tijuana. He also took pictures of people on a donkey. I was supposed to smile and wink at the American sailors who came down from San Diego to have a good time. Sometimes I would sit on the donkey myself to show them how much fun it was. I would giggle a lot until they almost begged to put on that silly hat and hang their long legs over the skinny ribs of that flea-bitten animal. For another fifty cents I would hop up in front of them and let them hug me around the waist. I was very good. Then your father came and had his picure taken. He was a blond sailor from Wyoming. I didn't know where Wyoming was."

When Bitsy's chubby figure came into view, Dee waved, but her sister didn't look up. She was munching on a taco, holding it away from her as the grease dripped down onto the cobblestones. Her brown slacks, one size too small, stretched across her hips and clung like plastic wrap to her legs. A white batiste overblouse floated loosely around her waist. A scuffed leather purse hung on one arm. Her face was carefully made up, lavender eyeliner accenting the blue of her eyes, bright red lipstick contrasting with her pale skin. Although she was twenty-eight, she wore her blond hair straight and thick to her shoulders like a teenager. "I'm gorgeous sitting down" was her favorite phrase. She didn't resemble Dee at all. She didn't have the broad forehead or arching black eyebrows. Her mouth was not as generous and she lacked the bony shelf atop her cheeks and luminous dark eyes that gave Dee's face its Mexican cast.

Bitsy took one more chomp out of the taco, tossed the remainder into a garbage can, then walked quickly toward the restaurant.

"You've spoiled your lunch," Dee said as she hugged her sister.

Bitsy turned her face away. "You can smell the cilantro on my breath."

"There was a smoking gun. I saw the taco."

"I was starving," Bitsy said, fishing in her purse for a tissue. "I dieted all day yesterday and half of the day before."

"Don't explain. It's none of my business."

"Of course it's your business. If you want to know anything about me, just ask."

Dee grinned at her affectionately. "You goof."

The hostess sat them in a corner of the patio where mariachi music streamed down from an upstairs banquet room. Bitsy snapped her fingers in time to the music. "I love the holidays," she said. "I love the shopping, the wrapping, the cooking—"

"What happened to your eye?" Dee turned her sister's face toward her.

"Nothing."

Dee took a deep breath. "That maniac's going to kill you."

"It was an accident. I was eating an ice cream cone. Leon goes, 'I thought you were on a diet.' So he tries to knock the ice cream cone out of my hand, misses, and gets me in the eye."

"You know you're scaring me, don't you?"

"Oh, Dee."

"If it were my husband—"

"He's not." Bitsy opened her purse and pulled out a folded newspaper clipping. "Have you seen this?"

"Don't change the subject."

"I'm not. You should have taken your glasses off. It would have made a better picture."

Dee took the clipping out of her sister's hand, glanced at the photograph of her in her judge's robes, a pen in her hand, her reading glasses hiding her large, dark eyes. "I left my glasses on and took my earrings off. I wanted to look serious, not so young. As it is, the reporter spends half the story talking about Hispanics in the judiciary and the other half on how I decorated my chambers. She asked me if I ever wore anything besides sensible pumps and brown suits."

"Well, I think it's a good article. I like it."

"You like everything."

"I suppose." Bitsy refolded the article and placed it carefully in her purse. "Want to come to Mexico with me?" she asked, popping a handful of nachos into her mouth.

"What are you talking about?"

"There's a place called Rancho Mirada in Ixtapan de la Sal

where they guarantee to take fifteen pounds off you in four weeks. I've got to do it. I'm bursting out of all my clothes."

"Leon's paying?"

"Only 'cause it's cheap." Bitsy picked up the menu. "Just as I thought. No cottage cheese." She looked pleased when Dee laughed. "Well, what do you think about coming with me to Mexico when the trial's over?"

"Sounds wonderful, but I can't. I'm hearing the Valley rapist case next."

"Really? The one where that guy—"

"That's the one."

When the waitress came for their order, Bitsy ordered enchiladas and beans with a side of guacamole.

"The broiled chicken looks good to me," Dee said.

"You obviously aren't aware that murderers and rapists prefer skinny women," Bitsy said. "Did I tell you about the Chinese acupuncturist who almost cured me of my craving for food?"

Dee grinned. "No. Tell me."

The two sisters were like skaters gliding smoothly over concentric grooves laid down in the ice long ago. First Dee would play big sister and fuss over Leon's cruelty, and then Bitsy, all sunshine and denial, would charm her sister with stories.

After the story about the Chinese acupuncturist, and one about a neighbor who trained her cat to use the toilet, lunch was over.

"I'll walk you back," Bitsy said.

In front of the courthouse they stood together for a few moments. "Give me a kiss," Bitsy said. "You look a lot better than you did an hour ago. You really looked frazzled. So what about Christmas?"

"What about it?"

"Come with us to San Antonio. Leon's sister's going to have the family, and they're going to do the whole Mexican thing."

"Sounds nice, but I'd rather not. 'The whole Mexican thing' doesn't appeal to me."

"But you'll be alone."

"So what else is new?"

3

Dee poured herself another cup of coffee and drank it standing at the sink staring out the window at the dark canyon. Her house, which sat atop a bluff in Bel Air, had survived a brush fire in 1978 when nine homes had burned down around it. The following winter, when torrential rains coursed down the denuded hillsides and earth turned to Bel Air lava, relentlessly moving muddy ooze, her house had held fast. The house two doors down the hill had been completely buried in mud, the television antenna the only thing visible, the muffled sounds of a soap opera the only thing heard.

"You ought to sell the place and move down to the flatlands," her ex-husband, Stan, had said when he moved out. "I don't know why you want to battle it anymore. The damned patio and swimming pool are going to slide down into the Greater Los Angeles Basin one of these days."

"I think better up here," she had replied.

Dee's first-grade teacher had a house like this, on a hill in City Terrace, not too far from the barrio.

"How did you escape the barrio?" Vickie Ortega had asked her when she interviewed her for the article. "Off the record. I won't put it in if you don't want me to."

"You can use anything you like," Dee said. "A teacher named Selma Boyd took an interest in me in grammar school. She'd take me home with her after school and let me help correct papers. She's the one who blasted the world open for me. I'd never even seen Anglos up close before. Selma and her husband and children ate their meals together, all sitting down at the same time, at a table, with napkins and knives and forks. There were no open cans, no tortillas, no empty pop bottles on the sink, no framed pictures of Jesus on the walls. They listened to opera broadcasts on the radio and read the newspaper. There were books around, fresh milk in the refrigerator, crisp cookies on the counter. I'm not saying that Mexicans don't live like that. I'm saying that in *my* house we never lived like that. Then when I was seventeen, I won a National Merit Scholarship—two thousand dollars, not much, but Selma helped some, mostly with encouragement. And then there were grants and loans—I even waitressed at Fat Burger. Do you want me to go on?"

"Not unless it's interesting or special in some way."

"It wasn't—that is, it wasn't to anyone but me. I met my husband my senior year at Berkeley. He was going to law school—Boalt Hall. I thought I was going to teach math in a high school somewhere, but he changed my mind. We got married in my second year at Boalt."

"What about sisters or brothers?"

"One sister. Beatriz. We call her Bitsy."

"Did she go to college, too?"

"Bits? No. My mother died when I was at Berkeley. Bitsy was only twelve. When I petitioned for guardianship, the judge said I was too young. He placed her with a foster family. She kept running away. The father was abusing her."

"Sexually?"

"Sexually. She got married at seventeen. I tried to stop her, but there was nothing I could do about it."

Miss Ortega didn't use any of it in her article.

Dee turned away from the sink, pulled her bathrobe tighter around her, and carried the coffee cup back to the bedroom. She put it on the bedside table and climbed into bed. The entire history of the trial lay in piles on the floor. Psychiatric reports in one pile, twelve thousand pages of daily transcript in another, photographs in still another. The photographs were horrifying. Dee had thought when the trial began that she would never get used to the shock of seeing them, but she had.

"Blunt affect," she said aloud as she turned the pages of Dr. Gershon's testimony. "I can certainly understand that."

MR. BLEWETT: WHAT ARE THE CRITERIA FOR JUDGING A
PERSON INSANE?
DR. GERSHON: FIRST THERE IS CONTINUOUS DISCOMFORT,
SUCH AS ANXIETY OR DEPRESSION. SECOND, THERE IS BI-
ZARRE BEHAVIOR, SUCH AS DELUSIONS OR HALLUCINATIONS.
THIRD THERE IS INEFFICIENCY, INABILITY TO PERFORM
ADEQUATELY IN LIFE.

Maybe she'd make an appointment with Dr. Gershon when
the trial was over and ask him about Stan. Not exactly change
psychiatrists; she'd already spent two years with Dr. Levy.
Just test out a man's viewpoint. Linda was too easy on her,
too agreeable, too ready to shoot Stan down at every turn.

"So Dr. Gershon, what about my ex-husband?" she'd ask
him. "He wears tennis shoes, cotton ducks, cuts his hair with
a manicure scissors, and has long since given up trying to
conform to other people's perceptions of him. He was Law
Review at Boalt, so passionate in his convictions that he met
with General Ngai in North Vietnam to try to stop the war.
He gave up a senior partnership in a Century City law firm
and now plays tennis for a living, if you can call it that, and
hasn't joined a protest group or read a newspaper in two
years. He may not even know who the president of the
United States is. Could you tell me, or would you mind
giving me an opinion—it won't change anything, you understand, since the divorce is final, and I'm getting used to living
alone—but, for the record, and so maybe I'll get something
useful out of the ten years we spent together—who fucked
up? Him or me?"

She put the piles of photographs and documents and transcripts on the floor beside the bed and turned out the light.
She slept fitfully, moving from position to position in the bed.

"Insanity!" she shouted, and then sat up in the darkness,
her heart pounding. A warm leg was pressed against hers.
She felt along the covers for the rest of the body.

"Jesus Christ, Stan! I could have shot you."

"You don't have a gun."

"Your behavior is so abnormal, so psychotic—" She fell
back against the pillows. "Where were you, anyway, this
morning? I called around ten."

"I had a game. Why'd you call?"

"Bill Blakiston wants to talk to you about doing some work
for him."

"I told you not to head-hunt for me, Dee. I don't want a job, I don't need a job, and Blakiston's an asshole." He put his arms around her, and she could feel the soft hairs against her nylon gown. "I'm sorry I scared you."

"I was having a nightmare."

"I saw the pictures. No wonder."

They had been divorced a year and a half now, but still the lovemaking persisted.

"It isn't exactly passionless," Dee had told her psychiatrist, "it's more mechanical than anything else. Bitsy says it's weird that I let him come over, and I'm beginning to think so, too, but he *was* my husband. We don't hate each other. He's a nice guy sometimes."

"People get used to one another," Linda had said. "It's like trying to stop a car. You can't jam on the brakes all at once."

He pulled her crosswise in the bed, then draped one leg over hers and made quick, thrusting movements until she cried out in pleasure. Then he rested a moment, his legs rigid against hers, before he began again.

His skin, the texture of his hair, the smell of his body, even the heat he generated, were familiar to her. The positions they took when they made love were as commonplace as the pattern in the quilt at the foot of her bed. Small stitches here, loopy ones there, a broad, swiping slide of blank material there.

"God!" he shouted as the shudder rippled through him.

They lay sprawled on the bed, now both separate again, his audible breathing not synchronizing with hers.

"Got anything in the fridge?" he asked. He rolled over to the edge of the bed and hung his arms down toward the carpet.

"I haven't been to the store."

He edged back up onto the bed and turned on the lamp. She squinted at him in the sudden brightness. His body was tanned and the worry lines that had once etched his thirty-four-year-old face were gone. His hair, which he had always kept so neatly trimmed, now curled at his neck and temples. Even the asthma that had plagued him all his life had disappeared. How could she argue with him about the way he lived when it so obviously agreed with him?

He got out of bed and began putting on his clothes.

"Linda says we're marking time together," she said, "trying to postpone the inevitable."

"Oh, yeah?" He glared at her. "Linda doesn't know shit."
He knelt down and looked under the bed.

"What are you looking for?" she asked.

"My shoes."

"Try the bathroom."

She lay in bed, eyes open, listening to him as he slammed
doors and drawers.

"Your shoes wouldn't be in my bureau drawers," she said.

He came toward the bed and stood over her. "Life's too
short, Dee. Marriage was predictable, boring. I told you that
before."

"I know."

"I bored myself silly. My ideas bored me, my life bored
me." He slammed the shoe that he had in his hand down on
the bed. "You bored me!"

"I didn't bore you a minute ago."

"That's different."

"I don't think you'd better come over like this anymore."

There was silence from the side of the bed.

"Do you mean it?" he finally said.

"I mean it."

4

The courtroom was filled to capacity and people were standing in the back. Every few seconds the door opened and hands shoved a camera through the opening. Before the flash went off an armed deputy grabbed the cameraman and pushed him and his camera out the door again.

"All rise," said Sid, as Dee came out of chambers and took her place on the bench. The noise of a courtroom full of people rising and standing and waiting and sitting down again sounded like sandpapering and hand clapping and air being let out of tires all at once.

"Mr. Carrington, would you please stand," Dee said in a firm voice.

The defendant, immaculately dressed, impeccably groomed, thin hair glistening in the courtroom lights, stared up at her dispassionately. His hands, resting nonchalantly against the edge of the counsel table in front of him, were almost feminine, with oval nails that had been buffed and then polished with clear lacquer.

"I've reviewed the trial testimony in the case of *The People versus Farley Carrington the third*," she said, pronouncing her words slowly and carefully. "It's been a complex trial that's taxed the energies of everyone concerned. I'd like to compliment counsel, who've done a fine job of organizing evidence and presenting exhibits. I realize that it's been a monumental undertaking. I haven't envied you your job. I'd like to particularly thank Mr. Fineman and his staff for their presentation of the defendant's case. I'm sure that much of the psychiatric testimony will stand as a model for similar cases in the future."

She scanned her notes, then took off her glasses and looked at the defendant.

"Mr. Carrington, I have not come lightly to the judgment I am about to pronounce, but after weighing all the evidence and reading all the cases, it is my opinion that you were not insane at the time you committed the murders in this case."

Reporters ran for the doors.

"Order!" She banged the gavel on the desk. She saw the defendant's lips moving, but couldn't hear what he was saying.

"Order!" She waited for the commotion to subside. She envied the photographers whose faces were flattened against the glass windows of the courtroom doors. They were out there and she was in here with Mr. Carrington's noiseless, moving lips.

"I won't go to jail." She heard it that time.

"You'll have an opportunity to talk in a moment, Mr. Carrington," she said, feeling her pulse leap. "As to the penalty phase of the trial, we'll set a date on which to—"

"And I'm going to kill you, too," he said offhandedly. Then he smiled at her.

"Bailiff, would you remove Mr. Carrington from the courtroom." She cleared her throat. "We'll continue discussion of the penalty phase without him."

Carrington turned and waved agreeably to a few people in the third row. Then he whispered to his attorney while the guards put the handcuffs back on him. The last Dee saw of him he was being led through the holding area on the way back to his cell.

Dee dropped the bag of groceries onto the kitchen counter and then walked back into the living room and stared again at the peach-colored expanse of wall above the sofa. "You're next, you Mexican cunt" was written in big, thick, red letters.

She went back into the kitchen and put the milk and eggs in the refrigerator. She shook her head. It was a prank, some kids in the neighborhood. Or she was tired and just imagined it. The writing would be gone when she went back into the living room. She peered into the refrigerator. So many cartons of milk. Who do I think I'm buying milk for? I have no children, no husband to drink it. All the articles I've read lately say adults don't need milk. Twenty percent of adults are allergic to milk.

She went into the living room again and stared at the writing over the sofa. "Mexican cunt." She stepped closer to the wall and touched the letters, then pulled her hand away and studied the shiny redness on her fingertips. Lipstick. Probably one of her own from the bathroom vanity.

She picked up the telephone and dialed Sid's number at home. It was Saturday, golf day. The phone rang four times before he picked it up.

"Dee? Where you been? Carrington's loose. Swapped name tags in County with another guy."

"He was here. He wrote me a note on the wall."

"Oh, Christ. Get out of there. He might still be in the house."

"Uh-uh. He's not."

When she hung up the phone, she sat down on a chair facing the wall. She was mesmerized by the words, entranced by them. All the years at Berkeley, all that she had accomplished, and she couldn't even convince a mass murderer that she was anything more than a Mexican cunt. She was still staring at the wall when the police arrived.

Policemen roamed through the house, lifting up sofa pillows and peering under chairs and whisking bits of dust into envelopes. Sid had arrived with Judge Pelletier, the calendar judge in criminal. Someone had even called Stan off the tennis courts at El Rancho.

"Would you please turn on the heat, Stan," Dee asked. "I'm freezing." She sat scrunched into the pillows in a corner of the sofa, a coat thrown over her shoulders.

"It's seventy degrees in here. It's just nerves."

"I'm not nervous. I'm cold."

He walked toward the thermostat near the kitchen door, then bent and picked something up. "Here's the lipstick."

Dee glanced at it. "It could be mine."

One of the policemen took the flattened tube from Stan's hand and slipped it into a small manila envelope.

"He's very clever," she said. "Not only does he want to terrorize me, he wants to demoralize me as well."

"She means the 'Mexican cunt' part, Judge," Stan said.

"Please don't explain me, Stan. I'm perfectly capable of making myself understood."

"We're all concerned with your welfare," Judge Pelletier said. "I looked over your calendar this morning. Everything can be put over to the beginning of the year. Why not take a vacation till this thing's resolved. Visit relatives, go skiing—"

The telephone rang. One of the policemen picked it up, said a few words into it, and handed the receiver to Dee.

Bitsy's voice, trembly with concern, floated through the wires.

"No, really, I'm fine, Bits," Dee said. "Can you hold on a minute?" She turned toward Judge Pelletier. "Ixtapan de la Sal. It's a health spa near Mexico City. Is that far enough away?"

The judge nodded. "I'd say so. By the time you get home, we'll have him back in custody."

5

"Get up, sleepyhead, you're missing all the fun of this place." Bitsy pulled at the drapes of the bungalow, and sunshine streamed into the room.

"My God, what are you doing?" asked Dee, opening one eye and using the sheet as a shield against the sun.

Bitsy plumped herself down at the foot of the bed. "While you've been sleeping, I've hiked, yogaed, ate, I had something called an 'Egg Surprise.' The surprise is there's no egg in it. Not even the whites. Someone said cornstarch and water. It tasted like glue."

"Why are you so happy so early in the morning?"

Bitsy tugged at the sheet. "Dancercize starts in ten minutes." She sucked in her stomach. Tight black leotards smoothed out her fleshy hips. "What do you think? Have I lost weight?"

"It's too soon." Dee's eyes were half-shut as she walked into the bathroom and closed the door.

"Everyone's wondering what you're doing holed up in the room," said Bitsy over the sound of running water.

Dee came out of the bathroom, rubbing her face briskly with a towel. "What do you tell them?"

"That you came down to rest and read. What if they catch Carrington before I hit my target weight?"

"If they found him tomorrow, I wouldn't hear about it for a month with the way the phones work here. Did you get ahold of Leon?"

"Yes, and I wish I hadn't tried so hard. He just continued where he left off at the airport, telling me what to eat, what to buy his nieces and nephews for Christmas, when to call him next."

"Why doesn't he write it all down and mail it to you?"

Bitsy followed Dee back into the bathroom and watched while she combed her hair. "There's a celebrity here."

"Who?"

"Chayo Sedano."

Dee stared at her image in the mirror for a few seconds, the comb poised in midair. "The actress?"

"One and the same. Played Dolores del Río's daughter in *Mexican Spitfire*, starred as the doomed mistress in *My Mexican Lover*—"

"Sang and danced in *My Heart Is Mexican*. Right after Stan and I got divorced, I started going to the Saturday matinees at the Real just to pass time. I saw them all. *Mexican Ranchero*, *Song of Mexico*—there's another one, the girl's an orphan—"

"God, yes, I remember that one. Oh, what was the name—" Dee snapped her fingers. "With José Comacho—"

"No, that was—"

"*Sins of Our Father*."

"That's it!"

"Her early movies were pretty bad," Bitsy said.

"Embarrassing," Dee said. "Still, there was something about her personality that kept you from laughing. Sincerity, maybe. The best one was the one she made for that Mexican director—"

"Ramón Mendoza. She was married to him then. After they started making soap operas together, they got divorced. Some people said it was because she hated playing the part of Angelina, the mother, and wanted the daughter's role. But the truth is that Chayo never really loved him. She never got over the death of her lover in 1968."

Dee smiled. "How do you know all this stuff?"

"Fan magazines. Chayo's pretty big in the Mexican soaps." Bitsy walked to the window and looked out at the rolling green hills and stands of laurel trees. The weather had been tropical since they arrived, even though it was the beginning of December.

"Remember when Mama took us to the Real, and we'd bring a sack of tamales to eat while we watched the movie?" Bitsy asked wistfully.

"And mothers pushed their babies up and down the aisles in their strollers to keep them quiet," Dee replied. She was beside Bitsy now, her arm around her shoulder.

Out on the grass below the window, several Mexican women walked toward the exercise pavilion. Their bodies were smaller and rounder than the bodies of Anglo women. Gold bracelets jangled on their wrists and the sounds of Spanish trailed after them.

"This isn't Mexico," said Bitsy.

"Those movies weren't either. They were corny, sappy, drippy fantasies."

"I loved them."

"So did I."

6

"Up, down, now-two-feet, up, down, now-two-feet." The tile-roofed exercise pavilion, a padded terrazzo square in the middle of the lawn, was crammed elbow to elbow with women bouncing and gyrating to the cha-cha music on the stereo cassette.

"*Cinco minutos*," called out the dance instructor as the tape ended.

"It feels wonderful when you stop," exclaimed Bitsy, collapsing backward on the exercise mat.

"Look, it's Chayo Sedano," said Dee as a slender woman in purple leotards strolled into the pavilion.

Bitsy stood up to get a better look. "She has freckles. And I think she's had breast implants. Her hair's blonder than on television. She looks too gorgeous to be thirty-nine."

The instructor was standing on the table that held the coffee and diet sodas. "*Muchachas*, if you will stop shouting, Chayo will lead us in a little exercise."

"To begin is always difficult," Chayo said when the commotion had quieted down. "In *Mexican Spitfire* I danced every day for ten hours, but I was so young and stupid, I didn't know how hard it was." She did a few waist bends, then stood with her hands on her hips, waiting for the music to start.

"*Bueno*. We'll begin. Kick, one-two-three. Bend, one-two-three . . ."

When the exercise was over, Bitsy jockeyed skillfully through the crowd surrounding the actress while Dee got a can of soda and sat down on the mat to drink it. In a few minutes, Bitsy was skipping back across the pavilion with Chayo beside her.

"This is my sister Dolores—we've always called her Dee," said Bitsy. "She's a big fan of yours, too."

Chayo's smile was practiced, but still captivating. "You speak Spanish?"

"I'm very rusty," Dee said.

"I watch *Es Mi Vida* faithfully when I'm home," said Bitsy, jumping in. "Will Concha marry Eduardo?"

"If I tell you, then it will spoil our surprise." Chayo's eyes were wandering. She blew a kiss to someone across the lawn. Her eyes were back to Dee and Bitsy again, but her right foot was out, her body moving forward. "Well, is so nice to meet you."

"Where did you learn to speak English?" Dee asked, and Chayo stopped and turned around again.

"I live in New York for a little time, and also Los Angeles," she said.

"Your accent sounds Southern," Bitsy said. "We were both born in Los Angeles. Dee's a superior court judge there. She's been hearing a gruesome murder case, and the murderer escaped and is after her, so she—" She froze. "Oh, God, Dee, I'm sorry. I did it, didn't I?"

"It's okay."

The absent expression in Chayo's eyes was gone.

"You are a judge?" Her eyes were bright and focused now.

"That's right."

"I think it is not easy for a Latina to become a judge in the United States."

"It's easier than becoming a movie star."

Chayo laughed. "You are *muy amable*, señorita."

"I'd love an autographed picture," said Bitsy, her face flushed with excitement. "Do you think it would be possible? If you don't have any available, maybe someone could take a Polaroid shot and you could sign it, or—"

"I will give you as many photographs as you want," said Chayo. "You and your sister will have dinner with me in my little house that I have here. Seven-thirty, is that a time for you to be hungry, or is it early?"

Dee was stunned by the transformation that Bitsy's little piece of information had wrought in Chayo. It had acted like an open spigot to Chayo's charm. Is she impressed by the fact that I'm a superior court judge, she wondered, or by the fact that I'm being chased by a murderer?

"It's perfect," said Dee. "We'd love to come."

Neatly clipped lawns and towering laurel trees surrounded Chayo's pale-pink house. A bougainvillea vine trailed down over the red roof tiles and dropped its bright purple blossoms in a soft pile next to the heavy Mexican door. Bitsy knocked. In a few moments the door was opened by a Mexican in his early thirties, with a thick wavy mane of black hair above his broad brow.

"*Bienvenidos,*" he said, and opened the door wide for them to enter.

They ate dinner on a glassed-in lanai overlooking the greensward. Candles flickered on the ebony table and fragrant gardenias floated in crystal bowls. Chayo had introduced the young man, Carlos González, as a dear friend, and he sat down at the ebony table with them, smiling often and listening to the conversation, but not joining in.

"Carlos does not speak English," Chayo explained, as a young Mexican girl in a white huipil served them bowls of creamed soup.

"Oh, God, its heavenly, real food," Bitsy said.

Dee glanced at Carlos, who sat listening to the English conversation around him, occasionally responding to a question or comment of Chayo's in Spanish. In profile, his nose was high and straight like a Spaniard's, but when he turned toward her she saw the Indian in him in the full cheek and wide mouth.

"Did you live in Los Angeles long?" asked Dee, turning to Chayo again.

"A year. When I am making my pictures, I live in Eagle Rock. You know where is the zoo?"

"Griffith Park?" prompted Bitsy.

"*Sí*, near the—*tiovivo*—what is the word—"

"Merry-go-round."

"*Sí*, the merry-go-round. So much work to say a few little words. But near the merry-go-round is where I play tennis all the time when I was in Los Angeles and was making my movie career."

"Our mother was Mexican," Bitsy said, spooning up the last few drops of soup.

"But the blue eyes—"

"I look like my father."

"So there was a *rubia* daughter for your father and a *morena* for your mother. You are both married?"

"Dee's divorced. Leon and I are still married." She smiled. "Sometimes I think just barely."

"Children?"

"We had a daughter—Vickie—but she died in 1975. April twentieth, to be exact. Leon sells beer. He was top salesman last year in the western division. We won a trip to Las Vegas."

Chayo reached for a cigarette on the buffet table next to a silver tray piled high with pearly seashells. The soup bowls were taken away and plates of rare roast beef with béarnaise sauce were put down in their place. Carlos took out his lighter and lit her cigarette.

"I have no children either," Chayo said.

"*No los tengo tampoco,*" said Dee. "I'll speak in Spanish. It isn't fair to exclude Carlos from the conversation."

"And my poor head was beginning to ache trying to think in English," Chayo said.

"I don't speak Spanish much in Los Angeles," Dee said.

"It's more acceptable in the States if you speak English," said Bitsy.

"Is it necessary to forget your Spanish language in order to succeed in the United States?" asked Carlos.

"You don't understand, Carlos," Chayo said. "What do you know about the United States? You can't even speak English." She turned her radiant smile toward Dee. "Don't mind him. He likes to discuss philosophical matters, but I have no patience with that. He's a graduate of a Jesuit seminary and sees life in ways that the rest of us don't."

"You don't dress like a priest," Bitsy said, staring at the open collar of his white shirt.

"Not a priest," Carlos replied. "Almost a priest, but to be almost something doesn't count."

"Carlos works for me sometimes," Chayo said. "He drives the car, smooths the way, arranges planes. My life is very full. I need someone to take care of the things that don't interest me. Besides, he's very handsome. If he had become a priest, what would I have done?"

The dishes were cleared again, and demitasse cups of coffee brought in on a tray. Dee watched Carlos's easy warmth with Chayo, their familiarity, and wondered whether they were lovers.

"Maybe another place would be safer for you from this murderer," said Chayo. "We're going back to Mexico City on Wednesday. I'd like you and your sister to come with me, to be my guests in my home."

Dee laughed. "We just met you today."

"I always know immediately whether I like someone or not. I always have guests in my home. It's a natural thing with me. Isn't it, Carlos?"

"Very natural," he said.

"Then we are agreed?" asked Chayo.

"Bitsy's got to get back," Dee said, "and I—"

"I can go," said Bitsy quickly.

"Then it's settled," Chayo said. She held up her wineglass. "To our friendship."

"To our friendship," said Bitsy, holding hers up.

Dee felt the room expanding and contracting in waves of perfume. Crystal gleamed, and sharp edges of light bounced off the table's ebony surface. The stars outside were twinkling in just the same way that Chayo's eyes were. Dee looked first at Chayo and then at Carlos. There was no danger here. Danger had been left behind in Los Angeles. This was only Mexican hospitality carried to the extreme.

Dee lifted her glass up and clinked it against the others.

"I won't be a spoilsport," she said

7

Just as they had arranged, on Wednesday morning, at ten, Carlos pulled the black Lincoln sedan up to the cottage steps at Rancho Mirada.

"Chayo is waiting in the car," he said when Bitsy opened the door.

Dee, who had the telephone clenched between shoulder and ear, looked at him across the room and smiled.

"I've been holding this phone for a half hour," she said, "and people keep coming on and asking me if I need assistance, and then nothing else happens."

"Sometimes the telephones are very Mexican," Carlos said as she hung up.

"Leon always says I'd lose my head if it weren't attached," Bitsy said, her face flushed. She had made a last run through the cottage to see if they had forgotten anything. She tugged at her blouse, which had hiked up in back, before she ran down the steps to get into the car.

Dee tossed the cottage key on the bed and turned to where Carlos waited for her at the door.

"I never do impulsive things like accepting invitations from movie stars," she said as he picked up their suitcases. "But these are impulsive times, I guess."

"I'm glad to see you again," he said as she closed the cottage door behind them.

"I'm glad to see you, too."

Before they started down the steps Dee looked out over

Rancho Mirada. Sturdy laurel trees ranged across the slope of grass like a battalion of soldiers, the breeze brushing their leaves and carrying the scent toward her in a fragrant stream. She could see Chayo in her red silk blouse bending over the front seat of the car to kiss Bitsy on the cheek. Everything seemed so ordinary, so safe. Mexico was where her mother was born. *Mi tierra,* she always called it. My land. Nothing bad could happen here.

They left Rancho Mirada and drove through the old town of Ixtapan de la Sal, past the flower-bordered public baths and the whitewashed stores. From there the road curved through pine forests, the hidden villages in them revealed only by funnels of gray smoke that rose above the trees. Then began the gentle spiral past hillsides cascading with crimson poinsettias, through pastel meadows of wildflowers into a valley of sugar cane, a reassuring green against the violent jumble of color that had come before. They got out of the car several times so that they could enjoy the view of snow-capped Popocatepetl from different angles, and by noon were traveling through the tree-shaded streets of a village on the outskirts of Cuernavaca.

Carlos stopped the car in front of a run-down wooden house. Children's voices flowed through the open windows of the car from a small amusement park in a grove of trees.

"When Maximilian was emperor of Mexico he came to this village," Chayo said as they walked through the broken wooden gate into a yard overgrown with zapote and coffee trees. Shingles had fallen from the roof. The house itself seemed to sag in sadness at its neglect. "He built this house."

An old man was reading a newspaper in a chair on the porch, and as they approached he got up and began waving the paper at them.

"No se permite pasar," he shouted, but when Chayo took off her dark glasses, the loose sheets flew out of his hands into the yard.

"¡Chayo. Qué sorpresa!" He hurried across the porch to open the door for them. *"Pásele, pásele."*

"Emperor Maximilian was my great-great-grandfather," Chayo said.

"You're descended from Emperor Maximilian?" Dee asked in surprise.

"I am," said Chayo, and she gave a throaty, proud laugh.

"But I'm sure my Austrian relatives wouldn't welcome a visit from me. Only my mother Lidia and I are left as proof that he deposited his seed in Mexico. My great-great-grandmother Concepción was a beautiful Indian girl, a gardener's wife. The emperor gave her this house and two children."

There was the smell of dust and rotting boards in the dark rooms. Ceilings were spotted where rain had come in. Curtains, gray and lifeless, hung crookedly across clouded windows.

"The government keeps the people from entering the house," Chayo said. "I don't know why. No one wants to come here. Very few people remember Concepción or care about Maximilian. Look how the furniture is falling to pieces. I offered to replace it and restore the house, but they won't let me. They'll be happy when it crumbles away to dust."

Near the back of the house was a room larger than the rest. It was empty of furniture, except for an ornate desk. One leg of the desk was missing, causing it to slant toward the floor. Dusty books with broken spines and torn covers were balanced precariously on its cracked leather top.

"This was Maximilian's study," said Chayo. "You can see the small chapel in the Borda gardens through this window." She rubbed at the fogged glass with the palm of her hand. "See, through the trees, that's the Borda house and gardens, the place where Maximilian fell in love with Concepción. Here in Acapatzingo the people speak of Concepción's trysts with Maximilian as though they happened yesterday." She put her finger to her lips as if listening for something. "They say his spirit comes here at night, and that if you stand still and hold your hand on your heart you'll smell the gardenias that he pressed to her breast and hear the hammock sway in the breeze as they made love."

She looked at Bitsy, who had been listening raptly. "Do you believe that love between two people dies when they die?"

Bitsy thought a moment. "No. I think it lives on after them."

"It's a nice idea," said Dee, "but I'd need scientific proof."

"You believe in the hereafter, don't you?" said Chayo.

"No, I don't."

Carlos stepped up to the smeared window and looked out. "Chayo is proof that their love has lived on."

"Well, yes, of course," Dee said, "in that sense love never dies."

Chayo smiled at her. "But that's all I meant to say."

*   *   *

From Concepción's house in Acapatzingo they drove to Cuernavaca. Narrow streets tumbled into one another and wound around flower-splashed sidewalk cafés and pocket parks. The light hand of decay peeked out from beneath the trumpet vine that blanketed everything. As they passed the bandstand in the tiny *zócalo*, there was a whiff of car exhaust and rotting garbage in the air. But the laurel trees draped their branches romantically over adobe rooftops, and as Carlos pulled up in front of the rusty gate of the Borda gardens, the air was warm and lushly fragrant.

"We're closed for repairs," said the guard inside the gate.

"When will you be open?" asked Carlos.

"Next year or the year after that."

"Please let us in," Chayo said. "Don't you know me? I'm Chayo Sedano, and these are my friends from the United States. They've come all this way to see the gardens and now you say they're closed. Don't be that way. Open up. Who will know?"

"It's the government," said the guard, shaking his head and shuffling from foot to foot. He pointed to the plaster arch above their heads. "The bricks are falling. One fell on a German tourist last year."

"*Por favor*, old one, we'll stay away from the walls, I promise," wheedled Chayo.

"I'm not permitted."

Chayo glanced at Carlos, and he took out his wallet and held a five-hundred-peso note through the iron bars. The guard stared at it for a moment, then snatched it between two fingers and opened the gate. "But away from the walls," he called after them.

The gardens were overgrown, huge trees blocking the sun, their heavy roots jutting up through jagged cracks in the walk. Shrubs crowded together, partially covering the broken skeleton of a carriage beside the ruins of a small chapel.

"The mosquitoes are hungry," said Bitsy, slapping at her arm.

"They've been waiting for us," Chayo said. She walked ahead to the edge of a reflecting pool. "All of this was Maximilian's garden. They say it was Empress Carlota's, but it was really his. He invited the French officers here on Sundays, and they wore their dress uniforms and rowed in the pool.

The ladies wore stiff white dresses with their hair in long curls. Sometimes Carlota came, but it wasn't really a place for her. Maximilian preferred Concepción to any of them. I'm named for Concepción, but no one has ever called me that except for Father Cristóbal when I was at the convent school."

While Bitsy and Chayo took one last look at the gardens from the bridge, Dee and Carlos waited at the car. "You're not like a Mexican woman," he said.

"What is a Mexican woman like?"

"Like your sister, pliable, eager to please others." He took Dee's hand in his. She wore a man's tank wristwatch, with no rings on her slender fingers. The nails were neatly manicured, but without color.

"Your fingers are warm," he said, and as he touched them to his lips, he looked at her from beneath dark lashes.

"There's no one in my life now," he said. "And you?"

"No one."

8

The highway to Mexico City was smooth and well paved, with a clear view of mountains and valleys. By the time they arrived in the city it was late afternoon, with bumper-to-bumper traffic and thick yellow smog that hung in front of the surrounding mountains like dirty bedsheets. Christmas ornaments trailed from lampposts down the Paseo de la Reforma all the way to the Zócalo, and shoppers, arms burdened with packages, hurried along beneath the giant ash trees, sidestepping the fruit vendors and beggars who got in their way.

"So many people," said Bitsy as they sat trapped at an intersection in front of Alameda Park. A fire-eater blew a stream of fire in front of the Lincoln's windshield, and when Carlos leaned out and handed him a few pesos, a swarm of clowns and Chiclet sellers and windshield cleaners surrounded the car.

At La Fonda del Recuerdo, a Yucatecan restaurant with orange awnings and grillwork windows, they ate their lunch in the lower-level dining room. Cutout paper decorations drifted overhead and a band on the balcony, light on guitars and heavy on trumpets, blasted the music of Veracruz into their ears.

"The noise in here is deafening," Bitsy shouted.

"That's why everyone comes here," Chayo shouted back. "They talk and nobody listens. Good things and bad things are said, and nobody cares. At the Christmas season everyone forgets their problems and has a good time."

At the next table a young woman chugalugged a tumblerful of rum and Coca-Cola while her companions urged her on with chants of *"Bebe, bebe."* Then she looked over at Chayo and screamed.

"My God, is she all right?" asked Dee. She stood up and started toward the other table, but Carlos had his hand on her arm.

"She recognized Chayo," he said.

The chant of *"Bebe, bebe"* turned to *"Chayo, Chayo,"* and in a few moments the whole restaurant was echoing with Chayo's name. Dee looked around her at the adoring faces turned in Chayo's direction. The band had stopped playing and was chanting her name along with the others.

"I've never seen anything like this," Bitsy shouted above the din.

"They love her," Dee yelled.

"Everyone in Mexico loves Chayo," Carlos shouted.

As Chayo hopped up onto her chair and held out her arms, Dee thought she had never seen a more exultant look on anyone's face.

"Chayo, Chayo, Chayo," they chanted, and the love rippled and curled through the room. It beat against the walls and tore the air.

"¡Viva Méjico!" Chayo cried out to them.

At the sound of her voice the chanting stopped, and a trancelike silence fell over everything. There was not even the sound of a glass hitting a table or an ice cube tinkling or a shoe sliding. The silence was like a living thing hanging thick in the air. Then suddenly, as if they had been dreaming, the crowd roused itself and screamed in one voice, *"¡Viva Méjico!"*

Chayo's house was in the Pedregal, once an ancient lava bed on the southern outskirts of Mexico City. *Palos locos*, their twisted branches nearly bare of leaves, were espaliered against the lava rock fence that encircled the compound. Carlos got out of the car and spoke to someone through an intercom at the gate. Then the gate swung open, and guards armed with Uzi machine guns waved the Lincoln through. The private drive wound past bronze lions on pedestals, over wooden bridges that spanned reflecting pools, through gardens of flaming azaleas. They passed a hedge of red-beaded holly and suddenly the house appeared, a Japanese-style mansion, all glass and sloping roofs and native stone.

"My house," said Chayo proudly. Her eyes were bright and full of grace. "Now it is your house."

"I want you to meet my father, Conrad Whitworth," Chayo said when the wiry man in cotton twill pants and a battered corduroy jacket joined them on the Japanese veranda in the early evening.

He refused a drink, but sat at Chayo's feet on the edge of her chaise lounge, shoulders sloping forward, hands clasped loosely between his knees.

"Chayo tells me you're from California. A judge, is it?"

"Yes."

The question was an innocent one, but there was an acuteness in his steel eyes that alerted Dee.

"My son went to medical school in Los Angeles."

"Does he live there now?"

"He was killed in 1968."

"Oh. I'm sorry."

Armed guards, like those at the gate, walked up and down between the stone statuary in the azalea garden below, their figures growing shadowy as fast-moving rain clouds swallowed up the light. Before Conrad appeared, Chayo had been calling Dee and Bitsy *manita*—little sister—and chattering about her movie career. Now she was strangely subdued, and Dee had the distinct impression that the taciturn old man was there to pass judgment on her two house guests.

"I couldn't be more thrilled to be anywhere than I am to be here," Bitsy said. "When I told Leon where I was, at first he was pretty mad about the fact that he had prepaid my stay at Rancho Mirada, but then there was dead silence, and I thought, oh-oh, either he's going to kill me or the phone's gone dead, but then he said, 'Get an autographed picture of her. Nobody's going to believe this.'"

"Then you're going to stay for a while?" said Conrad.

"I'm—" began Bitsy.

"Bitsy has to get back to Los Angeles by Christmas," interrupted Dee.

"Carlos, I wondered where you were," Chayo exclaimed as Carlos walked through the french doors and sat down in a wrought iron chair next to Dee.

"There was a problem at the gate," he said. "It's taken care of."

"There must be a lot of danger from overzealous fans," said Dee, cautiously.

Conrad, who had been studiously examining a stain on his corduroy pants, looked up. "You're wondering about the men with the machine guns."

"Yes. I've never seen so much armament in a private home before."

"Chayo's a big star. People want to touch her, maybe even hurt her." He put his hands on his knees and gave a little grunt as he boosted himself up. "The dampness affects my rheumatism. I hope you'll all excuse me if I don't come down to dinner, but I think you'd do well to go inside, too, before it begins to rain."

When he was gone, Chayo seemed relieved, as though a great chore had been gotten out of the way. "Since his wife died, Conrad lives here with me. He was Chico's father, whom I loved so very much. Now he's my father, too."

9

The decision to go to Cancún with Chayo was sudden and unexpected and would not have been made if Farley Carrington III had not still been on the loose.

"Stay another week," Sid said when Dee finally got a call through to Los Angeles. "Christmas in Mexico. Can't beat it, they tell me."

"I've taken advantage of your hospitality long enough," Dee told Chayo. "Bitsy's going back to Los Angeles, and I think I'll just find someplace in Cuernavaca and relax until it's safe for me to go back to LA."

"But you can't go," cried Chayo. "I have a treat in store for all of us. We're going to do what they call in Hollywood *"los pickup shots."* Ramón needs a jungle background for the scene when Concha runs off with Eduardo, and what can we do if the jungle of Yucatán is so very near to the Caribbean, *manitas*? No one says that I must work, work, work, and not play and have fun on the beach with my sisters from the United States. Ramón and the rest of the crew have things to do in Mexico City for a day or two, so we'll have fun together before he arrives, eh? We'll stay in Cancún, *muñecas*, and I promise that you've never seen water so blue or so warm, beaches so white and soft, until you have been to Yucatán."

"But it's almost Christmas," Bitsy protested halfheartedly. "Leon and I haven't spent a Christmas apart since we were married. His family is expecting us in San Antonio."

"Christmas is five days away," said Chayo. "You'll be home

by then, and your husband will love you all the more because he missed you so much."

"What do you think, Dee?" Bitsy asked. "Should we go?"

"It's up to you."

Chayo put her arm around Bitsy's shoulder. "Your husband won't refuse you if you tell him that Chayo Sedano sends him her love."

"Well—"

"I'm so happy," said Chayo. She put her other arm around Dee. "Do you know how happy I am?"

"I look terrible in a bathing suit," Bitsy said, but she already had the look in her eyes of someone who could feel the sand between her toes.

"My name is Jesús, but I'm called Chucho by my friends," the hollow-cheeked Mexican said when he appeared on the beach in the morning with Chayo. He was in his thirties, thin in his bathing trunks, but with a lightly muscled upper body.

"He's my friend," Chayo said, as she and the young man joined Carlos and Dee and Bitsy beneath a thatched palapa. Carlos appeared not to have met him before.

"I remember Chucho Cisneros," Bitsy said, digging her feet into the powder-soft sand and pouring some of it on top of her thighs to hide the dimples. "He was the greatest Don Quijote of the Spanish screen."

"I'm not Don Quijote," Chucho said. He pointed to a wooden platform that floated a few yards off-shore in the transparent waters of the Bahía de Mujeres. A parachute sailed into the sky, a man suspended below the billow of silk. "I strap people into the harness and pull them out of the water when they're done."

"It's glorious what you can see from the sky," Chayo said. "Little people running all over the beach. You can see the jungles, the beaches, all the little fishing villages along the coast. You ought to try it."

"Come on, Dee, do it," urged Bitsy. "I want to see you do it."

"You just want to see me make a fool out of myself," said Dee. She shielded her eyes from the sun as she watched the parachute swoop across the sky.

"It'll be fun."

"Then you do it."

"We'll use Carlos for ballast," Chucho said. "He'll sit above you on the lines so that you don't fly away."

Bitsy coaxed and Chayo went up first to prove it was safe. Then Dee and Carlos waded out to the launching platform, put on Mae Wests, and listened to Chucho's instructions. When he shouted "*¡Listo!*" the speedboat zoomed away from the platform, and Dee and Carlos were yanked upward, beach and palapas dropping away. The lines jerked unevenly above the harness, slackening and tightening as the parachute filled. Then they straightened out, and Dee and Carlos were zipped smoothly sideways, the wind like a hand against their backs, gusts of air kissing their skin. Carlos touched her shoulder and she looked up and smiled, but his words were distorted, the things he had to say lost in a sleek ribbon of air. Below them a slash of highway followed the Caribbean coast to the south. To the west, an ant's trail of a road severed the jungle fastness. They floated lazily now in a bowl of blue sky, ocean and bay and lagoons like a saucer beneath them.

"I knew you would love it," Chayo said, when they had landed and were wading through the surf back to the beach. "Sailing in the sky over Cancún always makes me feel that I am a child again, swimming on the reef in Puerto Morelos," and she slipped her arm through Dee's as though they were the oldest and best of friends.

"You'd better hurry. It's going to be a beautiful sunset," called Dee from the balcony. Brown pelicans and white-tailed kites did acrobatics over the water a few feet from the sand.

"I'll be right there," Bitsy called from inside. "I hope you want orange juice and tequila, because that's all that's in the refrigerator."

"That's perfect."

When they had arrived at the pastel pink and blue Fiesta Americana, the desk clerk had said that the hotel was full. But when Chayo walked up to the desk after making a phone call, three bay-view rooms had suddenly materialized.

"I like traveling with Chayo," said Bitsy, handing Dee her drink. "Things that are filled up or sold out always stay that way when I'm with Leon."

On the drive up from Mexico City, Chayo had taken them shopping for huipils. "When you are in Yucatán, the heat is so intense you have to wear a huipil," she told them.

Now Dee and Bitsy, each in an embroidered huipil and sandals, sipped their drinks and gazed out over the bay.

"These dresses were designed with me in mind," said Bitsy, looking down at the full-cut chemise. "Every bit of fat is hidden, and the breeze goes right up your legs to cool you off." She leaned back in the chair and sighed. "This is glorious. Who would have believed that we'd be guests of Chayo Sedano, sitting on a balcony in Cancún, the ocean at our feet—"

"What do you think of her, Dee?"

"She's very nice to us. I always put that at the top of my list. She does smoke too much. And I kind of feel sometimes like we're being dragged along behind her. And she is a little gushy—I mean, I'm not saying it's not sincere, it's just that she hardly knows us, and—I don't know. Maybe she's like that with everybody. What do you think of her?"

"The same as you."

They sat quietly now and watched the sky turn red and gold as the sun went down.

At seven o'clock, Carlos appeared at the door in a white guayabera and tan slacks.

"You look different somehow," Dee said.

"So do you," he replied.

The evening began at a small Yucatecan cafe near the workers' city of Cancún.

"I thought there were no mosquitoes in Cancún," said Bitsy, swatting at one as it bit her leg.

"A few escape now and then from the exterminators," said Carlos, "but they're innocent. Just a little prick, a tiny itching, but no malaria like there once was here."

The waiter brought some salve to the table along with the lime soup.

"I like to bring my friends to the authentic Maya places to eat," said Chayo. "You can eat French food in Paris, but in Cancún you must eat *cochinita pibil* with a few mosquitoes."

After dinner they drove along Paseo Kukulcán, the bay on one side, the ocean on the other. The palm trees in front of the hotels had been strung with Christmas lights that blinked and twinkled in the balmy night.

"We'll try all the discos, *cuates*," Chayo announced. "Cancún wakes up at night when the dance music begins."

At Friday Lopez, they danced the salsa with a crowd of

young Mexicans who were well dressed with plenty of money to spend.

At the Club Marimba, the dancers were mostly Anglo and the music was Billy Joel and Michael Jackson.

At four in the morning at La Estrella, with Anglos and Mexicans dancing to the frenzied beat of hard rock, perfume and cologne and perspiration steaming up out of the floor like a witch's brew, Dee and Carlos whirled hypnotically around each other, the strobes fractionating their bodies into bite-size bits of light.

"I want to take you to Puerto Morelos," she heard him say above the noise.

At the banquette, Chayo and Bitsy had been joined by Chucho and a husky, round-faced Maya. Chayo introduced him as Pepe, "my wonderful friend from Verecruz." They all had to shout to be heard.

"I'm taking Dolores to Puerto Morelos," said Carlos.

"Well, don't worry about me," Bitsy replied. "Chucho just told me I have a beautiful face and he's in love with me. I told him I was married and needed to lose at least twenty pounds. He said he likes curvy women and that he's willing to wait for my divorce. I'm having a great time." Chucho put his arm around her and they danced off together while Carlos took Dee's hand in his and led her out into the starry Cancún night.

10

From Cancún they drove steadily down the straight, well-paved road that follows the Caribbean coast. There were no other cars on the road but theirs, and, except for an occasional fishing village, the scenery was the same. Stark ceiba trees spread their limbs toward the ocean spray on their left, and the jungle, acid green beneath the shrouded treetops, stretched out on their right.

"What part of Mexico was your mother from?" Carlos asked.

"Chihuahua. Her parents took her to Tijuana when the Revolution started. My father was from Cheyenne, Wyoming. They barely understood each other. Literally."

He turned toward her as she spoke, and she felt a burst of pleasure at the way he looked at her.

The sun had come up by the time they reached the high stone wall on the ocean side of the highway. A sign in Spanish said Private to Members of La Ceiba Explorers Club, Puerto Morelos, Quintana Roo. Carlos got out, unlocked the gate, and they drove for a few miles along a private road, past gardeners weeding carefully tended lawns beneath the poinciana trees.

At the end of the road Carlos stopped the car. Sprinklers misted the hibiscus beside thatched cottages that faced the ocean. Two gnarled ceiba trees guarded the entrance to a two-story building shaped like the prow of a ship. A small sign on the door said in Spanish and in English, Office Opens at 8:00 A.M. Do Not Disturb Mr. Frankle.

"Andre is Chayo's father," Carlos said.

"Andre Frankle?"

"Yes. You've heard of him?"

"I saw an exhibit of his paintings at the Los Angeles Museum of Art. I'm sure the brochure said that he had died in a concentration camp during the war."

"I don't know where they could have gotten such information. He lives right here in La Ceiba and paints every day. I'm sure he would be surprised to hear that people think he's dead."

The door to the office was open. A switchboard blinked unattended.

"Do you think we ought to bother him so early?" said Dee.

"Andre will be up."

He led the way up the stairs and knocked on the door and an elderly man, paint-stained sweater enveloping his slender shoulders, opened it.

"Andre, *cómo estás?*"

Andre nodded and shrugged and twisted his face expressively, but said nothing.

"I've brought a friend of Chayo's to meet you. Dolores Guadalupe Sorenson."

Andre's hand was soft against hers, but the grip was firm. Dee saw the well-healed scar that braided across his forehead into his curly gray hair.

"I've admired your work for a long time," she said, and when he smiled, but still said nothing, she realized that he could not speak.

The studio was bright with the light that streamed in from a skylight and oceanside windows. There was a bed and dresser, closets along one wall, a small bathroom in a partitioned alcove. And in front of, on top of, and beneath everything were paintings. Some finished, some in progress. They leaned against walls, were stacked against furniture, stood on easels, lay flat on the floor. They were mostly of Indian women, except for one of a blond child barefoot on a sweep of purple beach. She held a fishing net in one hand and a spear in the other.

"Anyone could tell that it's Chayo," Dee said. "The face is the same."

When they had left him and were walking through the pool area down to the beach, Dee said, "What happened to him?"

"A terrible accident many years ago," Carlos replied.

*　　*　　*

"This whole coast was nothing but a Maya ruin when I was born," Carlos said as he guided the aluminum boat over the choppy surf toward the dive boat that rocked at anchor beyond the reef line.

The dive boat was a floating Maya cottage, its thatch roof and sapling walls weathered to a silvery gray, and as Carlos helped Dee up onto the deck, she said, "It looks like it ought to be planted in a village somewhere."

But as they bent forward to enter the cabin beneath the loose fronds, everything became modern, square and plastic, with refrigerator and cushioned bunk, a bookcase with diving magazines, a tiny head, and a table with three cardboard cartons of bathing suits, marked in Spanish and English, Men; Women; and Stretches, One Size Fits All, then in parentheses, Within Reason. There were fins and snorkels and masks and a cupboard stuffed with packages of cookies and marshmallows, bags of potato chips, cans of tuna and string beans and fruit cocktail.

"By the look of the food, they get a lot of Americans at La Ceiba," Dee said.

"They do." He opened the refrigerator and looked in. "Would you like Coca-Cola, Pepsi, *cerveza*, or orange juice?"

"Orange juice."

A cork bulletin board had slips of paper thumbtacked to it, some yellowing, others fresh.

" 'Heaven on earth with Carlos and Keh in the dive boat, Jean and Don Shreve, Anchorage, Alaska,' " she read aloud. " 'Lidia, can we come and live with you at La Ceiba? We'll clean the kitchen, iron the sheets. Rachel and Frank Modena, El Monte, California.' 'When I think of La Ceiba, I'll always hear the sound of Carlos's voice reciting in Spanish his poetry of Yucatán. Hilda Schlamme, Wiesbaden, West Germany.' "

"So you're a poet and a scuba diver, as well as a priest," she said when he handed her the orange juice.

"The diving is what everyone in Puerto Morelos does. And the poetry is just a beautiful thing to do."

"I like that." She smiled. " 'A beautiful thing to do.' Why did you ever think you wanted to be a priest?"

"It was my father's idea. There were thirteen children in my family, including nine boys. He wanted at least one of his sons to be a priest like he was, and so I was chosen, but I had no vocation. The world tempted me too much."

"Are things so different in Yucatán that the Church allows priests to marry?"

"No, but we're very far away from Mexico City, and my father was the only priest from Playa del Carmen to Cape Catoche. Nobody paid attention to him. I think he felt abandoned by the Church, and saw that abandonment as God's permission to tailor the Catholic religion to suit himself. At the end of his life he had become more Maya than Spaniard."

"And your mother?"

"She was a Maya. My father didn't marry her, but he was faithful to her, so in that way I suppose he was a good Catholic." He laughed, his teeth a blaze of white in his tan face.

"Well, my life certainly hasn't been that interesting. My father was a chief petty officer in the Navy. He was killed when I was ten."

"He was killed during the war?"

"No. A freak accident. He was on a boat in San Diego Harbor riding back to his ship. He leaned too far over the gunwale and was decapitated by a Japanese freighter. The officer who came to tell my mother about it said that the fog was so thick in the harbor you could spoon it into a jar. I'll always remember that expression, my mother repeated it often enough. After that my mother just went to pieces. We wandered around for a few years, spent some time with her family in Chihuahua, and then came back to Los Angeles. She died of liver disease when I was eighteen. When she was drinking she claimed that the Virgin Mary spoke to her. Her parish priest sent her to a doctor who told her she should be glad, that the voices would be a comfort to her when there was no one around to talk to." She smiled. "Bitsy likes to tell that story."

She changed into a bathing suit in the tiny head, then sat down on the toilet lid and stared at her toes. He had, without any embarrassment at all, taken off his clothes, and with the little gold cross blinking on a chain against his copper chest, pulled a pair of trunks out of the bin and put them on.

There's no doubt about it, she thought. We've come here to make love. But who is he? A priest? A deep-sea diver? A poet? Chayo's chauffeur? Why am I so uneasy with this whole

Chayo adventure? And why does she really need men with machine guns to guard her?

She stood up and looked out the portal at the ocean. Stan's right, she thought. All I do is categorize, memorize, synthesize, and generalize.

"It's not the most beautiful suit in the world," she said when she came out.

"You're beautiful."

They swam on the surface, facedown, fins slicing smoothly through the water. On the ocean bottom the purple tips of the fan coral, streaked with gold where the sun's rays caught, swayed softly in the wave surge. Carlos took Dee's hand and they floated downward to where a moray eel, mottled brown and white, perched in its hole, its jaws opening and closing menacingly. They hovered near it, holding perfectly still, watching. For an hour they explored the reef, resting occasionally on mounds of brain coral.

"I'm very tired," she said the last time they surfaced. He steadied her as the waves pushed against them.

"We'll rest a minute," he said. Their hair was shiny, slicked down by saltwater, beads of salt on their faces. He put his arms around her, and they balanced against each other on the gritty furrows of coral.

He licked a bit of salt from her lips. "Have you seen enough of the reef?"

"Let's go back now," she said.

Dee had been in love with a Mexican boy when she was seventeen, before she escaped the barrio. She had forgotten the Spanish words of love he would whisper in her ear until now as she lay with Carlos's amber legs twining hers and heard his voice like a sinuous thread weaving its web around her.

"*Te quiero*," he murmured.

They lay crossways on the bunk, slipping against each other, his gold cross warm between her breasts, the scent of the ocean blooming around them.

"I like when you touch me there," she whispered, as she saw the young Mexican girl reflected in his eyes.

Her arms were above her head as she drifted on a stream of sensation. She remembered that time of abandon vividly now, the lustful afternoons with the soft-voiced Mexican boy. Carlos stopped and looked down at her, his eyes like a dark well, full of mystery. Everything and nothing is revealed in his eyes, she thought dreamily. They are deep and inviting, drawing me in, telling me to drink my fill, that my thirst is over. They are full of secrets and pleasures I had forgotten existed.

11

Hidden by ceiba trees and tucked behind an outcropping of rock a few hundred yards from the rest of the compound, Lidia's house was invisible until Dee and Carlos had walked the last few yards up the powdered-sand beach. Then it sprang up suddenly beside the Caribbean, its huge, wave-licked terrace a jaw jutting into the ocean.

"Chayo sends you an *abrazo*," said Carlos as he hugged Lidia, "and said to tell you she'll be here when the work in Cancún is finished."

He drew Dee toward him. "This is Dolores Guadalupe Sorenson, a friend of Chayo's from the United States."

"And now your friend, too, I see," said Lidia. "I'm Chayo's mother."

She was in her early sixties, her olive skin finely lined but delicately pretty. A braid of soft gray hair wound around her head. She wore a simple white huipil and sandals, no jewelry and no makeup.

"Paco saw you take the boat out," she said, "and so we waited to have breakfast with you. Adelita is preparing it now in the *casita*. Please sit down. Keh is getting dressed."

They sat on comfortable couches facing the oceanfront terrace, where a servant was sweeping with a long-handled broom. The house was spacious but stark, the only decoration a crucifix on the wall in the entry and a gilt-framed Renaissance painting of the baptism of Christ in a niche in the living room wall.

"Keh didn't sleep well again last night," Lidia said. "When he went with Andre to the doctor in Mérida, he was given vitamins, but they haven't helped him."

"But Andre seems well," Carlos said.

"Ah, Andre. He has more energy than any of us. He's making sketches for a series of paintings of Maximilian and Concepción. He has never painted them before."

"Chayo took us to Concepción's house in Acapatzingo," Dee said.

Lidia looked over at her, a distant expression in her eyes. "Andre always liked the idea that I was Maximilian's great-granddaughter," she said. "I think he fell in love with the idea before he fell in love with me."

A husky, dark-skinned Maya entered the room, and he and Carlos embraced and slapped each other on the back. Lidia introduced Keh to Dee, with no explanation as to who he was or why he had come out of a bedroom in her house and touched her cheek and kissed her on the lips.

"We missed you, Carlos," Keh said. "The fishing is very good. You always know the exact time to come to La Ceiba."

"Adelita is famous for her *huevos motuleños*," Lidia said. A buffet table had been set up in an open-air *casita*, a thatch-roofed arbor a few yards from the ocean. Adelita, in huipil and apron that strained across her big belly, presided over a silver chafing dish piled to the brim with layers of tortillas, fried eggs, black beans, and tomato sauce, over which had been sprinkled bits of ham and cheese. A platter of artfully arranged papaya and mangos and melons sat in the center of the buffet, next to an ice-frosted pitcher of orange juice.

Andre was already seated at the long table. Lidia prepared a plate and set it down in front of him, and when everyone was seated, their plates piled high with food, Dee said, "Carlos showed me the reef this morning. It's beautiful."

"Where did you take her?" asked Keh. "To the shrimp beds?"

"No. I wanted her to see the coral gardens."

"Andre needs another glass of orange juice," Keh said, looking over at Andre's empty glass.

Adelita brought the pitcher to the table and poured Andre some juice. Lidia rearranged his napkin on his lap and watched him pick up the glass and take a drink before she turned back toward Dee.

"You speak Spanish like a Mexican," Lidia said.

"They call us Latinas or Chicanas in the States."

"But you're a Mexican?"

"I'm a Mexican."

"Chayo lived in the United States. In Los Angeles. Do you work in motion pictures, too?"

"Dolores is a judge in Los Angeles," said Carlos.

"Ah, a judge," Lidia said, her face lit with admiration. "Mexican women are not only God's gift to their families, but to their communities as well. Some may sing more loudly than others, but they all sing. Are you in Mexico alone?"

"No, my sister Bitsy is with me. Beatriz."

"Family is an important thing," Keh said.

"Yes, it is," said Dee, and as she speared a piece of melon with her fork she saw Keh's weathered hand cross the table and cover Lidia's small tan one. The unconventionality of Chayo's parents' living arrangements—the Mexican mother with her Maya lover and the Jewish father sitting mutely by—struck Dee as something she would have considered bizarre in Los Angeles. Here on this isolated stretch of beach on the east coast of Mexico, it was not only acceptable, but oddly touching.

"I was telling Carlos that I saw an exhibit of Andre Frankle paintings in Los Angeles," Dee said. "They called him a seminal figure in the German expressionist art of the thirties."

"We don't hear about things like that here," Lidia said quietly. She glanced at Andre, who was now gazing out over the ocean. "But I'm glad that Carlos thought to bring you to Puerto Morelos," she continued. "He's like my own child."

"Keh is the divemaster here at La Ceiba," Carlos said.

Dee looked up from her plate and smiled at him. "The one who taught you to dive," she said.

They drove for a long time without speaking at all. Every once in a while Dee turned and looked at the painting sitting upright in the back seat. It was of a woman holding a child in her arms. The face was Lidia's, but much younger.

"I feel like I've taken something under false pretenses," Dee said finally. "They don't know how valuable his paintings are."

"And if they did, they would have given it to you anyway."

His hand rested now on the inside of her leg.

"Did you love your husband?" he asked.

"Yes. I thought he was a wise and benevolent Anglo god. I was a Chicana who had grown up in a neighborhood where the girls tattooed their boyfriends' names on their fingers when they were fifteen and got married at sixteen."

He glanced at her slim fingers.

"No, I didn't do any of that."

"The love is over?"

"The things we had looked for in each other weren't there anymore. Yes, the love is over."

He kept his hand on her leg as he drove, and she felt the essence of him through the pressure of his fingers. Los Angeles and Stan and escaped murderers belonged to another world. And the troublesome thoughts about Chayo had lost their significance. She was sunburned and happy, and as keenly as she tried to call the worries back, they refused to come. All that mattered were Carlos's skin against hers, the sun-streaked ocean and glistering sand, and the ceiba trees bursting with kapok.

12

When the telephone rang and the operator said someone was trying to place a call from Los Angeles, Bitsy panicked. "If it's Leon, tell him I took a walk. All he does is yell at me long distance."

But it was only Sid Schwartz, Dee's court clerk in Los Angeles, speaking fast, as though afraid he'd be disconnected before he could get out what he wanted to say.

"They caught Carrington," he said.

It was eerie how clear the line was, as if in one perfectly connected telephone call all the broken connections and static of the past week could be atoned for.

"Where?" she asked.

"In a joint in Redondo Beach. He was eating crab legs and drinking Chablis. Didn't give anyone a bit of trouble. In fact, I heard that the arresting officers even let him finish his dinner. You can quit worrying, he's back in jail." Dee could hear paper crinkling and then the phone being dropped.

"You there?" he asked.

"I'm here."

"He sent a note over for you. 'Dear Judge Sorenson, sorry if I caused you any trouble, but I have some difficulty with self-control. Sincerely yours, Farley Carrington III.' "

"That was very nice of him."

"You don't sound too thrilled."

"But I am. He's very thoughtful."

"When you coming back?"

"I don't know."

There was silence.

"Something the matter?" he asked.

"Uh-uh."

"You must be having a hell of a good time."

"Just trying to relax a little."

"You'll call?"

"I'll call."

On the Saturday before Christmas Ramón Mendoza arrived from Mexico City to shoot the pickup shots for *Es Mi Vida*.

"Ramón says that there's no more dramatic place to show Concha running off with Eduardo than at the sacred well in Chichén Itzá," Chayo said, when she had introduced the dapper man with the small mustache to Dee and Bitsy. "It's an hour away. You'll love it, *manitas*, and you'll love seeing how Ramón directs me as the wonderful Angelina. Ramón was once my husband till God released him from his torture. We weren't so good as husband and wife, but I owe my life as an actress to him."

"Chayo exaggerates," Ramón said.

They left Cancún early in the morning. Chucho Carrillo, the parasailing attendant, and Pepe Montoya, Chayo's round-faced friend from Veracruz, rode in the truck along with the cameramen and sound technicians, while Carlos drove everybody else in the van.

"What a place!" exclaimed Bitsy when they reached the ruins of the Maya city, a calcified garden of skyscraper temples and pyramids and observatories growing out of the heart of the jungle.

The cameramen trundled their equipment down the path to the sacred well while Chayo and Ramón and the other actors worked in the plaza across from the ancient Maya ball court rehearsing the scene in which Concha and Eduardo run off together into the jungle.

"Don't go too far," Chayo called out as Carlos and Dee and Bitsy went off to see the ruins.

"We won't," Bitsy said.

The plazas were sun-scorched, the grasses so dry they crackled beneath their feet. Bitsy lagged behind as they climbed in and out of crumbling buildings. Carlos and Dee had to help her up the last few steps to the top of the observatory.

"The Maya were great astronomers and mathematicians," Carlos said as he looked out the observatory window to the plaza below. "But they also practiced human sacrifice. They believed that eating the corpse and smearing its blood on them was a way to draw the person's spirit into their own bodies and make them stronger."

"Ugh," said Bitsy, who sat slumped against a broken balustrade fanning herself with her purse.

"How long ago was that?" Dee asked.

"Chichén Itzá was probably built around the fifth century A.D. and the human sacrifices continued until Cortés arrived in the sixteenth century."

"It's almost as old as I feel," Bitsy said. "Well, it certainly is a sight to see all of this out in the middle of nowhere. I'm really enjoying it. Believe me, I'm more impressed by all the sacrificing and bloodletting than I can say, but I don't know when I've ever been so hot or my feet have ever hurt so bad. Every teeny pebble in this place feels like it's going right through my sandals."

Carlos bought them Cokes at the shaded refreshment stand beneath the trees, and they sipped them while they browsed through the trinkets and tourist books. Then they came back to the ball court and watched Pepe demonstrate its perfect acoustics by standing at one end of the 550-foot field and carrying on a conversation in a normal tone of voice with Chucho at the other end.

"We're almost through with our rehearsal, *manitas*," Chayo shouted to them.

"Let's climb to the top of the Temple of the Warriors while we're waiting," said Carlos suddenly.

"Not me," Bitsy said.

"I don't know if I want to either," said Dee, looking at the steep steps. Although she was much thinner than Bitsy and in better physical shape, the implacable heat was beginning to take its toll on her, too.

"You'll be happy you climbed up once you get to the top," Pepe said. He and Chucho sat cross-legged on the grass beside Bitsy.

"I'll watch you from here," said Bitsy, her fair skin blotched red. "I sure wish I had a camera to take a picture of you two up there."

"Wait here," said Carlos. "There's one in the van."

"It's Chayo's," he said when he returned with a small Polaroid camera.

"I'll be so careful with it," said Bitsy, taking it from his hand.

"Don't stay up there too long," said Chucho nervously. "They're almost ready to shoot the scene."

"I think the heat's gotten to Chucho, too," said Dee as she and Carlos headed toward the pyramid. "He looks jumpy." There was no vegetation on this side of the plaza, except for an occasional weedy clump and a few old trees, and Dee could feel the hot ground baking the rubber soles of her tennis shoes.

The stairs were steep, and as they climbed they kept their hands on the step above to steady themselves. Carvings of plumed serpents, mouths gaping, fangs in readiness, lined the way.

"It *was* worth the effort," said Dee when they reached the top and all of Chichén Itzá lay below, clutched in a jungle wreath of green. There was Bitsy, blond hair shining in the sun, waving up at them. Dee waved back.

"She thinks she's going to get our picture," Dee said, sitting down on the flat stomach of the stone idol, "but all she'll get is two ants on top of a stone molehill. I hope I'm not committing the equivalent of a Maya sin by sitting here. What is this thing, anyway?"

"That's Chac-mool's stomach, where they offered up the victim's still-beating heart," said Carlos, grinning at her.

"Oh." She stood up and brushed the seat of her pants with her hand.

He put his arms around her waist. "When do you have to go back?"

"Next week."

"We have very little time. You haven't really seen Mexico. You haven't—"

He looked over her shoulder.

"What's the matter?" she asked as she caught the worried look on his face.

"Nothing."

She swiveled around to see what he had been looking at. Bitsy was holding up the camera now.

"You saw something that disturbed you," she said.

"I didn't."

"Then why the change in expression?"

"Sometimes my expression changes. You trust me, don't you?"

"Of course."

"Good." He took her hand and pulled her toward the stairs. "They're leaving for the well to shoot the scene. We'd better go down now."

Chayo led the procession down the path away from the ball court. She had one arm around Jaime Delgado, the young Mexican actor who was playing Eduardo, and the other around Luisa Sereno, the show's Concha.

"Did you get any pictures of us?" asked Dee.

Bitsy handed her three photographs.

"You can hardly see us." Dee gave the pictures to Carlos, who looked at them and then slipped them into the pocket of his shirt.

"Chucho just told me that the Maya thought more of cacao beans than they did of gold," said Bitsy as they marched along the rock-strewn path. Maya vendors had stationed themselves every few feet along the way, offering for sale crudely carved Mayan gods, thin silver bracelets, and onyx Chac-mools.

"I wouldn't try giving any of these people cacao beans, no matter what Chucho says," said Dee.

A barefoot Indian boy stepped in front of Bitsy and held out three Chac-mools for her inspection. "Fi', fi', señorita," said the child, who was probably no older than five himself.

"¿Cinco pesos?" asked Bitsy, bending toward the dirty child.

"No, no, fi' dolla."

"It's not very well made, Bits," Dee said.

"I know, but look at him. What's five dollars, anyway?" She opened her purse and took out a two-thousand-peso bill and handed it to the child, who stared at it and shook his head.

"He thinks you want change," said Carlos.

"Or eight Chac-mools," said Dee.

Bitsy pressed the bill into the child's hand and took one of the Chac-mools. "Para ti," she said.

"You could use it for a doorstop, I guess," said Dee as they continued along the path, walking faster now to catch up to Chayo and the others.

"Did you see his face, how happy he was?" said Bitsy.

"You can buy Chac-mools on Olvera Street for two dollars apiece," Dee said.

"That's not the point."

Pepe had disappeared. Bitsy and Chucho walked on ahead, talking and laughing together as the procession continued on toward the well.

"Since Vickie died, Bitsy goes crazy over every child she sees," Dee said.

"I sense a great sadness in her," said Carlos.

"Bitsy?" An alarm rang in Dee's head. It was startling, disorienting. Maybe the heat had finally melted her brain. "Bitsy's the happiest person I know," she murmured.

"How deep is that thing?" asked Bitsy, peering into the scum-covered well. Chayo was having her hair fluffed by the makeup woman while Luisa Sereno and Jaime Delgado went through the scene one last time with Ramón. The heat was less intense here beneath the trees, but the dust kicked up by the television crew was making everyone cough.

"About thirty-six feet," said Carlos. "Those who didn't get their hearts torn out were thrown into the well."

"Great," said Bitsy.

Chayo did a few knee bends, licked her lips, and nodded to Ramón.

"¡Silencio!" shouted Ramón, and the cameras began to roll.

"What a time and place you've chosen to reveal your feelings for this wastrel," Chayo as Angelina said.

"You have no right to call me a wastrel," replied Eduardo, his handsome features contorted in anger. "You and your 'Sancho.' "

"What's a 'Sancho'?" whispered Dee.

"Someone you have a love affair with while you're married," Carlos replied. "An amante. It's almost always death to the woman if her husband finds out she has a 'Sancho.' If a husband has a mistress, we call that a second front, a segundo frente. But the husband is in no danger of death unless his second front also has a husband."

Concha had stepped to a precarious position on the precipice. "You want me to choose between my family and my lover, Mamá. What choice is it that you give me? Either you will give me your blessing to be with Eduardo, or we will run away together."

Dee smiled at the lugubriousness of the scene, and Carlos

said in a low voice, "Mexicans who have no money for anything else can usually find some to pay for a second front or to be someone's 'Sancho.'"

"Have you ever been someone's 'Sancho'?"

"Once, but I escaped unharmed, and she went on to someone else."

Ramón Mendoza yelled "Cut!" and the cameramen and technicians began to pack up their equipment.

"Was it beautiful, *muchachos*?" asked Chayo. "Did I dazzle you with my acting or is that the sun that has caused tears to come to your eyes?"

"It was wonderful, wasn't it, Bits?" Dee turned toward where Bitsy had been standing, but she was gone.

"She must have gone back to get another drink," Chayo said. "Her face was so red that I could see the color of it the whole time we were filming."

"Did you see which direction she went?" asked Dee.

"No, but Chucho was with her. I'm sure she's not lost."

Carlos had walked away and was talking to Jaime Delgado. Dee felt frightened as she stared at the back of his head. "I'll just go on ahead, Carlos, and see if she's feeling all right," she said.

She started out walking, then sort of trotting, and soon she was running over the ruts and rocks of the path back toward the restaurant. At the fork that went off farther into the ruins, she stopped, hesitated, and then continued on. No, she thought, Bitsy wouldn't be interested in seeing any more ruins than she's already seen. Of course she and Chucho have gone back to the refreshment stand and are at this very moment sipping Cokes while I'm running frantically down a dangerous path, risking heat stroke.

At the restaurant, Dee asked the man behind the counter, "Have you seen a blond, blue-eyed, chubby woman in a white huipil? She has a very pretty face."

He shook his head. "Not here, señorita."

"She was with a young man, tall," persisted Dee. "His cheeks were sunken in, gaunt-looking, and he was wearing blue jeans and a T-shirt with an alligator on the front of it." She had heard that sometimes before heat stroke your pulse becomes rapid and you feel as though you're going to faint. Her heart was beating so fast that she thought she could see the front of her blouse moving in and out.

"Señorita, drink something before you go out in the sun again."

"Yes, a Coke, please."

She paid for the Coke and sipped it slowly until she calmed down and the light-headed and nauseous feeling passed. Then she went into the restroom. "Bitsy, are you in here?"

There was no answer.

Once when she was a little girl her mother bought her a blue plaid jacket with a rayon lining, and the first day of school she took it off while she was sitting on a bench waiting for the school bus. The feeling she had when she got on the bus and realized that she had left the jacket behind was the same feeling she had now that Bitsy's voice didn't come back at her from one of the restroom stalls.

She walked out into the restaurant again, and the man behind the counter said, "Are you sick, señorita?"

"No, I'm fine."

The sun was high overhead and mercilessly hot as she ran across the empty ball court toward the van.

The van was empty.

Calm down, she told herself. She took the path to the ruins after all. She has Chayo's camera. She's in an adventurous mood. You're so smug, you think you know everything about her, that you even know what she thinks and what she's going to do next. But what was Carlos looking at? What the hell is going on?

She ran back down the path to the well. "Carlos," she said as he caught her in his arms. "I can't find her, Carlos. I can't find her."

"Come this way." They headed for the ruins that Bitsy would never have gone to, never, especially on a hot day with her face so red that Chayo had noticed it even while they were shooting the scene.

"Surely we'll find her," said Chayo excitedly when they met her and Ramón on the path.

Dee stared at her, at the perspiration that clung to the hairline of the wig she wore. Suddenly it was all there in Dee's brain. It had been there all along, just waiting for her to notice. She grabbed Chayo's arm. "Where's Bitsy? Where's my sister?"

"What are you doing?" shouted Ramón, pulling Dee's hands away. "¿Estás loca?"

Then he glanced at Chayo, who had begun to tremble.

"*Por Dios,*" he murmured. "*Por Dios,* Chayo, what have you done?"

"You said to trust you," Dee shouted as she and Carlos ran hand-in-hand along the path. "You knew something was going to happen to Bitsy." Her breath caught in her throat. "You knew Chayo was involved in it."

"I only knew that it would happen," he shouted back. "We had our men in Cancún, watching and waiting. No one expected that it would happen in Chichén Itzá."

She stopped dead in the middle of the path and pulled her hand away from his. "Your men!" she screamed.

He stared at her, his hands on his hips. He was breathing hard. He nodded his head. "*Sí,* my men."

At one o'clock in the afternoon two Mexican highway patrolmen, spiffy in their uniforms and dark sunglasses, joined the search.

At four o'clock in the afternoon one of the policemen said, "Your sister is not here."

"Yes," said Dee, "she's not here." She sat down on the ground and watched the ants crawl over her pants legs.

On the steps of the ancient stone observatory, before Chichén Itzá was locked in darkness, they found a Polaroid photograph of Bitsy. She was holding her purse in front of her, a frightened look on her face. On the back of the photograph someone had scrawled the words, "*¡Viva Méjico!* The Sons of Guerrero."

PART II
Maximilian's Garden

13

Rough seas and rain had dogged the six-week voyage of the *Novara*. Water had flooded the cabins of the seasick passengers, and Countess Paola Kollonitz, rather than remain below in the cramped and airless saloon with the rest of the royal entourage, had spent most of her time up on deck covered with blankets and tarpaulins. The seas were calmer now, and when the outline of land grew more distinct, the countess threw aside the coverings and ran to the rail to join Dr. Billimek, who had been studying and charting sea currents for Emperor Maximilian.

"Is that the New World?" the countess asked excitedly.

"Yes," said Dr. Billimek, and he clasped the countess's hand and kissed it. "Yes, my dear countess, the New World. And such a world it is we cannot even contemplate." Dr. Billimek was tall and fat, with gray hair that stood in wisps on his bald head. His eyes now sparkled with anticipation as the coast grew larger before them.

"I am fainting with the heat below," said a thin voice behind them.

The countess turned quickly and curtsied to the small, darkly pretty woman, who was swaddled in a billowing gown, a black bonnet tied tightly around her dark brown curls. Empress Carlota, as Charlotte now chose to be called, stepped to the rail and breathed deeply of the salt air.

"Your Majesty," said Dr. Billimek, bowing.

"I'm happy to see you are feeling better, Your Majesty," said the countess.

"Was I ill?" replied Carlota, pinching her lips together and gazing with red-rimmed eyes out over the harbor.

"No, Your Majesty," murmured the countess, who, with the fourteen other ladies-in-waiting, had taken turns for most of the voyage holding a basin to Carlota's chin to catch her vomit.

"Dr. Billimek, are you so selfish that you would keep the first sight of Mexico to yourself?" boomed the loud voice of Emperor Maximilian as he strode onto the deck followed by the royal entourage.

The emperor was in naval uniform, medals on his chest, balding blond hair and beard moist with the pomade that his valet had applied just moments before. His clear blue eyes and straight nose were handsome, but his full lip gave him a petulant look, and he had an undershot chin, only partly concealed by his sparse beard.

Dr. Billimek, flustered, began to stammer. "I would have called Your Majesty. I didn't intend—I didn't mean—"

"You're forgiven, Billimek." The emperor laughed. "I was only playing with you."

Since the *Novara's* departure from Europe in April 1864, the emperor had busied himself planning his court with his ministers, writing a manual of court ceremonial, and practicing his Spanish. Making jokes at the expense of others was one of the few indulgences he had permitted himself during the long voyage.

The *Novara* passed the rotting hulk of a French warship. All on board were silent now, suddenly mindful of the French soldiers who had died to make Maximilian's landing in Mexico possible.

"This is a day of rejoicing," said Maximilian jovially once the wreck was passed. "No sad faces. The tears are dried, and although there will be duty and travail, and although there have been some who have sought to dissuade me from this enterprise and some who have attempted to punish me on account of its undertaking, I, Maximilian, the new and future emperor of Mexico, lineal descendant of Charles V, the first true king of Mexico, do hereby decree sorrow to be banished from this land." He took Carlota's hand in his, and Countess Kollonitz caught a rare glimpse of tenderness as Maximilian gazed into his wife's eyes. The countess turned away, embarrassed by the look of adoring gratitude on Carlota's face.

The *Novara* anchored out in the mouth of the harbor, and the French naval commander, Admiral Bosse, came out to meet it in a small boat. Although the admiral was correct in his demeanor, saluting Maximilian and bowing to Carlota, he made it clear that he was annoyed that they had proceeded into port without his directions.

"We would have wanted your majesties to be escorted to anchor alongside the French ships in the harbor," he said. "This place that you have chosen is an ill-fated spot, marked by contagion and disease, and I would not want to have anything untoward happen to your majesties while I am port commander."

"We are quite prepared to deal with whatever comes," said Maximilian sharply. "God has guided us thus far; he will guide us farther."

"What is this contagion he speaks of?" whispered Countess Kollonitz to Dr. Billimek. "Can we die of it?"

Before Dr. Billimek could answer, the commander said, "It is yellow fever, madam, and death is a welcome release from its ravages."

When the countess shuddered, Carlota stepped from the shadow of Maximilian's arm. "You must not frighten the countess," she said reprovingly. "We are here for good and for ill, and here we will remain. Fevers do not daunt Emperor Maximilian."

"I will not be responsible," said the commander stiffly. "You may row ashore tomorrow morning."

"We will have a mass in the morning," said Maximilian.

"Then you may row ashore after the mass," said the commander in exasperation.

The countess looked from one to the other, a strange foreboding filling her at this confrontation between the king and the commander of his own naval forces.

Vera Cruz looked scruffy in the sunlight. Buildings needed paint. There were no people in the street to welcome the new emperor and empress of Mexico. And the heat. It reddened the women's faces beneath their stiff bonnets. It turned their tiers of starched crinoline petticoats into wet, limp rags, their bonnets into steaming turbans. The men removed their hats and wiped continually at the backs of their necks with linen handkerchiefs.

General Almonte, a mixed-blood Mexican whose dark skin brought whispered speculation from members of the royal party as to whether Mexicans might actually be Negroes, had come with a troop of soldiers from Orizaba to escort the new emperor and empress to Mexico City. He greeted the royal couple warmly and then stared in amusement at the young women in their heavy bonnets and dresses, and at the young empress, wilted and sagging on the arm of her lady-in-waiting.

"The train station is very near, Your Majesty," he said to Maximilian. "The journey will be quite warm, and we will not be out of the fever zone until we reach Soledad."

Without comment or complaint, the women lifted their soggy skirts and extended their damp, white-gloved hands for assistance, and then stepped into the rickety carriages, all of which were in varying stages of decay. Frayed venetian blinds flopped at the windows. Hard slat seats had been made not softer but merely lumpier by the addition of twisted straw.

Dr. Billimek, at Maximilian's invitation, and Countess Kollonitz, as Carlota's chief lady-in-waiting, shared a carriage with the royal couple, while the rest of the entourage, eighty-five in all, arranged themselves according to their own preferences. The five hundred pieces of luggage occupied eight wagons.

When the carriages had been loaded and gotten under way, Maximilian turned to Dr. Billimek and said, "This is an inauspicious beginning, Professor, not a sign yet that anyone is glad that we have arrived in Mexico. Has it been folly for me to think that I can rule what some have described as an unrulable country?"

"My knowledge of political affairs is so—that His Majesty would ask me such—greater minds than mine have—" The professor squirmed in his seat.

"Of course, of course, Billimek, I'm sorry I asked."

As they drove through the deserted streets, Countess Kollonitz fanned Carlota's face with a mother-of-pearl fan.

"Would you like to remove your jacket and shawl, Your Majesty?" asked the countess, who felt that she would faint if Carlota insisted on keeping the women formally dressed throughout the journey. Carlota seemed unperturbed by the heat, but the countess could see the moisture on her fore-head and upper lip.

"It is warm," said Carlota, "but not unbearably so. We must set an example of decorum for the people who will watch us pass as we travel."

The countess looked out the window. There was no one watching them pass, but if Carlota refused to remove any part of her clothing, then none of the other women in the party could remove theirs.

"Perhaps the natives are indoors," remarked Dr. Billimek. "It is very hot. People, as well as birds and butterflies, learn quickly the limits of their endurance in tropical climates."

Maximilian, who had been gazing morosely out the window, looking in vain for a banner or a sign of greeting, turned gratefully toward the professor.

"One gets used to the tropics," he said. "When I traveled in Brazil, I was struck by the way in which the people appeared immune to the heat. Of course, as you say, during the hottest part of the day, no one would venture out of doors."

"It is adaptation, nothing more," Dr. Billimek said.

"Does one's ability to withstand the heat have anything to do with the way in which the body is formed?" Carlota asked.

"Possibly so," Dr. Billimek replied. "It has occurred to me from time to time that God sets exactly the right creature down in the complementary climate."

"It seems a reasonable thesis to me," said Carlota earnestly.

"Yes, Your Majesty. Adaptation is one of the keys, albeit a minor one. But no one can exclude providence's plan, for it exists right down to the smallest ant in the most distant anthill." Dr. Billimek, an ex-monk as well as a naturalist, was in the habit of melding his religious and scientific selves.

"I'm sure, Your Majesty," continued Dr. Billimek, "that the flora and fauna of the tropics are amazing in their abundance and variety. I have looked forward to this trip with eager anticipation since the day that His Majesty invited me to investigate the creatures of Mexico." The professor leaned forward conspiratorially. "As a matter of fact, I have hope of discovering a new species of butterfly in the New World."

"I'm sure that there will be butterflies the match of those that we left behind at Miramar," Maximilian said.

"We will name a species after you," said Dr. Billimek,

noting the undercurrent of sadness in Maximilian's voice.
"*Lepidoptera maximiliano.*"

Maximilian smiled. "You must name one for Carlota," he
said, patting his wife's hand, "since it is she who convinced
me of the divine rightness of this mission."

When they reached the train, there was no station, no
signalmen, only a single-track rail through the marshes, with
open country on either side. As the caravan came to a halt,
there was a loud explosion. General Almonte rode up to the
royal carriage.

"What was the explosion we heard?" asked Maximilian
through the open window.

"It is not certain," General Almonte replied. "Possibly
fireworks in celebration of your arrival. Possibly *guerrilleros*.
The route of our travels is heavily populated by Juaristas.
This morning the mail coach was held up and robbed."

The two women looked out. There was no sound now but
the buzzing of mosquitoes.

"But I see no sign of *guerrilleros* here," the general said.
"It is on the long road to Mexico City that we will have to
keep vigilant. My men are familiar with the habits of the
Juaristas and are excellent shots."

Maximilian sighed. "Dr. Billimek, I believe that the Juaristas
have learned the rules of adaptation very well."

Carlota extended her hand to General Almonte to be helped
from the carriage. "It is my wish that you tell the others that
the explosion we heard was the sound of fireworks," she said.
"God's purpose is little served by idle speculation."

The train ride was short, as the French had laid track only
as far as Soledad, but it lifted Maximilian's spirits. General
Almonte had hired a band to accompany the royal party, and
whenever the train stopped the musicians got off and played
Mexican music until a crowd gathered. Against the general's
advice, Maximilian insisted on getting off the train at every
stop and walking among the people, most of whom had no
idea who he was.

Carriages and mules were waiting in Soledad, and once
again the royal entourage and their luggage were loaded into
lumbering, dilapidated conveyances for the last lap of the
journey. There was no longer any pretense at roads, merely
rocky ruts created by the carriages that had passed through
before. Dust swirled in through the broken windows and

covered the occupants with silt. The carriages, swaying and bouncing crazily, were constantly on the verge of toppling.

When Carlota began to choke and cough on the dust, the countess hung her shawl at the edges of the window, but as the material flapped back and forth in the breeze it merely carried the dust directly to their noses. There was no longer any discussion of natural history. Maximilian tried to maintain his dignity as he was jostled around in the carriage while Carlota struggled to keep from choking on the blowing dust. Dr. Billimek had removed his false teeth, which had begun to clatter, and wrapped them in his handkerchief. He held them inconspicuously in his lap with his mouth held shut so that his bare gums would not show. The countess battled with the shawl and finally gave up and draped it over Carlota's head until her coughing subsided.

At Chiquihuite it started to rain. Not a gentle rain that sounded like pine needles dropping on the roof. A rain that sounded like horses galloping over cobbled pavement. A rain that filled the dry riverbed along the side of the road with a raging torrent of water in five minutes.

The countess and Carlota huddled together as water streamed into the carriage. The muleteers hollered to the mules to go faster, and General Almonte rode his horse alongside and shouted through the noise of the storm, "I'd prefer Juárez to this rain. The road is washing out."

"Can we camp here for the night?" Maximilian shouted back.

"If we do, we'll have to swim the rest of the way."

"An impertinent young man," said Dr. Billimek through clenched gums.

"We'll drive through," shouted General Almonte.

The carriages slid and slipped along. At times they floated upward, free of the need for wheels. Then the water would pour in, and they would sink back onto the ground and the lurching, body-wrenching journey would continue.

"Would you say a prayer, Dr. Billimek?" said Carlota, peeking out from beneath the countess's shawl.

Dr. Billimek turned sideways on the seat and slipped his teeth into his mouth before he began. "Dear Lord, our Savior, in whose name all things are created—" His teeth clattered a rhythmic accompaniment to the words, but it was muffled by the general din of the storm and noise of the carriage. He spoke more loudly now. "We beseech you to guard and save our emperor and empress, Maximilian and Carlota, in this their divine mission to the people of Mexico. O Lord, let not the water overtake them when they are so young and have so much yet to give to these poor people in thy name."

The carriage began to slide. It slid sideways, then forward. General Almonte was at the door and had it open. He reached in and Countess Kollonitz pushed Carlota through the water-filled carriage and into Almonte's arms. Immediately behind Carlota was Dr. Billimek, who swam furiously through the carriage and out the door.

"Countess," yelled Almonte. The countess looked behind her at Maximilian, who sat in his corner of the carriage, a look of resignation on his face.

"Go, my dear," said Maximilian. "I'm responsible to your family for your well-being."

"But Your Majesty—"

"We must all accept our fate," he said, and he pushed her out of the carriage toward the waiting Almonte.

No sooner was the countess free of the carriage than it slid the rest of the way down the embankment into the swollen river and quickly sank.

"The king, you must save the king," screamed Carlota as the carriage disappeared from view. General Almonte's troops had gathered, and they all now stared glumly into the storm-whipped water.

Carlota pulled at Almonte's arm. "Do something, do something, do something," she shrieked.

One of the muleteers, a wiry little man, his Indian face set in determination, jumped from his wagon and ran toward the embankment. He looked into the churning water for a second, eyes blinking in the rain. Then he dived in and was gone. Moments later he reappeared, clutching Maximilian tightly to his chest.

Dr. Billimek began to crawl on his hands and knees down the steep slope. "Over here," he cried. "Over here."

The man swam toward Dr. Billimek, and when he was close enough the professor grabbed his hand and pulled it toward him.

"Hold tightly," yelled the professor. "It is His Royal Highness, the King of Mexico, that you have in your arms."

General Almonte and his men by this time had tied a rope

around the professor's waist and were dragging the three men back up the slick slope.

When they had pulled Maximilian alive from the river, Carlota fainted. While the countess attended to her and Dr. Billimek saw to Maximilian, the muleteer, Hector Sedano, went back to his mules. After a brief rest, during which time the rain stopped, the royal procession continued on its way.

In 1857, at the age of twenty-five, Maximilian—Maxl to his adoring family—a Hapsburg archduke and younger brother of Franz Josef, emperor of the fragmented, fragile, fraying Hapsburg dynasty, married Princess Charlotte, the motherless, quaintly unstable seventeen-year-old daughter of King Leopold I of Belgium. Her father said of her, "It is too bad she is not a boy, for she is more intelligent than her brothers."

Maximilian called Charlotte his "pretty little thing," and was fond of her, but Charlotte's affection for Maximilian was worshipful. He was her "brilliant one," her "adored," her "beautiful prince." The wedding was attended by representatives of all the royal houses of Europe, with Charlotte in a silver and white brocade wedding gown and Maximilian in the full dress uniform of an Austrian admiral. The Prince of Saxe-Weimar wrote after the ceremony: "Despite her elegant disposition and excellent figure, she is rather strange looking, and totally lacking in charm and grace."

Franz Josef appointed Maximilian as viceroy to Italy, and the young couple left for Venice. Italy was straining to overthrow Austria's repressive rule, but when Maximilian asked what his duties were to be, the dour Franz Josef replied, "You are to conduct a well-run court and set a good standard of behavior and manners for an unruly race."

Two years later Italy threw the Austrians out, and Maximilian and Charlotte retired to their castle of Miramar, an estate of lush gardens and crenellated towers built on a rocky promontory overlooking the Adriatic Sea, where Maximilian, a man of impeccable manners but frivolous habits, devoted himself to building castles and gardens and collecting exotic birds and rare plants. "I'm happy at last to be removed from the world," he declared unconvincingly.

By 1861, when Benito Juárez, a flat-browed, pure-blooded Zapotecan Indian, was elected president of Mexico, the bankrupt country had been involved in civil war for fifty years and had had thirty presidents.

"The Catholic Church and foreign bankers have been the ruin of Mexico," Juárez declared as he confiscated church property and suspended payments on foreign debts.

Enraged European bankers urged their governments to seize Mexico.

"There are riches to be mined in Mexico by someone who has the wit to conquer her," advisers told Napoleon III in France.

"Mexico will be lost to the Church," Vatican sympathizers told Empress Eugénie, Napoleon's Catholic wife.

A scheme was hatched to destroy Juárez, create a puppet monarchy, and find someone to place on the throne of Mexico.

"Maximilian is the only Austrian I have ever met with whom it is possible to carry on an intelligent conversation," Empress Eugénie told her husband. "He would make a most congenial Emperor of Mexico."

"It is a bolt out of the blue!" said Maximilian when asked by Napoleon if he would accept the Mexican throne.

"I have always been interested in Mexico as a bulwark against the encroachment of the Americans," Napoleon said.

When Maximilian told Franz Josef about Napoleon's proposition, the emperor, anxious to rid himself of his more popular brother, said, "Of course you will accept."

While Maximilian waited in the safety of his castle on the Adriatic, Napoleon's troops landed in Vera Cruz. As they marched toward Mexico City, confident of an easy victory, they were stopped at Puebla by a dirty, tattered army of Mexicans and defeated.

"It is a foolhardy venture," Maximilian's older advisers said. "The Americans will now come to the aid of Juárez. The clergy is utterly corrupt. You cannot trust the Catholic Church. This is a ghastly adventure born of a woman's whim. The Mexicans are rotten to the core and good for nothing but thieving. Tell Napoleon you have changed your mind."

But his younger advisers urged him on. "The Americans are too busy with their own civil war to interfere. If Napoleon can defeat Juárez, there are signs that the Mexicans will welcome you."

Napoleon sent troops to Vera Cruz again. When they reached Puebla, half of them having died en route of malaria and yellow fever, they laid siege to the city. The Mexicans held out for sixty days, and then, starving and outnumbered by an endless stream of French replacements, surrendered. Juárez's troops abandoned Mexico City and scattered over the countryside. He and his government escaped to the north.

Charlotte, isolated at Miramar with a husband who often left her alone while he pursued his own interests, was now convinced that Maximilian's true destiny lay in Mexico. "I see in this victory of the French forces the divine hand of Providence," she said.

Maximilian was not so sure. For weeks agonizing debate swirled above his head. He listened to everyone, vacillating between those who favored the venture and those who didn't. He could not sleep, lost his appetite, fell into deep depressions that not even the bawdy jokes of his courtiers could alleviate. He nearly collapsed with the strain. He worried that he would merely be Napoleon's puppet, and that he would be unable to withstand the power of the Catholic Church in Mexico. He fretted that friends and allies would not keep their pledges of support, that Napoleon would not keep his army in Mexico, that Mexican revenues would not repay the millions he had borrowed to finance the venture, that the Americans would intervene. And for all his aristocratic posturings, he was haunted by the thought that the people of Mexico did not truly want him.

"If you accept the throne of Mexico, I will never fail you," Napoleon said.

When the decision to go was finally made, Franz Josef said, "A Mexican king has no right to a Hapsburg inheritance."

"You cannot take away from me what is mine by birth," raged Maximilian at the betrayal.

"Devote yourself to Mexico," his brother replied, and the matter was closed.

13 June 1864

Leopold of Saxe-Coburg-Gotha
King of Belgium

Dearest Papa,
I hope you are well, as we are. The boat trip was strenuous, but not insupportably so. And even had it been, the reception that was accorded my darling Maxl made it all worthwhile. Flags waved, dignitaries were in attendance, and the festivities followed us every step of our journey from Vera Cruz to

Mexico City. The people, in their enthusiasm to touch their new king, grasp at him and touch him. They also hug me, much as one hugs a child. They are not yet educated to the ways of royalty, but that will come in time.

Our rooms, while not as elegant as those we enjoyed at the castle at Miramar, are quite adequate for our needs. I hardly notice the lack of amenities. Indeed, the shortage of silver and glass at the emperor's dining table is made bearable by the bouquets of flowers so charmingly arranged by our Indian servants.

Maxl still stings from the hurt he suffered at his brother's hands, but I console him by telling him that the loss of his hereditary rights will be more than repaid by the glory which will cover his reign in Mexico.

I have never felt so strongly the call to the throne as I do here in Mexico. An aura surrounds the two of us. The people around us feel it as well. Welcoming masses have been held in the churches, and Maxl is more convinced than ever that we did the right thing by coming here. The guerrilleros are in the countryside, shooting and robbing, but they do not have the sympathy of the people. The forces of Juárez have no power over he whom God has selected to rule Mexico.

One small incident occurred on the journey from Vera Cruz to the capital. Maxl fell from our carriage during a rainstorm. He landed in a puddle and was helped to his feet by one of the Indian muleteers, a man named Hector Sedano. Maxl was profusely grateful—out of all proportion, I might add, to the deed itself. Darling Maxl thinks of others sometimes to his own detriment and has insisted on repaying the man's helpfulness by employing him as a gardener. God will reward Maxl for his good heart.

Dear Father, how did I deserve to have a man so angelic, so pure, so selfless, for my husband? My happiness is overflowing. I only hope that I am his equal in this venture.

> My affection and love to you,
> Charlotte

14

When Maximilian and Carlota arrived at the Royal Palace in Mexico City, it reeked of recent occupation by unwashed Juaristas. Vermin crawled unmolested over and under everything, and the royal party, not having thought to bring insect powder with them to the New World, suffered from itches and rashes. Clothes had to be shaken before dressing and shoes inspected before being put on. Tile had fallen from the roof of the palace and littered the grounds. Parts of the palace walls had crumbled away, turning the rooms into drafty tunnels. The Creole women, in attempting to mask the dreariness of the place, had furnished the royal apartment before Maximilian and Carlota's arrival. The result was reminiscent of the waiting rooms of a run-down French hotel.

"It's lovely," said Carlota, as she swept across the filthy floor of her bedroom, her multitiered crinoline skirts scooping dirt and debris up into their Belgian lace borders.

"It is a gift from God how nothing ever deters Your Majesty's eternal optimism," said Countess Kollonitz.

"I hope that I have imbued you with the same spirit, my dear countess, for nothing worthy of effort should be described in less than exalted terms."

As for the city itself, it showed the effects of war and military occupation. Churrigueresque churches and colonial houses, long neglected, were falling in on themselves. Ornaments and tiles dropped from the plaster facades of buildings. Lepers begged on the streets. Stinking piles of garbage were left outside to rot and could be plainly seen and smelled from the eleven hundred windows of the palace.

"The Royal Palace is not a fit habitation for an emperor and empress," Maximilian declared. Within a few days of their arrival, he discovered an abandoned ruin on a hill not too far from the city and immediately engaged architects to transform the wreck into a castle. Before another week had passed, with only one wing habitable, with scaffolds and dust and gaping holes still in the walls, the royal couple and their entourage were in residence at Chapultepec. Carlota immediately began her royal entertaining and within a few months had conducted thirteen soirees, ten receptions, and five balls for the foreign dignitaries who were arriving in the capital. She also found time to dedicate an orphanage.

"Everyone pronounces my entertaining a glittering success," she wrote her father, "but I have yet to accustom myself to my guests' lack of manners. The Creoles, as those Spaniards born in Mexico call themselves, have welcomed us warmly, but their manners, at table and in the drawing room, are deplorable. I have been quite embarrassed to witness the gusto with which the men belch after dinner, and the concept of punctuality is entirely unknown to them. But it is the French who surprise me most. I had no idea until now that they could be so vulgar in their habits."

Maximilian removed himself from the city as much as possible. He would escape Carlota's functions by appearing for a few minutes and then slipping away to ride horseback with his secretary or chase butterflies with Dr. Billimek.

Meanwhile, the royal couple's Austrian retinue of attendants and courtiers and ministers and ladies-in-waiting, appalled by the filth and primitive living arrangements, complaining of drafty rooms and inedible food, began a steady exodus back to Europe.

"Your Majesty, I have decided to return to Austria within the year," Countess Kollonitz told Carlota.

"Well, then, when you go I'll say good-bye," Carlota said, and promptly brought Señorita Josefa Varela, a young Indian woman reputed to be a direct descendant of the Aztec poet–king Netzahualcoyotl, to Chapultepec to be her chief attendant.

Señorita Varela spoke little, but saw everything. She noticed that Maximilian and Carlota did not share the same bedroom.

"Why do the emperor and empress not sleep together?" she asked Countess Kollonitz one rainy afternoon.

The countess blushed and rearranged the brushes on Carlota's dressing table. "That is a question of extreme delicacy, Señorita Varela. Matters concerning the marriage bed are not to be shared with strangers."

"You are a stranger to the empress?" Señorita Varela asked, eyes sparkling. She wore a muslin gown with an embroidered, cinched-in bodice, an exact copy of the gowns of the other ladies-in-waiting. When Carlota was not in sight she would remove her leather slippers and go barefoot, so that her feet and the hems of her gowns were stained from stepping into the pools of stagnant water that collected in hollow spots beneath the leaky roof.

"This is not fit conversation," said the countess, as she fiddled with Carlota's gowns that hung on pegs above the cracked stone floor. "The empress does not confide in me or anyone. You are to see to her toiletries, help her in her bath, make sure that her clothes are laid out, that her hairbrushes are clean. Anything more than that will be an impertinence."

"I see," said Señorita Varela. "Then that is the reason for the sunken circles beneath the empress's eyes."

The servants spoke of it in the corridors. It was unheard of. Maximilian slept in a room at one end of the living quarters and Carlota slept in a room at the other end. And yet Carlota and he were openly affectionate. He kissed her hand. She stroked his beard.

"But she is only twenty-four years old," said Señorita Varela to José Blasio, the emperor's private secretary.

"And he is only thirty-two." Blasio shrugged. Blasio, a twenty-two-year-old Mexican, fluent in Spanish and German, had been called to take the place of the emperor's Austrian secretary, Captain Poliakowitz, who had fractured his arm in a riding accident. The emperor was so impressed by the skills of the young man that he engaged him permanently.

"Perhaps the emperor has a disease," Señorita Varela suggested.

"Or she wants no children," Blasio said.

"Or he likes boys," said Señorita Varela slyly.

Blasio sat beside Hector Sedano on the wagon seat, rosebushes and gardeners and tools crammed into the wagon behind them. Maximilian and Dr. Billimek rode their horses on ahead.

"He's a fine figure of a man," Blasio said.

"He has a fine figure," agreed Sedano, watching the way Maximilian sat his horse. "And he is a great king."

Blasio nodded. "If it were not for him, Juárez would have already destroyed Mexico. He thinks only of the Mexican people. He has told me that he will build an imperial library that will contain all the ancient works of Mexico."

"That's very good," said Sedano.

"We are very lucky to have been chosen by such a man," said Blasio.

"Yes, we are lucky," said Sedano, staring at his hands, which were the same color as the leather reins he held.

"An artist has also come from Europe to paint the portraits of the emperor and empress for the Mexican people."

"My, my," said Sedano.

"The empress, on the other hand—" Blasio shook his head sadly. "She discusses things she should not discuss, about the war and the generals and money. She talks to the emperor's ministers behind his back." He paused. "All these things interfere with a wife's true functions."

Sedano stared at Maximilian, who galloped ahead of the wagon, back erect beneath the flopping brim of his charro hat. The sunlight on the emperor's white merino suit finally blinded Sedano, and he turned toward Blasio, eyes blinking. "God pity him."

Dr. Billimek, in linen duster and cork helmet, gamboled over the cypress-covered slopes of Chapultepec, Emperor Maximilian close behind him. Blasio ran alongside, holding a large yellow umbrella over Maximilian and the professor to protect them from the sun. Periodically the professor would stop, bend down, and peer at something through his thick glasses, using his walking stick to poke into holes and push foliage aside.

"You see this," said Dr. Billimek as he pinned a centipede to the lining of his duster and then petted its wriggling body with a grimy fingernail. "The markings are different from the Brazilian centipede's." Maximilian bent closer to inspect the insect, which now lay quiet beneath the impaling pin. Blasio shuddered and turned away.

"Blasio has a sensitive stomach." Maximilian laughed. "That

that should be so after the awful Mexican food he has had to eat all his life is a mystery."

"Ah, but the centipede cannot think, therefore it does not realize that it is in pain," Dr. Billimek said.

"Yes, dear professor," said Maximilian, "but Blasio, thanks to his fine Jesuit education, can think, and he feels pain for the centipede."

"That is another matter entirely."

While the professor walked on ahead of them to resume his attack of the underbrush, Maximilian and Blasio paused and gazed out over the valley of Mexico, at the spires and domes and fields of maize that lay in the verdant bowl beneath the snow-capped volcanoes Popocatepetl and Iztaccihuatl.

"I'm informed by my generals that the guerrilleros are in the hills surrounding the capital and that they only wait for the appropriate time to come down and kill us all," Maximilian said quietly.

"Your Majesty should not listen to his generals, then," said Blasio. "The Army will protect you at all costs."

"It's Napoleon's Army. Why should they continue to fight and die for an Austrian archduke?"

"It is not my place to argue with Your Majesty, but the people of Mexico love you. You must listen to your Mexican generals. General Mejía would give his life for you. The Mexicans have always wanted a king. You are no longer an Austrian archduke, but the true king of Mexico."

Dr. Billimek had retrieved a folding butterfly net and a glass bottle from the capacious pockets of his linen duster, and as he ran, tripping over roots and rocks, he shouted back to Maximilian, "A yellow-banded butterfly, Your Majesty. I am on the trail of something truly extraordinary."

Maximilian stepped through the brush toward him.

"Here, Your Majesty, you hold the bottle while I attempt to catch the specimen in the net," said the professor, and he took giant, stalking strides toward the butterfly. "It is almost within my grasp," he said, reaching for it with a gentle swiping motion of the net. "Ah-hah! I've got it."

Maximilian held the bottle while Dr. Billimek deposited the fluttering butterfly. Blasio stretched his arm out over the slope so that the professor and the emperor were safely in the shade of the yellow umbrella.

Maximilian clasped the lid tight on the jar and handed the

bottle to Dr. Billimek, who inspected the imprisoned butterfly more closely.

"You look disappointed, Professor," said Maximilian.

"*Limenitis archippu*," the professor said. "Ordinary. Quite ordinary." He opened the bottle and freed the butterfly. Then he trotted off again, stopping occasionally to poke at something with his stick.

"It's time to get back," Maximilian said. "The empress is giving a dance and a Cuban singer is to perform. I've promised to be in attendance."

When they reached the veranda of the castle, Maximilian stopped to watch the gardeners who were planting shrubs and flowers along the stone path.

"These men are fortunate in their choice of occupation," he said. "Perhaps I'm not as fortunate in mine." He turned to look at Blasio's face. "Have you heard the people speak harshly of Carlota?"

Blasio flushed. "Not harshly, Your Majesty."

"But they say she usurps my duties. Is that not so?"

"Some may say that."

"Without her I could not rule."

"But she is a woman."

"She would have made a better emperor than I. Sometimes I wish that—" He ran one hand across his forehead and sighed.

"Many people think that Your Majesty is in need of relaxation," said Blasio. "Hector Sedano has told me of a place where Your Majesty might have a respite from the cares and worries of government."

"Hector Sedano? I don't know the name."

Blasio pointed to one of the gardeners, a slight, dark-skinned man, whose hands worked deftly among the thorns of the rosebushes he was planting.

"Surely you remember him, Your Majesty. Hector Sedano."

Maximilian stared at the Indian.

"He is the man who pulled Your Majesty from the river. Hector Sedano. The man who saved Your Majesty's life."

"Ah, yes, Hector Sedano."

"He knows of a place where the Aztec rulers rested, where Cortés put aside the cares of the world. It is a place of kings, Your Majesty. It is called Cuernavaca."

"Cuernavaca," said Maximilian, his eyes seeing past the

valley to a place where kings rested. "How far is this place from here?"

"Several hours' drive."

"And the Juaristas?"

"The road is clear, Your Majesty. Nothing will disturb you there."

15

24 August 1865

Archduchess Sophia

Adored Mother,

I take this opportunity to send you greetings. Since the mails are susceptible to disruption by the guerrilleros, the Countess Kollonitz has kindly consented to be my messenger and to deliver this letter to you upon her arrival in Europe.

Charlotte and I have been welcomed as though we were gods sent to rescue this nation. Our initial fears of a less than warm reception have been allayed by the love shown to us by these simple and warm-hearted people. I feel that I have been a part of this country all of my life, and I spend as much time as I can traveling among the people so that I might personally acquaint myself with their thoughts and desires.

Charlotte and I have moved from the Royal Palace to a castle I am restoring on a wooded hill called Chapultepec, which is the Aztec word for grasshopper. There are minor renovations still to be completed, but all imperfections are whisked away when I stand on our hillside terrace, with the rosebushes fragrant around me, the feathery whisper of the cypress groves at my back, and the luminous city at my feet. It is my own, my Mexico.

There are not the cultural advantages yet to be found here, of course, but I have commissioned the poet José Zorrilla to form a national theater, and I have almost completed the lengthy manual on court etiquette which I began on the Novara. All the embassies of Europe have now established their legations in our capital, and since the restoration of the Royal Palace we have conducted grand balls and brilliant receptions that have set the whole city talking of the royal splendor of the Hapsburgs.

The Creole women—some call them White Mexicans—are a charming mix of Old World elegance and New World freshness. They have lost the haughtiness one sees in their sisters in Spain. The beneficial effect of Mexico on the natural arrogance of the Spanish is rewarding to witness.

Charlotte is much loved, as she is a good and kind hostess, a generous monarch, a devoted wife. When she goes for a drive in the countryside, the people doff their hats as she passes. Our happiness could only be more complete if God were to bless us with a child.

As for Juárez, I admire his tenacity. He is a noble adversary, and when the guerrilla war finally runs its course I am sure that I can find a place for him in the imperial court, for we both want what is best for Mexico. I can think of no one who would serve Mexico better than someone who has fought so diligently on her behalf.

Napoleon writes letters urging me on, so you need have no fear that the French will abandon me in this effort. The Americans will not remain opposed to my reign when they see how Mexico progresses under my rule. I do not underestimate the work that remains to be done here, but not for one moment have I regretted my decision.

Your most devoted son,
Maximilian I, Emperor of Mexico

26 August 1865

Archduke Ludwig Viktor

Dear Bubi,

Only with you can I speak of the things that concern me most. Charlotte and I are isolated here, cut off from family, with only servants around us. At times I feel close to a breakdown. I ask that you please not relate to Mamá what I am about to tell you.

The rupture with our brother is now complete. I blame

Charlotte and her father for it. I had determined to accept the loss of my birthright, since there was nothing to be gained by not accepting it. But Charlotte and King Leopold were enraged that I should have had to renounce everything when I came to Mexico. A petition to my brother that Charlotte wrote and had me sign was greeted by Franz Josef first with rage and now with bitter silence.

I could bear that if the purchase had been worth the price, but Napoleon has begun to write letters threatening to remove all military support unless the French debts are repaid. How can they be repaid? Where is the money to come from? Where is the gold and silver we were all led to believe is here? My fortune is spent in maintaining a court that is ill dressed, bad mannered, and eager to return to Europe.

And the treatment Charlotte receives is abominable. She is shunned by the Creole women, and when she passes in her carriage the men do not doff their hats. Instead of maintaining her dignity in the face of their insults, she humiliates herself further by calling "Remove your hats," as she passes. She has become an object of derision.

At first it was Charlotte who so loved Mexico and the Mexicans, and I who was indifferent. Now, although she retains a fanatic belief in our right to be here, she regards everyone and everything with disdain, whereas I find the Mexicans in general to be a charming race of people.

Of course, I am aware of their deficiencies. There is a strain of superstition among the Indians that is dangerous and deep. They see Juárez burning churches, and since God does not strike him down, they believe him to be stronger than our dear Lord Jesus Christ. And there is something in the Mexican character that tends to corruption and depravity when placed in a position of authority. The worst of the lot are the judges, the Army officers and, especially, the clergy.

Mark it well that my differences with the Catholic Church prefigure disaster. The Vatican demands that I rescind the reform laws, claiming higher rights to nationalized lands. They insist on full control of the private and public schools, and, to the dismay of those Protestants among the citizens, insist that I establish the Catholic Church as the only creed and exclude all others.

The Papal Nuncio has visited me. I had hoped that we might yet sign a concordat, but I found him intractable in his demands. I watch eagerly to see by what means the Vatican will attempt to pry me loose from this throne. Of course, in my handling of this matter, as in so many others, Napoleon disagrees. He advises appeasement of the clergy, and Empress Eugénie's Catholic sympathies estrange us even further.

The Americans are another source of anxiety. Juarista clubs have formed in the United States, and arms are being smuggled in. American Civil War veterans come to Mexico and join the guerrillas. I have again and again tried to explain my position to American journalists, but the story is always twisted, so that even I have difficulty defending my position to myself.

Our long-awaited contingent of Austrian and Belgian volunteer troops arrived, but now I have reports of dissension and fights among the men. They will not accept orders easily from the French, and fight continually among themselves and with the Italian and Hungarian volunteers.

As for General Bazaine, I have no control over him at all. He is unwilling to unite his Army with the native Mexican forces, and so his efforts are fragmented and unsuccessful. In place of wisdom and obedience to the crown, he substitutes such cruelty toward captured Juaristas that even his own troops are repelled and desert the ranks in great numbers. Behind my back he remarks at my inexperience, and to my face he humors me with flattery. Only the Mexican General Mejía is loyal. I wish that his forces were greater and better trained. I know that he will be faithful to me no matter what the cost to him.

Dr. Billimek saves my sanity. The simple professor has eyes and ears only for the kingdom of animals and plants. He does not bother himself at all with politics. Indeed, he makes no attempt at social refinement, and has not bothered to learn very much Spanish, as he hardly converses with anyone but me. When he is present at gatherings and is at a loss for a Spanish word, he replies in Latin, which amuses me but no doubt has puzzled a great many of my guests.

What more can I say? It is my duty that brings me here, although Charlotte tells me over and over again that it was God. She tells me to rule with an iron hand. She is stronger than I, and I am not alone in saying that she would have made a better ruler than I.

There are difficulties between Charlotte and me—past indiscretions on my part, a reluctance to forgive on hers—which bear directly on the question of an heir. The throne demands it. The Mexican people merit it. Since it is unlikely that Charlotte will ever provide that heir, I have brought Agustín Iturbide, the two-year-old grandson of the late Emperor Iturbide, to Mexico City. His mother, who now lives in the United States, at first resisted giving him up and begged for a few more years of his company, but when offered a handsome settlement to relinquish him, promptly sent the child on to us in the care of his aunt. Charlotte pretends he is to be with us temporarily, and I let her have her pretenses. It serves no purpose to confront her on the issue.

On the journey to Mexico City from Vera Cruz I was saved from drowning by an Indian muleteer. He works now as a gardener at my castle in Chapultepec. He has told my secretary, José Blasio, of a place called Cuernavaca where I might rest my nerves and regain some semblance of control over my affairs. Charlotte cannot leave the capital at present and will act as regent in my absence. No one will notice the difference, as most decisions are made by her in my name even when I am present.

I am still stung by Franzie's treatment of me. I cannot believe our estrangement, cannot understand why he regards me as a threat, when he sits on the great throne of Austria and I on the little wanted, much beleaguered one of Mexico. You are lucky, dear brother, that you are the youngest and have been spared the jealousy the king has always reserved for me.

A week ago I attended a regimental concert at which songs from the Wienerwald were sung. My longing for home became so acute I found myself weeping. I was only thankful it was too dark for anyone to see my tears.

I have not meant to disturb your peace, but lately I have been haunted with the thought that I will never see our mother and father again, and that I will never again see the hyacinths in bloom at Miramar.

      I remain your devoted and affectionate brother,
      Max

16

Dysentery was but one of the ills that befell Maximilian during the rainy autumn months of 1865 and prevented his leaving Chapultepec Castle for Cuernavaca. He also had a fever that persisted for weeks, subsiding in the mornings and flaring in the evenings, bringing with it sweats that drained him of energy and left him haggard and pale.

Then, in mid-September Napoleon sent a letter notifying him that there would be no more money coming from France, and that he was contemplating the withdrawal of his French troops. At the same time the European bankers began to demand repayment of the loans that Maximilian had made to finance the Mexican venture.

General Bazaine, who had taken a seventeen-year-old Mexican girl as his wife and was living handsomely on the allowance of a French general, came to Chapultepec one evening as Maximilian, bundled in blankets, shivered by the fireplace in his private sitting room. The general, a tall man with a small mustache and a contemptuous manner, brought a decree for Maximilian to sign. It stated that anyone belonging to a guerrilla band, or anyone so accused, or anyone found to be carrying arms, would, with no right of appeal, be shot within twenty-four hours.

"Juárez believes you are weak," the general said.

"At this moment Juárez is right," Maximilian replied.

The decree lay unsigned on the table beside Maximilian's bed until late autumn when Maximilian, partially recovered from his illness, read it again and showed it to Carlota.

"Sign it!" she said.

"But it's barbaric. I've come to Mexico to govern the people, not to oppress them." And he tossed the decree onto a corner of his desk and forgot about it.

In December Charlotte's father, King Leopold, died. Charlotte broke down in fits of weeping in the days following the news, and Maximilian, weakened by illness, was so overcome with grief that he took to his bed again. By the end of the year he was well enough to resume the daily routine that he had initiated when he moved into the castle at Chapultepec. He retired at nine in the evening, at which time his Austrian valet, Antonio Grill, read to him in German until he fell asleep. He arose at three in the morning, read his correspondence, and dictated letters to Blasio. At half past five he drank a cup of coffee and then rode his horse for an hour. At eight Carlota met him in his study and they had breakfast there together, with Blasio sitting on a straight chair near the window in case the emperor cared to dictate while he ate. Señorita Varela stationed herself on a small settee nearby in the event that Charlotte needed a fresh handkerchief, for in moments of distress she had taken to nibbling on the lace tatting of her silk handkerchiefs until they were in shreds.

"A most disagreeable man asked to see you while you were ill," Carlota said one morning at breakfast.

Maximilian drank down the glass of Seidlitz water, a potion of mineral salts that he took as a mild cathartic each day, grimaced, wiped his lips with his napkin, and said, "Disagreeable? How is he disagreeable?"

"Forward. He is a most forward, aggressive individual. He says that he is a priest, but he unnerves me, and priests have never unnerved me before."

"My dear, how could anyone unnerve you? If you have ever been unnerved, it is indistinguishable from your other modes of being."

A flush of pain reddened her cheeks.

"Forgive me," he said. "I'm being unkind, and I don't mean to be."

Señorita Varela rose silently and handed Carlota a fresh handkerchief, which she promptly put to her lips and began to chew.

"You were ill, so I took the liberty of investigating the gentleman's credentials," said Carlota, the handkerchief always in the vicinity of her mouth. "His name is Agustín

Fischer. He was born a Protestant, but converted to Catholicism and then became a Jesuit. There are rumors that he is a very sensual man, not priestly in his habits. He was secretary to the Bishop of Durango and was dismissed because of some scandalous acts which the bishop was too tactful to spell out in his letter to me. I see no reason for this man's visit, unless he has been sent by the Vatican to try to sway you from your proper course. If that's true, it's an insult. You must not see him."

"What other things occurred during my illness?" said Maximilian impatiently.

"I received a letter from Empress Eugénie. She hints that our financial difficulties are your fault, that if you would build fewer theaters and palaces, if you would control the greed of your ministers—"

"Napoleon's wife hints and I am supposed to obey."

"But she speaks for Napoleon."

"Napoleon is a dog barking after it has already bitten," said Maximilian bitterly. "He is preparing to withdraw from Mexico, Charlotte, but wants me to believe that if I do as he says he'll stay."

"But if you anger him, he will surely withdraw, and then what will become of us? Sign the decree. Show Napoleon and the Juaristas your strength. Take charge of the army—General Bazaine countermands you, he ridicules your orders—"

"You are overwrought."

"Why do you always dismiss me so cruelly? Why can you not listen to what I say?"

"Because you say too much, dear Charlotte. Far, far too much."

"You will cut us off from all help."

"When you have calmed down we will talk again."

Their conversation ended, as it invariably did of late, on a note of unresolved antagonism.

The next morning, contrary to Carlota's wishes, Maximilian received Father Fischer in the private sitting room of the castle. The priest was a robust man, with thinning brown hair and full lips. A sprinkle of broken veins ran across his broad nose and disappeared into his flowing mustache.

"Your Majesty," he said, bowing deeply. His fleshy body was girdled tightly into his black priest's habit. A gold cross hung from the black sash that encircled his huge waist. Highly polished, hand-stitched Italian boots peeked out from beneath his skirt.

"Sit down, Father Fischer." Maximilian motioned to a brocade chair across from his settee. Father Fischer ignored him and sat down on the settee next to Maximilian.

The emperor smiled icily. "The empress described you to me. She has not done you justice."

Father Fischer grasped Maximilian's slender hand in his large one and placed it on his chest. "Do you feel the beating there of my heart, Your Majesty? It beats with love for you. Our Lord Jesus has sent me to be with you in your efforts to save Mexico and the Church."

Withdrawing his hand, Maximilian said, "Mexico and the Church are not the same, Father Fischer. I have spoken to the Papal Nuncio. The Vatican's demands cannot be met."

The priest now knelt on the floor at Maximilian's feet. He looked up into Maximilian's face with a gaze so rapturous that the emperor began to smile.

"You must disregard what the Nuncio said," said the priest. "I have the means to settle the dispute between you and the Holy See. I will write a *concordat* that will satisfy the Vatican's requirements and that you will beg to sign. Do you believe me?"

"I want to believe you."

"Good. First we will pray." The priest, still on his knees, closed his eyes and bowed his head. "Dear Lord, Blessed Savior, we pray for Maximilian, emperor of Mexico." He opened his eyes and looked up at Maximilian. "Shall we pray for the empress, too, or is there a woman that the emperor would prefer to name in prayer?"

"This is really most unusual, Father Fischer. I should throw you out."

Father Fischer closed his eyes and bowed his head once more. "It is as has been rumored, Savior. Our beloved emperor's marital bed is smooth, the sheets unrumpled, the lace coverlet unstained by his manhood. Restore him, O Lord." Father Fischer touched the top of Maximilian's balding head with his fingertips. "Restore him, O Lord."

Blasio entered the room on hearing the priest's voice thundering through the corridors.

"You've broken the spell, Blasio," Maximilian said.

The priest shook his finger in Maximilian's face. "You are a frivolous man, Your Majesty. Do you believe that our Lord, Jesus Christ, died for our sins?"

"Of course," said Maximilian, taken aback by the abrupt change.

"Is it true that you have thought of leaving the throne, of abdicating your responsibility to the people of Mexico?"

"The thought has occurred to me."

"Do you feel that Napoleon is weakening and that all who surround you practice perfidy and betrayal?"

"I do."

Father Fischer was calmer now, the choleric flush of anger almost gone. "It is settled."

"What is settled?"

The priest stood up and placed his hands on Maximilian's shoulders. "You will be strong. Juárez wants to destroy the Church in Mexico, but you will destroy Juárez first. There is no longer any question in my mind. I had a vision of Juárez's corpse laid out on its bier just this moment as I knelt beside you. The Vatican will aid you. There are those that I can prevail upon in Rome to help you save yourself as well as the Holy Mother Church in Mexico."

Father Fischer turned to Blasio. "Señor, the emperor needs a place to restore his mind and body so that he will be ready to meet the challenges that await him in his renewed resolve. I will accompany him."

Blasio nodded dumbly. He had never seen anyone speak to the emperor in this manner.

"The countryside would be best," said the priest, "someplace well removed from the worries of the capital."

"The roads are no longer safe," Blasio said.

"Then we will take the Army with us," said the priest. "This is the emperor we are speaking of, Señor. We are concerned with the health of the man who rules Mexico."

Carlota, her small figure stiffly formal in its enveloping mourning dress, watched the preparations for departure from behind the gilded iron balustrade of the terrace. Behind her the Iturbide infant cooed contentedly in his elderly Aunt Josefa's arms.

"Take the child inside," said Carlota irritably.

The sight of the child always upset Carlota, but especially so this morning. General Mejía, who had arrived with his troop of Mexican soldiers to escort Maximilian to Cuernavaca, brought news of the ambush and murder of two Belgian soldiers on a road near the capital.

"Then the emperor must desist," Carlota had shrilled to the general, a dark, sharp-featured Indian, as he stood awkwardly at the side of the breakfast table in the royal dining room. "He must not leave the capital at this time."

"My life and the lives of my men are between the emperor and all harm," General Mejía had replied.

Carlota had turned to her husband. "Will you do this thing in spite of the dangers?"

"My dear Charlotte, Father Fischer has seen my life spread before him in a vision. He assures me that I will not die on the road to Cuernavaca."

The carriages were now ready. Dr. Billimek and Father Fischer were already seated in the royal carriage, a special design that had arrived from Europe several months before. It was black with gleaming brass fittings and side lamps of Venetian glass. It had lockers for provisions and a desk outfitted with writing materials. Twelve perfectly matched, snow-white mules strained against the blue harness.

Blasio put his hand on the emperor's arm to help him up. "A moment, please, Blasio," Maximilian said. He turned and waved to Carlota. At the flutter of Carlota's handkerchief in return, he let himself be helped up the steps into the carriage.

General Mejía and his soldiers rode across the square toward the iron gates. The royal carriage followed, then the carriage that held the emperor's valet and the imperial luggage.

"It is a good thing to leave the empress behind for a brief while," said Father Fischer as the emperor leaned his head wearily against the soft black leather seat. "You will be renewed and invigorated."

The gates were opened, and the road lay ahead. The gardener, Hector Sedano, rode alone, his slight figure hunched over the reins of his horse. The entourage followed him, because he alone knew the place in Cuernavaca where Maximilian would rest and restore his soul.

17

"These are my subjects, Father Fischer," said Maximilian, gesturing toward an Indian family at the side of the road. The husband sat on a donkey, while his wife walked behind him, a baby wrapped in the folds of her rebozo. "Do you think that their lives have changed for the better now that I have come?"

"Their lives are spiritually richer," Father Fischer replied. "An Indian does not feel or want the same things that men of breeding and education want. Their needs are simple, their wants few. But Juárez would take away their salvation, their belief in Jesus Christ as their only Savior. You will restore that faith, bring them back to God."

They had left the valley of Mexico behind them. The road turned upward, and the vegetation became greener, the shade denser, the air cooler. Patches of bright red blanketed the tall trees that grew on the hillsides.

"We must plant some of those trees at Chapultepec," Maximilian said. "What are they, Professor?"

"They are a species of coral tree, Your Excellency."

"Do you think that the Aztecs saw these trees when they traveled this road, Blasio?" Maximilian asked.

"I am sure they did, Your Majesty."

The plaza of an Indian village appeared through the blaze of blossoms. Maximilian thrust his head out the window and peered through the trees.

"Stop the carriage!" he ordered. "I want to walk about."

"Do you think it wise to walk in an Indian village when there are bandits about?" asked Father Fischer as the carriage came to a halt.

"But you agreed that these are my people, Father Fischer."

"Of course, but—"

"If I am their ruler in truth, then they will welcome me. If I am not—"

"*A sus órdenes*," said General Mejía at the window.

"We will get out and walk here," Maximilian said.

The general looked around him at the steep cobbled streets, at the quietness of the village. "*Sí.*"

Maximilian stepped down first while General Mejía's troops watched from their positions. Then the professor and Father Fischer got out of the carriage and trailed behind the emperor.

Plucking a flower from a roadside bush, Dr. Billimek said, "The climate is changing, Your Majesty. You see this shrub, the way the leaf is formed, it is indicative of a semitropical climate."

"And do you suppose we will find butterflies in Cuernavaca that are more brilliantly colored than in the capital?" asked Maximilian.

"It is possible."

"Blasio, you must find a copy of Lamarck's book on botany for me," Maximilian said. "The professor has said that I must read it."

Blasio withdrew a small notebook from the pocket of his black frock coat and wrote in it while Father Fischer looked around, anxiously fingering the cross that dangled from his waist.

The streets were deserted except for several old women who sat on the ground near the ancient plaza, small stacks of vegetables on brightly colored cloths in front of them. General Mejía's men had encircled the plaza, and the general himself, head swiveling at every sound, rode slowly alongside the emperor and his companions. Beneath a leafy tree not too far from the carriage, Hector Sedano sat on his horse and waited.

"Buy something, Blasio," Maximilian said.

Blasio bought a bunch of carrots and a handful of green and red chiles, and as he handed the coins to the woman, he shivered, although the day was warm.

"I think the emperor would be wise to return to the

carriage," said General Mejía, his eyes fixed on a stand of mango trees at the far end of the plaza.

"The Lord protects me," Maximilian said. "Isn't that right, Father Fischer?"

"To a point, Your Majesty," the priest answered.

Sudden sharp bursts of gunfire erupted from the vicinity of the mango trees, and General Mejía said, "Quickly, give me your hand, Your Majesty," and pulled the emperor up onto his horse.

"Courage, Blasio," shouted Maximilian as he and General Mejía galloped back toward the carriage. Blasio stared after them, the raw vegetables in his hands, a startled expression on his face.

"Lord save us!" yelled Father Fischer as he ran past.

Dr. Billimek, who had been kneeling in the shrubbery, his yellow umbrella unfurled above him, looked up in surprise.

Blasio threw the vegetables to the ground and grabbed hold of Dr. Billimek's sleeve. "The Juaristas are shooting at us, Professor."

"Juaristas?" Bullets whizzed by. One of them put a neat hole through the professor's yellow umbrella. "I left my pistol in my suitcase," he said. "But then I neglected to buy ammunition for it when I was in Trieste."

"Don't talk, Professor, just run."

General Mejía deposited Maximilian in the carriage, and then he galloped away to where his men had engaged the *guerrilleros*.

"Oh, my God, my God," said the professor as he and Blasio scrambled into the carriage behind the priest.

"Look at how my people love me, Father Fischer," Maximilian said. "They kill one another for me."

When the battle was over, two of the bandits lay dead on the cobblestones, and the rest had fled into the crimson hills. General Mejía arranged his troops in a cordon around the royal carriage, and the caravan continued on its way. Father Fischer gave a prayer of thanksgiving for the emperor's deliverance, but Maximilian brooded, not speaking, and when the prayer was concluded, he retreated from the others, his mood dark and pensive. Blasio held the professor's yellow umbrella in his lap and stared fixedly at the bullet hole.

After they had ridden for a while, the silence broken only by the creak of the carriage wheels and the soft whistles of Dr. Billimek's snoring, Father Fischer reached into the pocket of his voluminous skirt and brought out a worn book. The cover, black with age, had been patched with hand-woven material.

"I have been saving this for just such an occasion as this, Your Majesty," the priest said.

"I need no presents, Father."

The priest placed the book in Maximilian's hands. "It is a breviary, a book of hours, and very old. Look at it. Go on, open it, Your Majesty. You see the writing in the margins? That was written three hundred years ago by Brother Gerónimo de Aguilar when he and Gonzalo Guerrero were shipwrecked among the savage Maya."

Maximilian opened the book and turned the yellowed pages.

"It is a gift from God come to comfort you in an hour of despair," continued the priest. "Your ancestor, Charles V, discovered this land and Guerrero's descendants populate it. You have a right to be here. Do not hurry your reading, Your Majesty, for you will live to be an old man. I have seen the length of your life in a vision, a road with many successes to come. The breviary will comfort you in your long sojourn in Mexico."

They passed into a tropical valley, perfumed by flowers that bloomed all year long and cooled by currents of air that streamed from the slopes of the surrounding mountains. At an old stone church in a grove of poplar trees, the caravan stopped.

"How fortunate that we have found a church in which to refresh our spirits," Father Fischer said. "Is this Cuernavaca, Señor Blasio? For if it is, it bears no small resemblance to paradise."

"No, it is Acapatzingo, but Cuernavaca is very near," Blasio answered.

Hector Sedano conferred with General Mejía for a few moments and then rode off on his horse.

"If Your Majesty would like to visit the church," said the general, "we will wait there until Señor Sedano returns with his family, and then he will guide us to our destination."

"Family?" said Maximilian. "I had no idea he had a family."

"All Mexican men have families, Your Majesty," the priest replied.

Concepción Contreras de Sedano, one of seven children of a shoemaker, was sixteen when she married Hector Sedano, an Indian muleteer from Vera Cruz who had come to Acapatzingo to buy a mule. Concepción had golden brown skin and ebony hair and carried herself with such graceful sensuality that Hector brought his mother from Vera Cruz to guard her when he was away.

Before the marriage Concepción's mother had given her advice on how to make her husband happy. "Always let him lie down with you when he wants to. Kiss him and tickle him and excite him with your tongue. And rub your body against his, because you will feel heat there which is pleasurable. If you do these things, your husband will not leave you, and you will not get tired of his attentions."

Now that Hector worked in the gardens at Chapultepec, he came home rarely, and so Concepción was startled to see him standing in front of their adobe house near the arroyo in Acapatzingo.

"Hector, *querido*," she said, and hugged him to her eagerly.

"We have very little time," he said. "Emperor Maximilian is waiting at the church for us."

"Emperor Maximilian is here in Acapatzingo? But why would he come to such a simple village as this?"

"He is in need of rest."

"But where will he rest here? We have no room." She called out to Hector's mother, who was patting masa into tortillas in the yard. "Mamá, Emperor Maximilian is coming here."

"Not here," said Hector. "I'm taking him to the gardens of José de la Borda."

He pulled Concepción into the small room where the two of them slept. "Quickly," he said, "pull up your dress and bend over." He unbuttoned his pants and let them drop to the floor. "I was in danger of treating my mule like a woman," he said as he prepared to enter her from behind.

"Wait, let me lie down."

"Hurry, hurry," he said, collapsing on top of her.

She wriggled her hips, tried to feel the exquisite sensation, but in four thrusts he had begun to breathe heavily, and by the fifth, he was through.

Concepción covered herself with the bedclothes as Señora Sedano looked in at them from the doorway.

"Why would the emperor come to such a place as this?" the old woman asked.

*   *   *

The church was bare of ornament, except for the fresh flowers that stood in earthen jars on the altar.

"A humble place," said Dr. Billimek as he surveyed the hard wooden benches and whitewashed walls.

"God resides in humble places as well as palaces," Father Fischer said.

Maximilian had knelt down on the stone floor beside the benches and was reading from Brother Aguilar's breviary.

"You must collect your aphorisms in a book, Father Fischer," he said without looking up, "for they are bound to amuse the general populace as much as they do me."

When Sedano returned, the afternoon light that had illuminated the church was nearly spent.

"You have been a long time in finding your family, Sedano," said Maximilian irritably. He looked toward the door where the light still lingered. An elderly woman, head and body wrapped in a black rebozo, stood with a girl of about seventeen years of age. A violet chemise hung demurely from the girl's shoulders to her ankles and her black hair was twisted into a coronet of braids. As the receding light played on the girl's oval face, Maximilian let out a gasp of pleasure.

"She's beautiful, isn't she?" said Father Fischer. "I prefer the women of Mexico to those of Europe. There is mystery in the Mexican woman's face, a promise of delights that one can only dream of."

When Dr. Billimek looked at him in surprise, Father Fischer shrugged and said, "Priests are men. God has forgiven me my transgressions. I have named my children, had them baptized, and confessed my sins."

The light seemed to draw Maximilian. The hard blue eyes that habitually looked past objects in his path were now fixed on the young girl's face.

"Is this your daughter, Sedano?" he asked.

"No, Your Majesty. This is Concepción, my wife."

Vines climbed untended up the walls of the Borda house. Lily pools were choked with weeds. A toppled laurel tree rotted in the courtyard. But wild orchids grew beside the fountains and thickets of mango and magnolia trees scented the air, and the moment Maximilian stepped past the gate he changed. His face, still wan from illness, took on an excited glow, and he walked briskly up and down the paths, stopping only to admire another vista, to dip his fingers into another fountain, or to stare up at the rainbow of vanishing light that streaked the mountains.

"My poet's soul is stirred by this place," he exclaimed. "This is more than I could have dreamed of. How have I not known of this place before? Smell the fragrance, Father Fischer, the perfume."

"It is very run-down," the priest said.

"I will rebuild it. The tiles will have to be replaced, and of course, we will bring in stone urns. There, along the path, just as you enter, will be a wishing well. The gardens will be replanted." He turned to Dr. Billimek. "We will bring nightingales here from Miramar—thousands of nightingales. And I must have a water garden, with pale lilies floating on leafy green carpets."

"We will need the botany book by Augustín de Candolle," said the professor.

"Blasio, write that down," said Maximilian. His face was animated, his eyes a brilliant blue. "The botany book by Augustín de Candolle." He turned toward Sedano, who had been trailing behind the others. "Sedano, is the climate always so temperate here?"

"It is, Your Majesty, as you see it now. There is very little change."

"Astounding! Where is the owner of these gardens? I must speak to him."

"The owner, José de la Borda, died a hundred years ago, Señor," said Sedano, embarrassed to be talking directly to the emperor.

"Were there any heirs?"

"Only the government, Señor."

"And you are the government!" said Dr. Billimek.

Maximilian spun around to Blasio. "Is that true, Blasio? These gardens in this heavenly place are mine?"

"Everything is yours, Your Majesty," Blasio replied.

The house was littered with debris, and velvety cobwebs hung from the ceilings and grayed the available light. Concepción set to cleaning while Sedano's mother went into the kitchen at the rear of the house and started a fire in the grate. Sedano brought the pots of food from the wagon and hung them from the rusted iron in the kitchen hearth.

Later, in the balminess of the tropical evening, while crickets sang in the weed-choked gardens, the royal party ate their dinner by candlelight on the spacious veranda. Concepción served the food, and as she brought the plates and removed them from the table, Maximilian's eyes followed her.

A hammock was strung for the emperor in one of the empty rooms of the house.

"Are you comfortable, Your Majesty?" asked Father Fischer as the emperor swung gently, eyes closed.

"Most comfortable."

"Have you prayed?"

"I have thought about praying. But I'm testing God. If he is as powerful as they say, then he knows my wishes without my prayers."

Father Fischer followed the path past the carriage house to the chapel where the Sedano family was spending the night. Hector Sedano sat on a stone bench outside.

"Ah, Señor Sedano, you are taking some air, I see," the priest said. "I too am enjoying the fragrance of the evening." He threw his head back as though gulping pockets of fresh air into his lungs. "Perhaps you would join me on a stroll and we could enjoy it together."

They walked back toward the small lake near the mango grove.

"You have done a great service to your country by acquainting the emperor with this place," the priest said. "Are you a Catholic?"

"*Sí.*"

"Then I will mention you in my prayers."

"*Gracias.*"

"Do you believe that without the Church your soul will not reach heaven?"

"I believe that."

"You know that Juárez wants to destroy the Church, don't you?"

"It will not be permitted."

"Who will not permit it? You?"

"*Sí.* If it has to be me, then I will not permit it."

"Let us sit and look at the lake," the priest said. "See the designs that the moon makes on its surface."

"*Sí.*"

They sat together on a bench, Sedano's earth-stained hands on his lap, grimy toes protruding from his sandals.

The priest sighed heavily and then said, "The emperor's wife does not please him."

Sedano nodded and swallowed audibly.

"He looks at your wife with longing."

Sedano nodded again.

The two men stood up and walked along the bank. The water was an oily stain beneath the trees.

"I have had a vision this very moment, Señor Sedano. I see God welcoming you into the gates of paradise and preparing a special place for you in heaven."

The chapel, except for the candles that Señora Sedano had lit on the ruined altar, was in darkness when Hector Sedano entered. His mother snored in her hammock, while Concepción, wrapped in a rebozo, slept on a bench near the door.

"Get up," he said, shaking his wife's shoulder.

"But I have only just gone to sleep." Her words were slurred by drowsiness.

He shook her again, and she sat up. "Does the emperor eat breakfast at midnight?"

"Leave your shoes," he said. "You don't need your shoes."

"But where are we going? Why must you pull my arm so sharply?"

She followed her husband out of the chapel and down the path past the small lake, running to keep up with him. At a fountain near the open door of the Borda house, he stopped.

"The emperor is in the room at the end of the veranda," he said. "When he is in Cuernavaca, you will stay with him."

She began to cry. "Have I done something to displease you?"

"He wants you in his bed. He is the emperor. The priest has given me dispensation to give you to the emperor."

"But how—what did I do?"

"You did nothing. This has to be done for the Church and for Mexico."

"But he has a wife. Whose wife will I be?" She clutched his arm. "Come into the chapel with me. We will lie down together in the corner. I will be better than I was today." She cooed in his ear, tickled his groin with her fingertips, tried to lick his lips with her tongue, but he shoved her away.

She stared at him, her heart beating wildly. "It's a sin."

"Tell your confessor. It has to be done." His mouth was tight, his eyes averted.

"And if I have a child—"

"It will be his. I will find someone else to satisfy me."

Maximilian was not able to sleep. The swaying of the hammock did not lull him, nor did the breeze that drifted in from the open doorway. He thought of what he would do with the Borda house, of the repairs that would be made, of the twisted cane furniture with chintz covers that he would have sent from Vienna. He would plant rare orchids in the gardens, and a species of gardenia whose aroma had haunted him since he had smelled it in the jungles of Brazil. There would be boats for rowing in the large pool, and he would order nightingales sent from Miramar to sing him to sleep at night. He turned in the hammock. He would not bring the Creole women here to this tropical garden. He tired of their artificial games. He wearied of the pretenses, of the witty talk, of the forced declarations of love. When he was in their company, he was in the world, not safely away from it. They talked of politics, of who slept with whom, of who flirted the most outrageously at what soiree. They made demands, and entreaties; created difficulties and entanglements; elicited false promises; brought out his disloyalties; spread rumors; unleashed his cutting tongue. They brought jealousies with them. His marriage did not contain half the jealousies that these casual liaisons did.

At thirty-three he had become old in Mexico. The doctors dosed him with iron and quinine, but fevers and worry had made him thin and nervous. He had grown jaded in his passions. His senses had become dull. He feared the loss of potency, the diminishing of desire.

"Oh, God," he groaned.

He heard a woman's voice, soft and beguiling, on the walk outside the door. Then a man's, low and insistent. He sat up in the hammock trying to hear what was said, but there was nothing but the swish of leaves against the roof.

"Concepción," he said in the darkness.

"Sí."

In the moonlight he saw her raise her violet dress above her head and drop it to the floor. She walked toward him, breasts high and undulating slightly as she moved.

"Concepción," he said again, and put his arms around her waist and laid his head against her breast.

"Sí."

She stepped into the hammock beside him. She had let her braids down, and her black hair was silky over them both. He kissed the cool skin of her belly while she massaged his penis with fingers as soft as the magnolia petals outside the door.

He slipped high inside of her and came rapidly, then lay back again, bathed in her scent.

She studied his face in the moonlight, the narrow nostrils, the full lips, moist and partly open, the blue eyes melancholy even now. He had finished. There would not even be pleasure for her from this man. The anger inside of her at Hector and the priest burned her stomach and made her head ache.

"Maximiliano," she said, and he looked at her in surprise.

She kissed him on the lips, then stroked him until he had grown hard again, then rubbed him against her until she felt her own exquisite release.

"Concepción," he sighed.

She took his penis in her mouth, and Maximilian closed his eyes and dreamed of Miramar and nightingales, of pleasures too delicately beautiful to last.

18

"There is no point in keeping the Iturbide child here in Mexico any longer," Maximilian told Blasio. "Make arrangements to send him back to the United States. As matters stand now, concern for an heir to the throne of Mexico seems little more than an absurdity."

Maximilian's personal fortune was dwindling away as debts mounted and guerrilla attacks increased. News came from Europe that Franz Josef, at war with Prussia, would send no more troops to Mexico. Charlotte's brother, Leopold II, new king of the Belgians, notified Maximilian that he would have to withdraw his soldiers also. And in France there were cries that Napoleon be done once and for all with the Mexican adventure.

"Sign the decree which General Bazaine has drafted for you, Your Majesty," Father Fischer advised Maximilian. "It will help you destroy Juárez. No one will ever say again that you are weak, that you cannot control your subjects. Show them how strong you are, how you will not tolerate insurrection, how you will govern this country, you will rule it, and that you have no fear."

Maximilian signed the decree. Ordinary soldiers now had the power of life and death over anyone found bearing arms. Common citizens used the decree to rid themselves of their enemies. French soldiers, ordered to execute bandits on the spot, without trial, without clemency, without appeal, deserted in increasing numbers. Father Fischer had predicted that the decree would destroy Juárez, but it was destroying Maximilian instead.

The gardens of José de la Borda in Cuernavaca became a refuge for Maximilian from the chaos.

"It is like May in Italy all year round," he wrote his youngest brother.

In the mornings he would rise early and by eight o'clock had crossed the road to the castle that Cortés himself had built during the Conquest. There he worked at his desk for an hour, after which he rode his horse or walked through the gardens with Dr. Billimek and Blasio. He lunched al fresco on the veranda of the Borda house, and then took a short nap.

In the afternoons he went to Acapatzingo to be with Concepción. He had built an Indian chalet there for her that he called El Olvido, forgetfulness. Unlike the Borda house, with its gardens that now resembled a European summer retreat, the small estate in Acapatzingo had an uncared-for easiness. There was no scheme in the plantings. Flowers, flamboyant and randomly scattered, were permitted to tangle into thickets of blinding color, the mango trees allowed to ripen until the smell was sweetly dizzying.

"I love you as I have never loved a woman before," Maximilian told Concepción. "I have never known such joy, such happiness with anyone else."

Carlota sometimes accompanied Maximilian to Cuernavaca, but would sit wan and unsmiling, lost in her own thoughts, not interested enough even to ask him where he went in the afternoons. Since her father's death, her pretty face had aged, become pinched in an expression of permanent sorrow. She had begun to suffer from delusions.

"You want to be rid of me, I can see it in your eyes," she told Maximilian. "You hate me. I know that you do."

"I don't hate you."

"You do. And it is because I have not been able to bear you a child."

The chalet in Acapatzingo was safe from all intruders. There was no one there but the two lovers and an Indian servant. Maximilian and Concepción bathed together in the brass tub he had brought from the castle at Chapultepec. They lay together beneath the coffee trees on fragrant beds of fallen leaves in the cool afternoons.

"My misery was so profound, the sadness that had engulfed

my soul so deadening," Maximilian said, "I would have left Mexico forever if I did not have you."

Then the word came that Napoleon was about to begin withdrawing his troops and all other support.

"I would welcome you back as a gallant monarch who has had to face insurmountable obstacles," he wrote Maximilian. "Let us not think of the past, but look to the future."

Maximilian, shocked by the news, sank into a depression that paralyzed his spirit and rendered him helpless. It was as though this moment had not been foretold, as though he had imagined he would have endless years in which to linger in the sweet gardens of Mexico.

"General Mejía supports you, Your Majesty," said Father Fischer. "There are Mexicans who would rally to your side if you would lead them. Tell them you are willing to fight for Church and country. You must fight. How else can you fulfill the destiny that I have seen stretched out before you?"

"I have tired of it all," Maximilian said. "Leave me in peace."

"How can you tire of it?" screamed Carlota. "It is God's wish that you be here."

"Hear how she speaks for God, Father Fischer."

"How can we know she doesn't? Listen carefully to Her Majesty, for she has the welfare of Mexico firmly in her heart."

"I do," cried Carlota, "oh, Maxl, I do. I will go to Europe. I will talk to Napoleon. The pope will receive me. He won't turn me away."

"I won't permit it. No one will beg for me."

"But I must go. Of course I will go. There will be enemies in my path, of course, I know that, but the angels of heaven will protect me, for my mission is to save you, darling Maxl, my adored one. How can I fail in such an exalted endeavor?"

Perhaps it was Carlota's crazed determination that rallied Maximilian's spirit, for he wrote to Napoleon: "A gradual withdrawal will not be necessary. Withdraw immediately, if it pleases you. I will defend my honor and my empire with the help of my new countrymen."

In July 1866, against Maximilian's wishes, and with occasional moments of delusion in which she confided to her ladies-in-waiting that Maximilian was plotting to kill her, Carlota left on her mission to Europe.

19

A wan, frail Carlota arrived with her retinue of servants and Mexican ministers in Paris on a warm day in August 1866. Due to a mixup in telegrams, Napoleon's representatives were sent to the wrong station, and when Carlota's train arrived, only a handful of Mexican supporters were there to greet her.

"Napoleon wants to shame me," she told her Mexican lady-in-waiting, Señora del Barrio, as they stood on the station platform, steamer trunks piled around them. "It is a failure before it begins."

When they arrived at the Grand Hotel, her spirits revived when she was informed that the entire first floor had been reserved for her and her party. There were baskets of fruit and bottles of wine waiting, and bouquets of flowers stood in silver vases in all the rooms. Napoleon's ministers crowded around the doors, waiting their turn to present their cards.

In the afternoon, a note arrived from Napoleon inviting her to the palace in St. Cloud the following day.

"Oh, we *will* succeed, Manuelita," said an exhausted, but happy, Carlota. "I am confident of that now."

The next day Carlota rose early and sent Señora del Barrio to buy a new hat for her. "Empress Eugénie is very elegant. She will be pleased to see that I did not lose my sense of fashion in Mexico."

After lunch a carriage arrived, and Carlota and Señora del

Barrio left for St. Cloud, traveling through streets lined with cheering crowds waving Mexican flags.

"This surely shows how much the French people love Maximilian," said Carlota, turning and waving back.

An honor guard greeted Carlota when she arrived at the palace, but as she and Señora del Barrio ascended the grand staircase, she heard the household staff and aides-de-camp commenting on her thin appearance, remarking about her black dress, still wrinkled from traveling, and the ugliness of her new hat, a monstrosity of bows and feathers and swaths of tulle. And when she heard them whispering that her dusky-skinned lady-in-waiting resembled an orangutan, she asked Señora del Barrio for a handkerchief, which she placed at her mouth and began to nibble.

Señora del Barrio was escorted to an antechamber while Carlota was taken directly to Napoleon's study.

"My dear Empress Charlotte," said Napoleon when she entered the room, "it is so very nice to see you again." He wore an elegant uniform and a cluster of gold medals across his chest. His mustache was long and pomaded and he had combed his shiny brown hair onto the sides of his cheeks.

"I prefer to be called Empress Carlota," she said sweetly, and placed one gloved hand in his.

"What a lovely hat," murmured Empress Eugénie, kissing Carlota on both cheeks. Eugénie was radiant in a gown of Valenciennes lace, her sloping bosom powdered white, fresh flowers twined in her golden curls.

"Maximilian sends his greetings and inquires after Your Majesty's health," Carlota said.

"I accept his greetings, and send mine in return," said Napoleon. "As for my health, I suffer the tortures of gallstones and have spent the past month taking the waters at Vichy."

"Perhaps you are being poisoned," said Carlota. Napoleon, who had heard rumors of the Mexican empress's mental instability, glanced at his wife.

"The question of poisoning has never been mentioned by the doctors," Eugénie said.

"Doctors are notorious for poisoning people," said Carlota. "I never permit doctors to minister to me." She straightened her hat and smoothed the folds of her wrinkled gown with the moist handkerchief. After a few moments in which no one spoke, she said, "The people cheered us in the street. They adore Maxl as I do."

"The news of your arrival has been much in the newspapers," Napoleon said. "They cheer your courage, nothing more."

"Did you find your sea voyage enjoyable?" asked Empress Eugénie pleasantly.

"I hardly slept," Carlota said, "I was so filled with worry and anticipation. Of course you know that Maximilian speaks of abdication."

"An unfortunate ending," Napoleon said, "but Maximilian must be encouraged to leave Mexico. It is a desperate enterprise, a forlorn hope."

"I told him that only old men and idiots abdicate," said Carlota.

Napoleon looked uncomfortable as he straightened his shoulders against the back of the sofa.

"Your advice, while well intended, may prove disastrous for you both," said Eugénie. Carlota looked sharply at her, and without replying turned toward Napoleon. "You must save him, Your Majesty."

"He is beyond saving," Napoleon replied.

"If your husband were only less extravagant," Eugénie said. "He spends money for theaters and museums and parks when half the population is illiterate and the other half has no need of them."

Carlota got up suddenly and knelt at Napoleon's knee. "We are surrounded by enemies, Your Majesty. My darling Maxl is so beloved by his subjects. The Americans will not dare go against us if you remain steadfast."

"My dear Charlotte, Mexico and your husband will drag me down with them. My power ebbs away in Europe while Mexico drains me of men and money."

"But Juárez is Satan. He plots our downfall. He begrudges our happiness, would destroy what we have worked for. Another three years is all that we will need. But you must remove General Bazaine. I will not rest until you do. Bazaine plots with Satan also, and would destroy my brilliant Maxl. He has henchmen here in France who are watching me, trying to ruin my mission, trying to poison your mind against me. But I bring documents from Maxl that will prove that the financial situation can be reversed, that Juárez can be defeated, that the throne of Mexico can be saved, that—"

Carlota's words, so precise at first, tumbled over one another now. "Oh, you must, you simply must save him. He is my adored. We have no children, but he is not bitter. He loves me more now than I thought it was possible to be loved. I love him. Of course I love him. I love him. He is adored. I adore him. He is adored." Her voice grew faint, her eyes jittered, and then she lay prostrate on the carpet, the monstrous hat lying like a funeral wreath beside her.

Tears coursed down Napoleon's face and Eugénie wept openly.

"You must care for this poor woman," said Napoleon when Señora del Barrio was brought from the antechamber. "What possessed Emperor Maximilian to permit her this voyage, this embarrassment, this strain? What can be done to preserve what sanity she has left?"

"Come, Your Majesty," said Señora del Barrio gently, and she took Carlota's hand in hers and led her from the room.

There was yet another visit to Napoleon. This time Carlota, instead of delivering a meek and rambling speech on her knees, arrived brandishing the document in which Napoleon swore he would not abandon Maximilian.

"You see what you have written," screamed Carlota. " 'No matter what happens, if you accept, I will never fail you.' What of this? Is your word worth nothing? Are you a liar and a coward, unable and unwilling to support your friends? And what of the money that was sent to Mexico to help us, which has cost us so dearly that we are bankrupt with the effort to repay it? Your bankers have stolen it. They have grown rich on it. Their perfidy and fraud will destroy us. We are destitute. Where will we go? What will we do?"

Eugénie fell to the sofa in a faint.

Napoleon's aide-de-camp entered the study from the antechamber. "She is distraught," Napoleon said. "There is no hope for her, no means to make her understand."

The news of Carlota's mad journey spread through Europe. Father Fischer, who had arrived in Europe shortly before Carlota, received daily reports at the Vatican of her growing insanity. He had heard that she accused those around her of trying to poison her, that she ate nothing but nuts and oranges while traveling, that she kept live chickens in her hotel rooms, to be cooked as needed.

"She will come here next, Holy Father," Fischer said one afternoon after lunch with the seventy-four-year-old pontiff and Cardinal Antonelli, the pope's closest adviser.

"She dreams of convincing you to abandon the clergy and Church property in Mexico as Napoleon is abandoning her husband."

"I hear she is mad," Cardinal Antonelli said.

"Her madness is tinged with shrewdness," said Father Fischer. "She understands the duplicity of those around Maximilian. His own French General Bazaine conspires with Juárez behind the emperor's back. Maximilian's innocence, his lack of understanding of these matters, is startling."

"I say leave him to his fate," Cardinal Antonelli said. "While his country collapses around him, the bishops in Mexico report that he watches birds and hunts butterflies. Two thousand nightingales were delivered to his gardens in Cuernavaca while Juárez was leading his troops against the imperial forces."

"Is this true?" said the pope.

"I'm afraid that it is, Holy Father," Father Fischer replied, "but you must understand that Maximilian's constitution is very delicate, that his nerves cannot be strained constantly without respite. I have learned his habits well this past year. He must be handled with care, praised and encouraged. His love for beauty nurtures him. If he were to be denied it, his usefulness would soon be over."

"His usefulness is already over," the cardinal said. "He speaks of abdication."

Father Fischer smiled. "He will not abdicate. There is a girl in Cuernavaca, the wife of the emperor's gardener. I encouraged Maximilian's interest in her."

"A gardener's wife?" snapped the cardinal. "You think an emperor will stay in Mexico and risk death for a gardener's wife?"

"And the gardener?" said the pope. "Is he a Catholic?"

"He is, Your Holiness, and I gave him holy dispensation in your name. He fully understands that his gift is a gift to the Church rather than to Maximilian."

The room was very quiet. Father Fischer toyed with his crucifix.

"Go on," the pope said. "Go on."

"Maximilian was suffering from what appeared to be nervous prostration before he met the girl. He was often ill with fevers and drank excessive amounts of sherry. I had to find a way to soothe him, calm him, and when the girl appeared and I saw the look in Maximilian's eyes at the sight of her, I knew immediately that a liaison between the two would be profitable. Time has proven me right. Maximilian is entranced by her. When he has been with her, his eyes are brighter, he speaks with more confidence of the future, he agrees more easily to the solutions I suggest for his problems. She has had a child. A boy. I have seen him. He resembles the emperor and has blue eyes. All is not lost."

"Your blessing is eagerly sought by Emperor Maximilian, Holy Father," Carlota said. She bent her head beneath the black lace mantilla and kissed the pope's ring. She had been lucid and extremely calm from the moment she and Señora del Barrio were admitted to the Vatican. Señora del Barrio had been whisked away on a tour of the Vatican while Carlota, escorted by velvet-robed papal chamberlains, was led past the Swiss Guards up the stairs to where the pontiff, a heavyset man with a kindly expression, sat waiting for her on his golden throne.

"God is watching and will look after your husband," the pope said.

"Oh, I believe that, Holy Father, I do believe that. I felt the call from God even more strongly than Maximilian, and so I led him to Mexico."

"I have heard how valuable you have been to him."

"I have tried to be. I have wanted to do what is right. How could he have remained at Miramar, living a life without meaning, growing old without purpose? I am the daughter and granddaughter of kings. I have always been stirred by the sight of soldiers marching in defense of their monarch."

"Yours is an illustrious family, one which I have mentioned in my prayers from time to time."

Carlota looked up at him timidly. "If Maximilian is forced to return to Europe, the humiliation will be more than he can bear. Will you speak to Napoleon, Holy Father? Will you intercede on Maximilian's behalf? Will you agree to relinquish your claim to Church property in Mexico?"

"I pray for Maximilian every day, my child, but I cannot do what you ask. I would help you if I could, but I cannot."

Carlota's eyes filled with tears, but she made no sound.

The pontiff stood up and took her by the hand and they walked out into his private garden.

"Your burden is very heavy," he said as they stood looking out at the colonnade of the Basilica of St. Peter.

"Yes."

"Maximilian is fortunate to have a wife such as you."

At dinner that night in the dining room of the hotel, in the presence of a group of Maximilian's Mexican supporters, Carlota refused to eat.

"It is obvious that someone is trying to poison me," she said.

The following day she would eat nothing but oranges, examining the peels carefully for signs of tampering.

The next morning Carlota called Señora del Barrio to her room.

"Have a carriage brought, Manuelita." Her eyes were bright, her cheeks a feverish crimson. "I am going to the Vatican."

The pope was eating his breakfast when Carlota rushed into his room. She fell on the floor at his feet, flung her arms around his knees, and began to sob uncontrollably.

"I attempted to dissuade her," said the purple-robed Cardinal Antonelli, wringing his hands and shouting to be heard over Carlota's shrieks and wails. "There was nothing to be done with her. She is quite hysterical."

"My child, my child," said the pope. He tried to pull her arms away gently, but she shook her head and cried even louder.

"All right, you may stay, it's all right."

The tears suddenly stopped and she lifted her tear-stained face. "I'm starving, Holy Father. Napoleon's spies have followed me from Paris. They poison my food. Protect me, Holy Father. Let me stay here with you. I'm so hungry, so hungry."

She put her head to his knees again and began to whimper.

"Here, now, you shall have food." A chamberlain filled a plate with fruit and a portion of omelette and set it down next to the pope's place. "You see, here is a plate of food. You may eat as much as you like."

Carlota raised her head and sniffed at the food. "It's poisoned. Everything they give me is poisoned."

She jumped up, dipped her fingers into the pope's cup of hot chocolate, then stuck her fingers in her mouth and sucked on them. "Oh, I'm so hungry, so hungry. I'm starving, Holy Father. I will starve in front of you." She snatched bits of food from his plate and popped them into her mouth.

The pope motioned for another cup of chocolate to be brought.

"No, it's poisoned," she cried, and insisted on drinking only from his cup.

When she had eaten her fill from the pope's plate and drunk what she wanted from his cup, she became calm, and was even persuaded to go on a tour of the Vatican library. She spent the rest of the day happily exploring the frescoes and busts and paintings in the Vatican museums, and that evening, assured that all the assassins who had followed her from Paris had been arrested, agreed to be taken back to her hotel suite.

When she reached the hotel she broke down again. "Assassins! Assassins!" she screamed. "I must be with the Holy Father. Only the Holy Father can protect me from death, can protect me from assassins, can feed me."

A doctor was called.

"Hysteria," he said.

At ten o'clock in the evening, ranting uncontrollably, Carlota was returned to the Vatican, where the pope was awakened from sleep to find the raving empress beside his bed.

"She has gone mad," Cardinal Antonelli said. "In eighteen hundred years, this is the first time that someone has gone mad in the Vatican."

"The poor thing," said the pope.

"Oh, Holy Father, let me stay, please let me stay. Promise me that you will let me stay."

A bed was prepared for Carlota in the Vatican library, and the pope's doctor, disguised as a palace chamberlain, brought a cup of hot milk laced with a powerful sedative to her bedside.

"Look, it's not poisoned," said the pope, taking a tiny sip of the milk.

"Then you may hold it to my lips," she said, and drank it down. A few minutes later she went meekly to sleep.

The next day Carlota vacillated between clear-eyed sanity and wild-eyed paranoia.

"Has she departed yet?" the pope asked, as he tried to avoid her in the corridors.

"Not yet, Holy Father," the cardinal replied.

In the afternoon she consented to be driven to see an

orphanage, where, at first, she behaved nicely and even gave the mother superior a donation. But during a tour of the orphanage kitchen she became unhinged at the sight of a dirty knife.

"Poison! Poison! I'm starving, and everything is poison!" She ran to the stove and plunged her hand into a boiling cauldron to pluck out a piece of meat, fainted, and was carried unconscious back to her hotel.

"The condition of the empress of Mexico breaks my heart," the pope told Father Fischer that evening. "I offered to send my doctors to see her, but she refused and departed suddenly for her estate on the Adriatic. I sent a letter of blessing to her hotel before she left."

"She is insignificant in the scheme of things, Holy Father," Father Fischer said.

"I want you to return to Mexico," said the pope. "Your talents are unique. I hope through your charm and geniality you will succeed in inducing Maximilian to remain in Mexico after the French withdraw."

"I will try."

10 October 1866

Beloved Maxl,

I was received in Europe with open arms. Everywhere I went there were receptions and ceremonies. You are loved by the people of Europe as only a monarch on the throne of a great country is loved. They see your struggle and hold you higher than the Pope.

But it is Napoleon and his Forces of Evil that would cast their spell on all that is good. He will not listen to argument, he will not back down from his Satanic position.

I am starving. Napoleon's Evil Henchmen are everywhere. Only Pope Pius, Holy is his name, gave me shelter and protected me from my enemies. He fed me from his own plate, and I had no fear. No one has yet been able to penetrate the Vatican to poison the Pope's food.

I try very hard, my beloved. You have always made me so happy that I want to repay you in some small measure before I die. Evil Forces prevent me. They are everywhere.

But I was happier with you in Mexico than if we had stayed at Miramar and watched each other grow old. I am wife to the greatest monarch of all. You are no mortal man, but an angel who will save Mexico. I am heiress to jewels and palaces on every side.

The fan palms and weeping willows have grown tall at our Castle of Miramar. I have examined every bush and tree that your loving hand planted, and when I sit beneath your ivy bower by the summerhouse and look across the terrace to the sea, I feel that your own dear arms have reached across the oceans to enfold me. Everyone greeted me warmly. It is useless.

Your faithful wife,
Charlotte

20

By 1867 Maximilian was a man under siege from within and without. Wracked by fevers, afflicted with mysterious stomach pains, unable to decide whether or not to abdicate the throne, he received the crushing news from Europe that Charlotte had been committed to an asylum. Shortly after that came the information that Napoleon, enraged by Maximilian's equivocation, had ordered all troops out of Mexico immediatley, including the Foreign Legion.

"I have sent Professor Billimek back to Austria," Maximilian wrote his mother. "He takes with him a few of my books and all the butterfly specimens that we collected together, since I have no place to store them. The castle at Chapultepec has been looted and destroyed, my personal belongings stolen. Even my beloved house and gardens in Cuernavaca are lost to me, vandalized by bandits. I have taken up residence in the La Teya hacienda, a simple dwelling loaned to me by a Swiss merchant who, unlike some, is not afraid of Juarista retribution.

"I feel myself being torn from the Mexican throne bit by bit, piece by piece. Napoleon's anger extends to the horses and rifles of the French soldiers, which he insists on removing from Mexico lest my remaining imperial forces make use of them. Mexico attempts to vomit me up, and yet I resist. Tell me what I must do."

"The die is cast," she wrote back. "Hapsburgs do not abdicate."

Marshal Bazaine began removal of his troops from the

north, and rebel forces spilled through the opening and headed south toward the capital. As each town and village was evacuated by the French, it was promptly taken by the Juaristas. Father Fischer returned from Rome and resumed his place at Maximilian's side.

"You must have courage," Father Fischer advised him. "I see a vision of you on the throne of Mexico for years to come."

"Your visions are too convenient," replied Maximilian witheringly. "There is no throne."

"I tell you, he is on the verge of mental collapse," Dr. Samuel Basch advised Father Fischer. Dr. Basch, a young German–Jewish doctor, had recently come from Europe to take over as Maximilian's personal physician.

"He is stronger than he realizes," Father Fischer replied. "He will prevail."

"He will not prevail if he continues on in Mexico," retorted Dr. Basch, who was the first one to confront the priest on Maximilian's behalf.

"And can he return to Austria, where his own brother forbids his name to be spoken in his presence? If he dares to return he will be persona non grata."

"And here? What of here? The French are evacuating. No one pretends politeness to the emperor any longer. He is booed in the streets, his wife's name is defiled. Is he not persona non grata here?"

"Here he is a hero," said the priest.

On the eve of departure of the final contingents of French troops from Mexico, Marshal Bazaine came to say good-bye to Maximilian.

"If I have shown you any disrespect, I apologize," the marshal said. "I hope you will not regard me with bitterness."

Maximilian put his arms around him.

"An *abrazo* for an old friend," he said, and tears came to the French officer's eyes.

"We have seen much together, Your Majesty," said Bazaine, as they walked together in the cramped garden of the only home Maximilian now possessed. "We have disagreed in the past, and my loyalties have been to Napoleon, but my men have died here, I have fought here, and now I am heartbroken that it has all been for nothing and that I must leave you in such a condition. Come with me now. Leave Mexico. There is nothing left here for you. The priest leads you on with false promises."

"No longer," said Maximilian. "He has left for Durango on some mission of mischief for the Church. I will not welcome him back. His charms grow tiresome, his deviousness unbearable. I know now that he deceived me."

"Then come with me."

"I cannot abandon my post."

"But you have nothing left. Juárez will ride into the capital soon. Everything is gone."

Maximilian, drawn and pale, his hands shaking with weakness from his last illness, took the marshal's hand in his. "You have done your duty. I will do mine. I will personally lead what is left of the Army. We will go to Querétaro, where General Miramón is waiting with his men, where I have my staunchest supporters, the nuns, the humble priests, the defenders of the empire. We will last as long as we can. If we are victorious, then Juárez will have to deal with me as an equal. If we are defeated, then no one can say that I did not do my best."

Seven thousand men were left behind to defend the capital, and Maximilian, accompanied by Blasio, his valet Grill, and Dr. Basch, rode to meet the rest of his army on the outskirts of the city. But where he expected to find ten thousand men waiting for him, there were only sixteen hundred.

"I am a Mexican," he told his troops. "We can do without the French. We will fight as Mexicans."

Maximilian wore his military uniform, his medals on his chest. There was color in his cheeks, and his hands did not shake as he held the reins and led his men toward Querétaro.

At the end of the first day, Maximilian sat with his men around a campfire. He joked with them and ate the same food they did. Later he rolled up in a blanket on the ground, ready for sleep.

"I've brought Your Majesty's medicine," said Dr. Basch, kneeling down beside him.

Maximilian waved him away. "Take your potions yourself, my dear doctor. This is the medicine I have been needing all along. To take command of my own destiny."

On the morning of the second day, they were attacked by a

band of rebels. Maximilian threw himself into the fighting. His bravery astonished his seasoned soldiers. While shells exploded around him, he jumped from his horse and led his men across the fields, shouting words of encouragement to them as they went. The Juaristas retreated, and an exhilarated Maximilian, too energized to sleep, walked among his wounded with Dr. Basch.

"No commander could hope for more than I have received from you," Maximilian told his men. "Our numbers are small, but with victories such as this they will grow larger, and the people will join in, and the crown will be saved."

"His mood has changed drastically," said Blasio to Dr. Basch when Maximilian finally consented to get some sleep before the next day's march. "Can it be that he was happy to be in battle?"

"Yes, I think so," Dr. Basch replied, "for the outcome of battle is clear-cut. Indecision and inaction have almost destroyed him, but I have hope for him now."

The next day they reached Querétaro, its whitewashed buildings rising out of the valley to greet them. General Mejía and General Miramón met Maximilian and his men at the entrance to the city. As they were escorted through the streets, cheering throngs lined the road shouting "¡Viva Max! Viva Méjico!"

Maximilian turned to Dr. Basch, his eyes glistening. "You see, Doctor, this is why I am here."

21

General Miramón, wounded, his forces cut to pieces at the battle of San Jacinto, had brought what remained of his army to Querétaro. General Mejía had brought his Indian troops and the remnants of the foreign battalions. In total there was an army of nine thousand men.

On a promontory called the Cerro de las Campanas, the Hill of the Bells, Maximilian made camp. Here he had a commanding view of the mountains of the Sierra Corda and the fertile valley that surrounded the colonial city of Querétaro.

On March 14, 1867, Juárez's army, led by General Escobedo, attacked Maximilian's army. Sixteen thousand men converged on the city from the north and another ten thousand approached from the west.

On the first sortie Maximilian's forces won. And on the second and on the third. But Maximilian's generals disagreed on whether to counterattack. Unable to make a decision, Maximilian faltered and Escobedo's forces regrouped. By the end of March there were forty thousand rebels ringing the surrounding hills.

All his life Maximilian had been an actor waiting in the wings to come on stage and recite his part. Now in high boots, spurs, and wide sombrero, he led his men fearlessly in every battle. Faced with the guns of the opposing forces, their grenades exploding at his feet, he became a miracle of bravery. The greater the danger, the more tenacious and reckless he became.

"His eyes are different somehow," whispered the men among themselves. "There is a mysterious light in them," they said.

He carried a strange elation within him that no one could fathom, and rather than a defeat, his retreat to Querétaro became his epiphany.

Grill shined the emperor's boots and spurs each night, and every day Maximilian, his enthusiasm never wavering, marched along the lines of fortifications, ankle-deep in mud, his sombrero on his head, Blasio at his side.

"How are you faring?" he would ask the soldiers in the trenches. "Are you well treated? Do you receive the rations that are due to you?"

Blasio would write down the complaints of the men, and when they returned to camp at the end of each day Maximilian would see to it that all complaints were reviewed and any injustices righted.

In mid-March Maximilian, in a special ceremony on the battlefield, honored his troops for their bravery and devotion by presenting them with medals of valor.

He shook each man's hand, then hugged him, as he presented the medals.

"You are the glory of Mexico," he said to each one of them, his voice choked with emotion.

When the ceremony was over and Maximilian had turned to go, General Miramón stepped forward, and pinning a medal on the emperor's jacket, said, "No, Your Majesty, you are the glory."

A month later the news came to Querétaro that Mexico City and Puebla had fallen to the rebels and that General Marquez, entrusted by Maximilian to bring reinforcements to Querétaro, had looted the custom receipts and fled for his life. At first no one would believe it. And when they did, the men's mood turned from hopefulness to dark depression. Desertions increased from virtually none to as many as fifty a day.

By May, the water supply cut and his men eating roast mule, Maximilian faced the possibility that his forces would be defeated by disease and starvation before they were destroyed by Juarista bullets. He moved his stronghold from the rocky Cerro to La Cruz, another promontory above the city. Here, in the Convent of the Cross, whose high stone walls and spacious patios were once a Spanish colonial fortress, he made his headquarters. Here he gave heart to those who still remained. And when the nuns gave him bread from the dough used to bake the holy wafers, he shared it with his men and told them not to despair.

Maximilian was awakened by the shout "Save the emperor!"

He rose and calmly dressed in his uniform. He stood by the window a moment and felt the chill of dawn on his face, then threw a greatcoat over his shoulders and, taking a pistol in each hand, walked out onto the patio.

The guards were gone, and the gates of the fortress were open.

"Your Majesty, this way, hurry!" came a voice from the shadows of the chapel where General Mejía and several hundred soldiers waited.

"Where is General Miramón?" Maximilian asked.

"He was wounded and has been taken to a doctor," said General Mejía. "You have been betrayed. The defenses have been opened and Escobedo's troops have broken through into the city. Your horse is waiting to take you to the safety of the Cerro, Your Majesty, but we must hurry."

"Are there horses enough for all?"

"No."

"Then we will walk."

Escobedo's forces opened fire on the Cerro, and Maximilian's men, bodies flattened against the cactus-covered earth of the rocky hill, fired back. General Mejía, looking through his glass at the city below, watched as the rest of the Imperial Army was rounded up and taken captive.

"Have they started up the hill yet?" Maximilian asked.

"Not yet, Your Majesty, but they are approaching."

"Is there any way to break through?"

"Their guns are too close. It is useless to try."

"How long do you estimate it will be before they storm the hill?"

"Very soon, Your Majesty."

"So be it. Let us hope for a lucky bullet."

Maximilian, as emperor of Mexico, held Querétaro for seventy-two days. Then he surrendered and was imprisoned in La Cruz in the same room he had occupied during the siege. It had been ransacked, his possessions stolen, the mattress ripped, but the people of Querétaro brought him his meals and provided whatever he needed for his comfort.

"I have never had so much underlinen in my life." He laughed, and everyone marveled at his lightheartedness.

Maximilian was moved from place to place over the next few days. Then one evening he, his two generals, and Dr. Basch were taken to the crypts of the Convent of the Capucines. The emperor lay down to a wakeful sleep on one of the tombs and Dr. Basch chose as his bed a table used to lay out the dead. The wives and children of Miramón and Mejía had accompanied them to the convent, and the sounds of their wailing resounded throughout the stone building the whole night long.

The next day Maximilian and General Mejía and the wounded General Miramón were given adjoining cells on the second floor of the convent. Dr. Basch was on a floor below them, but free to minister to the emperor. Maximilian's cell barely had room enough for a bed, a chair, a washstand, and two wooden side tables. A crucifix hung on the wall and four silver candlesticks sat on one of the tables.

The cleanliness of the convent and the solicitous attitude of his guards gave Maximilian hope. "This is not as lovely as the gardens of Cuernavaca," he told Dr. Basch, "but it is a place in which one can anticipate the future. Perhaps when I return to Miramar, I will write a history of my reign in Mexico—not an instructional and boring treatise, you understand, but one which will enlighten and entertain."

"Who better to do it, Your Majesty," the doctor replied.

"Yes. I have always written very well."

On a sunny afternoon, General Mejía walked in the cloister garden with the emperor.

"When I return to Miramar, I want you to be with me, you and your family," Maximilian said.

The general was so moved he could not speak.

A trial was held, and Maximilian and Generals Miramón and Mejía were sentenced to death. Telegrams of protest flowed in from all over the world pleading with Juárez to spare Maximilian's life.

Agnes Salm, an American circus rider who had married

one of the emperor's officers, rode to Querétaro from San Luís Potosí in a tiny fiacre accompanied by her maid and small terrier dog. She visited her husband in prison and then went to meet with Juárez.

"I will give my life in place of the emperor," she said.

Juárez's Indian features were blunt and pockmarked, his black eyes cold. "It is not I who demand his life. It is the people who demand it. I have sympathy for you and will release your husband, but I cannot spare the life of Maximilian, for if I do not do the will of the people, they will take his life and mine as well."

On the day set for his execution, Maximilian took communion early in the day, and Blasio was brought from his cell at La Teresita Convent to write some letters for the emperor and receive instructions.

"I entrust the gold from the war treasury to you," Maximilian said. "See to it that the families of the generals are taken care of, as well as Concepción and the child."

He then turned to Dr. Basch. "You are to supervise the embalming of my body. I want to be presentable when my mother sees me in my coffin."

"Let us think of the possibility of a reprieve," Dr. Basch said, "so that none of these instructions will have to be carried out."

"I am a dead man. I have already departed this life in my mind. It is strange, but from my youth I have always known that I would not die a natural death."

At midday General Escobedo visited General Mejía in his cell.

"I owe you a debt," General Escobedo said. "I was once your prisoner and you allowed me to escape. Now I offer you that opportunity. I will provide a horse and wagon for you and your family and in a few days' time you will be safe in your home in the Sierra Corda."

"I will accept the offer if you let the emperor and General Miramón go free also," said General Mejía without hesitation.

"You are a fool, you and your emperor!"

"Then we will be shot together."

The execution was set for three o'clock in the afternoon. Daylight grayed into dusk. Maximilian, who had sat in silent meditation all day, his eyes flying to the door at each rasp of footsteps in the corridor outside, now sighed and said, "It seems that I am not to die today."

*   *   *

There were rumors of reprieves and intercessions, of special emissaries from the United States, of protests from the royal houses of Europe. The convent was searched again and again for sympathizers who might have been smuggled in to help the emperor escape.

"I have received a letter from Franz Josef," Maximilian told Dr. Basch. "He has restored my hereditary rights to me. Perhaps I have been reprieved."

But it was merely a three-day postponement. The new day of execution was set for June 19. At three that morning Maximilian arose and dressed in black civilian clothes. Mejía and Miramón were brought to the emperor's cell and a priest came and said mass. The priest, near collapse as he conducted the service, broke into tears several times. The guards could be heard crying in the corridor. At the elevation of the host, Dr. Basch sobbed out loud and had to be comforted by Maximilian.

After the mass, Maximilian ate a breakfast of bread and chicken and washed it down with a bottle of red wine.

"When you see Blasio again, Dr. Basch, remind him of the duties I have entrusted to him," Maximilian said. He handed the doctor his wedding ring and rosary. "Give these to my mother and tell her I died a good Christian and a dedicated Hapsburg."

Maximilian watched the dawn sky from his window. Dr. Basch sat hunched in a chair, his head in his hands. When the jailers came, Maximilian smiled at them, and then they escorted him down the stairs and through the cloister garden. He stopped momentarily and looked at the sparkle of dew on the leaves of the peach trees, at the cat that dozed in a spot of early sun. He could see the light-ringed mountains, numinous clouds suspended above their defiles.

He turned toward his jailers. "It is a beautiful day," he said. "I have always wanted to die on a beautiful day such as this."

The emperor and his two generals were put into separate carriages, each man accompanied by his own confessor. Dr. Basch, too distraught to witness the executions, stayed in his cell in the convent. As the procession moved through the streets, Maximilian peered out from the gloom of his carriage. There were few people about, and the doors of the houses were draped in mourning. Then he heard the shriek of Mejía's wife, and looked back to see the young woman, her baby in a rebozo on her back, trying to catch the wheels of her husband's carriage with her hands. The soldiers pushed her aside with their bayonets, and she ran screaming her husband's name through the deserted streets.

At the foot of the Hill of the Bells, the men were helped out and each handed a crucifix. Maximilian was pale, but his step was light and springy with life. Mejía, the faint cries of his wife poised in the clear air, could hardly stand upright. Miramón, although not completely recovered from his wounds, was composed.

They walked to the top of the hill where the soldiers were waiting. The breeze played with the fine golden hair of Maximilian's beard as he looked down one last time at the spires and domes of the colonial city.

The commander of the firing squad stepped toward Maximilian. "Please forgive me," he said.

"Forgive you?" said Maximilian. "This is your duty. Do what must be done." And he handed a gold piece to each of the seven riflemen.

"Aim carefully," he said calmly. "Do not destroy my face. I do not want my mother to cringe when she looks at it."

As the young officer raised his sword, Maximilian said, "I hope my blood will bring peace to Mexico," and then he shouted "¡Viva Méjico! ¡Viva independencia!"

Shots rang out and Maximilian fell to the ground.

Miramón and Mejía were each brought forward.

"God Bless the emperor!" they both shouted before they were shot.

Maximilian lay in the dirt, his body twitching. The young officer, hands trembling, pointed with his saber at Maximilian's heart. And there, where the steel blade rested, a soldier took aim. A shot was fired. Then all was quiet.

Maximilian's body lay in its coffin in a cell at the Convent of the Cross. The heart, lungs, liver, and intestines had been removed and the eyes replaced with black glass marbles. Then the frame had been varnished twice and hung like the carcass of a steer to dry. When the embalming process was complete, the body was dressed in black trousers and a military jacket with gold buttons. Army boots were placed on its feet, black kid gloves on its hands and a black tie around its neck.

But chloride of zinc instead of naphtha had been injected into its arteries, and within three weeks the body began to turn black and exude the unmistakable smell of putrefaction. When pleas began arriving from Europe requesting the return of Maximilian's body, Benito Juárez, unable to justify the delay, but unwilling to relinquish the body in its present condition, ordered the remains sent to Mexico City for a second attempt at embalming.

At one o'clock in the morning on the day after the corpse had been delivered to the San Andrés Hospital in Mexico City, Benito Juárez, his squat body encased in an ill-fitting suit, a felt hat in his hands, met Dr. Basch in the chapel of the hospital. Juárez was accompanied by his personal physician, Dr. Ignacio Alvarado.

"I am a humanitarian, Dr. Basch," Juárez said. "I do not want to be accused of having mistreated Maximilian's corpse."

"The emperor was an admirer of yours."

"He was not an emperor, merely an archduke of Austria."

Dr. Basch nodded solemnly. "The archduke's body is being worked on now by Dr. Andrade and his two assistants, Dr. Montano and Dr. Buenrostro. Do you want to see it, or will you wait here while I take Dr. Alvarado into the room to make his examination?"

"I have come to see the archduke," Juárez said acidly. "I'm not afraid to look at corpses."

The doctors had removed the bandages that had been wrapped around the body, and the stench in the dissecting room was overpowering.

"I see that souvenir hunters have taken away pieces of him," said Juárez noting the chunks of hair missing from the corpse's scalp and beard.

Dr. Andrade looked up from the dissecting table. "We have guarded against it as best we could," he said, "but there have been times when the body was left unattended."

"It is of no interest to me if he leaves Mexico with less hair than when he arrived," Juárez said. He moved closer to the table. "His legs are too long for his body, and the forehead gives an impression of intelligence, of which he showed very little."

"I beg your indulgence, General Juárez," said Dr. Basch. "The archduke was a poet and a philosopher. His death was a noble one. I am proud that the family has designated me to accompany the body to Austria. I consider it to be an honor."

"As honors go, you are ill served by the Hapsburgs," said Juárez. "They sent a prince of Europe to be martyred. What can he have known of Mexico?"

"You were a formidable opponent."

"You dignify him too much. This is my country. I defended it against the enemy."

Dr. Andrade uncorked a vial of arsenic and poured it into a dish. Then he and his assistants sponged the solution on the blackened corpse.

"The smell is much better," said Juárez when the process was complete. "What will be done to him now?"

"He will be hung from the ceiling to dry," Dr. Andrade replied.

"Will he then look better than he does now?" asked Juárez.

"He will be fit to travel," the doctor said.

Juárez and Dr. Basch left the room and stood together in the cold corridor.

"I have one favor to ask of you," said Dr. Basch. "The archduke's secretary, José Blasio, still languishes in prison. He is a Mexican. What purpose does it serve to keep him there?"

"None."

"Then you will free him?"

"On the condition that he leave Mexico."

Dr. Basch looked pained. "How can I agree to that condition for him?"

"How badly does he want to be free?"

Dr. Basch thought for a moment. "He will leave Mexico," he said.

On a rainy morning in November, Blasio was set free from La Teresita Convent. He was given his knapsack and a horse and was pointed in the direction of Vera Cruz, where a ship waited to take him to Europe. When he was a safe distance from Querétaro, he stopped his horse and opened the knapsack. The gold that Maximilian had given him was gone. In the bottom of the sack was the tattered prayer book that Father Fischer had given Maximilian. Blasio pulled at the horse's reins, kicked its flanks, and turned in the direction of Cuernavaca.

22

Hector Sedano's mother sat in a wicker chair on the shaded patio while a small boy played at her feet. As Blasio approached, Señora Sedano rose.

"Buenos días, Señora," he said.

"She has been waiting."

"I knew your voice at once," said Concepción, appearing in the doorway. She was wrapped in a shawl, her black hair unbraided.

"The child has grown," Blasio said.

Concepción was silent, her eyes expectant, her fingers tight on the fringes of the shawl.

"Juárez would not spare him," he said, "but never has Mexico had such a hero as he was at the last."

Concepción stared at him dry-eyed. "Is there anything for me and the child?"

"He gave me gold to bring you, but it was stolen by the Juaristas." He reached into his knapsack and took out the breviary and handed it to her.

"What is this?"

"A book to bring you comfort. An ancient prayer book."

She turned it in her hands. "Is this all?"

"Well, there's—the emperor said to—that I should—"

"A book," she said dully, and let it drop to the floor.

Blasio picked it up, dusting its worn edges with his fingers, smoothing its creased pages. "The book belonged to Brother Gerónimo de Aguilar. He was a prisoner of the Maya and has

written somewhere in the margins of the book where a fortune in gold was hidden in Yucatán."

She wrapped the shawl tighter around her and turned
toward the house.

"Wait!" he said. "There is another message."

Her back was to him.

"The child is to be sent to Europe to be raised."

Señora Sedano screamed. Concepción made no sound, did
not turn around.

"There is no alternative," Blasio said. "Juárez doesn't want
him here as a pretender to the throne. He'll kill him if he
remains in Mexico. The boy will have everything that the son
of an archduke of Austria should have. The Bringas family
will take him to Paris with them. The Archduchess Sophia
has promised to see to his education."

Concepción swiveled around. The shawl flared and then
settled down at her sides. "Will he be called the emperor's
son, carry his name?"

"No."

She bent down and picked the boy up. She wrapped him
in the shawl and walked up and down the veranda, crooning
to him while her mother-in-law wailed.

"This was a terrible thing, a terrible thing," Blasio mut-
tered. "Oh, how brave he was, Concepción. Dr. Basch told
me that his jailers cried at his death. He spoke of you, of the
boy. His thoughts were of others at the end, never for himself."

Concepción paced with the child for a long while. Then she
stopped in front of Blasio. He had never seen such fury in a
woman's face before.

"Here," she said, and shoved the child into his arms. "Go
away."

Blasio was startled. He looked down at the child and then
at Concepción. "But I can stay for an hour, and you can
hold him a while longer. I don't have to leave this minute.
If you have a bit of something for me to eat, I'd be grateful.
The road was long and dusty, and I haven't—"

Her gaze on him was contemptuous. "Go away," she said
again.

"Sí, I'll go," and carrying the child, who had begun to cry,
he hurried through the garden without looking back.

Concepción packed their clothes. A baby cried in the next
room. Hector sat in a chair staring at the carpet.

"It's done," she said. "The boy is gone. But we still have the girl, and if we don't take her away they'll find out about her, and then we'll lose her, too. What child of yours could have blond hair and blue eyes?"

When Hector began to cry, she stopped what she was doing and stood beside his chair and caressed the back of his neck with her hand.

"It was God's will," she said.

PART III
Andre
and
Lidia

23

Artur Frankle, painter's smock bunched over his heavy sweater, red beret at the usual angle on his clump of brown curls, set up his easel and paints in his customary place in front of Da Vinci's "Mona Lisa" in the Grande Galerie of the Louvre. Rene, one of the gallery guards, winked at him, well satisfied with his commission for the month. By paying Rene a percentage on his sales, Artur Frankle was permitted to keep his spot and discreetly sell his paintings. He was a very hard worker, churning out reasonable facsimiles of La Gioconda day after day, except for Rosh Hashanah and Yom Kippur and the days the museum was closed. He was very cautious, and never accosted anyone, but would quietly slip one of his cards out of the pocket of his paint-spattered smock and into the hand of anyone who inquired if his Mona Lisas were for sale.

"She's beautiful, isn't she, sir?" he asked the distinguished-looking gentleman who had stood at his elbow without moving for the last half hour.

"Beautiful?"

"The 'Mona Lisa,' " said Artur, putting a few quick brush strokes to the corners of the enigmatic mouth.

"Yes, very beautiful," said the gentleman, whose eyes were on the doorway to the gallery and not on the paintings.

"It was quite a scare we had, sir," said Artur, lonesome for someone to talk to. The task of painting four Mona Lisas a day no longer challenged him, and when business was as slow as it was today, with a light rain falling and the galleries half empty, he would often strike up a conversation with anyone who stood close to him for more than a few minutes.

The gentleman, dressed in a dark suit with a white carnation in his lapel, appeared annoyed.

"She was stolen," Artur said.

"Who was stolen?"

"The 'Mona Lisa.' La Gioconda. Surely you read about it in the newspapers. An Italian did it. A workman they say. Took it straight off the wall and carted it off to Florence, Italy. It was revenge, he said."

The gentleman was quiet a moment, as though deciding whether or not to encourage the conversation. Then he said sharply, "Revenge? What nonsense are you talking about?"

Artur smiled a lopsided smile that exposed his crooked teeth. He knew the way to draw people out. It was almost as great a talent as his talent for artistic mimickry.

He mixed some paint, rolled a brush in it, then dotted a strand of Mona Lisa's hair so that it sparkled in the gallery light.

The gentleman was looking at his painting now. "It's too bright," he said. "Don't you see the original there? It's soft and muted. Don't you see where the light and dark colors intersect?"

"My, if you aren't right," said Artur, rubbing at the offending paint.

He stepped away from the easel. "Is that better?"

"Much. Now, what about the revenge?"

"Oh, the Italian? Well, he said the French had stolen enough Italian paintings over the centuries; he thought he'd just even the tally." Artur laughed till he coughed. The grooves in his cheeks, mere feathery tracings when his face was in repose, folded up like the bellows of an accordion when he laughed.

"When did this happen?"

Artur thought a moment. "I was painting Rubens's second wife from 1911 until 1914 when the war began. It's not half the painting the 'Mona Lisa' is. Yes, 1914 is when they got it back. Three years ago next month."

The story seemed to have interested the man, but he still glanced periodically at the door to the gallery, as though expecting someone.

"The war news is not too good, is it, sir?" said Artur. "I

mean, what good was the little advance in Champagne when we lost all those men?"

"It was a pity."

Artur took a rag from his pocket and wiped his hands, then stuck his right hand out toward the man.

"Artur Frankle, originally from Warsaw, later of Strasbourg, and currently of Paris."

The gentleman studied the paint-stained hand a moment before he finally offered his own gray-gloved one.

"Count Sedano y Leguizano, son of Maximilian I, emperor of Mexico." He withdrew his hand from Artur's. "I didn't know they allowed Jews to make copies in the Louvre."

"Between us, sir, you and I are the only ones who know that I'm a Jew or that you are the son of an emperor."

"You're being impertinent."

"Impertinent? Me? God forbid I should be impertinent. Jewish, maybe; impertinent, never."

"I'm sorry if I insulted you."

"If you buy a Mona Lisa, I won't be insulted."

Sedano looked toward the door again. A man in a dark-gray overcoat stood there staring into the gallery.

"Is that the man you were waiting for?"

Sedano turned quickly, as though to hide his face. "No."

"He's looking at you."

"I don't know him. How much?"

"How much what? You change conversations too fast for me to keep up."

"The copy. I'd like to buy one."

"Four francs."

"I'll take it."

"Wait, wait, now, you can't take it here. I have to walk outside with you and conduct the transaction there. If I walk out with a canvas, it's okay. If you walk out with one, they'll arrest me."

"Then let's go outside." Sedano took some money out of his pocket and gave it to Artur, who began to sort through the stack of paintings that leaned against his easel.

"Hurry," said Sedano nervously.

"I'm picking out a good one for you."

Sedano had gotten halfway to the door at the other end of the gallery when Artur caught up with him, a painting beneath his arm.

"Hurry, hurry," mimicked Artur. "You're some art lover, aren't you?"

When they reached the outside of the Louvre, Artur handed the canvas to Sedano. "It's yours. Look at it in good health."

The man who had been in the gallery stepped into view again.

"Do you live near here, Mr. Frankle?" Sedano asked.

"Not far."

"Would you like company for supper?"

"Hoo-ha, what is this? Has that man come to take you back to sit on the throne of Mexico?"

"It's not a joke."

Artur leaned toward Sedano and put his hand gently on his arm. "Listen, something's upsetting you. A blind man could see that. You'll come home with me. Will that make you happy?"

"Yes."

"Good."

Artur retrieved his easel and paints, and he and the count walked hurriedly down the street in the direction of Artur's apartment.

"Did you say something?" asked the Count when they had walked about a block.

"It was nothing. I only said kings have to eat, too."

The aroma of roast chicken and kasha varnishkes wafted sweetly through the small apartment. Five-year-old Andre and four-year-old Oscar sat in the parlor with the tall blond stranger while Brina basted the chicken one more time and turned the steaming kasha with a spoon to keep it from sticking to the pot.

"You've never brought one home before," said Brina, peeking out the kitchen door into the parlor.

Artur took off his stained smock, dropped it on the floor in a corner of the kitchen, then put on the black silk robe that hung on a hook behind the door.

"He's harmless," he said. "Like Aunt Sadie. He thinks he's the son of the king of Mexico."

Brina wrinkled her forehead. "Is there a king of Mexico?"

"Not anymore. And so what if there was? Do you think his son would want to eat kasha varnishkes in such a place as this?"

Artur tied the belt on his silk lounging robe and walked into the parlor. "My dear Count, supper is almost ready."

Sedano looked up at him and smiled at the sight of the luxurious robe in the shabby apartment. "Your sons are very intelligent."

"Of course."

Andre held out a book for his father to see.

"What is this?" said Artur, taking the book from the child.

"It's a history of the Hapsburg reign in Mexico," Sedano said. "My father's reign. The emperor. Emperor Maximilian."

"Oh, yes, yes," said Artur, handing the book back to the boy. "Look, there is no need to give the children gifts. You bought a painting. That's enough. Do you always carry books around to prove you're the son of the king of Mexico?"

"Would you believe me without it?"

"Look, Count, you're making me very nervous. Eccentric people are interesting. I have many eccentric relatives myself. But sons of kings—" He shook his head.

"Why aren't you wearing a crown?" asked Andre.

Sedano patted the boy's head. "I'm the illegitimate son of Maximilian. Some call me the imperial bastard."

"Sha, this is a child!" exclaimed Artur. Then he took the book back and began to leaf through it. "Maximilian I, Emperor of Mexico, by Father Agustín Fischer," he read aloud. He looked up at Sedano. "You're serious."

"I am."

"But why here? What do you want?"

"Kings have to eat, too," said Sedano sardonically.

During dinner, Sedano carefully went over the history of Maximilian's three-and-a-half-year reign in Mexico and his heroic death at thirty-five. When he related how he himself had been taken away from his Mexican mother and brought to Paris, Brina began to weep and had to go into the kitchen to blow her nose.

"I never knew my mother, Concepción," Sedano said, "having been very young when I was taken away. She died of fever in Yucatán a year after my father's death, leaving my sister María in the care of the Sedano family."

"Have you seen her?" asked Artur.

"Who?"

"Your sister."

"No. She remained a Mexican. I have no interest in that.

Of course, I would have some interest in the prayer book that Father Fischer says he gave Maximilian. Father Fischer kept all of my father's personal papers, but the book was never found. It was a book of hours of a lay priest named Gerónimo de Aguilar, who was shipwrecked with another man in Yucatán in the sixteenth century. Brother Aguilar kept a diary of his experiences with the Maya in the margins of the book, and some people say that he wrote of a hidden treasure of gold in the jungle." Sedano sighed. "Perhaps the book was buried with my mother."

"She went to this place looking for gold and died?" said Artur.

"Of fever, yes," Sedano replied.

The plump chicken had become a bony carcass now. Artur poured out the last of the wine.

"This is a very strange story, Count. And no one knew any of this until the priest's book was published?"

"There were rumors, but no one knew the true story."

"And you believe it's true just because a priest wrote it in a book? Personally, me, I'm always suspicious. I never make up my mind so quick. Lots of things are written in books. For money. Maybe even for revenge. Tell me, did this Father Fischer get rich from this book?"

"I suppose he thought he would, but nobody cared about Maximilian and his illegitimate children."

"Not even with the story about the gold?"

Sedano shook his head. "Father Fischer was a parish priest in a Mexican village when he died."

"Which proves my point."

"What point?"

"That nobody believed him enough to buy his book."

"I believe him," Sedano said. He took the book and flipped the pages open. "Look at that picture of Maximilian. We are the same, down to the upper lip that is fuller than the lower. Look at the narrowness of the face, the sad droop of the eyes."

Artur studied the photograph, making clucking noises with his tongue as he compared the features of the man in the photograph with those of the man opposite him.

Sedano wiped his mouth with his napkin and smiled at Brina. "Those were wonderful noodles."

"Varnishkes," murmured Brina, who was timid with strangers.

"You know, I believe you," said Artur, closing the book and slamming his fist down on the table so that the wine glasses jumped and spilled red wine on the white tablecloth.

"I believe him, too," Brina said, "but they are only varnishkes."

"No. I'm talking about being the emperor's son. I believe you." Artur tapped his forehead with one finger. "I am a perfect judge of character. The moment something doesn't make sense, I know it. Falsehoods are trapped right here and rejected. I'm nobody's fool."

"I knew that when I saw you in the Louvre," Sedano said.

"Let me see. If Maximilian was a Hapsburg, how are you related to Archduke Francis Ferdinand, the one who was shot at Sarajevo?"

"I'm his first cousin."

"And the man that you were to meet, the one who didn't show up, who was he?"

"That's difficult to explain."

"You've explained everything else. Why not that?"

Sedano stared at him.

"All right, all right," said Artur, "I'll tell you what, I'll make it easier. The man who did show up, who was he?"

"That, too, is difficult to explain."

"You've explained how a king is a king and yet not a king. What's so difficult about a man who shows up at the Louvre and one who doesn't?"

Andre and Oscar laughed at their father's question, which was phrased like the puzzles with which he always teased them.

"Well?" said Artur. "I'm waiting."

"And so am I," said a man at the door, which was open now and could be seen clearly from where the Frankles and their guest sat at the dining room table.

Artur jumped up from the table. "What is this? Who are you?"

With a few quick strides the man at the door was at Sedano's side and locking handcuffs on his wrists.

Two more men appeared in the doorway.

"My God!" said Artur, backing toward the kitchen.

"What have you brought home with you, Artur?" shrieked Brina, and she pulled the two little boys out of their chairs and huddled with them against the wall.

"For you, too, monsieur," and a fourth man appeared,

yanked Artur out of the kitchen, and handcuffed him. "I arrest you both for espionage."

"Espionage?" shouted Artur. "Espionage? I am innocent. How could this happen? I am a painter, a copyist. There has been some mistake, a horrible misunderstanding. My wife will tell you. Tell them, Brina, that I'm innocent."

"He's innocent," said Brina, her voice a whisper.

"Tell them, Your Majesty, tell them that I'm merely a lowly copyist."

"He's merely a lowly copyist," Sedano said.

"I can prove it," said Artur excitedly. "Look, look at the walls, filled with fake masterpieces. Would I spend my days copying paintings for four francs apiece if I was a spy?"

The fourth man appeared to be considering what Andre had said. Then he shook his head. "I'm sorry, monsieur. It's not my job to have opinions on things like that."

"But who'll have an opinion, if not you?" demanded Artur as he and the count were pulled out the door and dragged along the street to a waiting automobile.

"Artur!" Brina screamed from the apartment window. He looked up and waved at her and the two boys. Then he turned to the men who had arrested him.

"My sons," he said proudly.

24

"I'm innocent, I'm innocent," Artur shouted as he and Count Sedano were locked into the same cell in the Sante Prison.

"Calm down," Sedano said. "They'll soon find they've made a mistake and release you."

"Calm down? Calm down?"

"Must you say everything twice?" Sedano inspected the gray linens on his cot. He walked to the washstand and picked up the cracked cup that sat on the edge of the basin. "We'll need another cup," he said.

"We'll need another cup? We'll need another cup?"

Sedano turned to him and smiled. "I hope you aren't released too soon. You amuse me."

That afternoon Count Sedano had a visitor, a gray-haired man with a heavy beard and mustache. He carried a gold-handled cane and nodded his head once as Artur was introduced to him.

"This is Miguel Bringas, the man who cared for me when I was a child," Sedano said.

"I'm very pleased to meet you," said Artur.

"Artur is an innocent, a painter," said Sedano. "He's been caught in something that doesn't concern him. But we may speak freely in front of him. He's harmless."

Bringas sat down on the only chair in the cell and rested his hands on his gold cane. "I have endeavored to contact everyone that I know in Paris to see whether we can have these preposterous charges dropped."

"And?" prompted Sedano.

"They say that the trial is a formality, that you must go through it in order to clear your reputation."

Sedano laughed. "They won't execute me because of a dishonored reputation, monsieur. They'll execute me because I spied for the Germans."

"But you didn't, did you?" interrupted Artur, who sat on his cot listening to the two men. "You couldn't have, could you? I mean, that's treason. The Germans are the enemy. Why would you do such a thing?"

"For money," Sedano said.

Bringas turned pale. "Then the charges are true."

"Of course. I've known for the past month that I was being followed, that it was only a matter of time before I was arrested. They have the evidence and now they have my person. It's finished."

"What evidence?" asked Artur.

"Letters in which I communicated French intelligence to my principals in Germany. They were written in disappearing ink."

"Between the lines of a regular letter, of course?" said Artur.

"No. Blank sheets of paper."

"Wait, wait. What kind of spy is this who writes with disappearing ink on blank sheets of paper? Of course they would become suspicious. How could you think that they wouldn't become suspicious? Who sends blank pieces of paper through the mails?"

"You should have done my spying for me," said Sedano dryly.

Bringas shook his head. "I can't believe any of this. I'm at a loss to understand your actions."

"They were merely the actions of a desperate man, one who found himself without funds," said Sedano.

"But to betray your country for money—" said Bringas.

"Not *my* country. I'm an Austrian, remember."

"You are an idiot."

"Not exactly."

"I think exactly, Count," interjected Artur. "How many letters were there?"

"Twenty-nine. The only possible defense I have is to say that I was posting them for a friend."

"What friend?" asked Artur suspiciously.

"Don't worry. You're not implicated and won't be."

Bringas stood up and called for the guard through the cell door.

"Will you attend the trial?" Sedano asked. "I would like you there."

"I'll attend," Bringas said. The guard appeared, and Bringas and Sedano looked at one another mournfully and then embraced.

"He seems like a father to you," Artur said when Bringas had gone.

"He is a good man."

Witnesses were notified and documents and letters were gathered to make the case for espionage against Count Sedano y Leguizano. Artur, for whom no witnesses and no documents or letters could be found and no case made, remained in custody also, since the prosecuting attorneys were hopeful that some bit of evidence against him would eventually materialize.

On the eve of the count's trial, Bringas sent a bottle of champagne to the cell that the count shared with Artur.

"He's a thoughtful man," Sedano said. He uncorked the champagne and poured out two glasses.

"Very nice," said Artur as he sipped the champagne. "Tell me, are you frightened?"

"No, but I think of my father, Maximilian, often. He was executed by the Mexicans and now I face possibly the same fate with the French."

"Yes, it's a striking coincidence," said Artur. "I've been reading that book that the priest wrote. I have to tell you I find this whole thing very interesting. Tell me, my dear Count, why did you really do it?"

"I needed money for gambling debts."

"Was there no other way than this?"

"I tried every way I could think of. I even went to Belgium, to the castle of Bouchout where Empress Carlota is confined. She cried and called me Maximilian when she saw me. She stroked my beard, but there was nothing in her eyes, no understanding of what I was saying. That whole castle for Maximilian's mad wife and not one franc for his bastard son."

The next morning, before the trial began, the guards came for Artur. They took him to the prison office and returned his black silk robe to him. He put it on over his trousers, and then, looking around him as though waiting for someone to stop him, walked out of the prison and went home.

Every day Artur brought his son Andre to court. They sat in the fourth row where Sedano could see them. Artur brought Father Fischer's book and a map of Mexico, and when there were breaks in the testimony, Artur would read to the little boy out of the book, and they would trace Maximilian's odyssey in Mexico on the map. He no longer spent his days in the Louvre copying the "Mona Lisa." He had become obsessed with the history of Maximilian and the fate of Maximilian's son. Brina nagged him, complained that she didn't have money to run the household. She threatened to take the children and go back to Warsaw to live with her parents.

"Besides you shouldn't take a small child to such a place," she said. "He should be in school."

"This is a school," Artur said. "This is history. Tell me when again he will be so close to history. I want him to understand things. My God, Brina, this is Maximilian's son. The father was used by Napoleon and the son is used by the Germans. The parallels, Brina, the parallels. And the World War, do we know why there's a World War? No. We're pawns, like Maximilian and his son. We don't act; we are acted upon. I want Andre to understand that there are things over which we have no control, things which are out there in the world separate from us but which determine our lives more certainly than anything we ourselves do."

"Andre is too young to understand," said Brina. "Besides, Sedano is a criminal. That's all I know."

"No, Brina, Sedano is playing out his destiny."

Sedano was found guilty of espionage and sentenced to death by firing squad. He was transported from the Sante Prison in Paris to the military prison at Vincennes, where the sentence was to be carried out.

Artur rose early on the morning of October 10, 1917 and tiptoed into the bedroom that Andre shared with his younger brother.

"Shh, we mustn't wake Mama or Oscar," said Artur, picking the child up out of the down-filled bed.

"Where are we going?" asked Andre.

"We're going to take a trolley ride to Vincennes."

Artur prepared a picnic lunch. Cold meats and cheese, bread, and a bottle of red wine. The day was frosty, and he bundled the boy in a sweater and coat and put woollen mittens on his hands and a stocking cap on his head that came down over his ears.

They sat in the back of the trolley, the picnic basket between them. Andre stood on the wooden seat and gazed out the window as they left central Paris behind them. Five miles outside Paris they entered Val-de-Marne. Through the woods rose the great tower of the fortress of Vincennes, once the residence of French kings, then a hunting lodge, and now an army barracks and prison.

"That's the Château of Vincennes, Andre, where they're keeping Count Sedano."

"I'm sad that he is in this place, Papa."

"I'm sure he's sad, too."

The trolley let them off and they walked through the woods toward the château.

"Here's a good place for a picnic," Artur said, placing the basket beneath a wide-spreading oak.

"Will Count Sedano die today?"

"Yes," said Artur, and he handed his son a chunk of bread.

When they had eaten, they walked through the tall grass. Artur kept the tower of the château in sight, and then suddenly before them were the walls and the castle keep.

"I'm a friend of Count Sedano," Artur told the guard at the gate. "He has asked that I be here to witness his execution."

They were taken to an observation room above the dungeons where prisoners were kept. The room overlooked an inner courtyard. Monsieur Bringas and the official witnesses were already there when Artur and Andre arrived.

"A child has no business here," Monsieur Bringas said.

"He is being educated, monsieur," said Artur, and he lifted Andre to his shoulder so that he could see better.

In a few moments Count Sedano, in dark trousers and a white shirt open at the neck, auburn beard long and untrimmed, appeared in the doorway across the yard. A priest, his breviary in his hand, was beside him. Sedano ran his hand across his eyes to shield them from the sudden brightness of the autumn sun, then lifted his head and saw the faces at the window.

"Oh, my," Artur murmured.

"I want to go home," said Andre, and he began to cry.

"Shh, this is very important. The priest is praying that Count Sedano will go to heaven quickly."

"Sedano y Leguizano," shouted an officer in the courtyard, "son of Archduke Maximilian of Austria, you will be shot as a traitor."

Sedano stood in front of the wall, his shoulder blades lightly touching the stones. Andre had stopped crying, but had buried his head in his father's neck and wouldn't look up.

"Come, come, Andre, pick up your head," Artur said. "If he can do this thing, you can watch him. Look, he's looking straight at you. Wave at him, Andre, throw him a kiss."

Andre slowly raised his head.

"He's smiling, Papa. Why is he smiling?"

"Maybe he's happy."

The volley of gunfire echoed through the yard, bounced off the stone walls of the castle, and vibrated in the air. Sedano's white shirt turned pink, then red, and he slumped slowly down the wall to a sitting position.

"God forgive him!" shouted Monsieur Bringas.

Artur kissed his son's cheek. "You see how easy it was?"

"Yes."

"You will remember what you saw today?"

"Yes." Andre shivered in his woolen clothing.

"Nothing worse than that can happen to anyone, so you have a lot of room to make mistakes in. Do you understand what I'm saying to you?"

"Yes."

"Good. Then your purpose in life, no matter what you do or where you go, is not to make as big a mistake as he did."

25

On a frigid winter evening in Oslo, Norway, twenty-four-year-old Andre Frankle, wearing two suits of clothes against the cold, and carrying nothing but what was in his pockets, was smuggled aboard the Norwegian tanker *Ruth* bound for Tampico, Mexico. He had no documents and no passport and had bribed his way aboard.

"It's only a supply closet that I have found for you," said Christian, the sailor who had met Andre at the dock and brought him on board. They stood now near the winch on the deck of the tanker and talked in low voices. "I'll bring you your food and remove your slop at night. You'll probably be discovered before the voyage is over, but by then it will be too late to turn back. You'll have to be very quiet, no talking, so ask what you have to ask now."

Andre pulled his snow-covered cap off and smoothed his hair back from his forehead with the palm of his gloved hand. His brown hair, uncut during the months he had been running through Europe looking for a hole through which to escape, looped and curled against the back of his neck. He wasn't handsome. His nose was too prominent. But the arrangement of his features was not unpleasant.

"Well?" said Christian. "We'll be frozen corpses if we stand here in the cold any longer. Do you have any questions?"

"How long till we get to Mexico?"

"Three weeks, if the weather is good."

Flecks of snow fell around them. "I can't think of any

questions," said Andre, and then he added affably, "Can you?"

"Peers said you were a Jew. Is that right?"

"Yes."

"But you're not a Stalinist?"

"That's a strange question. Why would you ask me a question like that?"

"Because there are two other passengers aboard, and the captain has told us that every seaman on the ship will be held responsible if they're assassinated, and that we're to keep an eye out for Stalinists."

"Who are the two passengers?"

"Leon Trotsky and his wife."

"Oh." Andre nodded and pursed his lips knowingly.

"We're not carrying petroleum, only Trotskys," said Christian with a chuckle.

"The ship is going to Mexico, though, isn't it? I paid Peers good francs to—"

"Don't worry, it's going to Mexico, but I'm warning you that this isn't an ordinary voyage. President Trygve Lie himself chartered us to take the two Russians out of Europe. No one wants them. Even Norway is throwing them out."

"So this is their own private cruise ship that I'm on."

"Not so private. There's also a Norwegian policeman, Jonas Lie, who's guarding them. But the whole ship runs for their benefit."

"Well, they needn't worry about me. I can assure you that I'm not a Stalinist, and certainly not an assassin. I'm a refugee, a stateless person, a man without a—"

Christian had already opened the hatch, and Andre, bending to accommodate his lanky frame, followed him noiselessly into the passageway.

Snatches of conversation from the cabin adjacent to his hiding place tantalized Andre. Through the holes for the electrical wiring he listened to Trotsky and his wife, Natalya, as they talked to each other in French with barely a trace of a Russian accent.

Andre knew when Trotsky was trimming his beard, because he could hear the clicking of scissors as Trotsky stood at the mirror. And he knew when Natalya was dressing, because he heard hangers rattling on a metal rod and her words became muffled and indistinct, as though dampened by layers of clothing. Trotsky also read aloud to Natalya from books on Mexico, and he would quiz her when he was through, as if he were the schoolmaster and she the pupil.

The Trotskys' daily routine became Andre's also. He slept when they slept, was awake and listening when they were awake and talking. When the ship rolled in heavy seas, and he heard the sounds of vomiting, he would retch into his pail. When it was quiet in the other cabin, he read from Father Fischer's memoirs of Maximilian.

Andre's hiding place was a narrow cubicle, four feet by eight feet, his bed a pile of empty burlap sacks behind stacks of cartons containing canned goods and toilet paper and soap. The soap's pungent aroma seeped through its wrappings and blended sickeningly with the locker air. When Christian brought Andre's food in the evenings and exchanged the full pail for an empty one, he made a show of holding his nose at the stench.

"You are too fastidious," Andre wrote on a piece of toilet paper.

"Your nose is dead," Christian wrote back.

"God has arranged it," wrote Andre.

The weather continued intermittently stormy in the Atlantic, and the Trotskys rarely left their cabin, except for meals with the captain and short walks on deck when the seas were calm. By the fifth day Andre felt himself an occupant of the Trotsky cabin.

"What does he look like?" he wrote when Christian brought his food one evening.

"Short, swaggering, big head, thick mustache, goatee, wide forehead, wild hair, flaring nostrils," Christian wrote back.

"Do you have a pad of drawing paper?" wrote Andre.

Christian shook his head.

"Letter paper?"

The following night Christian brought several sheets of stationery with him. All the next day Andre worked on a portrait of Trotsky, and when Christian came in the evening, he showed it to him.

"The chin is wrong," Christian wrote. "He has a Jewish chin."

"A Jewish chin?" exclaimed Andre out loud. "Please tell me what a Jewish chin looks like." He laughed and shook his head. "A Jewish chin," he said over and over.

"Shhh," hissed Christian.

On the eighth day for the first time Andre heard the Trotskys quarreling.

"Seva must stay where he is in Paris," Natalya said.

"But Lyova can't care for him indefinitely," Trotsky replied. "He's safer with our son than he is with you."

"How can you speak of safety, Natalya? Stalin is hunting my children as diligently as he hunts me. Do you think I'm not torn with worry over Seryozha's fate? He's my son. There is no safety anywhere in the world for my children. Why shouldn't I have my grandson with me while I still live?"

"Lev, Lev, why must we argue?"

Andre kept his ear to the steel bulkhead, wanting to hear more, but there was nothing but silence.

Fear of discovery left Andre halfway through the voyage. It will be too late to turn back, Christian had said, and Andre longed to be outside in the air, to exercise his legs, wash his face in salt spray.

"I'm going out on board tonight," he whispered to Christian on the eleventh day of the voyage.

"Then the meals will stop. When you're caught, I don't want the captain to associate me with you. I'll tell him I didn't know you were here, that you must have come on board yourself and hidden."

Andre waited until it was quiet in the cabin next door to his locker. No sounds of water running or hangers rattling. He grasped the handle of the door, stopped to enjoy its coldness and solidity. He realized that he had not opened a door in almost two weeks. He stepped out onto the deck and the sudden draft of chilled air stung his eyes and bit at his lungs. He stifled a cough and leaned out over the rail to watch the steel-gray water slide over the hull of the ship.

"I wondered when you would come out of there," said a familiar voice behind him.

Andre spun around. "Eyeglasses," he said. "Christian said nothing about wire-rimmed eyeglasses."

Trotsky's guard, Jonas Lie, stepped toward Andre, grabbed his arm, and twisted it behind his back.

"For God's sake, I'm not an assassin," Andre cried. "I don't know anything about Russian politics."

Jonas Lie let go of him, and Andre leaned against the rail. "Who are you?" asked Trotsky.

"My name is Andre Frankle, born in Warsaw, brought up in France, but I lived in Berlin until I was hounded out. I'm an artist, a Jew, a refugee like you." It was rattled off, exhaled in a monotone of pain.

Trotsky was at his side now. "I'm sorry. I hope he hasn't broken any bones."

"I don't think so."

Andre sat down on the cold deck and massaged his arm. "How did you know I was hiding?"

"I saw someone bringing food to you. Then I heard you laughing over someone's Jewish chin."

"That was yours."

"Oh? And is it Jewish, do you think?"

"No more than your fingers."

"You remind me of my grandson Seva. He's only thirteen, but very playful. Like you. Do you feel better?"

"Yes."

They walked along the deck, Jonas Lie following watchfully behind them.

"Seva is my daughter Zina's child," Trotsky said. "She's gone now—committed suicide. Seva is with my son Lyova in Paris."

"I thought of going back to Paris," said Andre, "but anti-Jewish feeling is almost as strong there as it is in Berlin. Then I thought I would join my parents and brother Oscar in Warsaw, but"—he shrugged—"I've changed too much."

"I know exactly what you're saying. I was born in a shtetl in Gromokley. I couldn't stay there either. My father was a farmer. But I've erased that time from my mind."

Andre glanced at Trotsky's face occasionally as they walked. Then he drew the sketch from his pocket and handed it to him. "It was a challenge to draw you without seeing you, but Christian described you very well, I think."

Trotsky stopped walking and studied the sketch. He stroked his chin, and then laughed. "It's very good. You *are* an artist."

"I said I was. Hitler said I wasn't. Being a Jew and a certain kind of artist is a fatal combination. I was expelled from the Berlin Academy of Art because I was Jewish. Then a painting of mine won first prize in the Young German Artists exhibit at the Stadtmuseum in Dresden. Hitler had it removed and exhibited in Berlin as an example of degenerate art."

Trotsky handed the sketch back.

"No, no, you may have it."

"Thank you. Natalya will be pleased. She was once an art student, and has a great appreciation of artistic talent."

Trotsky turned toward Jonas Lie. "You can go if you want to."

When the policeman had disappeared into a passageway, Trotsky said, "I detest that man. He regales me with stories of assassination plots, of Soviet tankers that will meet us in the middle of the Atlantic and drag us back to Stalin. He is supposed to guard us, but his real mission is to ensure that I don't get off the ship before I'm safely gotten rid of in Mexico." His voice was hoarse with anger. "And I detest the Norwegians because they're in thrall to Hitler. In Sundby they kept us like prisoners in a house with twelve policemen guarding us. No visitors, no telephone calls, no radio, no newspapers. I wanted to see my son and grandson in Paris before we left. What was the harm? Instead I am shoved aboard a tanker with Natalya, with no opportunity to collect my papers or arrange my affairs, no time to find out what has become of my youngest son Sergei."

Trotsky sighed and shoved his hands deeper into the pockets of his overcoat. "Stalin tries to make me a nonperson. He says that I have betrayed Russia and plotted with Hitler to overthrow the Soviet government. I'm tried in absentia and convicted, and I know that when my usefulness as a scapegoat is over—" He ran his finger across his neck.

"There's safety in Mexico," Andre said.

"Stalin's arms are very long," said Trotsky. "But what do I care? A little more time is all I need, time to complete my writings, and then Stalin can do what he wants. And you, what will you do in Mexico, how will you live?"

"I'll do whatever I can. I'm told that the atmosphere in Mexico is very congenial to artists."

The cabin was as Andre had pictured it, except for the papers and books on the floor and on the two beds, and the ashtrays filled to the brim and overflowing. Cigarette smoke hung sheer and milky in the stale air. Natalya sat in a corner of a small overstuffed couch reading, a flowered dressing gown tied around her plump figure, a cigarette held between nicotine-stained fingers. She was middle-aged, with high cheekbones and deepset eyes.

As Trotsky introduced Andre to her, she said, "I'm happy

for company," but the hand she held out to him trembled, and she withdrew it quickly.

"Andre will have his meals with us until we get to Mexico," Trotsky said.

"That would be very nice," she replied.

Trotsky showed her the sketch Andre had made, and her eyes brightened, but "It's very nice" was all she said.

"Natalya suffers the most," Trotsky said. Natalya was inside the cabin, the door closed. "Never once has she complained. I never married her because I'm still married to my first wife. But Natalya bore me two sons. She treats Seva as her own grandson. Everything of mine is a part of her. Please forgive her for not greeting you more warmly."

"She looked at me strangely," said Andre. "My presence disturbed her."

"She is just reticent, afraid of strangers. She is very cautious, very protective of me. The fear you saw in her eyes was not for herself, but for me. But you will have your meals with us, Andre. On that I insist."

26

The port of Tampico lay off the tanker's bow. Andre and Trotsky had been up since dawn watching the landmass grow larger. Flat marsh and palm trees anchored the coastline, and out in the harbor fishing boats scooted haphazardly between rusty tankers.

"It's too big a change in weather for me," said Trotsky irritably as the tropical heat floated off the land toward them.

As they had drawn nearer to Mexico, Trotsky's moods had become mercurial, shifting rapidly from unruffled acceptance of his fate to spells of railing rhetoric against Stalin's treachery. For the past few days, Andre had been unable to predict how he would find him when they met for meals. Natalya bore his moods and ill humor stoically, hardly responding when he snapped at her, which would goad Trotsky into even crueler insults. But this morning he had appeared at the rail early, dressed nattily in tweed knickerbockers and cap, his face composed, his eyes alert behind their thick glasses.

"I've found you a welcome companion on this voyage," Trotsky said, turning his eyes away from the harbor and toward Andre. "You'll promise to visit Natalya and me when we're settled."

"I have no idea where I'll be," Andre said. "It's always difficult to make promises."

"We'll expect to see you. I've enjoyed our conversations.

Do you deny that I've had an impact on your thinking during this voyage?"

"You still haven't made me into a communist."

"I haven't put my mind to it."

"You'll never change my opinion that art shouldn't be regulated by governments."

"I never said the artist should be deprived of artistic liberty. I only said that he must not use that liberty to attack the revolution."

"I won't argue with you. I told you, I'm not a political man."

"You're a revolutionary and don't even recognize it. You paint pictures that make you a fugitive. You smuggle yourself aboard a ship headed for Mexico. Those are the actions of a revolutionary. As for arguing with me, I wish my son Lyova had your independence of mind. Some day I'd like to meet the parents who raised you. Especially your father."

"My father?" Andre laughed.

"Why is that funny?"

"You wouldn't like my father. He would waggle his finger in your face for causing the deaths of all those peasants. He would tell you how to handle your children and your wife, what to eat to make your bowels move, and then he would sit you down and give you a lecture on how you should have handled Stalin. He's not afraid of anyone."

"And you think I wouldn't want to meet such a man?" They had entered the harbor, and Trotsky's eyes and attention had already turned away from Andre and were occupied with what was happening on the docks.

"Diego Rivera will be here to meet us. He can help you. Not only is he a committed communist, but he knows all the artists of importance in Mexico—Siqueiros, Orozco—" His eyes scanned the crowd of people standing on the pier. "I dread this, Andre. It's always the same, the pushing, shoving, shouting. We're like rodents being chased by elephants."

"Madame Trotsky must leave her cabin now," said Jonas Lie, who had come on deck while Andre and Trotsky were talking.

"Let her rest a while longer," Trotsky said. They spoke in German, since Trotsky knew only a smattering of Norwegian. "How can it disturb you? We've come to Mexico with the purpose of getting off the ship. I assure you that that is still our intention."

* * *

"Mr. Lie wants you on deck," Andre said. A steward was in the cabin loading boxes and suitcases onto a cart. Natalya, in striped blouse beneath her trim suit, a cloche hat with dotted veil balanced girlishly on her head, sat forlornly on the bed, suitcases and boxes stacked around her.

"I'll walk out with you," he said. "Is there anything you want me to carry? These books, you'll want them." He picked up the twine-wrapped books that Trotsky and Natalya had been studying.

"They'll kill him on the pier, I know it," Natalya said, her eyes beneath the veil clouded with fright. "I'll wait here. I don't want to see his death. I'm so frightened, Andre. We have no friends on the ship to help us. I won't leave until I see the faces of our friends."

"I'm your friend, Natalya." He sat on the bed beside her. "I can't assure you that nothing will happen to him, but I can assure you that I'm your friend. Once you're out in the air and see the green trees lining the harbor and feel that wonderful warm Mexican air, you'll forget Norway and Stalin and everything else."

Her hand trembled on his arm. "This is no life, Andre. It is purgatory. They are killing L.D. inch by inch. First his daughters, Nina and Zina. Then our Seryozha has disappeared. I fear for Lyova's safety in Paris. And our grandson Seva—it is like what Ivan the Terrible did to Prince Viazemsky. Every day the prince found several more of his servants dead in the courtyard of his palace. Then one by one his brothers were murdered. The prince begged to be killed himself, but the murders continued until all of his relatives and friends were dead. Maybe Lev won't be assassinated; maybe they'll kill me instead. It will be the same to Lev. The pain will be more than he will be able to bear."

The loud voices of Trotsky and the policeman could be heard arguing outside the cabin, and then Lie burst in.

"Madame Trotsky, if you don't come out onto the deck at once, I'll have to use physical force to bring you out. The Norwegian government demands that you leave this ship, that you land in Mexico. Those are my orders."

"She's coming," Andre said. "Give her a moment to compose herself."

"You will come now, madame," said the policeman.

He stepped across the room and lifted her bodily from the bed.

"Leave her alone," shouted Andre, and he pulled the policeman's hands away.

"I haven't dealt with you yet," said Lie menacingly.

"How will you deal with him?" demanded Trotsky, who now stood in the opening to the cabin. "I'll send a letter to Trygve Lie telling him that you were paid to bring him aboard."

Natalya straightened her hat and picked up her purse. "Don't worry, Lev, I'm quite all right now."

"No, I won't go with them," Natalya cried. "Lev, what are they saying? What do they want me to do?"

Two Mexican policemen had come up the gangway and taken hold of Natalya's arms. Trotsky looked around him in confusion as a line of policemen, their arms protectively extended in front of him and Natalya, led them down the gangway. "What are they saying, Andre?" he asked. "They're talking too fast."

"They just want to help."

When they reached the pier, the policemen shoved their way through the crowd of reporters who had begun shouting questions at Trotsky the moment he was within earshot. A microphone was standing on the dock, and Trotsky, shrugging off his police protectors, clutched at it as though it were a life preserver.

"I'm happy to be in Mexico in the warm sunshine after the cold Norwegian winter," Trotsky said in a loud voice. "It was a difficult crossing, but Natalya and I are glad to be here. We especially thank President Lázaro Cárdenas for his hospitality in permitting us to come to Mexico. We are especially grateful to Diego Rivera for asking President Cárdenas to invite us. Thank you."

As Trotsky finished, a tall woman, dark eyes shaded by heavy brows that merged over the bridge of her nose, appeared out of the crowd. Ropes of glass beads and colored stones jangled around her neck, and layers of petticoats swayed across her slim hips. She tossed one end of her shawl over her shoulder, then embraced Natalya and kissed her on both cheeks. "Welcome to Mexico, my dear Natalya," she said in husky-voiced English. "I'm Frida Kahlo, Diego Rivera's wife." Then she turned to Trotsky and grasped his arms. "Welcome to Mexico, Comrade Trotsky. Diego could not come to meet you, as he has been ill. He apologizes that he could only send a wife, but I bring with me all the good wishes that he would give you if he were here in person." Then she kissed him on each cheek, as she had Natalya. "President Cárdenas has sent the presidential train, *El Hidalgo*, to take you to Mexico City. From there it's a short ride by car to our home in Coyoacán, where Diego waits for us."

She let loose a barrage of Spanish at the policemen and they made room for her to walk alongside the Trotskys as they continued up the path. Suddenly she turned and looked back at Andre, who still stood on the gangway.

"Who is he?"

"He crossed with us on the *Ruth*," Trotsky replied. "In the excitement of landing I forgot about him. His name is Andre Frankle. He's an artist."

"Come on, Andre Frankle, the artist," she called to him gaily. "Will you stand at the dock all day, or will you come with us to see Mexico?"

El Hidalgo carried its occupants through the Mexican countryside in portable opulence. Everything had been provided to make the Trotskys comfortable during the trip. Servants served their meals in the luxurious private dining car. Cigarettes were offered, brandies poured. The rest of the time was spent in the lounge car, with Frida and Natalya on one side of the aisle chatting about Mexico, while Trotsky and Max Schactman, an American friend who had joined them in Tampico, sat talking on the other side. Andre took a seat in the corner and drew sketches of everyone.

"The greenery everywhere," Natalya exclaimed. "I hadn't realized how starved I was for the sight of living plants. Norway is so cold, so forbidding." Her lip quivered. "You're so kind, Frida, so very kind."

Trotsky had stopped talking and now glanced often at the two women across the aisle. Andre sketched quickly, trying to catch the look of tenderness as Trotsky looked at Natalya, then the animal hunger as his gaze lingered on Frida. Natalya looked up to say something to her husband and saw him staring at Frida's full bosom.

"I must excuse myself now," Natalya said. She walked across the aisle, and bent to kiss Trotsky's forehead. "You mustn't stay up too late, Lev. It's been an exhausting day."

Andre made more sketches now, of Trotsky and Schactman engrossed in conversation, of Frida Kahlo's coarse beauty as she stared expressionlessly out the train window, her chin resting on her hand. He struggled to capture the arrogant tilt of her head, the volume of hair impaled by a tortoiseshell comb, the strips of bright yellow wool that she had coaxed into her braids. In the daylight he had noticed a shadowy mustache above her pointy lips, but in the compartment's dim light, it was barely visible.

"I think I'll say good night, too," said Trotsky when it had grown dark. He left the lounge car, followed by Schactman. The porter walked through the car removing empty glasses.

"Are you content with what you have drawn tonight?" Frida asked in English.

"Quite content," Andre answered in Spanish.

"So you speak Spanish as well as English."

"I'm a Jew without funds. My only treasure is my knowledge of languages. Yes, I speak Spanish. I lived in Madrid for a time."

"And did you fight the fascists?"

"I left for Germany before the Spanish Civil War. I don't involve myself in politics."

She laughed. "So you come to Mexico with Trotsky. Tell me, don't you know that he's a communist, that I'm a communist, that Diego Rivera and all the painters you'll meet in Mexico are communists, and that we don't make distinctions between art and politics?"

"I've heard that, but I'm interested only in cubism, surrealism, and expressionism. No other isms interest me."

"Then you're not an intellectual like the Europeans I saw in Paris, those who sit and talk, but do nothing?"

"No, I'm not an intellectual."

She reached into her shawl and brought out a small flask and took a quick drink from it. "Mexican artists are activists, not intellectuals. Perhaps you'll fit in after all. Rivera despises intellectuals. Rivera shits wherever and whenever he wants to shit, and he doesn't ask the permission of the intellectuals. That's why his alliance with Trotsky will be short. Rivera is larger than life. His murals are bigger than the sun. His appetites are like mine, gargantuan, insatiable. He and Trotsky will be enemies after they've lived together only a short time. You'll see."

She waved the flask in front of him. "You're unshockable."

"I'm observing."

"I'm something to observe, I can tell you. I had an accident on a motorbus when I was eighteen. Impaled by a metal rod. My pelvis and spine were splintered, my right foot shattered. I live with the pain still." She held up the flask. "My medicine." At the look on Andre's face she said, "So suffering moves you. I'm glad to see that there's a person inside that unshockable body." She took another drink and placed the flask back in her shawl.

"So what do you think you saw today that intrigues you so much, Andre Frankle, the artist?"

"The way Trotsky looks at you frightens Natalya."

"That old man?"

He handed her the sketches he had made.

"Hmm, you have captured it very well. The poor soul. She's broken and sad, and he hurts her more by panting for me. As for your ability, I will say that you're original. You draw well—economically—not prettily. There's a hint of the German expressionist there, certainly. I can see that Beckmann is a strong influence on you. It doesn't take an expert to see that. And, of course, you have an infallible eye." She handed the sketches back and said dismissively, "It takes more than an eye to make an artist."

"What does it take?"

She touched her chest. "Heart. Here. That's what you'll see when you look at my paintings. I bleed, I weep, I moan, I scream, I scratch. And when you look at Diego Rivera's paintings, you'll cry because of the compassion they reveal. You'll see the pain of the people for whom the Revolution has never ended. No one can know the suffering of Mexico. No one. Rivera and Siqueiros paint that suffering on the sides of buildings, and even they cannot capture it. It squeezes out the sides of the paintings and runs out onto the ground. This is a country that has bled, Andre. It has been stolen by many, but no one has been able to keep it for long. Kings have tried, but it has stained and corrupted them and their puppets." Her tone turned mocking. "So tell me, do you have a heart as well as an eye, Andre Frankle, the artist?"

"Some say I have a heart. I think I have one. I feel it beating."

"I don't think you do," she said imperiously. "Maybe when you grow as old as I am, you will."

"You forget, I've been studying your face. You're not much older than I am."

"But I'm old in spirit. So tell me why you've come to Mexico."

"The Nazis saw something in my paintings that offended them. I thought it best not to aggravate them further. Mexico offers me the artistic freedom I need."

"Be careful in your relationship to Trotsky or your freedom will be short."

"We're only acquaintances."

"He treats you like a son. His sons won't live long."

"I think the danger to him is exaggerated. Stalin is glad to be rid of him. Why should he want to harm him now? He's an old man with few followers."

"Trotsky didn't blink when the czar and his family were murdered. Others won't blink when Trotsky and his family are murdered."

"If I'm in danger for speaking to him, then Diego Rivera is in more danger for helping him."

"Of course he is. I told him he would be. But he's Diego and will do what he wants. Danger to a Mexican is excitement, the possibility of death, freedom from the shittiness of life."

She looked down at her long flounced skirt, then touched the silk fringes of her shawl with beringed fingers. "This is my Tehuana costume, but I'm not wearing all my finery today. I wanted to dress conservatively in honor of the occasion. Don't smile. I usually wear more colors, and I twist my braid with bits of mirror and paper flowers and jewelry. I like to remind everyone who looks at me that I have Indian blood. Of course, it's mixed with Jewish blood."

"You're a painting."

"I am, am I not? It excites me to look this way. It's an erotic thing, like touching yourself." She hesitated. "Or touching another woman."

Andre turned his face toward the window, as though to look outside, but all he saw was the dark glossiness of Frida's image reflected in against the dark glass.

"I see I go too far too soon," she said, and he knew she was gloating at his discomfort. "Some say that we Mexicans run in fits and starts, like the jumping bean. You have to catch us, Andre, to even begin to understand the Mexican."

"There's no need to patronize me."

Her shoulders stiffened beneath the shawl. "You hurt my feelings. I'm being a friend."

"You're not my friend yet."

"You say that so that later you can insult me with impunity."

"I say that so that when we become friends you'll let me paint your portrait."

"You may paint whenever and whatever you like. I don't care. But why are you looking at me so intently? Do you also pant after me like the old man?"

"No. I admire the way you look. I've been thinking all day how I can get you to pose for me. I was also thinking about what you said of Mexico and the Mexicans. I've studied Mexico since I was a boy in Paris and my father brought the illegitimate son of Emperor Maximilian home to dinner."

Her eyes ignited with interest. "There was a son?"

"He called himself Count Sedano y Leguizano. He was executed by the French for espionage. My father took me to see it."

"What a cruel thing to do!"

He smiled. "It wasn't cruel at all. It made a lasting impression on me. My father believed that we learn everything there is of importance in life from what happens around us. I've never been able to erase that day from my mind. It's strange what a child will remember. We ate cheese in the forest and then we were in a big building looking out the window. I watched them shoot him. He was very heroic, almost nonchalant. I'll never forget it."

"Then you must know that there was an illegitimate daughter also."

"Yes."

"María. She's an old woman now."

"You know her?"

She pressed his knee with her fingers. "My dear Andre Frankle, I not only know her, but I know her granddaughter Lidia. But since you won't permit me to be your friend, I'm not going to introduce her to you."

Lights spun by the train window. Frida's mouth was open, revealing small white teeth beneath the dark upper lip. The sketches lay on the seat. They were suddenly dull and insipid, of no interest to him at all. "I had hoped to trap your personality in a bottle, and you have trapped mine instead," he said.

"That's what I told you," said Frida, "to know the Mexicans first you must catch the bean." She tweaked his cheek affectionately. "I like you. There are not many that I like. But you, *cuate*, will be my friend."

27

Magdalena Carmen Frida Kahlo y Calderón was born in a blue house on Londres Street in Coyoacán in 1910. Her father, Wilhelm Kahlo, a German Jew, had come to Mexico in 1891, changed his name to Guillermo Kahlo and opened a photography studio. His first marriage ended with the death of his wife, leaving him with two daughters, María Luisa and Margarita. He then married Matilde Calderón y González, a Mexican woman from Oaxaca, who bore him four more daughters, Cristina, Matilde, Adriana, and Frida.

The blue house in Coyoacán was the seat of Frida's personality, the place that harbored her fantasies, nurtured her art, bore her stamp of fable and imagery. Her homoerotic paintings of fetuses and flowers and bleeding wounds covered the walls along with her collection of ex-votos, tiny paintings with handwritten prayers celebrating miraculous rescues from death. Frida's art and the ex-votos were grotesque, dreamlike, absorbed with self, their perspectives skewed but naively charming. Like Frida.

Throughout the house, in the kitchen, bath, bedrooms, studio, were colorful oddments, bowls, dishes, rocks, fans, pre-Columbian figures and Indian handcrafts, as well as dolls, paper flowers, combs, bits of jewelry, and fragments of embroidery.

Frida and Rivera lived there briefly at the beginning of their marriage before their adjoining studios were built in San Ángel. After his wife's death, Frida's father lived there

alone, at times joined by children and grandchildren. It was a
house that Frida always came back to, a house in which in
1937 she settled the Trotskys.

Frida gave Andre a room in her studio in San Ángel and
got him a job as an assistant to the artist David Siqueiros. She
affectionately called Andre her young Jew. Trotsky cringed at
the term, but Rivera laughed at it. "Frida says and does what
she wants," he said. "She once asked Henry Ford if he was
Jewish. She is afraid of no one."

The Trotskys and Riveras saw each other often. There were
picnics in the hacienda at San Miguel Regla on the outskirts
of Mexico City, and outings to the lava beds of the Pedregal,
where Trotsky liked to ride horseback over the rocky ground
and dig cactus specimens for replanting outside his and
Natalya's bedroom in Coyoacán. There were parties in Frida's
studio in San Ángel, where Frida's raucous laughter and
provocative behavior with guests produced a chilly aloofness
on Natalya's part.

In public Rivera remained a staunch Trotskyite, a fervent
anti-Stalinist who refused to speak to David Siqueiros because of Siqueiros's efforts to have Trotsky ousted from Mexico. But in private Rivera excoriated Trotsky, found fault with
his theories. Trotsky in turn galled Rivera by calling him a
philistine and declaring his political views middlebrow. They
hectored each other like young bulls.

"How can I help it if Trotsky fondles my knee under the
table?" Frida protested to Andre. "He's an old man who can
probably not raise his tiny thing an inch above his lap." But
she didn't discourage Trotsky's attentions, kissing him on the
lips when she greeted him, and calling him *mi amor* in a
seductive manner, all of which caused Natalya great distress.
Diego, who himself had only recently broken off a long affair
with Frida's sister Cristina, sniped more heatedly at Trotsky
and fell more often into spells of melancholia. The sixty-year-
old Trotsky assumed the expression of a lovesick boy when
Frida was around, and he and Rivera, as Frida had predicted,
came to detest each other.

In April of 1937, while the purge trials and executions of
Trotsky's followers in Russia continued, the American educa-
tor John Dewey came to the house in Coyoacán. Dewey
chaired a commission to decide if Trotsky was guilty or innocent of the charges that Stalin had brought against him in

absentia. The commission consisted of six Americans, one Frenchman, two Germans, an Italian, and a Mexican.

After thirteen sessions, concluding with an impassioned speech by Trotsky in which he urged the workers of the world to unite, John Dewey declared that Trotsky had proven his innocence of Stalin's charges beyond a reasonable doubt. The findings of the commission did nothing to change Trotsky's status as a hunted man, but it gave Frida a perfect excuse for a party.

The fiesta was held in the blue house, where Frida greeted her guests in a purple flounced skirt and red blouse. A bright yellow rebozo hung from her shoulders and yellow hibiscus blossoms twined through her braids. Loops of colored stones circled her neck. Fingers and wrists were adorned with rings and silver bracelets set with jade and carnelian.

"*Mi querido*, I'm so glad to see you," Frida told Andre when he arrived. "Everyone is here. No one has dared to refuse Diego's invitation."

Armed men patrolled the fence and the walkways of the garden and mingled with the guests while flashbulbs, sounding like muted gunfire, popped intermittently. Mariachis in silver-encrusted blue suits and tasseled sombreros played *jarabes* and *jaranas* in the flower-filled courtyard off the gallery, but no one danced, since none of the guests knew the Mexican dances.

"Everyone thinks you're my new lover," said Frida, pulling Andre through the throng to where Rivera and Trotsky stood in a circle of admirers near the fireplace. "But of course it's the old man that Diego worries about, not you. Already he's beginning to hate the old fart. I told you it would happen. Diego tells such fantastic stories, and it disgusts Trotsky, whose eyes see nothing but the floor beneath his own feet. But the greatest insult of all is that he no longer laughs at Diego's jokes."

Frida kissed Rivera juicily on the lips. "Take care of my young Jew, Diego, while I see to my other guests." Rivera was an enormous man, over six feet tall, with a monstrously fat belly that hung over his belt and frog eyes that peered crookedly from the sides of his face. A ridiculous floppy sombrero roosted on his huge head.

"This party was a mistake," said Rivera sullenly. "Frida's instincts are those of the bullfighter, not the diplomat. This is not a time to rub the Stalinists' noses in the dirt."

"What better time can there be," retorted Trotsky, "than when these accusations against me have been exposed as lies?"

"Maybe they're not such lies," Rivera said. "After all, if a man brings potatoes to market in a wagon, it's a good guess that he's a farmer."

"Ach! You don't know what you're talking about," said Trotsky. He turned to Andre. "I hear you're working with David Siqueiros on plans for a mural at the Electricians Syndicate."

"Yes, I am."

"So you've involved yourself in proletariat art at last."

"I've sold none of my own paintings yet. Putting propaganda on the walls of buildings is preferable to starving."

"I've been warned by my advisers that Siqueiros is dangerous. There are those who say my end is more likely to come at the hands of Siqueiros than Stalin."

"Advisers? *Gringos?*" snapped Rivera. "What do those damned *gringachos* know? They exaggerate everything. Siqueiros talks a lot, but he'll never do anything to you. He's just the same *loco* he's always been."

"I agree with Diego," Andre said. "Siqueiros is an artist. All the rest is theatrics."

"A man whose grandfather fought with Juárcz against Maximilian at Querétaro, a man who himself goes to Spain to fight Franco, is a man who would kill for his beliefs," said Trotsky.

"What do you know of David Siqueiros?" grunted Rivera. "I've known him since we were young. He's an actor. He loves drama. He'll soon tire of his threats against you."

Screams and shouts erupted from the vicinity of the courtyard. A man in a white shirt and white pants burst through the gallery doors and ran toward Rivera.

"You are the traitor because you give him sanctuary!" the man shouted.

One of the guards pulled Trotsky out of the way as the man in white hurled Rivera's gargantuan frame to the floor and began to pummel him with his fists.

"Stop him, Andre," Frida screamed.

Andre heaved himself onto the man's back. Several more guards ran in through the open doors and helped pull Siqueiros away and pin him to the floor.

"*Mi amor*, what has that crazy Siqueiros done to you?" crooned Frida, as she sat on the floor, Rivera's bulk cradled in her arms. She kissed his protruding eyelids and fleshy mouth and wiped his bleeding nose with the fringes of her yellow rebozo.

"Andre, get Siqueiros out of here," she said. "He's a *pendejo*, a fool. He doesn't know what he's doing."

Natalya, who had complained of a headache and had been resting in the bedroom, came running out and threw her arms protectively around her husband as Andre and one of the guards dragged Siqueiros toward the door. As they passed Trotsky, Siqueiros shouted, "You don't belong in Mexico, señor."

"And do you?" asked Trotsky calmly.

When they reached the sidewalk, Siqueiros was thrown, blinking and sputtering, into a taxicab. Andre climbed in beside him.

Frida, who had run after them, bloodstained rebozo flapping limply against her shoulders, now leaned into the window of the cab. "Take him home, Andre," she said. "He's a bad boy. It's the fault of those *gringos*. They make him crazy."

Siqueiros leaned forward and kissed her hand. His face was scratched, eyelids narrow slits sliding into swollen craters. "*Adiós*, Frida, *adiós*." Then he sat quietly back against the seat and let himself be taken home.

Frida's affair with Trotsky began several weeks later in her sister Cristina's house in Coyoacán. Although Frida and Rivera often took lovers, Rivera was complacent about Frida's affairs only when they were with women.

"She's highly sexed," he said proudly whenever anyone remarked about his indulgence of her.

When her lovers were men, Frida would warn them that secrecy had to be maintained.

"You know he has pistols," she would tell them. "He likes to shoot them off in the Pedregal, watch the bullets spin off the rocks. He'll murder us both if he catches us."

The affair with Trotsky had an added fillip.

"He's old and sweats a lot," Frida told Cristina, "but because Diego loathes him so much, it's very exciting. And besides, Diego made love to you here. It's only fitting that I should make love to the old one in the same place."

Frida and Trotsky also met in Frida's studio in San Ángel, making love next to the enclosed alcove that Andre occupied.

Just as on the crossing on the *Ruth*, he could hear Trotsky's voice through the thinness of the studio walls. But in San Ángel the answering voice was not Natalya's, but Frida's, and the sounds were not of Spanish being practiced and family matters being discussed, but rather the passionate and pathetic gruntings of an old man making love to his benefactor's wife.

"I'm ashamed before you," Trotsky said when he and Andre finally met face-to-face on the stairway, the smell of Frida still on Trotsky's body.

"I've seen nothing," Andre said, but he too was embarrassed.

"It will soon be over. Frida says it will ruin us both, that she wants only passion from me, not love, that she loves only Diego."

"Please don't explain to me. You have no reason to think that anything you do—"

"Anyway, it's gone too far. My advisers warn me that if it becomes known, it will be a scandal that will discredit me to the world. And, of course, there's Nata, whose silent reproaches make my guilt all the more excruciating." Trotsky's lip twitched. "I have just left her bed, Andre, and already I mourn the loss of her. Such lust, such appetite she has. Even more than Nata had in her youth. She holds nothing back, hides nothing. Ay, love at any age is exhausting, but at my age it's a disaster."

The affair ended shortly after that. The Trotskys stayed on in the blue house, and the Riveras still visited them there, but, as Frida reported back to Andre, dark eyes dancing with delight, "Natalya goes around looking like a wounded bird, and Trotsky stares icily at me in her presence. We tried to protect her, to keep it from her, but how could she not know, *querido*? Things like that are not easily hidden from someone who knows you as well as Natalya knows Trotsky."

They were in the San Ángel Inn, eating lunch, the mariachis playing in the patio. Frida leaned across the table. "Now that things have ended between me and the old one, I have time for you." She kissed him on the lips. "We kiss, but there is nothing."

"Diego is a friend. I won't offend him by making love to his wife."

"Ay, you have more scruples than the old one did."

"Besides, you're a Catholic and I'm a Jew."

"But I don't want to marry you, *querido*, I only want to

make love with you. And when you're tired of me, you can throw me away. You find me desirable, don't you?"

"Very desirable. The thought of making love to you has occurred to me from time to time."

She ran her tongue over her lips. "Were the thoughts exciting?"

"Yes."

"What did we do together?"

"All the things that men and women do."

"But you don't have to dream it, *querido*, we can do it."

"They were just thoughts. I don't act on every thought I have. If we have a love affair, when it's over we won't be friends. You said you wanted us to be friends."

"You use my own words against me, and just when I have come to burn with desire for you." She shrugged and patted his face. "Ay, *chulo*, you have such control. Never in my life have I seen anyone like you. You want me, but will do nothing about it." She brought his head down close to her mouth. "Listen to me, Andre, I want to see the girl you take to your bed in spite of everything you know to be wrong, the one you cannot say no to, because it will be like an explosion, an earthquake, a stick of dynamite in your penis. And then I want to hear about friendship and complications and Catholics and Jews."

In 1939 Frida went to Paris and then to New York to exhibit her paintings. While she was gone, Trotsky had a bitter argument with Diego Rivera, and he and Natalya moved into a house of their own on Avenida Viena in Coyoacán while Rivera started divorce proceedings against Frida. Andre, who was now living and working in an apartment studio in an old colonial buidling overlooking the El Carmen Church in nearby San Ángel, was occupied with sketches for a projected series of paintings on Mexican village life.

On those afternoons when Andre would visit the Trotskys in their house on Avenida Viena, armed guards, mostly Americans, would interrogate him through a peephole before they would let him in the gate, and he would come away with the disquieting sense that Trotsky was as much a prisoner in Mexico as he had been in Norway. Then the news reached Mexico that Trotsky's two sons by Natalya had been murdered by Stalin. Andre visited the Trotskys a few more times after that and met Seva, the young grandson who had finally come to live with them. But after each visit, Andre was so shaken by the cheerless house and the haunted faces of the Trotskys that he longed for a way to sever the relationhip.

"My dear Andre, do you think that all of these precautions protect me from Stalin?" asked Trotsky one afternoon as he and Andre walked in the shaded garden of the Avenida Viena house. Trotsky, who had taken up cactus gardening seriously and was raising rabbits in hutches near the wall, had greeted Andre in overalls, a black and white spotted rabbit snug in the crook of his arm. "No," said Trotsky, answering his own question. "His agents are everywhere. Perhaps the corner baker is a member of the GPU and is planning to put poison in my *pan dulce*."

"Now that the war has started in Europe, Stalin will forget all about you."

"What Stalin has set in motion against me cannot be stopped."

They walked toward the house where Natalya was preparing tea and sandwiches for their lunch. At the steps, Trotsky paused. "We mustn't alarm Nata," he said. "Now that Seva is here she is happy for the first time. All of our children are dead. He is our future."

Natalya and one of the Mexican maids served lunch at the long table in the kitchen.

"I'm hard at work on the biography of Stalin," said Trotsky, pointing to the piles of books and papers and notebooks stacked at the end of the table. "Some might find it ironic that I'm devoting my energies to writing about the man who will no doubt cause my death. But who better than I to write the book? It will be the definitive book on Stalin, the one that explains him to the world."

The exterior wall around the property blocked out the afternoon sun so that the air in the house, with its limited number of windows, was sodden and dank with the trapped moisture of steam from cooking pots and the sour smell of perspiration deposited on overstuffed furniture. There was no ornament anywhere in the house, no color. Except for the books that filled the bookshelves, there was nothing on the walls.

"Frida has taken some paintings of mine with her to New York," Andre said.

"We would love to have something of yours," said Natalya,

ignoring the mention of Frida's name. Natalya now felt such bitterness toward her that she had scratched out her face in every photograph in which she appeared with Trotsky.

"The house is so bare," Natalya said. "There," she said, pointing to the wall that faced the dining table.

Andre took a piece of paper from an open notebook that lay on the table. "This is a painting that I owe to L.D. and Natalya Trotsky," he wrote on it, and then signed his name.

"I'll tack it up right there on the wall until the painting arrives," she said.

When lunch was over, Trotsky walked with Andre through the cloistered garden to the padlocked gate. "Stalin is keeping a list of all my friends and associates. There have already been assassinations in Europe. I expect that there will be some in Mexico, too. Perhaps you should not come again, Andre."

Andre nodded. "I'll send the painting."

One of the guards bent and released the padlock.

Trotsky shook Andre's hand. "I hope your parents survive the war in Poland. Hitler hates the Jews more than Stalin hates me. That's a big hatred."

"My father has always known how to protect himself."

"Cleverness is sometimes not enough."

When the gate was locked once again behind him, Andre felt an enormous relief. In recent months his father's voice had come to him at odd moments asking the same question over and over: "They say that Stalin made the Norwegians throw Trotsky out in exchange for a load of Russian herring. Tell me, my son, how many herring is a man worth?" Andre no longer had to worry about the answer. He would not have to visit Trotsky again. He was free of the obligation of being his friend.

28

In early April 1940 Frida telephoned Andre with the news that the Samuel Waxman Gallery in New York had sold three of his paintings of Indian women. "Waxman says he has never seen a fresher talent," said Frida. "He called you a visionary. He said your portraits of Indian women strike at the heart and make one cry at the humanity of the poor Mexican. He said, 'Send me more.'

"I told him that you may be a visionary, but you're so poor you have to take buses to the villages and are in danger of losing life and limb with one of those crazy matador bus drivers, that you need a car, and fast.

" 'Buy one,' he said.

"I said, 'With what? The three paintings you sold won't buy him a car and paint brushes, too.'

" 'Then I'll give him a stipend,' he said.

" 'How much?' I asked him.

" 'Fifty dollars a month,' he said.

"I said, 'One hundred and he's yours.'

"So I got you the money you need and you can buy a car. I find you money and I'm broke, *cuate*. Diego's run off to New York with Paulette Goddard, the American movie star. It's time to take care of Frida now. But I still love you, so come over tomorrow afternoon. I've decided that the time is right for you to paint my portrait."

"What did I tell you, *cuate*?" said Frida when Andre arrived at the blue house. "How about that Sam Waxman loving your paintings? Is my eye good or not? You'll see, before I'm through you'll be more famous than Rivera, and you aren't even a Mexican. But you'll become one, *cuate,* and then they'll give you more walls to paint than they give Rivera. Did I tell you that you would make lots of money? And dollars at that."

"For a communist, you're a great capitalist." Andre laughed.

"Until the world is perfect, we need dollars." She was dressed in reds and blues today and wore Mexican huaraches, which squeaked on the wooden floors of the yellow-walled kitchen.

"A little *cocktailito,*" she said, pouring him a glass of scotch. She picked up the bottle and took two quick swigs. "To success," she said.

"To success," he said, lifting his glass to her bottle.

"So, *cuate,* have you met the girl yet, the one you can't say no to?"

"Not yet."

"Not even one little Mexican love affair have you had since you came to Mexico?"

"Not even one little Mexican. Not even one little Indian either."

"I told you before, you have no heart, Andre. You will never become a Mexican until you find a heart. So how's Trotsky, have you seen him?"

"Trotsky is well for now. I think it's best that you're done with him."

"Regardless of what people say, the break between him and Diego was political, not because I let Trotsky fuck me. Ay, but I do miss his friendship. And Siqueiros, have you heard anything about that maniac? He no longer calls or sends me notes. I've known him since I was so young. Now our friendship too is over."

"I've seen him," Andre said. "He's back from Spain, acting more and more like a politician and less and less like an artist. He's blaming Spain's defeat on Trotsky's refusal to support Stalin. I try not to talk about politics with him, and we get along well."

"He knows you have European sensibilities and need things to be scientific," she said. "So he puts his revolutionary talk aside."

"Whatever his reasons, he's been very pleasant to me, but

I think he still views me as the enemy because of my friendship with Trotsky." He gave a quick laugh. "He called a painting that I did of an Indian village 'a fascistic interpretation of the Mexican proletariat.' But he smiled when he said it."

"His sense of humor," said Frida. "Finish your *cocktailito*. It's time for you to begin my portrait."

She led him thorugh the art-filled gallery to the studio, which was light and airy, the floor a mosaic of Mexican pavers, waxed and buffed to a high gloss. An easel with a half-finished painting of a nude woman sat in the middle of the room facing the model, a girl about nineteen years old. The light was on the girl's face, her profile tipped to the right.

"You can work over there by the light while I work on my own painting," said Frida. "But don't talk to me unless I talk to you. And don't touch my model, since I pay her salary, and she is nontransferable."

An easel had been set up for him, complete with paints. He tripped over a chair as he walked toward it.

"I think she's beautiful, too," Frida said. She moved the position of the girl's upper torso with her hands. "Look at her breasts, how they tilt upward."

Andre turned away. He had been drawing nudes from life since he was twelve, but still he felt his penis rising in his pants.

"Don't worry, Andre, it happened many times to Diego, and he's seen many more nude women than you have."

Andre busied himself checking the brushes. Then he squeezed a few blobs of paint onto the palette.

"She's a very good model," said Frida. "It's the color of the skin when light hits it, very fine and translucent. I found her in Cuernavaca when Diego did the mural in the Cortés Palace there. She was only ten years old, but already she was a beauty, with the Indian blood bringing great mystery and strength to her features. I began to paint her there, and when she grew up and came to Mexico City to study acting, I painted her here, too, from time to time."

"You're an actress, then?" asked Andre, turning toward the girl. She had finer features than the Indian women he had been painting, yet her face was not European. The eyes were spaced wider apart, the cheeks fuller, the brow less round.

"*Sí*," the girl said.

"She just completed a small part in a Dolores del Río movie," Frida said. "It's only a matter of time before she gets starring roles. Lidia, this is Andre Frankle."

"Lidia." He took her hand and kissed it.

"*Buenos días*, Andre," she said, smiling at him.

"What a sight, Andre," Frida exclaimed. "I should paint you two just like that. I'll call it 'Jew Kissing Indian Hand with Two Breasts.' Actually, I think you've stared at her long enough. Her parents are very strict. It's not a wealthy family. Her father owns a small furniture factory. But there's only the one daughter, and so they're particularly careful of her."

"Is posing in the nude and acting in the movies being particularly careful of her?"

"*Tonto*, you of all people," remonstrated Frida. "This is art. They trust me. As for her movies—" She turned toward the girl. "Have they ever seen any of your movies, Lidia?"

"Only one. They liked it very much."

"You see, Andre, they're proud of her. And you can remove the lecherous look from your face, because she's leaving all this behind soon and going back to Cuernavaca to be married. She's known the young man since childhood. The families have arranged it."

Frida talked as though the girl weren't there. Andre began sketching Frida's profile as she worked, but he kept glancing at Lidia.

"Aren't you curious why I chose today when Lidia was posing to ask you to come here and do my portrait?" Frida asked.

"All right, I'm curious. You never do anything without a plan, and never concoct a plan without wanting everyone to know about it. So tell me why today in particular."

"Come, come, think, Andre. You don't remember what I said to you on the train from Tampico, do you?"

He put his head back and shut his eyes. "You said that I could paint your portrait. You said that I had no heart. You said—" He opened his eyes and looked at the girl. "You said that you knew Maximilian's great-granddaughter." He moved closer to the girl. "It's you."

"*Sí*," the girl said.

"This is Lidia Machado Ramírez, the great-granddaughter of Maximilian, emperor of Mexico," announced Frida.

"You met Count Sedano y Leguizano in Paris," Lidia said. "So Frida told you about me, too."

"You can dress now, Lidia," said Frida brusquely.

When the girl had left the room, Andre said, "Why did you do that?"

"You were making me jealous the way you looked at her."

"But you had her here, you asked me to come."

"Hmm, maybe I made a mistake. I'm always playing games, hoping to surprise people, to give them a little variation in their ratty lives. I knew you would enjoy seeing her body, not only because you knew Maximilian's son, but because you appreciate beauty. But the look on your face when she was here was—well, *cuate*, what can I say? I hope that it was just the beauty of her body that overwhelmed you and nothing more."

"Then this was some kind of joke. You brought her here just to see my reaction?"

"No, no, it's nothing like that. But why are you so upset? She's a child. Your experience has not been hers, Andre. She's an innocent. Her career in the city has been an interlude, and soon she will return to Cuernavaca and marry her *novio*. If you think there is anything you can take from this girl, then I truly made a mistake in asking you to come here."

He threw the brushes to the floor, his face flushed and angry. "You knew about my interest in Maximilian's family, so you invite me here while his great-granddaughter is posing for you in the nude. Now you pull her away as though I were a murderer of babies."

"I've insulted you," she said, and she turned away and busied herself at the easel. "Is it too late to keep you for myself, then?" she asked, her back to him.

When he didn't answer, she turned around and embraced him, her bracelets jingling musically in the still room. "Ay, forgive me, *querido*. I don't always understand what I'm doing or why. I want only the best for my friends. I don't mean to harm anyone. If I hurt you, it is unintentional. What can I do to make you forgive me?"

"Ask her if she'll pose for me."

She leaned back in his arms and looked at him. "What are you saying?"

"I'm an artist. She's a model. I'd like her to pose for me. She poses for you."

"But for me it's different. I don't look at her the way you were looking at her."

She put her lips to his and kissed him. "You make me

jealous," she said. "You're cruel and heartless, but what am I to do?"

Lidia came to Andre's studio in San Ángel on Saturday afternoons. He looked forward to it throughout the week, so that by Thursday he could no longer concentrate on the mural sketches he was doing for Siqueiros. He found himself standing at the window in the apartment of the old colonial building in which he lived and staring out into the street, as though by watching he might hurry her arrival, might catch a glimpse of her silhouette as she walked past the bookstore and the restaurant and then the gate of the courtyard. Watching for her became a pastime of his, and when the afternoon light in the studio grew weak, he would put on a jacket and sit outdoors on a bench near El Carmen Church and look for her among the parishioners entering for late afternoon mass.

On the mornings of the days that Lidia came to pose, he would shower, then dress in clean pants and shirt and walk to the market for flowers to brighten the studio. He noticed the drabness of his studio more now than ever. The worn daybed, the limp curtains, were a reproach. Even the light displeased him as he tried to catch her likeness in daubs and swirls of paint.

She would arrive in her smart city clothes and change into a cotton smock. The high-heeled shoes would disappear, and she would walk barefoot, her perfectly shaped toes a rebuke to the scarred wood beneath her feet. She would smile at him and ask, "Have you had a good week, Andre?" as she removed her makeup with cold cream and pulled the pins from her hair so that her dark-brown locks hung thick and straight to her shoulders.

"I have had a very good week," he would answer. And she would open her smock, and the sight of her would make his heart pound.

When he had a cold, she brought him *tisanas,* teas made of orange leaf and orange flower and chamomile.

"Your throat is sore because you drink water with ice in it," she would caution, "and because you leave your windows open at night. The bad airs, *los males aires,* enter through the windows. That's what makes you sick."

One afternoon as they strolled through the Saturday market, Andre impulsively picked up a silver bracelet. "Do you like it?" he asked.

"*Sí*, it's very pretty."

He paid the vendor and put the bracelet on Lidia's wrist.

"*Qué linda*," she said, but then she took it off and handed it back to him. "My *novio* would be angry."

"You've become a madman," said Frida one morning when she came to look at Andre's portraits of Lidia. "Does she know that you love her, *cuate*?"

"No. I'm afraid I'll scare her away. I've had no experience with innocence. The women I've known have all been knowledgeable about life."

"You have never so much as touched that satin skin?" she asked in amazement.

"I know every contour of her body without ever having put my fingers to them."

Frida shook her head, her chunky silver earrings clanging against her cheeks.

"But what do you talk about, then?"

"Things that I suppose an innocent girl would be interested in talking about. I ask her questions about Maximilian and Concepción. She tells me about Concepción's house in Acapatzingo, of how her family returned there after the Revolution, of what their lives there were like. I tell her about Europe."

Frida sat down on the divan that served him as bed and couch. "Come, sit down beside me, *chulo*." Her perfume and the noise of her jewelry crowded everything else out of the small room. "I shouldn't tell you how to win Lidia, but how can I help myself when I see that she will be so well loved by you. *Bueno*. You must assert yourself with her. Don't permit her to turn you away. And if the *novio* fights you for her, you mustn't show weakness in any way. Lidia will spurn you if you're weak. You must be strong, *macho*. You mustn't show that you want what's best for her, only what's best for you. If someone fights you for her, remember that he's afraid of you, afraid that you have more strength than he does."

"All of this is foolishness, Frida."

"Ah, foolishness? If you want a Mexican woman, you'll listen to what I say. I'm telling you that right now, she's watching carefully to see what you do. She has to be led to love. You're not in Europe now, *cuate*, with your models spreading their legs for you because you give them a look that says that they should. Here a woman—particularly a woman who has lived most of her life in a small village—must be carefully educated as to the kind of man you are, that you are brave and will fight for her, that she can depend on you for protection, that you will never leave her."

She caressed his cheek with her hand, and her bracelets were cold against his skin.

"But perhaps it's not Lidia at all that stops you," she said. "Perhaps it's something else that prevents you from defeating everyone and everything and taking her for your own."

At the end of April, Andre finished the series of nude portraits of Lidia and sent them to New York. Lidia appeared on Saturday, as she always did, but this time she didn't undress. She sat opposite him on the daybed.

"I've brought you something," she said, handing him a small plaster figurine. "San Pedro. He's my patron saint. Now he's yours. He'll watch over you like he watches over me. He'll keep the evil eye away from you and see to it that you eat well and don't get so many colds."

"You're leaving."

"Sí. I waited until your paintings were finished. Now they are, and the film I'm making will soon be over. We only have to shoot some additional scenes in the Alameda on Thursday, and then there's no longer anything to keep me here. My *novio* has written me that he's becoming impatient. He's worried that if I stay longer in Mexico City I'll never return to Cuernavaca."

"Well, then, that's that. I've enjoyed painting you, Lidia. You're a beautiful girl." He looked down at the ugly plaster figure. "I hope you have a wonderful life, with everything you want."

"I hope that you do, too, Andre."

Artur's voice had been particularly strong the past few days. "Careful, my son. Being a Jew is difficult enough, but being a refugee Jew, an outsider, sooner or later the Mexicans will turn on you just as the Germans did. For the moment, the Mexicans think you're a poor soul in need of salvaging, someone who only needs to be brought to God to be saved. But how will you fare in the midst of all this pagan superstition? Can you really love a woman who believes that the Aztec gods send bad air to make people ill, that omens are always present in advance of misfortune?"

He could hear his mother's voice all the way from Warsaw. "She isn't Jewish, my son. You break my heart. Can she clean a herring or make a *brocha* over the candles? And what of the children you'll have?"

"Well, you shouldn't cry over it now, *cuate*," Frida had said when he told her Lidia was leaving. "I told you what to do. Anyway, it's much fuss about nothing. If you had slept with her once or twice, the madness would have dissipated and you would have been able to go back to your work."

"But I can't work. I don't care that she's going. It's just that I can't work. I haven't been able to pick up a paint brush or look at a canvas."

They had been drinking wine in Frida's kitchen, the ridge of pain gone from her forehead. "This is the earthquake I predicted, the dynamite in your penis. Maybe it's not too late. Maybe she likes you, too. Who knows?"

"It would be a catastrophe for both of us."

"Maybe it would be a catastrophe if you were together, and maybe not. Maybe you'll forget her in time, and maybe not. But not to work? *Madre de Dios*, what is there but work? But listen to me, *chulo*, if you decide to go after her, beware of the world she lives in. Even I have never lived in the world that Lidia inhabits. I talk of the beauty of Mexican life, about Indians and their incorruptibility, about villagers and their simple ways, but I'm a fake, a poseur. I've wanted to be someone else all my life, but I've never had the strength. Lidia is genuine, *cuate*. She'll lead you to the true Mexico, into a life that Rivera and I exalt in our work. I have no way of knowing, you understand, but that world may be too much for you. So do this thing with your eyes wide open. Take care that you understand what you're giving up, that there may be dangers. I'm not even smart enough to tell you what the dangers are."

Across from the Palacio de Bellas Artes was the Alameda, a green oasis in the middle of concrete and asphalt and honking horns. On Avenida Lázaro Cárdenas the traffic was backed up behind a donkey that had tripped on a piece of broken asphalt and now lay sprawled on the street while its owner and several policemen tried to coax it up onto its feet. From Lázaro Cárdenas to the Paseo de la Reforma nothing moved. The drivers of the stalled cars read their newspapers, yelled advice to the policemen, and heaped abuse on the owner of the donkey.

Andre maneuvered his 1933 blue Chevrolet coupé into an opening on Hidalgo Street, then parked the car and ran across to the Alameda. The park was cool in the afternoon heat. A few children wandered on the fringes selling Chiclets. Several hundred feet into the park was a barricade and a sign, No Pasar. Two guards in police uniform lounged on camp stools at the barricade.

"You can't come in," one of them said.

"Diego Rivera sent me over," Andre replied.

The first guard looked at Andre suspiciously while the second one whispered something in his ear and then disappeared into the trees. When he returned, he pushed the barricade aside so that Andre could enter.

Movie cameras had been set up near a fountain, and the actors were getting last-minute instructions from the director. Lidia, in a tiered red skirt and puff-sleeved pink blouse, stood next to the director listening intently to what he was saying. With the tan makeup on her face and her braided hair pinned to her head, she looked very Indian. Behind her, seated on a horse beneath the trees, was a bearded man, his bearing erect in his military uniform, his blond hair and beard dusted with a gold powder to make them glisten. The set was chaotic, with extras milling around, people talking, someone playing a guitar.

Lidia nodded to the director. Yes, she understood what he wanted. The guitarist stopped playing, the voices grew quiet. The director raised his hand and said "Action" in English. Lidia walked toward the horse. When she was within a few feet of it she stopped and looked up at the man in the saddle. And then Andre remembered the chipped and faded mural in the government office in Cuernavaca depicting Maximilian's entry into Mexico, and the panel showing Maximilian's first glimpse of Concepción in the Borda gardens, he seated on his horse, she standing on the path across from him.

Andre was so caught up in watching Lidia that he tripped over the tripod that held the sound equipment. The sound engineer caught the recording device with both hands, but the tripod clattered to the pavement. The director turned in Andre's direction, raised his hand, and said "Cut."

An assistant came over to where Andre was standing. "Who are you?"

"A friend of Lidia's. I hope your equipment isn't broken."

There was a hurried conversation between the director and Lidia, and then the director called a recess.

"I never thought of you as Concepción," said Andre when she was standing next to him, her face still animated and flushed with the excitement of the scene.

"I made my skin darker with makeup," she said. "The costume isn't authentic, but it's a movie after all." She touched his arm. "Are you ill? You look so pale, so tired."

"I didn't sleep very well last night."

"You need a *calmante*, a tea to rest you. You work too hard at your paintings."

"If you stay here in Mexico City, I'm sure I'll be cured."

She smiled shyly. He had seen the Indian women smile like that in the villages when he asked if they would sit for him while he painted their portrait. They would say yes and smile that shy smile. He would begin to paint, and before he had finished they would gather their rebozos around them, smile again, and disappear.

"My family is waiting for me," she said. "My *novio* is waiting." She looked pained. "I told you, Andre, that I had to leave."

"I want to do another series of paintings of you."

"Frida can find many who will pose for you."

"But they aren't you. That's the problem."

The director was calling her back to redo the scene. The stricken expression on her face now mirrored Andre's. She looked as though she were going to cry. "But you knew, Andre. Frida told you that I was betrothed."

"It wasn't important then." He took her hands in his. "You were happy to see me just now. I could hear it in your voice."

"I was happy to see you."

"Then stay. You've never told me that you love this man. I don't believe you want to go through with it at all."

"If it makes someone unhappy to hear some things, then I don't say them."

"Do you love him?"

"Of course."

"Do you love me?"

A tear escaped and slid down her cheek. She tried to catch it with one finger. "My makeup," she said.

"I'm pleading with you, Lidia. I'm making a fool of myself here in the park in front of everyone."

"You don't understand Mexico or Mexicans. I'm betrothed."

"All right, you're betrothed. You haven't married him, so there's still time."

She moved toward him and pressed her face against his chest.

"My heart is bursting, Lidia," he said as he put his arms around her.

"*Oh, Andrito*, don't make me feel so sad."

The director called her again, and she pulled away, patting her wet cheeks with the palms of her hands.

"I'm leaving tomorrow," she said.

"I'll drive you to Cuernavaca."

"Nothing will be accomplished."

"We'll see."

"Lidia, *ven acá*," shouted the director.

"The Del Prado Hotel," she said, and then she ran toward the set.

"What time?" he called after her.

"Ten o'clock," she answered.

29

By the time the last penitents had crossed the square on their way to eight o'clock mass, Andre had bathed and shaved, loaded a box with clothes and paint supplies into the rumble seat of his car, and was headed for the Del Prado Hotel. When he entered the lobby he saw Lidia near the elevators talking to the actor who had played Maximilian in the film. Gone were her well-tailored suits and high heels. Her hair hung down her back in a single braid and she had draped a mauve rebozo around her slender shoulders. A heavy woven bag with her belongings lay on the polished floor near her sandaled feet.

"Nando, this is my friend, Andre Frankle," she said.

"*Buenos días*, Nando," said Andre as he picked up her bag.

"What kind of name is Nando?" Andre asked when they had gotten in the car and were on the road to Cuernavaca.

"It's short for Fernando."

"It made me jealous to see him." He glanced at her. "Is that how you dress at home?"

She looked down at the bare toes peeking out of her sandals. "This is how I looked when I left home. This is how my mother and father expect to see me when I return."

"I don't think you can turn back into what you were when you left Cuernavaca just by changing your clothes."

They left the city, and the road began its ascent into the Ajusco Mountains, the cool breeze washing the air with the scent of pine. In the distance sheer cliffs and mountain peaks grew up out of the forest. They had been climbing for about fifteen minutes when the car began to falter. Instead of its former *chug-chug*, there was now a listless *chug-ping-chug*. Andre looked nervously at the dials on the dashboard.

"They watch to see the buses go by on the way to Cuernavaca," said Lidia as they passed an Indian family squatting on their haunches at the side of the road. "It entertains them."

"Uh-huh. You know you won't fit in, don't you? I mean, village life is fine for someone who hasn't lived in Mexico City and been an actress and an artist's model, but how you're—"

"You think I'm sophisticated, but I'm not. I've always wanted to come home. Frida's life is not for me. She talks about the beauty of the Mexican people, but she lives like an American."

When they arrived at a place on the road where the granite cliffs sprinkled with forest green disappeared into the clouds, there was an ear-splitting bang from the right rear tire of the coupé. The car swerved crazily from one side of the road to the other while Andre wrestled with the wheel. Then it stopped. No *chug-chug*. No *chug-ping-chug*. Nothing.

"No spare," said Andre tersely.

"Tires are not to be trusted," Lidia said by way of comfort.

"Is there a village nearby, somewhere that I can get the tire fixed?"

"We're not very far from Tepoztlán. It's always possible that someone knows something about tires there, even though they have no automobiles."

They retrieved their belongings from the rumble seat. Andre balanced his box on one shoulder, Lidia her string bag over hers, and they set out down the road. It was early afternoon and the cornfields lay freshly plowed in the May sun.

"Have you been to this village before?" he asked.

"Once with my *novio*."

"You came here alone with him?"

"No, no. We came to meet his brother Juan, who's married and lives here with his family. We'll go to his house and see if he can help us."

Two Indian men, their faces shielded from the sun by large sombreros, stooped in a field at the side of the road fixing the handle of a plow. They wore the traditional white pantaloons and white overblouse of the peasant. Lidia asked them something in a language that Andre didn't recognize. One of the men squinted at her suspiciously and then answered.

"He says we don't have too far to walk," she said.

"What language was that?"

"Nahuatl, the language of the Aztecs. I speak it because my father is an Indian. When he was a little boy he lived in Tepoztlán." She pointed to the mountains. "My father said that during the Revolution all the people left the village and climbed up into the *cerros*. They left their fields and their houses behind. Zapata had come here to take the land away from the rich landowners, and then the Federales came to get rid of Zapata, and everybody fought with everybody, and the village was destroyed. My father said that his family would only come into the village at night to forage for food or to hunt the deer that had come down into the village and taken the place of the people. It was a terrible time. My father and his family finally left for Cuernavaca and never came back to Tepoztlán."

"But your *novio*'s family stayed?"

"*Sí*. My *novio*'s father fought with Zapata and lived like a criminal during the Revolution. But when he returned to the village he was very clever. He built a mill where the women could come to have their maize ground for tortillas. At first the men of the village resisted him. They wanted the women to grind the corn by hand. They were afraid their wives would look at other men if they weren't busy all day grinding corn for tortillas."

She turned toward him as they walked. "You'll know everything about Tepoztlán by the time we get there, eh, Andre?"

"Go on. Tell me more. I want to know everything."

She laughed. "Andre, Mexicans can't be studied. They just are."

"I want to know everything about the *novio* in Cuernavaca. I want to know all the rules."

"There are no rules," she said. "Señor Lewis worked very hard, and finally the villagers accepted the mill, and he became a rich man."

"Lewis?"

"*Sí*. Benito Lewis is the name of my *novio*. His father was an American and his mother Carmen was a Tepoztecan girl, a niece of Zapata. Señor Lewis and Carmen were killed by the peasants not too far from here. They were on their way to a fiesta in Tres Cumbres. No one knew why they were killed, but Benito says it was because the villagers were jealous of his success and bitter that he had become one of the hated *caciques*, the headmen who control the land and the village like those they had fought during the Revolution. Now Benito's brother Juan runs the mill and sends money to Benito for his share of the inheritance."

The road became steeper, losing its way at times in thickets of trees where the air was dense with the pungent smell of pitch-pine kindling fires. The first house, a simple square of rough stones set in mortar, appeared suddenly from behind a screen of ciruelas and coffee trees. Boards leaned against the side of the house to shelter the maize that was stored there. Chickens cackled in the fowlhouse, which held an assortment of old oil cans on its roof, the plants in them top-heavy with flowers. From the open door of the stone house came the slapping noise of tortillas being formed by hand.

As they continued on, gradually more houses emerged through the thin veil of trees, like animals in hiding, and then the dome of the church and the convent appeared above the flat roofs. The village ended abruptly at the base of a granite peak that stood like a silver shield between the houses and the sky, and was now turning to amber as the sun went down.

"Look at those colors, Lidia."

"Maybe you'll have time to paint them tomorrow if we can't get the tire fixed."

"What about your parents? Shouldn't you telephone them?"

"There is no telephone."

He looked at the poles spotted in the fields and at the lines strung between them.

"The telephones haven't worked for a long time in Tepoztlán," she said. "No, no, my family doesn't worry."

"Is Cuernavaca like Tepoztlán?"

"All Mexican villages are alike."

The village was quiet except for the occasional sound of a child at play or the bark of a dog. A woman, head and shoulders wrapped in a rebozo, walked barefoot ahead of them leading a burro from which hung two *ollas* of water.

"Let's ask for some water here," said Andre, stopping at the doorway to one of the houses. Perspiration had stained his light-blue shirt an indigo color.

The woman inside saw them through the open door. Lidia asked her in Nahuatl if they could have some water, and the woman answered in Spanish.

"Sometimes they're ashamed to speak Nahuatl," said Lidia, as the woman ladled water into a tin cup from an earthen container. Lidia drank half of it and then handed it to Andre. He looked at her as he put his lips to the spot where hers had been.

"The plaza is straight ahead," Lidia said. "Juan's house is near the center of the village."

The woman had been observing them quietly.

"*Muchas gracias*," said Andre, handing back the cup.

"*No hay de que*," she murmured.

Some children were playing cat and mouse in the empty plaza. An old man dozed on a stone bench. Over everything was a sleepy watchfulness.

At the edge of the plaza, in front of an unpainted adobe wall with a wooden door and two grilled windows, Lidia said, "This is Juan's house." She tugged on the rope that hung beside the door, and a bell rang inside. "The mill closes in the afternoon," she said. "Juan will be here."

Dogs barked and a baby cried somewhere behind the wall. Then the door was opened by a husky man in his thirties. Heavy lips curled upward to show his gums. His eyes were the color of tea leaves in his faded leather face. Brown hair hung uncombed on his forehead, but he wore store-bought pants and a shirt with buttons. He gave no sign that he recognized Lidia.

"Juan?"

"*Sí.*"

"It's Lidia. Lidia Machado, Benito's *novia.*"

"Ah, Lidia, *cómo estás?*"

"Bien. I was on my way home to Acapatzingo, but the car wouldn't go any farther."

"*Sí*, I understand." He looked over at Andre.

"This is my friend, Andre Frankle," she said. "He's a great artist, a friend of Diego Rivera. He's coming with me to Cuernavaca to paint my wedding portrait."

"*Sí*, I understand."

Andre stepped forward. "Is there someplace we can spend the night until we can get the car fixed?"

Juan's face was impassive as he stared at the two of them. Then he pulled the door open.

"*Pásele*," he said in flat, uncadenced Spanish, "welcome to my house."

30

Juan led the way through a jungle garden of yellow hibiscus and pink oleanders. Parrots chattered in cages suspended from the mango trees. A child's wooden swing swayed gently back and forth in the afternoon breeze. Inside the house a tiled corridor wound past cool, well furnished rooms all facing an inside garden where a monkey jabbered in its cage. Crimson bougainvillea trailed up a whitewashed wall to spew its color over the tile roof.

It was dusk. A kerosene lantern had been lit in the kitchen, where a young pureblood Indian woman patted *masa* into tortillas at a polished table, copper pots swinging from the ceiling above her. On the floor near her bare feet, a baby slept in an ornate cradle while a little boy, black hair thick around his olive face, played with a wooden top.

The young woman turned away from the stove. She smiled shyly at Lidia and spoke to her in Nahuatl, but kept her eyes averted from Andre's.

The kitchen table was large, and there were chairs for all to sit down. "Please," said Juan. He motioned for Andre to sit in the chair opposite him, but ignored Lidia, who had already picked up the little boy and was talking to him in Nahuatl.

Juan poured some colorless liquid into two glasses.

"Brandy?" Andre said.

"Pulque," Juan answered. He downed his in one swallow and then looked at Andre, who now put the glass to his lips and swallowed quickly.

Juan filled the glasses again. "Do you know my brother Benito?"

"No, I don't."

"I see." Juan raised the glass and the pulque disappeared down his throat. "Where do you come from? Your Spanish is not like the Americans'."

Andre stared at the glass of liquor for a moment, then drank it down. "I'm from Europe."

"When are you going back?"

"I'm not. I suppose you don't get any newspapers here or you'd know there's a war on in Europe."

"I get a newspaper twice a week. You're not in the home of a dumb Indian." He filled the glasses again. "Drink," he said, and he lifted the liquor to his lips.

Andre drank up, and then set the empty glass down on the table, his eyes watering. He turned to look at Lidia, and it seemed to him that her skin was as luminescent as the copper pots that hung above her head.

Juan leaned back in his chair. "So you're an artist. Do you paint pictures like the communist Rivera, all over the buildings of Mexico City?"

"No. I'm an easel painter." Andre's words were slightly slurred.

"That Rivera, he's a communist, an anti-Christ, a nonbeliever. He thinks the Indian is higher than God."

"And what do you think?"

"I think the Indian is losing his faith in Christ. He's looking to false gods. When the son of Cortés lived in this village, he spread the word of Christ, but then the Revolution came and war was declared on the Church. My father was a Cristero who fought to restore Christ to the peasants. I'm a Sinarquist, who knows that our only salvation is the Catholic Church. Are you a Catholic?"

"I'm a Jew."

Juan coughed and spit a gob of heavy phlegm into a handkerchief. "I think it's dangerous for you to take Lidia for a ride in your car. There are some people who say that a man should be killed if he talks to another man's *novia*. There are some people who say that a man should be killed if he is a Jew or a communist."

"I feel in no danger."

"I think you're probably a *tonto* like the Indians in the next village."

"If I'm stupid, then so are you."

Juan's wife placed a bowl of chiles on the table and a dish of boiled meat with *mole verde* beside it. Next to the dishes she stacked the hot tortillas as she took them from the griddle. Lidia stood near the stove, the little boy still in her arms.

"Our family is well known in this village," Juan said. "My father fought with Zapata."

"My father fought with no one," said Andre, "and he never hid food and riches behind high walls while his neighbors went hungry."

Juan bent forward, his hands clutching the table. "A mass is said in my father's memory every year in the chapel of Santa Cruz. You have insulted his honor."

Andre shrugged. "It seems strange that he fought with Zapata and now his son is the richest *cacique* in Tepoztlán. But you can live as you please." He leaned toward Juan until their foreheads were almost touching. "Don't push me. I don't like it."

"You entered my house."

"You invited me."

"I didn't invite a Jew." He downed another glass of pulque, then poured one out for Andre.

"I've had enough."

"Drink!"

"I said I don't want any more."

Juan stood up and glared at Andre. "If my brother Benito saw you here with Lidia, he would kill you, because you've dishonored him. Some say that Zapata is still alive in these hills. Some say that Zapata is in Germany fighting with Hitler, and that's why Hitler is winning the war. You've run away from Europe because you're a coward."

Andre wobbled unsteadily as he got to his feet. "Let's go, Lidia."

"Lidia will stay here until Benito comes from Cuernavaca for her."

"Lidia will come with me." Andre turned toward her, his eyes wavering, dizzied by the brilliance of her hair in the lamp's glow. "Give me your hand."

They walked through the house as quickly as Andre was able. "You are so crazy, Andre, so crazy," she said when they reached the garden.

Suddenly stones began landing with heavy thuds around

them. Andre picked one up and threw it back toward the house just as Juan disappeared inside.

"Hurry," said Lidia as Andre staggered and fell.

"The pulque," he said, holding his head.

"Get up, Andre, get up." She pulled on his arm. "Juan will kill you."

Juan had reappeared with a shiny machete in his hands.

"You're drunk," Juan said. He swiped at Andre with the machete and missed.

"So are you." Andre stumbled to his feet, leaned toward Juan, and shoved him sideways. The machete dropped, clanging once as the metal blade bounced against the trunk of a mango tree.

"You dropped your machete," Andre said.

"I can kill you with my hands," said Juan. He lunged at Andre, and they both wobbled against each other for a few seconds, and then collapsed onto the ground, rolling together beneath the oleanders, punching each other drunkenly. Juan's heavy body didn't move as easily as Andre's. He couldn't escape the blows with the agility that Andre could. He grunted and farted, his fists unraveled, and as a gash opened over his right eyebrow and spurted blood into his eyes, he rolled onto his stomach, his face buried in the broken hibiscus blossoms that carpeted the ground.

"Can I stop now?" said Andre as he sat on Juan's back. Juan turned his face to the side, coughed, and a bit of yellow flower dribbled out of the corner of his mouth.

"I guess we're through," Andre said. He wiped his nose with his shirtsleeve, and then looked up at Lidia. "He's tired."

"Sí, he's tired."

Juan's wife emerged from the house, Lidia's bag in her hand and Andre's box balanced on top of her head. She stepped gracefully past where her husband lay, past Andre and Lidia, to the gate, where she bent straight-shouldered toward the earth and placed the things carefully on the ground. Then she moved toward her husband and helped him up, and the two of them went quietly into the house.

Lidia glanced at Andre often as they walked back up the dusty street with their belongings. The church bell in the chapel of Santa Cruz was ringing and villagers streamed out of their houses, lit candles in their hands. The procession

grew and surrounded Andre and Lidia, pulling them up the
street and into the church.

"It's the festival of saints," she said. "We'll pray to San
Pedro."

She lit a candle for Andre and one for herself and placed
them on the church altar. "You were very *macho*, very brave,
Andrito."

As he watched her in prayer before the candlelit saints, his
head still ringing with pulque, his body sore from Juan's
punches, his ears suddenly turned hot, as though a mosquito
had entered and was trapped inside. Through the buzzing of
the insect his father's voice came to him again. It was so dim
that Andre could barely hear what he was saying.

"She prays to idols, my son. Not very well carved idols.
And she looks at you in admiration now, but what did you do
but save your own life? Run, Andre, run, before it's too late."

After the festival, as fireworks lit the granite cliffs, Lidia
and Andre climbed the dirt path to the *cerro* behind the
village, using the makeshift rope ladder that had been placed
on the trail where the climb was the steepest.

"You see the shrine of Tepozteco up there, Andre." She
stopped and pointed to the stone temple above them. "My
father told me that when he was a child in this village that it
had not rained during the whole month of June, and that the
corn would not grow. The god Tepoztecatl was angry with the
people of the village because they hadn't given him a good
celebration in September before the planting season. So the
people brought Tepoztecatl food and pulque, and in two days
it rained so hard that the village was flooded."

When they reached the top, the temple, which had seemed
majestic at a distance, looked battered and forlorn, its stones
blackened by incense. Dry flowers drooped from empty soda
bottles.

Lidia spread her rebozo on the ground and laid out the *olla*
of *mole verde* and the cloth-wrapped tortillas that they had
bought at the festival.

"You must be hungry," she said as she deftly scooped a bit
of *mole* into a tortilla, rolled it, and handed it to him. When
she was satisfied that he had eaten his fill, she prepared one
for herself and began to eat.

He lay back and looked at the night sky. The dizziness and
ringing sensations in his head had subsided in the clear, thin

air of the mountain, so that his father's voice came through with no interference. "You see, my son, how comfortable she is here in this village that has no electricity and no automobiles, how little she worries about telephone lines that hang useless from the poles they tie their burros to. And such stories she tells. Such superstitions she believes in. How will you live with a woman like this? What will become of you?"

"What are you thinking of, Andrito?" she said.

"You," he answered, and feelings of love for her swept over him.

She lay down beside him and spread her rebozo over them both. "Are you trembling because we are close together?" she said.

"I'm trembling because of what I want to do."

"If you do it, it will be all right." She took his hand and placed it beneath her shift, against the warm breasts that he had painted over and over but had never touched.

"Have you ever—" he began.

"No, never."

"I'll go slowly. I don't want to frighten you."

"I'm not frightened, Andrito."

Beneath the warmth of the rebozo he lifted the shift over her head, so that the perfume of her skin filled his nostrils. He moved gently across her body, now sucking softly on the nipples of her breasts, now running his tongue over the skin of her stomach.

"Andrito," she murmured, and turned to stroke him. He felt dizzy again, disoriented by her sudden response, breathless at the seductive swaying of her hips.

He arched his back, attempted to enter, but her fingers spread and clutched at him and her whimpers of pleasure turned to shallow breaths of pain.

"I'll stop, I'll stop," he gasped.

"No, Andrito, you mustn't."

He rested a moment, his lips on hers.

"I loved you in Frida's studio," he said.

"And I loved you."

"I wanted to do this then."

"I know. And I wanted you to do it. Try again, Andrito."

"I'll hurt you."

"It will be over quickly."

He was poised above her, torn between his urge to protect her and his own selfishness.

"Please, Andrito, you must do it."

He pushed once, hesitated, and then pushed again, more sharply. She was shaking, but did not cry out. Once more and he was smoothly in, deliriously in, safely in.

"You are so *macho*, Andrito," she said, and her words intoxicated him more than the pulque had.

"I love you, I love you," he said as he reached his climax. Then he lay pressed against her, quivering with the power he had unleashed, drunk with his achievement.

He could not sleep, but lay with his arms around her, gazing with wonder at the brightness of the stars. He tried to ignore his father's voice, but he could hear him mumbling in the darkness of the shrine of Tepozteco, somewhere in the vicinity of the altar, near the incense residue and the burnt offerings.

31

The next morning they climbed down from the *cerro*, stopping at each turn of the trail to kiss and caress each other.

"Will you tire of me like Diego tired of Frida?" she asked.

"Men sometimes do," he said, his heart pounding with love for her. "But I'll always take care of you."

When they reached the plaza, Andre glanced around for signs of Juan, but there was only a cluster of Indians squatting in the shade of the laurel trees, their parcels in the dust beside them. Chickens squawked in homemade cages. An old man held two piglets tied together by their rear legs.

"No one pays any attention to us," Andre said.

"They see us," Lidia replied.

In a dilapidated shop on the edge of the plaza, Andre bought *churros* and hot chocolate, and he and Lidia sat on a stone bench and ate their breakfast.

"There's no reason why I should tire of you, though," he said as he kissed the sugar from her lips.

He listened for his father's voice, but there was not even a muffled comment, not even a whispered aside.

There were no tires to be had in the village, and no one who knew where any might be found. The villagers they spoke to told them to go to Cuernavaca, that it was market day, that surely tires could be bought there, and that the fastest way to get to Cuernavaca was to take the bus. So Lidia and Andre joined the waiting Indians and piglets and chickens at the plaza, and soon a rusted bus rumbled to a stop in front of them.

"Where are you going?" Andre shouted at the open door of the bus as Indians and animals clambered aboard.

"Cuernavaca." The driver wore white *calzones* like the Indians, but instead of a sombrero, he had a billed cap on his head with dirty gold braid encircling it.

Andre helped Lidia aboard, and then went back for his box.

The bus began to roll. Lidia stood at the door. "Hurry, hurry, Andrito."

He threw the box aboard and hung on to the rusty doorframe for a few seconds, and then the door closed behind him. Lidia hugged and kissed him, and the Indians turned away in embarrassment.

The bus labored its way around the plaza, lurching from side to side down the steep cobblestone streets, squeezing through narrow lanes meant only for burro traffic. Exhaust fumes entered through the broken windows and tree limbs rasped across the roof.

"Don't let the animals dirty the seats," the driver shouted without turning around.

As they passed the church, the bus slowed down and the Indians stood up en masse and crossed themselves. Then it started forward, gears grinding, and the Indians sat down again.

"A *la izquierda*," the driver yelled when the bus got stuck between the roofs of two houses. The Indians all stood up, leaned to the left, the bus cleared the roofs with inches to spare, and in minutes was traveling unimpeded down the highway to Cuernavaca.

A few miles outside the village, Andre, who had been scanning the roadside for sight of his car, let out a groan. "For God's sake, Lidia, look what they've done to my car."

The Chevrolet was where they had left it, but there was now a white wooden cross on the roof and a wreath of faded flowers. On the hood was a statue of the Virgin Mary, a row of half-burned candles, and the decaying carcass of a baby lamb. As they passed the car, the Indians on the bus stood up and crossed themselves.

"*Qué lástima*," Lidia said. "What a pity. Now you have no car and no need for tires."

Andre watched his car until they were too far away for him to see it any longer. Then he turned around in the seat and put his arm around Lidia.

"That's the first car I've ever owned and now it's a church," he said.

"They'll never give the car back to you now. But at least we're on our way to Cuernavaca. When we get there, I'll talk to my parents, explain to them how this happened between you and me." She nodded as though envisioning how she would do it. "I'll tell them that I can't marry Benito."

In Cuernavaca the Indians and their livestock got off the bus at the zócalo. The streets were clogged with wagons and peasants on foot carrying produce and animals to market from neighboring villages. A vendor came aboard with a tray of sliced fruit, and Andre bought a stick of pineapple to share with Lidia.

Acapatzingo was five minutes from the zócalo. The driver let them off in front of a small park, and they began to walk down the shaded street.

"That's Concepción's house," Lidia said as they passed a wooden structure half hidden by trees and vines, "the one Maximilian built for her."

"It's a ruin."

"The government guards it so that it's not destroyed any further, but slowly it decays, a little bit more each year. It breaks my grandmother's heart to watch it. This is the house in which she was born."

A short distance from Concepción's house was the plaza of Acapatzingo, and off to the south of the plaza the street wound steeply upward past a deep ravine and came to a stop at a yellow wall with a carved gate.

"My father made the gate himself in his factory," she said.

"I'll come in with you."

"I have to explain to them first. They'll have to make an excuse to Benito so that he's not disgraced. And the priest must be consulted—"

"They'll make you change your mind." He drew her into the shadows so that they were hidden from the street. "Do you still love me?"

"How can you ask me?"

"Then don't go in. What does it matter what anyone else says? I want you with me. Forget about Benito and the priest." He held her in his arms, touched her breasts, pressed against her leg, felt his power over her slipping away.

She ran her hand across his cheek. "I love you, Andrito. There are rooms at the Posada Cuernavaca. Come back this evening at nine o'clock."

The Posada Cuernavaca was a small hotel with heavy oak furniture and tile floors. Andre's room had a balcony overlooking the reflecting pool and patio restaurant.

After a bath and a shave he went down to the restaurant and ordered red snapper and a small bottle of wine. As he ate he looked around him at the people at the other tables. Some wealthy Mexicans up for the weekend from Mexico City. A well-dressed American couple with a little boy at the next table.

"The little black things are beans, Bix," the mother was saying. She had a sweet face and a rosy flush to her fair skin. Wisps of permanent-waved brown hair had escaped the sun hat she wore and spiraled onto her forehead and around her ears. The husband was intent on his food, his panama hat concealing all but his large nose and prominent mouth.

"Don't like," said Bix, who was in a sailor suit and had his mother's good looks. He pursed his lips and shook his head from side to side.

The woman looked over at Andre. "I don't know how a person's supposed to travel in Mexico with a three-year-old child," she said in English. "If I force him to eat, it either makes him cry or vomit."

Andre nodded and smiled. He hadn't seen many Americans in Mexico. At a table on the other side of the pool a man in hiking boots and sweat-stained clothing sat alone. He had bold features and slightly bulging eyes beneath a sheaf of uncombed gray hair. An Italian, Andre decided, until he heard him speak to the waiter in German-accented Spanish.

When the waiter came back to his table, Andre said, "Is the man over there staying at the hotel?"

"I don't know, señor, but I can ask him."

The waiter talked to the man, pointing in Andre's direction, and then came back and said, "He is staying here, señor."

The German finished his lunch and strolled toward Andre's table. He was tall and sturdily built. Pens and scraps of paper and notebooks stuck out of ink-stained pockets, and he wore a metal watch on each wrist. A man in his late forties, thought Andre.

"*Buenos días*," the man said.

"*Buenos días*," Andre replied.

"You speak Spanish with an accent. German perhaps?"

"I lived in Germany," Andre said in German. "Please sit down. My name is Andre Frankle."

"And I'm Professor Hans Kobermann. Forgive my appearance, but I've just returned from the Xochicalco ruins near here. It's very dirty work."

"You're a scientist?"

"An archaeologist. The Mexican government has kindly permitted me to come here and explore their Aztec and Maya ruins, but Xochicalco hasn't yielded as much as I had hoped it would. Are you interested in archaeology?"

"I'm an artist. I know very little about it."

"And I know very little about art."

The woman at the next table was listening to the German words with an interested incomprehension on her face.

"Oh, Mrs. Whitworth, I am so sorry," said the professor in English. "Permit me to introduce you to—"

"Andre Frankle," Andre said.

"This is Mrs. Theodora Whitworth," the professor said.

"I'm delighted," she said.

Her husband looked over at Andre.

"And Dr. Conrad Whitworth," the professor added.

Dr. Whitworth stood up and leaned over the table to shake hands with Andre.

"Dr. Whitworth is on his way to Yucatán to do research in tropical diseases," the professor said. "Since I am also leaving for there tomorrow morning, we have decided to go together."

"We did have a car," Mrs. Whitworth said, her eyes round and bright. "It brought us here all the way from Atlanta, and then something happened to the engine. The pistols or something went out."

"The pistons," her husband said.

"Then Connie decided we'd go on from here by bus and train," she said, "but the professor convinced us that buses run when they want to run and trains sometimes don't run at all, and that we should go with him. He has more courage than I would have, offering to ride all the way to Yucatán with Bix in the car."

"I've made the trip to Yucatán many times alone," Dr. Whitworth said, "but I've never taken my family with me before."

"I'm afraid I don't even know where Yucatán is," Andre said.

"Somewhere to the south," said Mrs. Whitworth with a wave of her hand. "Isn't that right, Connie?"

"The southeast."

"Of course. I knew that."

"It hasn't belonged to Mexico very long," said the professor. "It was once a protectorate of Guatemala. Then the Spaniards who controlled it were so afraid Juárez would swallow them up or the Indians would kill them, that they asked the United States to annex them. The Americans said it was too far away." The professor's laugh was a truncated snort.

"Mommie, pee-pee," said Bix, holding one chubby hand to his crotch.

"Oh, dear." Mrs. Whitworth swung the child into her arms. "So nice to have met you, Mr. Frankle."

"Maybe we'll see you again," Dr. Whitworth said.

"A very nice family," said the professor when they had gone. "I took pity on them, actually. I can remember very well my own first experience here in Mexico, attempting to travel by train. It was shortly after the Revolution and bandits were still robbing the trains, and—" The professor interrupted himself. "You see how one talks on and on when faced with another human being who speaks your language. I have struggled many times to say something in Spanish only to find out later that I've said something else. Have you come to Mexico to stay?"

"Yes, I have."

"I've been here since 1935. I get mail from Germany telling me that I must come home, that we are at war. I ask jokingly, 'What war?' and, of course, I receive no answer. Therefore, I ignore the letters, since they choose to ignore mine. But what of you? You must have similar problems."

"I have no problems to speak of," Andre said.

"So far Mexico appreciates Herr Hitler, and so we go on our way unmolested, eh?"

"They may appreciate Herr Hitler, but whether they want an undocumented Jew in Mexico is another question."

"Ah, I see."

"But as long as the Mexican bureaucracy remains as inefficient as it is, I have hope that no one will notice me."

"So you hope for their bureaucracy to continue on its disorganized way, and I hope that Mexico will stay out of Europe's war so that I may yet uncover some important archaeological sites."

"Good luck to both of us," Andre said.

32

The night air was warm, with a hint of a breeze. The path from the gate meandered through a well-kept garden to the veranda. In the temperate climate of Cuernavaca, the Machado family spent most of its time on the veranda rather than in the somber darkness of the house. Socorro, Lidia's mother, prepared meals on a range beneath the eaves. The family ate at an oak table and sat on oak chairs whose seats and backs were webbed with flat brown strips of leather. Visitors sat on the leather couch facing the garden. Leather and oak were the hallmark of the furniture made at the Machado factory.

"This is Andre Frankle," said Lidia, when Andre arrived at nine o'clock.

Lidia's mother, a demure woman with tight gray braids encircling her head and a blue cotton dress on her plump figure, sat in one of the oak chairs. She was darker than Lidia, but had the same soft gray eyes.

Lidia's father, Victor Machado, was dark-skinned and thick-featured, with a thatch of black hair that grew straight back from his forehead. He was short and husky in his brown slacks and starched white shirt, and his hands were permanently stained from the tanning solutions that he used in the making of his leather furniture. He seemed ill at ease when he was introduced to Andre.

Lidia's grandmother, María Sedano y Leguizano de Ramírez, sat in the largest chair on the veranda, her tiny feet propped up on a tapestry-covered footstool. She said nothing to Andre when he took her delicate hand in his, but her eyes, a piercing blue, followed him as he shook hands with Señor Machado, said a few words to Señora Machado, and then sat down next to Lidia on the leather couch.

Señora Machado had set out hot chocolate and a plate of candied cactus.

"Lidia went to the market to buy the *nopales* this afternoon," Señora Machado said. "They are very sweet, very good to eat. Do you like *nopales?*"

Andre munched on the sticky fruit. "It's very good."

"You are a friend of Frida's?" Señor Machado asked.

"Yes, we are good friends."

"But you do not know Benito?" said Señora Machado.

"No, I don't." He glanced at Lidia. "Did you tell them?"

"I told them some things," she said.

"What things?"

"That you painted pictures of me and they are in a gallery in the United States."

"The church needs painting," Señor Machado said.

"Andre only paints pictures, Papá," said Lidia.

"The priest would like more pictures of the saints," Señor Machado said. "Are you a Catholic?"

"No, I'm not. I'm a Jew."

Señor Machado's face lost its shallow politeness.

"Lidia is going to be married soon," Señora Machado said. "Benito Lewis is the name of her *novio*. The banns have been posted. I have been sewing the wedding gown."

"There's a problem, Mamá," said Lidia. "I can't marry Benito."

Señora Machado shook her head vigorously. "I won't listen to talk like this. Benito is your *novio*." She began to cry, mopping her face and swiping roughly at her runny nose with a large white handkerchief. "He has brought gifts. Money has been donated to the church in your names."

"Mamá, *por favor*, Andre and I have—he has—we have—"

"Aieee!" Her mother screamed and dropped her head back against the hard wood of the chair.

"I will kill you!" Señor Machado yelled.

"Let him be!" came a jagged-voiced command from the shawl-covered figure in the shadows.

"He has dishonored her," said Señor Machado. "He has made her valueless."

"The devil has come in the form of a Jew and possessed you," cried Señora Machado as Lidia knelt beside her mother, her face hidden in the gathers of the blue cotton dress.

Andre backed away, stood near the steps, away from the chaos that he had created.

"They will soon recover," Lidia's grandmother said. "Come back in the morning."

There was a stack of newspapers on the tile floor of the lobby when Andre returned to the hotel. "Trotsky Assassination Attempt," said the headline. He snatched up one of the papers and opened it. Trotsky, the Jewish chin now covered by a spiky goatee, and Natalya, older and frailer, stared helplessly at the camera.

Leon Trotsky, the exiled ex-leader of Russia, and his wife, Natalya, were the targets of an assassination attempt in their home in the Coyoacán suburb of Mexico City. In the middle of the night of May 24, 1940, twenty-five men dressed in military uniform entered the house and machine-gunned the bedroom in which Trotsky and his wife were sleeping. Miraculously, the Trotskys were able to escape harm by hiding under their bed.

The would-be assassins also entered the bedroom of the Trotsky grandson, Seva, lit an incendiary bomb, and attempted to shoot the young boy, who thereupon ran into the garden, escaping with nothing more serious than a wounded toe. The identity of one of the invaders has been positively established to be that of David Alfaro Siqueiros, artist, war hero, and admitted communist. He escaped with the others and is now being sought for questioning.

The mystery of how the gunmen entered the closely guarded Trotsky home is one that has not yet been solved, although one of the guards who was killed by the invaders was thought to say before he died that the person who approached the heavily fortified house and gained entry for Siqueiros and the others was a man known to Trotsky, a German Jew by the name of Andre Frankle. While little is known about the background of . . .

From the front window of the hotel Andre saw soldiers on horseback, rifles on their shoulders. He dropped the newspaper to the floor and ran to the reception desk.

"I need to know the room number of Professor Hans Kobermann. It's very urgent, a matter of extreme importance."

"If you need a doctor, he is not a doctor, señor," the clerk said.

"No, no, I need Professor Kobermann. The number of his room, please."

The desk clerk looked through his book, and then said, "Room twelve, señor, but he asked not to be disturbed."

But Andre, not listening, was already racing down the corridor.

The professor peered out of the half-open door, one eye closed, the other blinking in the light. The sleeves of his pajamas were stained with marmalade.

"Herr Frankle, I'm sorry, but we're leaving very early in the morning. I'm trying to sleep."

"I must ask you a very urgent question. Were you merely being polite to me today?"

"Polite? Are you insane? I am sleeping and you pound on my door to ask me if I was polite to you today?"

The professor tried to push the door closed, but Andre leaned against it, holding it open.

"What are you doing, Herr Frankle?"

"I need to talk to you."

The professor stared in bleary-eyed astonishment at the agitation in Andre's face, at the frenzied determination with which he pushed against the door.

"All right, all right." He scratched his backside, opened the door wide, and stepped aside.

"Come in, Herr Frankle. Whatever has happened to you between this afternoon and tonight cannot be as bad as all that."

They sat on the tangled sheets of the professor's bed, and Andre related the story of his escape from Germany, of his meeting with Trotsky on board the *Ruth*.

"And you had absolutely nothing to do with this attempt on his life?" the professor asked.

"Absolutely nothing."

"How do you know that the soldiers outside the hotel are after you?"

"I don't know. But would you take a chance?"

The professor shook his head. "You're in trouble, Herr Frankle, there is no doubt about that. But why do you come to me for help? What can I possibly do for you? I'm here in Mexico on sufferance myself."

"I'll explain, but first answer my question. What do you think of Jews?"

"What should I think of them? I have excavated their bones in Palestine, and when left in the hot sun they bleach as white as a gentile's."

"You don't agree with Hitler, then?"

"Let me put it this way, Herr Frankle. I'm as tempted as the next man to believe Hitler and the others. Why shouldn't I believe that I'm special and you're not? Ah, what a blessing to be a prejudiced man, living out a simple existence with answers to every question." He gazed at the marmalade spots on his sleeve. "But what I would like and what I must do are two different things. For science I have had to make many sacrifices. I've had to discard anything that would interfere with pure scientific thought, or else everything I touch in my work would be tainted with bias. Then how would I discover the truth of anything? Tell me that." The professor sighed. "It was painful, but to be an archaeologist, I had to give up my prejudices."

"You make perfect sense, Herr Professor, perfect sense."

"You mean that you think I can be trusted, don't you?"

"I mean that you are a rational man, a believer in the truth, a man who—"

"Calm yourself, Herr Frankle. What is it you've come to ask of me? Ask it and we'll see if I have it in my power to accommodate you."

"You mentioned that you were traveling east tomorrow to Yucatán. I want to go with you."

"Hmm." The professor rubbed the gray stubble on his chin. "It could be dangerous for me."

"If we're stopped or questioned, I'll disappear, disassociate myself from you."

"There are the others, the American couple and their child, what of them?"

"What are your feelings? Do you think they would be unsympathetic?"

"I have had very little conversation with them, but I would judge, since they have a child with them, that their inclination toward foolhardiness is not as great as mine."

"Then don't tell them."

"You act as though it were settled between us."

"It is." Andre walked to the door and opened it. "I have a little money, so we'll share the expenses. What time tomorrow?"

"We planned to leave before the sun comes up so that we can travel a good distance before it gets too hot."

"I'll be ready," Andre said.

"Lidia." Andre's voice was a loud whisper.

"She's in the room at the end of the veranda."

The old woman was in the same chair, but now wrapped in blankets, a shawl around her head, her eyes pale rings of color in the candlelight. "I can only breathe sitting up," she said. "My heart. It's best to die before illness like mine comes. Here, come closer. It's not morning. Why have you come again so soon?"

"I've come to take Lidia away."

"Good. Benito is not for Lidia. I never thought that she should marry him. He's too weak to be married to the great-granddaughter of an emperor. Why do you want her?"

"I love her."

"I know that. I saw the look in your eyes. It's said that Maximilian looked at my mother like that when he first saw her in the church. Is that all?"

The old woman was staring at him, waiting. He couldn't remember what Frida had said. It was gone, dropped into the pit where all useless information goes.

Then it returned in a rush, punching him in the chest, and leaping up into his mouth. "I won't show any man any fear. I'll fight for her. I'll never leave her. I'll always protect her."

"Of course. But what of yourself? You must think of yourself first."

"Myself?" He looked around him, as though inspiration lurked in the shadows. "Life will be better," he said. "I haven't been able to work these past few months thinking that she would marry Benito."

"Go on."

"She'll take care of me." The old woman was smiling at him, encouraging him with her opaque eyes. "No matter what happens, she'll take care of me. If we encounter suffering, she won't complain because she'll know that I'm there with her until we die."

"Your understanding is rare for a *gringo*. Are you sure that you have no Mexican blood in your veins?"

"None."

"What is your mother's name, my son?"

"Brina."

"I will give you a blessing on her behalf."

And as he knelt at her side, she made the sign of the cross over him.

33

The professor, his fresh hiking clothes already stained with dirt and grease, was checking the ropes that lashed the luggage and supplies to the roof of his dented black Buick when Andre and Lidia appeared in front of the hotel.

"You said one person, Herr Frankle, not two."

"This is my wife, Lidia. She was visiting her family."

"When she visits her family, do you always stay alone in a hotel?"

Theodora Whitworth, who was sitting in the back seat of the huge Buick with her husband and little boy, rolled down the car window and called out, "Is there some problem?"

"There's a wife," the professor said.

"What's your name, honey?"

Lidia smiled, and Andre said, "Lidia. Her name is Lidia."

"Well, what's all the fuss? Plenty of room for a tiny little girl like her."

"I haven't told them about Trotsky or any of that business," the professor whispered to Andre, "but if there's any trouble, I'll have to, and then you will have to fend for yourselves. Do you still want to come?"

"What's the route?"

"Across country to Veracruz."

"I thought you said you were going to Yucatán."

"I am, but you can't get there from here by land. There is no highway. First we go to Veracruz, then we'll load the car and the supplies on a freighter across the Gulf of

Campeche to Progreso. From there it's a good road through
Yucatán."

As the night-tinged sky brightened, the professor hurriedly
rearranged everything on the car's rooftop rack to make room
for Lidia's suitcase and Andre's box. Digging tools and cases
of human bones dug out of the ruins of Xochicalco were
shoved up against Dr. Whitworth's cartons of medical equipment. Suitcases and empty five-gallon gasoline cans were set
on top and everything was tied down with double-knotted
rope.

"Tell you what," said Theodora Whitworth, "there's room
for Lidia back here, and Andre can sit up front with Professor
Kobermann. And what language are we going to be talking on
this trip, anyway? I sure hope it isn't German, but whatever
it is, we'll just have to do the best we can between us, won't
we? And aren't you the sweetest thing, Lidia?" She looked at
her husband as though waiting for him to chastise her for
talking too much, but he smiled at her indulgently. "Sit right
here in the middle next to Bixby. We call him Bix for short.
Bixby's an old family name, couldn't avoid naming him that,
but Bix is nice, don't you think? And please don't call me
Theodora, or I'll never know who you're talking to. The
name's Teddy, just plain Teddy."

There was lots of talk as they rode, mostly by the professor
and Teddy Whitworth, mostly in fractured Spanish. Conrad
didn't speak much, but glanced occasionally at Andre, a curious look on his face. The roads were good, but the professor
drove erratically, taking his hands off the wheel often to
gesticulate.

By the time they had driven an hour, Lidia had begun to
answer some of Teddy's questions, and by early afternoon
Teddy knew the entire story of Maximilian and Concepción.

"The conquerors left their sperm all over Mexico," said the
professor. When Teddy gasped, he said, "Is that the right
word?"

"*Children* would have been a better one," said Conrad.

They passed one dusty village after another, stopping often
to rest under the cedar trees at the side of the road and drink
water from the professor's canteens.

"Will you look at this poor child's cheeks," Teddy said.
"Red as a firecracker."

"Put him on your lap," said Conrad.

"What good's that going to do when he's so hot and cranky?"

She wiped his face with a dampened handkerchief and then she and Lidia took turns rocking him until he finally fell asleep.

"Are you a doctor of tropical diseases?" asked Andre as they drove the last stretch of road before Puebla, where they would spend the night.

"Yes," Conrad answered. "Mainly malaria, but some other parasitic diseases as well. When we reach Veracruz I recommend that you dose yourselves with quinine as a prophylactic against malaria. I can provide some for you and your wife."

The snow-capped volcanoes, Popocatépetl and Iztaccihuatl, loomed large above them as they drove the curving road into the mountains, the flat agricultural lands were transformed into a giant checkerboard on the valley floor below. The professor nearly drove off the narrow road several times, but no one in the car said anything, since he always managed at the last minute to bring the car under control.

"I'm feeling a little dizzy," Teddy said.

When she had closed her eyes and appeared to be sleeping, Conrad leaned toward Andre. "I saw your picture in the paper this morning. I haven't told my wife about it. I didn't want to alarm her."

"But you came on the trip, so you evidently don't think I'm guilty of anything."

"God no! The whole thing sounds like a comic opera."

"What opera are we all talking about?" asked Teddy, her eyes fluttering open. "What are you two whispering about? I hope it's nothing too interesting. My, but the air is cooler here. I think I just might live after all."

From the mountains they descended into the Valley of Puebla. It was raining lightly, and the blue and yellow tile domes of the churches glittered like mounds of colored ice. The houses were built in the Spanish style, with wrought-iron balconies dangling like filigree necklaces over their blue tile facades.

"This is where Juárez first fought off the French on Cinco de Mayo, 1862," said the professor, "but it was only a symbolic victory. Maximilian came anyhow. And I'm sure Andre is glad that he did."

At the *zócalo* men played dominoes at crowded booths beneath protective awnings. The professor stopped the car and they found a table out of the rain and ordered *mole poblanos* and *cervezas.*

"I don't believe in spoiling children," Teddy said. "My family thinks it's terrible that Conrad and I are taking Bix to Yucatán, with all those snakes and bugs and other terrible things, but I always say you can get bit by a bug in Atlanta, too, don't need to go to Yucatán to do it."

"Teddy means that we don't take unnecessary chances with Bix," said Conrad, "but we don't shield him from things either. My father took me to Africa with him when I was five years old. I credit that trip for my interest in tropical medicine."

"Conrad's father was a missionary," Teddy said. "Conrad likes to talk like an atheist, but I know that deep down in his heart he hears the angels as loud and clear as anyone else. He claims not to believe, but we were married in the biggest Episcopal church in Atlanta." She turned to Lidia. "Where were you married, honey?"

Lidia looked wistful.

"Oh, dear, you're not married at all, are you?"

"We intend to be soon," Andre said.

"Well, what's wrong with doing it now?" asked Teddy.

"A priest won't marry us without a posting of the banns," said Lidia.

"How long does it take to post banns?"

"Too long." Lidia opened her bag and took out a cloth-covered book and handed it to the professor.

"You can marry us," she said.

"But I'm not a priest."

"I know. And Andre is not a Catholic."

The professor stood in the Puebla church, the gray onyx altar behind him, the book in his hands open to the place that Lidia wanted.

"If everyone present agrees that in God's eyes we are man and wife, then we will be," Lidia said.

"I certainly agree," said Teddy.

"And I," said Conrad, who stood next to her, Bix in his arms.

The professor began to read from the book, stumbling over the words, but as Lidia looked up at him his pronunciation improved, his voice began to soar, and soon he was reading as though he had been ordained by the pope himself.

When the ceremony was over, the professor's eyes were

red, and he cleared his throat before he said, "I now pronounce you man and wife."

"I'll never forget this day," said Teddy, tears in her eyes as she watched Andre take Lidia in his arms and kiss her. "We'll all be friends forever. I can feel it like I've never felt anything in my life."

As they left the church, the professor turned the book over and over in his hands. He glanced at Lidia and flicked his tongue nervously against his front teeth. "This is a very old book," he said.

"Yes," Lidia replied.

"Very old."

"Yes, very old. Have you ever heard of Gonzalo Guerrero and Brother Aguilar?"

"Of course. The first Spaniards to land in Yucatán and live among the Maya. You don't mean to say that this book—" He looked at the pages again, at the tiny handwriting in the margins.

"It's a breviary, a book of hours," Lidia said, "an ancient prayer book that was given to my great-grandmother Concepción by Emperor Maximilian. It belonged to Brother Gerónimo de Aguilar."

34

For all his seeming inattention to detail, the professor was efficient in a way that was at once metaphysical and mysterious. Just as Andre had decided that he couldn't possibly have any idea where Yucatán was or how to get there, evidence appeared to prove him wrong: in Puebla there was a letter notifying the professor that when he arrived in Chichén Itzá a wagon and muleteer would be waiting to take him to the village of Xan-Xel; and at the dock in Veracruz a stamped document was in readiness authorizing the Mexican port officials to load the Buick and all its paraphernalia on board a freighter headed for Yucatán. But it was after the two-day voyage across the Gulf of Campeche, when they were still on board ship, anchored in shallow water several miles from the harbor at Progreso, that the professor's hidden competence was finally unveiled.

Lidia and Andre stood at the rail of the ship watching the tug approach. The professor had had his binoculars trained on it from the moment it left the palm-lined shore. Teddy Whitworth was playing a game of peek-a-boo with Bix to distract him while Conrad attempted to slather calamine lotion on the heat rash on the little boy's face.

"Immigration officials," said the professor. "They'll want to see your papers, Andre. Go below. When they're gone we'll hide you in the car and take you off that way."

"They won't let Lidia land alone," Conrad said. He had

hardly spoken during the voyage, leaving the conversation to
Teddy while he read medical texts and wrote in a large black
notebook that he carried with him everywhere, even to meals.

"She's not alone," Andre said. "She's with the four of you."

"It doesn't matter," said Conrad. "Archaic as it may be, in
order to land she must be a married woman traveling with
her husband."

"We can't hide the two of you in the car," the professor
said thoughtfully, "but go below, Andre. Something always
develops at the last minute."

A diminutive Maya, his hawk-nosed face hairless and chocolate brown, boarded the freighter.

"Documents, please."

The professor fumbled in his pockets, dropping things on
the deck as he searched for the right papers.

"Chichén Itzá?" asked the official.

"Yes, and this young woman is my assistant."

"Your papers don't say anything about an assistant." Long
spiky eyelashes shielded his almond-shaped eyes.

"Let me see them," said the professor, taking the papers
back. "Ah, here, you see this part here, 'will be permitted to
enter with automobile and equipment as necessary.' "

"But she is not an automobile, señor."

Conrad stepped forward. "I believe that's meant to be
loosely interpreted. The woman is as necessary to the carrying out of Professor Kobermann's work as any piece of equipment would be."

The official looked doubtful.

"My name is Conrad Whitworth. I'm a doctor of tropical
diseases. If you want to check my credentials, you may in-
quire with Dr. Campos at the Clínica Biológica in Valladolid."

The professor stared at the bottle of medicinal alcohol next
to the calamine lotion in Conrad's open black bag. "Maybe
the gentleman would like a drink, Herr Doktor," the professor said, and lifted the bottle out of the bag.

"It's not for drinking," Conrad said. "It's for insect bites."
But the professor had already wrapped a hundred-peso bill
around the bottle and handed it to the Maya.

At high tide the freighter moved into the Progreso harbor.
Lidia was permitted to disembark with the rest, and when
the Buick was driven down the ramp, no one checked the
lumpiness beneath the rug.

"Hurry," the professor said. "We don't want them to think too hard about how many of us there were when we boarded."

The Whitworths got in front with Bix and Lidia got in back. Andre emerged from beneath the rug, his face streaked with perspiration and his shirt and pants dotted with blue fuzz, and in minutes the professor was driving at breakneck speed down the highway.

Andre sat in stunned silence. It seemed to him that he had been running all his life.

"I won't leave Mexico, Lidia," he said stubbornly.

"We're together, Andre," she murmured.

They drove through endless fields of henequen plants, their blade-shaped leaves stabbing at the sky. As the heat rose off the highway, the spiked plants became apparitions that danced on either side of the car, fanned out, and then disappeared. Then the jungle was behind them and they entered the city of Mérida. The noise was the first thing they noticed. The city hummed with noise, a discordant symphony of honking horns, clanging trolleys, and ringing church bells. It babbled a medley to itself in a singsong of Maya and Spanish.

Along the Paseo de Montejo the descendants of the Spanish conquerors, grown rich on the golden sisal of the henequen plant, lived in art-filled mansions. They sent their children to be educated in Europe, called themselves Yucatecos, and thought of Mexico as another country. On the outskirts were the thatched houses of the Maya, descendants of scholar-priests, the history of their people erased from their minds.

The professor drove through the traffic to the Plaza de la Independencia, where they stopped to buy cool glasses of *horchata*, sugary drinks of almond essence and orange flower water. Andre and Lidia rented a horse-drawn *calesa* for a ride around the city, while the Whitworths sat in the shade of the Indian laurel trees and watched Bixby try to catch the grackles that flew in and out of the branches. The professor wandered the crowded aisles of the municipal market, amusing himself by speaking to the vendors in Spanish while they answered in Maya. In early afternoon, when everyone felt refreshed, they continued on their journey.

The rain that pelted the car all the way to Valladolid didn't relieve the heat, just liquefied it. Teddy periodically stuck a washcloth out the car window to catch some water and then doused Bix with it. She had removed all his clothes except for his underpants, and she made a game of wringing the cloth out over his head. Everyone's clothes were soaked, partly from perspiration, partly from the rain that came in from the half-open windows, and partly from Teddy's homemade showers.

The professor's driving had not improved, but there was little traffic on the road, which decreased the danger. Occasionally he stopped the car and everyone stood outside for a while, faces turned up to the cooling rain. Then they got back in and drove off again.

As they neared Valladolid they glimpsed the first of the pyramids of Chichén Itzá in the distance. The rain had continued unabated, and the road now resembled a river. Water was up over the Buick's running boards, and the car floated crazily along with the current.

The town looked uninhabited in the storm, its buildings all in need of repair, the door to the Church of San Cervacio open to the rain. The professor angled the car up over the water-washed curb of the plaza in front of the Clínica Biológica and Conrad and Andre ran into the building.

The building, once a Spanish *alcalde*'s home, was now a laboratory for the study of tropical diseases. Broken test tubes littered the floor. File cabinets, too full to close, hung open. Dr. Campos, the laboratory's director, was nowhere in sight.

"Shit!" said Conrad. "No matter how much work I do when I'm here, it always has to be redone when I return."

"What *are* you doing here?" Andre asked.

"Research, like I said. Dr. Campos keeps my records and supplies here, and I go out and do field work with the native population in the villages near Chichén Itzá. This is the first time Teddy and Bix have come along. I'm not sure how well it's going to work out."

While Conrad went in search of salvageable syringes and medicines, Andre scanned the pages of a newspaper he had found on the absent Dr. Campos's desk. He stopped. The paper grew slack in his hands. There was his picture. It was an afternoon shot. He and Trotsky were sitting side by side at a picnic table. There was also a picture of Diego Rivera and a woman getting off a plane in New York.

* * *

An informant, said to be a friend of the missing David Alfaro Siqueiros, who disappeared on May 25, has implicated Diego Rivera in the assassination attempt on Leon Trotsky on May 24, 1940. Rivera has flown to San Francisco with American actress Paulette Goddard. Andre Frankle, a German alien, who was also named by the informant, has not been located.

"Give me a hand, Andre."

Andre dropped the paper and took hold of one of the handles of the metal container.

"Did you get everything you needed?" he asked.

"I've filled this thing with as much medicine and supplies as I could find."

They carried the container out to the street, and the professor tied it onto the roof of the Buick with the rest of the supplies. The rain had stopped, but it was still overcast and steamy. People were out on the streets now, men in white shirts and pants, women in embroidered huipils and carefully draped rebozos. Both men and women were short, barely five feet tall. Their beak-shaped noses, flat brows, and close-set eyes were very different from the blended features of the Maya of Mérida.

"We're coming to the end of the trip, Andre," said the professor before he started the car. "I'm taking the Whitworths to the hotel in Chichén Itzá, and then I'm going on to Xan-Xel. You haven't told me what you are going to do. You could stay here in Valladolid. It's quiet, not too many people. The El Mesón del Marquez is a decent hotel."

"Where did you say you were going?"

"Xan-Xel. It's a Maya village."

"Do you mind if Lidia and I come along?"

"It's very primitive, very isolated. Are you sure you—"

"Yes. I'm sure."

The jungle road from Valladolid was rock-strewn, but passable, with glimpses through the trees of stone-dotted fields, their new growth of maize clean and green after the drenching rain. When they arrived at the Mayaland Hotel in Chichén Itzá, they walked up the steps through the Spanish portico to the lobby.

"My Lord, civilization in the middle of nowhere," exclaimed Teddy, as she looked down the long corridor of polished Mexican pavers to the garden, which replicated, in a tidy manner, the jungle they had just passed through. "It takes my breath away to see it. I had visions of grass huts and no running water and bugs everywhere."

"We'd like some supper," said Conrad to the Maya behind the registration desk. A plate of *panuchos,* small tortilla rounds covered with chicken and pickled onion, was at the man's elbow.

"Something like what you're eating would suit us fine."

They sat at a long dining table on the terrazzo, shaded by lacy acacias.

"There's no one here but us," said Lidia, as the food was brought. There were flowers and fresh linen on the table.

"I've seen this place filled with archaeologists," the professor said. "They use it as a base of operations for the ruins. But when the money runs out, so do they."

"Are you really going to take this fragile little girl out into the jungle, Andre?" Teddy asked. She had her fingers hooked onto the top of Bix's pants to keep him from crawling out of his chair and up onto the iron grillwork behind the table. "I'd love it if the two of you stayed here and kept Bix and me company while Conrad is out wandering around with his Indians."

"If archaeologists come here, then there must be journalists, too," Conrad said. "I think Andre would be wise to continue on with Hans to Xan-Xel."

In the late afternoon they stood on the steps of the hotel and said their good-byes.

"We'll come and visit you," Lidia said.

"I'll bet you won't," said Teddy as she and Lidia hugged. "We'll be here, don't you forget, so anytime you get lonesome—"

"Liddy, Liddy," cried Bix, holding out his arms.

"Oh, look how he loves you," said Teddy as Lidia picked the little boy up and kissed him. "Maybe you'll have a little one yourself. There's nothing so noisy and so much work, but nothing so sweet either."

Conrad handed Andre a small carton filled with vials of medicine. "There's alcohol in there. It's very good for ticks. And viperol for snake bite. There's some cotton and bandages. And quinine. Each of you take one every day. The Maya don't always cover their water cisterns, and the mosquitoes breed in them. They claim they get sick from the *mal aire*, but it's really the mosquitoes."

"But the *mal aire* causes illness, too, doesn't it?" Lidia asked.

"Only colds, Lidia. Fever and sweats come from mosquitoes."

"Will you be here if we need you?" she said.

"I'll be in the vicinity. You can leave a message with Teddy at the hotel. Don't forget to take care of cuts. Cover them and put iodine on them. Cuts turn into infections and infections turn into gangrene pretty quickly in the jungle."

Lidia put her arms impulsively around Conrad's neck and kissed him on the cheek. He looked surprised, but pleased.

"If anything ever happened to me I can think of no one but you that I would want to take care of me," she said. And then she added quickly, "But of course Andre's the one I would want to hold my hand."

35

A quarter mile from the hotel, at the edge of the jungle, the mule-drawn wagon was waiting. It was a square platform with three hard wooden seats. Red-striped awnings had been draped over four supporting poles.

"Señor Kobermann?" said the muleteer.

"Yes, and these are my friends, Señor and Señora Frankle."

"I am named Luís," the muleteer said, and he smiled, revealing two gold-rimmed front teeth.

"We'll want to get to Xan-Xel before dark," said the professor as Luís helped him and Andre remove equipment and suitcases from the Buick and load them aboard the wagon.

"We have enough light," Luís said.

When everything was securely tied down and everyone seated in the wagon, Luís hopped up onto his platform seat, pulled at the reins, spoke to the mules in Maya, and the journey began.

"Some of what you might think are grass-covered mountains are really the remains of pyramids," said the professor, pointing to mounds of verdure-covered stones that were barely visible through the dense brush. "No one knows how many Maya ceremonial sites there are out there, and there'll probably never be enough money to excavate them all. The roots of the trees break up more and more pyramids every year. Even if we could mark every one of them for further exploration, we'd never find our markers. The jungle grows about a foot a month."

"How frightened the Maya must have been to see the Spainards with steel plates on their chests come riding toward them on their giant horses," Lidia said.

"They must not have been too frightened," the professor replied, "when you consider that the Maya held out longer against the Spaniards than the Aztecs did. But so much is missing that we don't understand. The Spanish friars burned the whole body of Maya literature, which may have given us some answers. When they realized what they had done, it was too late to resurrect the memories of the surviving *halach uinics*, the scholar-priests." The professor shook his head in disgust. "Now the only thing we have to go by are a few remnants which escaped the flames, plus Father de Landa's account of his experiences in Yucatán."

"And Brother Aguilar's book," Lidia said. "On every page of the breviary he has written something about Maya life. It's in a tiny handwriting in a Spanish that's difficult to read and interpret, but it is a record of the Maya."

"It's not religious writing?"

"Some of it is religious, but much of it is a daily accounting of Maya life."

"*Mein Gott!* Do you know what might be contained in that breviary that your family has kept to itself all these years?"

"But there's no mention of gold. There's no map, nothing to tell the location of any gold. The book has been studied by my family for years. It's a Catholic book of hours and an account of Maya life, nothing more."

"Nothing more? This book is better than gold."

"How could it be better than gold?" asked Andre, catching the professor's excitement.

"Because there are no direct records of the Maya. We have only fragments of Maya writings, and Father de Landa's account. But Brother Aguilar and Gonzalo Guerrero lived with the Maya. Guerrero became a Maya. This is a priceless work. There are museums that would make you rich in exchange for this breviary."

"Where did you put it, Lidia?" asked Andre anxiously.

"I put waxed paper around it and then wrapped it in a huipil and put it in my suitcase."

"You've done exactly right," the professor said. "To think that you have such a book and no one has ever realized its importance."

"You make me ashamed that we have not given it the honor it deserves," Lidia said.

"Just guard it well," the professor replied.

The wagon bounced from side to side, tossing its occupants into the air and knocking their heads repeatedly against the awning. In a spot where the rock path curved, a limestone palisade rose in front of them, its face nearly obliterated by shrubbery. The professor asked Luís to stop the wagon.

"Look ahead of us," said the professor as they walked to the edge of the precipice. Below them was a small lake half hidden by low-hanging ceiba trees.

"The Maya called it the Sacred Well," the professor said. "They used it for human sacrifice."

Andre leaned over the edge and peered into the murky water.

"First the victims were cleansed in the steam of the *temescal,* and then they were thrown into the well. If the victim didn't drown, that meant that he had spoken with the rain god Chac, who lives in the depths of the well. The Maya considered such a person a divine messenger."

Andre threw a pebble into the water. "How do you know all this if the Maya left no records?"

"The fragments of writing I spoke about and an American named Edward Thompson. He bought Chichén Itzá from the Mexican government and lived here for forty years and dredged as much as he could from the muddy bottom of the well. He brought up gold objects and jewels and of course he sold them to museums to sustain himself. Perhaps he even grew rich. I don't dispute that. But he also brought up human bones, which was the first evidence that the well had been used for human sacrifice."

The professor gazed at the jungle around them, and, as though the motmots flying overhead were listening, he lowered his voice. "The Mexicans called Thompson a treasure hunter and threw him out of Mexico, but nothing would have been done here at all if it had not been for him." His voice descended lower still and he now spoke with great intimacy. "Like Thompson, I sell some of the artifacts I find. Nothing is sacred, since knowledge knows no motive. Great discoveries are made by treasure hunters, as well as by scientists, and so I'm proud to be both. I convey all of this to you in the strictest confidence, because if my activities were to be fully known, I too would become a fugitive."

The jungle encroached more closely on the wagon. In some places the trail disappeared entirely and the muleteer jumped down and chopped at the steely tentacles of the liana vines with his machete.

Suddenly the air grew thick and heavy, and the sun was blotted out.

"What is it?" Lidia cried as the sun was blotted out.

In seconds the air was black with gnats. A blanket of gnats, swarming, diving, buzzing.

"Oh!" Lidia cried, swatting at her face and ears. Andre covered her with his body, but the gnats crawled under their clothes. They clung to moist skin, were sucked into nostrils, clogged mouths and ears.

"Get beneath the seats!" the professor shouted. Andre pulled Lidia beneath the seat while the professor searched frantically through his crates until he found the mosquito netting.

"Here, quickly, put this over your heads."

The three of them cowered, choking and gagging, beneath the netting as Luís drove right through the blackest of the swarms, swatting the insects with his hand and spitting out those that had gotten past his gold-rimmed teeth into his mouth.

The gnats disappeared as quickly as they had come. The professor threw off the netting, and the three of them emerged red-faced and gasping.

"It's not much farther to Xan-Xel," he said.

Xan-Xel had a low limestone rock fence to mark its perimeters. It had no church, and there was only one well in the center of the small *zócalo*. Radiating out from the *zócalo*, nearly hidden in the jungle, were the thatch-roofed *chozas*, the doorless huts where the inhabitants lived.

They waited at the well where Luís had left them, their belongings on the packed red earth beside them. In a short while a woman, her lips and cheeks colored with the red dye of the achiote seed, a water jug balanced on her head, walked with graceful, flowing movements toward them along the jungle path.

"This is Juanita," the professor said.

She greeted them in Maya-accented Spanish and poured water into a cup for them to drink. When they had drunk their fill and the vermilion in their faces had begun to fade, the professor said, "Lidia and Andre need a *choza*."

"They will have mine," she replied.

"We can't do that," said Andre.

"There is no problem," the professor said. "Juanita stays in my *choza* with me when I'm here."

Juanita's *choza* had a hammock and a low table made of cedarwood. Cooking utensils were in a lean-to at the rear. Chickens and pigs wandered in and out.

"It's not as fancy as El Mesón del Marquez in Valladolid," the professor said, his arm around Juanita's waist. "But no one will bother you here."

"It's fine," said Andre. "I like it. Don't you like it, Lidia?"

"It's very quiet," she said.

As Andre stood in the doorway of the *choza* and watched the professor and Juanita walk off together along the jungle path, the lacy underskirt beneath her huipil draped so that it swayed seductively against her bare leg, he was struck by the fact that the professor's awkward behavior had vanished, had been replaced by an easy self-assurance, as though this small village in the jungle were his domain.

36

Visitors were rare in Xan-Xel, except for an occasional archaeologist like the professor who came to examine the stone pyramids. People didn't ordinarily stumble across the village, and it wasn't on any maps. The only way that anyone could find it was by following the ancient jungle-covered Maya road that once linked Chichén Itzá to Cobá in the interior and to Tulum on the Caribbean. Although the professor had come to Xan-Xel before, the arrival of the two young strangers was an event. Juanita, who herself was a special person in the village, having once attended *carnaval* in Mérida, brought the villagers a few at a time each day to stare at the woman with the light brown skin and gray eyes who had no children to care for and who spent long hours sitting on a stool in front of the curly-haired man while he painted pictures of her. Juanita explained that the man and woman were from Mexico, and the villagers imputed their strangeness to that.

In the early evenings the professor would come to the young couple's *choza*, and the villagers would hear the woman reading aloud from a book that she had brought with her. Sometimes they recognized a prayer that the priests read in the church in Valladolid, but mostly the words were of animals and *halach uinics*, the great Maya chiefs, and reminded them of the stories that the *h'men*, the prayermakers, recounted when they performed the secret Maya rituals. Sometimes they heard the professor's voice, and then there would be loud talking between the two men as they discussed the meaning of what the woman had read.

On the days that the curly-haired man didn't sit outside the *choza* and paint pictures, he would pack his colors in a box, and he and the Mexican woman would join the professor on his daily trip into the jungle. A mule carried the professor's supplies along with the curly-haired man's boxes of colors and cloth. They would walk in the direction of the green mounds that lay beyond the village near the cenote of Dzitnup. The mounds were buried beneath liana vines and zapotes and cedar trees that grew branch to branch over them. Ancient lore said that they were part of a Maya city even greater than Chichén Itzá.

Soon the novelty of watching the comings and goings of the strangers paled and life returned to what it had been for as long as any of the elders in the village could remember. The women rose early, when the day was coolest, and cooked a breakfast of tortillas and black beans and hot chocolate. Then the men went to gather firewood, returning with their backs straining beneath the weight of the heavy sticks, the tumplines tight against their foreheads.

Before the men left to cultivate the *milpas*, the fields where the maize was grown, their wives prepared a lunch for them to take with them. Sometimes it was *papadzul*, hard-boiled eggs chopped with pumpkin-seed sauce and rolled in tortillas, or *pollo pibil*, chicken in achiote spice and sour orange paste. If there was pork left over from the *cochinita pibil* of the night before, it too would be sent along. And there was always a bowl of chile peppers to aid digestion and prevent stomachaches.

When their husbands were gone, the women tended to the children and household tasks, preparing *masa* for tortillas, tending the apiary, trimming and watering the flowers that grew in profusion around the *chozas*. Then they did the family wash in a huge wooden trough filled with water that they had drawn from the well with a hemp rope. When their tasks were done, they gossiped together, and the clickings of the Maya language sounded like the chirping of crickets.

The rain god Chac had been good to Xan-Xel this year, and the maize had grown tall and green. In the early afternoons, when the sun blazed the brightest, the men returned from the *milpas* for the siesta, and then the village was at its quietest, as everyone sought refuge from the heat.

Each *choza* had a lean-to for cooking and two doorless openings, front and back, through which the available light and breeze could flow. Some men took their siesta dozing under the shade of the cedar trees. Some stayed in the dark interior of their *chozas* and swung half-dreaming in their hammocks.

In late afternoon, the men returned to the *milpas* and the women began the preparation of the evening meal. *Cochinita pibil,* if there was pork, or *pollo pibil,* if there was chicken. On special days X-Tabentum, a liquor made of fermented honey, was drunk with the evening meal, and there was always a plate of sliced mammee apples and papayas and bananas.

Before it was dark, the men returned home and their wives bathed them in the same wooden troughs in which they had washed their clothes. Then the men dressed in clean white cotton and ate their evening meal at a low table, seated on homemade stools, while the women served them.

When the meal was over, the women poured water from gourds onto their husband's hands to clean them. Only when the men left to talk with the other men in the growing darkness of the village did the women and children eat.

Sometimes in the evenings there were fiestas, and then people came from neighboring villages. They danced the ancient dances to the dissonant strains of Maya music. They drank *balche* until they were blind. Their frenzy knew no limits. They fell atop one another and howled. They took one another's wives and were as wild as the jaguars in the jungle, nipping at one another in ferocious abandon. And when they had slept and recovered, they were as passive as they had been before.

Lidia and Andre adapted to the village's rhythmic pattern. They learned to forsake the heat during the siesta and to lie together in the stillness of their *choza,* swinging in the large hammock. They spoke in whispers and laughed and made love.

Conrad stopped in every few weeks to see how they were, to refill their quinine bottles and give them news of the outside world, which sometimes arrived in Valladolid several weeks after the event.

The village seemed to Andre to be the safest place on earth. There was no Trotsky, no Siqueiros, no Stalin's GPU.

He was painting better than he had ever painted before, and the canvases piled up along the wall of the *choza*. He and Lidia drifted together, not needing or wanting or fearing anything.

Then one day he heard Artur's voice again.

"So I was wrong. You love her, she loves you. But what about the rest of the world? You think because you've decided that you won't be a part of it anymore that it will leave you alone? Things can happen, my son. You're too happy. No one dares to be so happy."

Gold flowers and crimson crosses illuminated the cursive script of the breviary, and in the wide margins was the delicate handwriting of Brother Aguilar. In some places the ornate line of the lay priest's lead stylus was fluid and dark and in other places water-spotted and faded, a victim of aging paper and four hundred years of neglect.

The breviary had been made for Brother Aguilar in Salamanca, Spain, and had the Roman calendar in it and an equation for figuring the dates from the year 1 through the year 1582. All the feast days were listed as well, as were the golden number and dominical letter for adjusting for leap year and determining the day on which Easter fell each year. Of course, not being an astronomer, Brother Aguilar's calculations of when the vernal equinox occurred in Yucatán had erred in favor of a late spring each year, and so his starting dates were not as trustworthy as they might have been. But otherwise, the breviary was as complete as any Catholic would want it to be. It had readings from the Bible, prayers, psalms, hymns, and canticles. It had the four Gospel lessons, the Hours of the Virgin, the Cross, and the Holy Spirit. It was weighted heavily in favor of prayers to the Virgin Mary, but also included the Penitential Psalms, Suffrage, and Office of the Dead.

Lidia alone was able to decipher the archaic Spanish in which Brother Aguilar had written his diary in the margins of the breviary. She thought parts of it so beautiful that she read and reread them until she had committed the words to memory.

*On This, the Fourth Day of May, in the Year of Our Lord
and Savior Jesus Christ, One Thousand Five Hundred and
Eleven*

I begin this diary on the sixth day adrift. We are eighteen,
including Captain Valdivia and two women. The seas are now
blue and clear and calm, with not a sign of the hurricane that
threw us into the treacherous shallows of Las Víboras and
destroyed the caravel. We have no sails, and only three oars.
The merciless sun has caused weakness and fever, and although
I resist drinking seawater to quench my thirst, many of the
others do not. If God will forgive me, I write on the margins
of my prayer book, which, with my metallic lead writing instru-
ment, is all that I have left to me, save for the clothes I wear.
If we should all die, then a recitation of the circumstances of
our deaths will be welcomed by those who find our bodies.

I am Gerónimo de Aguilar of Ecija, a small town near Seville
in Spain, a lay brother employed by Don Pedro Valdivia to
minister to the religious needs of his men on the long voyage
from Darién to Santo Domingo. Captain Valdivia's voyage
concerned a mission to settle accounts with a business rival.
A matter of loans not repaid. We also carried a cargo of cloth
and leather hides and ten thousand ducats destined for the king.

On the day on which the caravel was lost, I awoke prepared to hear confessions and to tend to the sick, but was
brought on deck by the lurching of the ship and the noise of
whipping sails and bellowing wind.

All was despair and confusion. Captain Valdivia held the
wheel while the ship rose and fell on mountainous seas. The
foremast had broken in two, killing four men. As I ran to
minister the rites, Gonzalo Guerrero, a young seaman from
Seville, came up beside me and called out, "The ship will
break up before their souls reach heaven."

Since his logic was indisputable, I abandoned my ministry
and instead endeavored to help him rescue our only passengers, an aunt and her niece, and to help them into the boat
that was being lowered over the side. The women scarcely
resembled the elegant creatures they were when they boarded
the caravel. Their hair was undone and snarled in seawater,
their long lace gloves torn from their fingers, their silk gowns
stiffening in the briny water.

Before the ship was lost, the young Guerrero bravely
entered the flooded hold and retrieved the king's gold.

On This, the Fifth Day of May, in the Year of Our Lord and Savior Jesus Christ, One Thousand Five Hundred and Eleven

Captain Valdivia at first told and retold the story of his business rival's treachery. But on this seventh day adrift he lies with cracked lips and barely speaks. When he does, his words, whether distorted by swollen tongue or muddled by delirium, lack meaning. He no longer bothers to assert his supremacy over us, and his corpulent body seems to shrivel more rapidly than do the bodies of the rest of us.

Since I hear the confessions of those who are still able to think clearly, this afternoon I asked Gonzalo Guerrero if he wanted me to hear his, and he replied, "I'm close enough to God now to confess to him personally."

On This, the Eighth Day of May, in the Year of Our Lord and Savior Jesus Christ, One Thousand Five Hundred and Eleven

The two women no longer cry and moan. The niece lies with her head in her aunt's lap. The aunt has torn away strips of their clothing to cover their sunburned flesh. Although leg and thigh are now exposed, the men do not look.

Captain Valdivia roused himself from his stupor this morning and said, "An umbrella for the ladies."

I did not reply, since I saw no purpose in pointing out to him that umbrellas could be found only in Santo Domingo.

Guerrero and I pass the time by praying. He is not a very religious man, and so I pray and he listens. We have also spent somber moments discussing the question of who among us will die first. I defer to his greater experience at sea.

"It is not a simple matter of mathematics," he told me today. "Captain Valdivia acts strangely, but strangeness is not a sign of impending death. Some of the others are very quiet, but quietness is also not fatal."

Guerrero's eyes are very clouded. I know he suffers from sun and thirst and lack of food as much as the rest of us, but he still speaks with remarkable authority. It is his belief that the women will die first.

*On This, the Ninth Day of May, in the Year of Our Lord and
Savior Jesus Christ, One Thousand Five Hundred and Eleven*

Today the first seaman died. He had not moved from his
sitting position for several hours, and when a gust of wind
moved the boat suddenly to the west, he toppled silently into
the water.

*On This, the Tenth Day of May, in the Year of Our Lord and
Savior Jesus Christ, One Thousand Five Hundred and Eleven*

Today the aunt of the young girl died. The niece is unaware of it, as she has fallen into a profound sleep.

*On This, the Eleventh Day of May, in the Year of Our Lord
and Savior Jesus Christ, One Thousand Five Hundred and
Eleven*

Four seamen died today. In the late afternoon, when balmy
ocean breezes came to cool those of us who remained, the
young girl sat up in the boat and smiled at me.

"It is much warmer here than in Panama," she said. "Tell
me, have we arrived yet at Santo Domingo?"

Her blistered hand moved delicately through the folds of
her ravaged gown as she spoke, and at the sound of her voice
Captain Valdivia said, "Attend to the young woman, Brother
Aguilar."

I spoke to her gently until she died, at which time Guerrero remarked, "Brother Aguilar, I don't believe that I have
ever seen a man so suited to his work."

*On This, the Twelfth Day of May, in the Year of Our Lord
and Savior Jesus Christ, One Thousand Five Hundred and
Eleven*

On this, the fourteenth day adrift, when I thought that the
shining light before me was the gate to paradise, to my
astonishment and great rejoicing, I realized that my eyes
were blinded by the shimmering sand of an island.

"Land," I croaked, and Captain Valdivia roused himself
from his dreams and stared at it with me. Then Guerrero
awoke, and the other men began to stir. Soon we were
pulling at the oars, eleven corpses suddenly come to life.

"Brother Aguilar, a prayer," the captain said when we had staggered ashore.

Such was my thirst that I hurriedly recited a prayer of thanksgiving and then with the others fell upon the coconuts that lay on the ground, breaking the husks on limestone boulders and gobbling up liquid and coconut meat with such unrestrained, ravening appetite that, bloated and belching, we collapsed onto the sand and vomited ourselves into unconsciousness. When we awoke, we were still in such a state of illness that we writhed in agony for several hours, after which, partially recovered, we set out for a well that one of the men had discovered a short distance into the jungle of trees.

The well was as large as a small lake, a water-filled limestone pit with scarified walls set in a grove of tall trees. Here we spent the afternoon, drinking, then sleeping, then drinking some more. At the first shadows of night Captain Valdivia ordered us back to the beach, where everyone, now in high spirits, set to gathering firewood. When evening came, it was no different than the day, warm and humid and thick with the cacophony of jungle birds.

One of the seamen caught a strange-looking lizard, and soon all of us were scampering after the creatures, and when the fire was hot we skinned the animals and roasted them. Only in Salamanca have I tasted meat as vile.

"The flesh of rodents and small animals does not agree with me," Captain Valdivia said, and he ordered Guerrero to catch him a fish for his supper. The captain has regained his arrogant manner, and his speech, which with bad fortune had fallen to the vulgar level of his men's, has risen once more to its customary high Castilian. He also now separates himself from us, eating his food and napping apart from the rest.

Captain Valdivia says that our salvation was guided by Divine Providence. Guerrero says that it was guided by the currents. I try not to take sides, but I think regularly of Saint Gregory, who said that to be born would be of little benefit to us if we were not redeemed by Christ, our Savior.

The captain spoke to us after we had eaten.

"We have seen the proof of prayer today. Our lives have been spared, we are on land once more, the king's gold has been saved, and we are in good health and fine humor. It is possible that Spaniards have come this way before and were helped by the inhabitants. Tomorrow we will walk inland through the jungle. If this land is like that of the others in the

Indies, there will be good fruits to eat and more wells with fresh water to drink and friendly natives to help us. I have calculated that we have drifted no farther than seventy leagues from Cuba, I am unable to state in which direction. Sleep well tonight. Be sure that in heaven God hears your prayers."

On This, the Fourteenth Day of May, in the Year of Our Lord and Savior Jesus Christ, One Thousand Five Hundred and Eleven

At sunup today we set off into the jungle, leaving surf and cool trade winds behind. Three men marched ahead, hacking at the tangled vines with tree branches. Behind them were two men, the sack of gold slung on two sticks that they carried between them. Then came the Captain, followed by the rest of us.

By midafternoon we were stumbling along in the suffocating heat. We tripped over scarlet bushes beneath the cedar trees and sank up to our ankles in the cumbrous swamps of the palmetto groves. Our faces were flushed and covered with welts from the hot pricks of mosquitoes and stinging ants. Spiders clustered thickly on exposed skin and crawled under leggings and up sleeves. Perspiration ran in rivulets beneath our wool tunics. We could not see the sun. Only a filtered shadowy light told us that it was still day. Occasionally one of the seamen fell into the soft vegetation and lay there panting for air. Only the captain's proddings made him rise again.

"We will find a village soon, and with it will come rest and succor and instructions from the natives as to which way Cuba lies," the Captain told us, and as he spoke I noticed that his manner had turned away from its pompous confidence and become ill-humored and sullen, an aspect of his nature which I had noted before, and so was not alarmed.

When we had struggled along for some distance, we began to separate, some of us sitting down suddenly in a thicket of bushes or lying down with our faces in the moist humus of the jungle floor. I am thinner than most and so kept to my feet.

Finally the captain himself surrendered to the heat and collapsed on the ground with red face and thumping chest. Having gained some knowledge of medicine during my stay in a Benedictine monastery in Italy, I ran to his side and patted his face with the damp leaves of a nearby bush.

"It is an infirmity of the veins that makes me weak," the Captain told me as I tended to him, and I replied, "We must also give some credit to the harshness of the surroundings."

Guerrero also called me to come to his aid. He sat among roots and leaves beneath a cedar tree, oblivious to the stinging ants that crawled along its trunk.

"I would as soon be bitten to death by a swarm of ants than die of a too rapid heart," he said, and I answered, "The heat causes the blood to thicken and move more slowly in the body. You will be better with a little rest."

It was but a short while later, as the men lay resting in the bushes, that there appeared through the haze of the jungle an apparition such as none of us had ever before witnessed. At first I thought it was a spirit, or perhaps a delusion due to the extreme heat. But all of us saw the same thing. A dark-skinned man with a wooden headdress that, rising to a peak from his flattened brow, trailed green iridescent feathers and bits of obsidian mirror down his back almost to the ground. The man's face was tattooed, his nose a hawk's beak of shaped clay. Ornaments and beads hung from his earlobes and nose, and gems studded his filed teeth. On his upper body he wore a cotton tunic and on his lower body a jaguar skin. He carried a spear in one hand and a shield in the other.

The figure moved toward Captain Valdivia, jewels and bits of obsidian mirror shooting fiery shafts of light into the jungle gloom. The captain, who had been fanning himself with a palmetto leaf, looked up, his mouth agape, and Guerrero shouted, "We must run away, Captain," and stood up as though to run, when there appeared behind the apparition a line of Indians in breechclouts and sandals carrying shields and spears like their leader. Tattoos and ornamental scars covered their bodies. Jewels and beads hung from necks and wrists and encircled their ankles. But they wore nothing on their heads, and their uncombed locks bristled out from their pointed brows.

"They are just curious, nothing more," Captain Valdivia assured us as the man in the wooden headdress lifted the captain's chin and looked into his eyes. "Soon their curiosity will be satisfied and we will give them some trinkets to show our friendliness."

"What trinkets will we give them, Captain?" Guerrero asked.

"A gold ducat or two."

At that moment the man in the headdress screamed and backed away from the captain. I crossed myself and said a prayer, for it was apparent that the cause of the man's consternation was the Captain's blue eyes.

The Indians then descended on the captain, each one poking a finger into his cheeks, then looking at his eyes and screaming. When everyone had taken his turn, the man in the headdress shouted a command and we were pulled to our feet and shoved into a circle. A litter was brought, and the captain and the sack of gold were hoisted onto it. Then the leader took one last look at Captain Valdivia's blue eyes and shrieked one more time before we were prodded by the howling Indians into the jungle.

I was surprised at the lack of fear on the captain's part. He floated above our heads on his litter, a look of immense pleasure on his face.

"Brother Aguilar, would you give these heathens your blessing," he said to me, "for you may soon get the opportunity to bring them to Jesus. Look how amenable they are. They carry me as if I were a veritable divinity come to earth."

Although I did not tell the Captain so, it was my thought that the proper time for blessings would be when I baptized them. I was sure now that the captain had lost his sense of balance, for in Madrid I have seen the bishop officiate at the burning of Jews who were as much heathens as these savages are, and it is my memory that the bishop did not give them a blessing before they were tied to the stake.

When we had been walking for several hours, the jungle grew sparser and we caught glimpses of a village of thatched-roof mud huts in the distance. The Indians, who had all day nudged us along with the sharp points of their spears, now walked alongside us and let us rest when we wanted to. They draped their necklaces around our necks and let us hold their spears and examine the jewels in their pointed teeth.

"There is a village, and perhaps there is also a bay," Guerrero told me. "Cuba cannot be too far from here. I have heard that the savages of the Indies possess the ability to make large boats that can carry men long distances."

We entered the village at dusk. There were no women or children to be seen, but men came to greet us, jumping and gesticulating at the sight of us. It was obvious that we were as alien to them as they were to us.

"We must just give them this moment to enjoy our strangeness and to comment on our dress," the captain told us as the savages crowded around him.

I noted their friendliness, but Guerrero pointed out to me that it was the captain who drew their attention the most.

A mat was brought for the captain to sit on, and when the Indian men approached him they hid their faces with their hands, peeking shyly between their fingers at him, and shrieking occasionally. By this time the women had come out of the houses, and they too stared at the captain and peered into his eyes. They were more demure than the men and hardly made a noise as they took their turn examining him.

I have never seen such women before. They are short and dark, but appear taller because of the erect manner in which they carry themselves. They move with long strides and graceful, swooping gestures and leave a sweet-smelling breeze in their wake. As for their faces, Guerrero and I argued as to whether or not we would describe them as ugly, and we finally agreed that if not ugly, their visages were certainly peculiar, since most of them had an affliction that caused their eyes to cross and their pupils to meet above the bridge of the nose.

If I were to compare them to Spanish women, I would have to say they are ugly. They have no refinement of dress or feature. Where Spanish women wear their hair in gentle curls beneath starched bonnets, these women part their long black hair in the middle and plait it over each ear. And where the gowns of Spanish women are of silks and velvets and sewn to enhance the body's shape, these women wear roughspun chemises that hang loosely from their shoulders with a tiny bit of fringed underskirt draped to show beneath the hem.

Their skin appears to be smooth, but the skin of Spanish women is pale and radiates light, where theirs is dusky and traps light just like the jungle that surrounds them. But it is their teeth, filed to sawtooth pointiness, and their noses, drilled and hung with ornaments of bone and colored stones, that are truly repellent.

When the women had their fill of looking at the captain's eyes, they disappeared, and when they returned their arms were laden with pots of food and gourds of water. I had never smelled spices such as these, and as the earthenware plates were heaped with the pungent-smelling food I hoped the taste would prove as agreeable as the aroma.

We were given a thick black soup of some variety of bean with a mound of meat on top. We had no utensils with which to eat, but the women passed around stacks of thin, round cakes and demonstrated how the concoction could be scooped up and the whole of it eaten at once.

I began a prayer, but the men, who had already snatched up the food and begun to eat, drowned out my words with fits of coughing and sneezing.

"It is very spicy," said Captain Valdivia when he had wiped his eyes, "but it is a feast like no other."

I thought at first that it tasted like the lizards we had caught and eaten when we first landed, and was relieved to observe that the spices finally deadened my tongue to the taste. While we ate, Guerrero, who uses his cleverness well, determined, by use of signs and gestures, that the place we had come to was called Cuzmíl.

The Indians watched us closely as we ate. No sooner was a plate emptied than one of the women piled it high with food again.

"Their attentions make me uneasy," Guerrero said, but the captain's contentment was obvious.

"Perhaps we will bring several of these friendly savages to Cuba with us," the captain remarked to me. "Their appearance is unusual enough to make money merely by exhibiting them."

As we lay like sated animals next to the overflowing dishes of food, the return of the Indian leader, his retinue of savages trailing after him, was heralded by the tinkle of bells and beating of drums. One of the savages blew into a conch shell and a husky, mournful wail drifted overhead.

What followed was an astounding spectacle. The savages formed a circle and began to chant and dance, with one group throwing spears at another group, who, with astonishing dexterity, caught them before they struck flesh. I, along with the rest, was enthralled by the entertainment and enjoying myself immensely when Guerrero pulled at my sleeve and said, "I propose that we take the sack of gold and while the dancing continues leave this place. The captain may speak of Cuba, but I have seen no bay, no native canoes to take us there. And the meaning of the savages' dance is clear. The savages are the hunters and we are the hunted."

I replied that he must be mistaken. "It is a demonstration of physical prowess and daring," I told him. "You mustn't search for meanings where none exist. These people are primitive. They have not found God as you and I have. They need someone to lead them to him."

"Is it possible that you intend to stay here?" he asked me, and I replied that I hadn't thought of it, but that it was a pleasant enough place.

The spear-throwing stopped abruptly. As the conch flute's wail grew louder and the stamping feet more insistent, the leader pulled a long flint needle from his tunic and held it up for everyone to see. At the sight of the needle, the music became frenzied and the dancers spun and twirled more wildly.

Then suddenly the sound of the flute trailed off, the dancers fell to their knees. Everything stopped, became quiet, as with one swift movement the leader bent forward, pierced his earlobes with the needle, then smeared his face with the drops of blood caught in his hands.

My shock was absolute. The seamen let out shrieks of horror. Captain Valdivia's face, illuminated by the firelight, looked distressed, and when the leader stuck out his tongue and slit it with one of his long jagged fingernails, then smeared the blood on his chest, the captain closed his eyes and looked as though he were going to faint.

Two of the dancers then entered the circle also, and the leader opened his jaguar-skin skirt, pointed to his penis with one hand and held the flint needle triumphantly over his head with the other. When he pierced the skin of his penis with the needle, I shrieked as though the mutilation were mine, and Guerrero said to me, "Do you still intend to stay and bring them to God, Brother Aguilar?"

The two dancers then pierced their penes, and a length of thread was slipped through the flesh of each man so that they were linked, penis to penis, the thread hanging loosely between them.

At this point I fell to my knees, numb to my surroundings, barely able to acknowledge what my senses had apprehended. As I knelt there praying, Guerrero tried to escape into the jungle, but was captured quickly and dragged back to the fire where the captain still sat, dazed and ashen-faced.

"You must lead us out of here, Captain," Gonzalo shouted at him, but the captain seemed unable to comprehend. As for the rest of us, we were paralyzed by horror.

"Brother Aguilar, tell them to run before it's too late,"

Gonzalo cried out to me, and I managed to reply, "Where will we run, Gonzalo?"

Suddenly the men awoke from their trance and attempted to flee, but they were clubbed to the ground, tied together by their necks with rope, and dragged onto a path into the jungle.

"Where is their friendliness now?" Guerrero screamed at the captain.

The sight of the captain, once again perched on the shoulders of the Indians, moaning and rocking from side to side in his litter, was a pitiful one. Although I had fear for myself as well, I was distraught by the agony in the captain's face. His cheeks shook, and he pulled at his hair and squawked to be let down.

After an hour's march we emerged into a clearing. A stone pyramid rose skyward, moon-tinged clouds licking at the faces of grotesque idols at its top. Carved serpents with cavernous mouths and elongated fangs lined the sides of the steep steps.

"Brother Aguilar, where are you?" the captain called out, and I answered, "I am here, my captain. Do not despair."

Torches were lit to illuminate the site and four of the seamen were tied to trees whose shaved trunks shone like bone-white sentinels at the foot of the pyramid. All the rest of us, except for the captain, were put into wooden cages at the edge of the clearing.

"You must hear my confession, Brother Aguilar," the captain cried out as his clothes were pulled off him. When he lay naked and wriggling on the ground, his captors brought a thatch brush and a container of blue liquid, and, just as if he were a fence post, carefully and methodically painted him blue.

I pulled at the bars of my cage and with a voice hoarse with fear, cursed the savages. "You are heathens," I cried, "and you will burn in hell."

But my curses were ignored. At the instant that the painting of the captain was completed, the savages gave a jubilant shout, and the leader pulled the string free that connected his penis to the penes of the two dancers. Then he strode across the clearing to where the four seamen were tied, and with the bloody string he marked a circle on each man's tunic where the heart would be.

Guerrero spoke the name of the Lord loudly, and all around me I heard the men begin to whimper.

"There is no need to baptize these savages, Brother Aguilar,"
Guerrero said, "for they are part Christian already. Is this not
an auto-da-fé, and are they not treating us as we would treat
blasphemers against Christ?"

The arrows struck at the seamen's legs first, then their
arms and shoulders. Everywhere but the blood-marked spot.
They screamed so shrilly, so piercingly, that the jungle birds
screeched in sympathy.

"Kill them, kill them, have mercy on them and kill them,"
I shouted, feeling their agony as my own.

"They are not yet ready," Guerrero said. "Don't you see
the design of it yet? Don't you see the splendor of the ritual,
the purposefulness of it, the logic and symmetry and mystery
of what they are doing?"

Captain Valdivia had fainted. The Indians jostled and shook
him until he regained consciousness and could stand without
falling. At the sight of the arrows piercing the bodies of his
men he began to cry, and although I shuddered at the comparison, it seemed to me that in his naked and blue-painted
condition he looked like an exotic animal, hopping and sobbing in the clearing beneath the stone mountain.

The leader raised his arm, the random rain of arrows
stopped, and with deliberate aim each of the four seamen was
dispatched instantly with an arrow in the center of the blood-
drawn circle.

I was dumbstruck, unable to move. In the cage next to me
Gonzalo collapsed onto the floor, his face pressed against the
bars, his eyes fixed on the dead men, still tied upright against
the posts, their heads slumped onto their lifeless chests.
Neither of us said anything. I did not pray. He did not speak
of God or design. Only the captain's hoarse voice hovered
over us as he was carried up the steep stone steps. "We are
crucified, we are crucified, we are crucified."

"It cannot be that we have died and are in hell, Brother
Aguilar," Guerrero said, "for see how my arm turns pink
when I pluck at the flesh."

When the Indians reached the top of the stone mountain,
Captain Valdivia's screams were fainter, his words gibberish.
He was thrown on top of an altar, his blue body barely
distinguishable from the dark blue of the dawning sky. The
Indians then moved quickly, and although I could not hear
a cracking sound, I concluded from the angle at which the
captain's body lay across the altar that his spine had been

snapped in two. At that moment the rays of morning broke through the gray clouds, and a storm of bellowing and howling erupted from the Indians who waited at the mountain's base.

"They see it as a sign," Guerrero said. "God has parted the heavens for them and shined his light upon them, and now they can complete their offering to him."

The leader made a swift stabbing motion with a stone knife into the captain's chest, splitting his rib cage in two. As I write this I try to remember if the captain screamed yet another scream after his heart was removed and held aloft in the leader's hand, but I believe that the shock of the moment left me senseless as to the details. But I do remember that the leader held the captain's still-beating heart in his hand and ran from idol to idol at the top of the stone mountain, smearing their carved faces with the captain's blood. And I remember that one of the other savages stripped the captain's skin from his body and put it on himself like a suit of clothes. I especially remember how the skinless, heartless body of the captain was tossed from the altar and bounced and slid down the stone steps to the Indians waiting below, each of whom cut out a part of the body and ate it with great shouting and celebration.

"Are they not partaking of the body of Christ, Brother Aguilar?" Gonzalo shouted as I wept. "Is this not his body and his blood and are these not his children?"

On This, the Twenty-first Day of May, in the Year of Our Lord and Savior Jesus Christ, One Thousand Five Hundred and Eleven

After Captain Valdivia's horrible death, I prayed fervently while Guerrero and the others rattled and tested the strength of their cages, which were so designed that when one part appeared to loosen, another part tightened, preventing escape.

On the second day of our captivity Guerrero and several of the other men fell into a feverish delirium, which, in my opinion, was a natural consequence of fright.

"God is testing us to see if we are worthy of paradise," I told Guerrero, and he replied, "Then I have failed. For I am still here."

Meanwhile the attention of the savage women remained constant. They brought fresh gourds of water to our cages and great quantities of food, and were always careful when they slid the dishes toward us not to touch our bodies or soil their hands with our fecal matter.

We began to eat not to satisfy hunger, but to banish boredom, and as we crammed our stomachs with food we became lethargic, falling asleep after we had eaten and waking up only to defecate and eat again.

"Look how docile we have become, Brother Aguilar," Guerrero said to me after we had stuffed ourselves for the eighth time in one day. "Do you not think it strange that they bring fresh plates of food before the ones we have before us are emptied?"

"Perhaps this is their means of repentance," I answered him.

On the fourth day, while eating, I was struck by a blinding pain in my head, accompanied by a vision of a man being devoured by a wild beast. I related my vision to Guerrero, who said, "That is the answer, Brother Aguilar. We are being fattened up to be eaten."

I alone still retained possession of a metal buckle, and so set its sharp edge to work immediately to cut the bars of my cage. I worked diligently through the night, and before dawn the saplings that had made my prison were nothing but a pile of loose sticks on the ground around me. Now proficient in the use of the buckle, I began to work on Guerrero's cage and was able to free him before the sun was up. But such strenuous sawing had dulled the edges of the buckle, and the bars of the cages of the other men resisted dissection. The men sobbed in anguish as they saw my efforts to save them coming to naught.

"What must I do?" I cried, and Guerrero replied, "You must save yourself."

Thereupon Guerrero and I left the clearing and ran through the jungle. The sobs of the others followed us, striking pain in my heart.

When night fell, we found ourselves on a beach whereat was located a hollowed-out cedar log and primitive oars. We climbed into the canoe, and, although our strength was diminishing, set out to reach the island which we saw across the calm water. We rowed as forcefully as we were able, but had gotten no farther than midway in the channel when we saw an armada of canoes coming toward us. The Indians in the canoes were as fearsome as the savages of the island we had just departed, and so we surrendered without struggle and were towed to the opposite shore, there to be poked and prodded as though we were specimens washed up from the sea.

The leader of the savages was as gaudily arrayed as the one we had left behind on Cuzmíl. His face was tattooed, and spinach-green jade was embedded in his filed teeth. Jewels hung from his wrists and ankles, and his earlobes shivered and danced as the sun ignited the opals fastened there.

He began to bellow and gesticulate toward the island of Cuzmíl, which gave me to believe that his anger was directed less at us than at the inhabitants of that island. When he had completed venting his displeasure, he beckoned for us to follow him. We entered onto a steep path from the shore which led upward to a broad plateau whereat there were towers and temples of stone overlooking the sea. There was evidence of savages having recently occupied the site, but we saw no one.

We did not remain there, but immediately set out for the interior of the island, traveling on a broad, smooth road in which evenly matched pebbles had been tamped into a bed of limestone. The road was in open sun, away from the humidity of the jungle. With sips of water offered now and again by the savages, the heat was bearable. Thus began an arduous trip, in which we were marched until we were faint from the heat, and then we were allowed to fall in exhaustion at the side of the limestone road, only to be dragged up again a short time later. Guerrero and I became giddy with fatigue, not knowing where we were being taken, nor what our fate was to be.

We traveled in that manner for several days and nights, when, in what seemed to me to be a phantasma or celestial phenomenon, a city appeared through the jungle green, its buildings suspended beneath the clouds. Its monuments were of such excellence and originality that we were struck speechless.

"Chichén Itzá," the head savage said, and he pointed proudly to the regal pyramids and lofty observatories that stretched out for miles before us.

We walked dumbly through the city, through vast public squares like those of Seville, with tall trees bearing blossoms of violent red. The buildings were embellished with carvings of monsters and serpents. Their gleaming white handsomeness was marred by paintings of torture and bloodletting and human sacrifice, but I was reassured to see that there were also ordinary scenes of mothers and babies, fishermen in their canoes, farmers in their fields.

"They cannot mean us harm," Guerrero said to me as we were allowed to rest in the shade of the trees, "for why then bring us to this beautiful place?"

We were once again pulled to our feet and led through a spacious public market, where Guerrero and I remarked to each other on the abundance and variety of goods piled beneath the cotton awnings. We were looked at curiously by the vendors, some of whom leaned toward us from their market stalls and spoke to us in a cricket-like language as they thrust bits of meat into our mouths.

On the edge of the city, when we had passed a circular observatory of gleaming stone, its windows open to the heavens, we entered a peaceful area where trees grew so dense that their limbs joined together overhead to create a cooling canopy.

Then suddenly the road ended. Ahead of us was a precipice and beyond that a sixty-foot, water-scarred limestone wall with trees and pendulous shrubs growing out of its crevices. At the edge of the precipice was a low stone structure where a fire burned beneath a mound of rocks. Attendants doused the heated rocks with water and billows of steam floated upward.

We were stopped. And as I looked out over the shadowed well, I had a clear and distinct premonition of impending misfortune, which was immediately substantiated when the head savage drew aside his jaguar skin and breechclout and exposed a penis so transmogrified by repeated bloodlettings that it resembled a lizard-skin pouch. He pricked his penis with a flint needle, just as the savage on Cuzmíl had done, and smeared the blood on his face and chest. I felt my legs abandon me, and only Guerrero's hand on my arm kept me from falling.

"Pray for me," Guerrero murmured. I wondered why he said such a thing to me, for I was in as much danger as he, but then I saw that the savages had hold of him and were pulling him away.

"It is a bath, only a lovely bath," he cried out to me as he was plunged into the steamy vapors of the stone enclosure.

Then I saw him lifted out of the chalky mist. He shivered momentarily in the sunlight. Arms supported him, raised him up.

"Our Father in heaven," I shouted as I saw that they

meant to throw him into the well, "take Gonzalo Guerrero to your bosom, O Lord, and make a special place for him in paradise."

I heard Guerrero scream "Thy will be done" as he soared through the air and into the water.

On This, the Twenty-sixth Day of May, in the Year of Our Lord and Savior Jesus Christ, One Thousand Five Hundred and Eleven

After three days, during which time the savages kept a vigil over the well, Guerrero rose from the water. So great was my happiness at seeing him again that I did not question the method by which he had survived. But as great as my happiness was, it was as nothing compared to that of the savages. They shrieked and wailed when they saw him, and when they pulled him out and raised him to their shoulders I knew that his rising alive from the depths of the well was proof to them that he was a god.

On This, the Twenty-ninth Day of May, in the Year of Our Lord and Savior Jesus Christ, One Thousand Five Hundred and Eleven

Guerrero has been given the house of a noble. A cluster of copper bells hangs on a string at the door, and the walls are painted with pictures in radiant colors. I was taken there this morning and made to sit in a corner near his bed, which was a straw-padded heap of saplings laced together by withes.

A young girl sat on a reed mat near the door rolling out the meal for the round cakes that the savages eat. She gracefully pinched a bit of dough from the grinding stone and mashed it between her palms, then patted it quickly from hand to hand until she had a flat cake, which she then laid out to cook on a heated ceramic plate. As each cake was finished, she piled a sauced concoction on top. Guerrero and I ate with great relish, and I remarked to him that the cooking of the savages was very refined.

When we had consumed all the cakes and were pleasantly sated, I asked Guerrero by what means he had remained submerged in the well for three days.

"I swam beneath the water until I reached the shelter of the wall," he told me, "and there I hid in the shrubs."

"They think you are a god," I told him, and he replied, "It was fear that kept me hidden. But then my legs grew numb and sleep overtook me and I fell like an ant into the water."

On This, the Thirtieth Day of May, in the Year of Our Lord and Savior Jesus Christ, One Thousand Five Hundred and Eleven

Today the headman Nachancán came to Guerrero's house. He touched the copper bells to announce his presence, and when he entered, accompanied by two savages, I sensed that some dreadful event was about to take place.

Guerrero was made to stand and pee into a gourd, and then without ceremony he was picked up and laid on his bed, whereupon Nachancán removed a flint needle from his skirt and pierced the cartilage at the base of Guerrero's nose and inserted a jade ornament. Guerrero screamed, but the two savages held him tight as Nachancán bent over him and with a flint knife cut circular holes in his earlobes and plugged them with gold disks. Then, with a fine flint needle dipped in blue liquid, Nachancán tattooed the figure of a jaguar on Guerrero's chest.

I was now trembling so violently that I was sure the savages could hear my bones shaking beneath my skin.

Nachancán then made a move as if to stick Guerrero's penis, but with a shriek that I have never heard from a man before, Guerrero grasped the soft skin and pierced it himself, and then watched weeping as his blood dripped onto the stone floor. When Nachancán had left, I tried to comfort Guerrero.

"You are still Gonzalo Guerrero, a seaman from Seville, a Catholic and a man of good nature," I told him, but he refused to listen.

On This, the Fourth Day of June, in the Year of Our Lord and Savior Jesus Christ, One Thousand Five Hundred and Eleven

Today Guerrero was taken to the *temescal*, where the steam is made. He sat in the cleansing mist, and when he emerged the savages dressed him in a breechclout and jaguar-skin skirt and put deerskin sandals on his feet. They plucked out his facial hair. They adorned his toes and fingers with rings and wound stone necklaces around his throat. Then Nachancán appeared and placed a green-plumed feather head-dress on his head. When they were through I was so fright-ened at his appearance that I shrank away from him. Only when he said, "Brother Aguilar, give me your blessing," did I awake to the knowledge that his fear was as great as mine.

On This, the Tenth Day of June, in the Year of Our Lord and Savior Jesus Christ, One Thousand Five Hundred and Eleven

In this morning's predawn darkness ten canoes filled with two hundred fifty savages of Chichén Itzá set out for the island of Cuzmíl. Halach Uinic Nachancán, the great cacique of Chichén Itzá, stood in the largest canoe, feathers cascading from his wooden headgear, his spear and hul-che at his side. Guerrero sat beside him in full warrior dress, but carried only a spear, since he is not yet expert in the use of the spear-throwing hul-che. As Guerrero's slave, I sat to the rear of him beside Nachancán's slave. We carried no weapons and wore nothing but breechclouts.

The flotilla of canoes creased the water rhythmically, oars dipping, scooping, rising to suck the air, then dipping again. As we journeyed, I wondered at the strangeness of the events and was preoccupied with thoughts of death. Guerrero, who has borne his travails exceedingly well, and for whom my pity increases daily, seemed resigned to whatever adventure lay ahead of him. His face is now a map of swollen, encrusted ridges where serpents and jaguars reside, pricked into the flesh of his face with sharp bones and made visible by the blue pigment that has been kneaded into the wounds. I try to remember his fair face as it was, how his eyes, the color of fresh-tilled earth, once gazed so charitably at everyone, but I am blinded by his ugliness.

When we reached Cuzmíl, the savages hid the canoes beneath the trees, and, since the inhabitants of the village still slept, Nachancán's men went freely from house to house setting roofs on fire. When the people emerged, coughing in the smoky gloom, the savages split the men's heads open with their half-moon palisades and ran spears through the bodies of the women and children. I watched as one watches a nightmare, my senses numb. The smell of burning flesh and the sight of bodies strewn over the ground sickened me.

At the house of Ah Balam, the savage who had torn out Captain Valdivia's heart, a hornet's nest was thrown inside. Ah Balam emerged, beating at his bitten skin and knocking the insects from around his face. He was naked except for the large ornaments in his nose and ears. Nachancán motioned for Guerrero to run Ah Balam through with his spear, and when Guerrero refused, Nachancán gave him a look of contempt, and turned and walked away.

At that moment Ah Balam made ready to fire an arrow into Nachancán's back, and I saw the agonized glance and felt the breath that Guerrero took as he drew his arm back and heaved his spear into Ah Balam's chest. I shuddered and collapsed onto the ground as Guerrero took the knife that Nachancán offered him and severed Ah Balam's head from its body.

Captain Valdivia's gold was retrieved, and Ah Balam's surviving men were taken prisoner. Nachancán sent men to investigate the fate of the seamen we had left behind when we escaped from Cuzmíl. There was nothing to be seen but empty, garbage-filled cages.

When we were once again in the canoes and rowing back toward Chichén Itzá, I stared as if bewitched at Guerrero. These others were savages, but he was a Spaniard. From whence comes this cruelty, this impulse to slaughter? I asked myself. Then I trembled at my own question.

On This, the Eleventh Day of June, in the Year of Our Lord and Savior Jesus Christ, One Thousand Five Hundred and Eleven

We returned to Chichén Itzá to great rejoicing. The market square had been cleared of its vendors and neat rows of colorful goods, and now the savages, drunk on a liquor of fermented honey and *balche* bark, reeled insensibly among vomit and broken pottery. As the captives were marched single-file through the square, their necks tied together with rope, the savages whipped them with tree limbs and jabbed at them with spears.

I feel very alone here. He who was so handsome of face and sweet in temper before he was pierced and tattooed is now turned to savage. I can only pray for the man that I know must still reside within that loathsome body.

On This, the Fourteenth Day of June, in the Year of Our Lord and Savior Jesus Christ, One Thousand Five Hundred and Eleven

I am still weak from fever. The curer saved me by administering a potion which he makes from the mold that forms on moistened cornmeal. Although these are savages, they are artful ones.

The nobles who created this great city of Chichén Itzá have disappeared, and their descendants live in grass-topped *nas* at the edge of the city. They do nothing but plan wars and fight battles, but I have seen the books of their ancestors. They revere these books as we do the Holy Bible. I am astonished by the riches they contain. My comprehension of their language is incomplete, but I believe they had knowledge of mathematics and invented a calendar to equal ours. Such degeneration of a great people cannot be explained.

On This, the Tenth Day of July, in the Year of Our Lord and Savior Jesus Christ, One Thousand Five Hundred and Eleven

I saw some savages worshipping today beneath a crucifix-shaped tree that they call *Yaxche*. I thought that they had knowledge of Christ, and so was overjoyed. My disappointment was great when I discovered that they believe that when one of them dies he climbs the branches of the tree to heaven.

There are places of burial nearby where the chieftains are lain. Maize and a few jade beads are dropped into the corpse's mouth, the maize to ensure that he will go to a place shaded by the first tree of the world, and the jade beads to guarantee that when he arrives there he will drink the elixir of the cacao bean for all eternity.

During festival months the savages make pilgrimages to the city of stone above the sea, where they worship the blue-eyed god Kukulcán. They call this place Tulum.

Although it is an ignoble comparison, the savages in some ways resemble Spaniards. They practice a form of baptism called *caputizihil*, and when they offer human sacrifices to their gods I am strongly reminded of our own Spanish inquisition and the burning of heretics.

Always with me now are the words of the psalm, "Some trust in chariots, and some in horses: but we will remember the name of the Lord our God."

On This, the Twenty-eighth Day of July, in the Year of Our Lord and Savior Jesus Christ, One Thousand Five Hundred and Eleven

In relations between men and women, I observe that customs in Chichén Itzá are different from those of Spain. The savages regard these urges as a necessary part of life and do not burden them with prudery. Of course, they have their injunctions, as we do ours. When planting their fields, the men abstain from union with their wives for many days beforehand and instead burn copal and pray to Xulab, god of the planet Venus and protector of hunters and agriculturists.

Since I promised God to be chaste, I am a great curiosity to the savages. They try in every way to tempt me, once by putting a woman in my bed while I slept. But my resolve is firm.

The savages believe that a man has not sinned until he has known a woman. In that way also they are like us.

On This, the Thirteenth Day of September, in the Year of Our Lord and Savior Jesus Christ, One Thousand Five Hundred and Eleven

Guerrero was given Nachancán's daughter Cuzam for his wife and I was given to the noble Taxmar as a slave. The savages have no draft animals, and I work as one in the cornfields. Taxmar is not cruel. He treats me no differently than a Spaniard treats his horse.

At the well today I saw my reflection for the first time since I was brought here. My hair and beard are long and matted. I wear breechclout and sandals and tie my hair back with a red leather thong. My skin has turned a deep brown from the sun. I have taken the Indian habit of squatting on my hind legs, which is more comfortable than standing for lengthy periods while waiting to be called by my master.

Not only does my appearance cause me dismay, but I am alarmed that when dealing with these savages I sometimes forget their barbarous natures. I pray for a miracle.

On This, the Fourteenth Day of July, in the Year of Our Lord and Savior Jesus Christ, One Thousand Five Hundred and Nineteen

I have not written in my breviary for eight years. There has been nothing to recount. But today while I worked in the fields, poking seed holes in the rocky soil with a sharp stick, I was summoned to appear in the house of Nachancán.

"A messenger came from the Mexicas with a letter from the captain of a giant canoe," Nachancán told me. "The captain of the canoe has come in search of two men with light skin." I struggled to control my tears, since crying is offensive to the halach uinic. "He has also sent me gifts," Nachancán said, and he held up a strand of green beads.

My joy was boundless. For eight years I have prayed morning, noon, and night that Guerrero and I would be rescued, and now a letter has come.

Noble Lords,
I have heard of the existence of two light-skinned men living among the Indians. By the description given me, I suspect that you are Spaniards. We come to explore and colonize these lands and are in need of people who can speak and interpret the native language, and will reward any fa-vors you grant us. I send you a map to guide your way to Cape Catoche, where our brigantine awaits your arrival. May the Lord be your protector and ours.

Hernán Cortés

The great Hernán Cortés!

On This, the Sixteenth Day of July, in the Year of Our Lord and Savior Jesus Christ, One Thousand Five Hundred and Nineteen

I have waited two days for Guerrero to return from Xel-Ha so that I may tell him of the letter. I worry that Cortés will leave without us. The letter was not dated. Perhaps it is months old. Or years old. I can wait for Guerrero no longer, but must make my way to Cape Catoche alone.

*On This, the Nineteenth Day of July, in the Year of Our Lord
and Savior Jesus Christ, One Thousand Five Hundred and
Nineteen*

I left Chichén Itzá at night, and, unseen by my master,
proceeded to where the canoes were kept beneath the trees
at the ocean's edge. I brought food and water, and God was
kind and sent a swift wind to blow behind me, so that by
dawn of the next day I arrived at Cape Catoche and there
found anchored the brigantine that Cortés had written of.

"*Dios y Santa María y Sevilla,*" I shouted to the men on
deck.

My appearance, to which I have not given any thought for
these many years, so shocked the seamen on board that when
I neared the ship they stared at me as though I were a
savage.

"It is I, Gerónimo de Aguilar of Seville. I am a Spaniard.
Do you hear me? A Spaniard."

My Spanish must have sounded as strange to their ears as
it did to mine, but finally, confounded at my image, but
convinced of who I claimed to be, they took me aboard.

I had carried *papadzules* with me to eat, but when offered
food by the brigantine's cook, I readily accepted, excited at
the prospect of once again tasting Spanish food.

"Just so did I stare at the Indians when first we came upon
them, Gonzalo and I," I told the seamen who crowded around,
faces transfixed, to watch me eat.

I was given smoked venison and a bowl of vegetable stew.
The meat was as stringy as a lute and the stew as bland as
marsh water. I was finally forced to spit the masticated venison onto the table.

"The Indians use a spice which makes their food very
tasty," I told them. "It is called *xnipec*—which means wet
nose of the dog, for it brings water to your nose when eaten.
But I do not recommend that you visit them just for the
tastiness of the food."

The seamen laughed at my wittiness, but as I stared at the
inedible fare in front of me, I felt an unaccountable sadness at
my own words.

On This, the Twentieth Day of July, in the Year of Our Lord and Savior Jesus Christ, One Thousand Five Hundred and Nineteen

I was brought before the great Hernán Cortés today. He is a short man with a long face and eyes that struggle to stay open beneath tight lids. Although the day was hot and his quarters on the ship airless, he was attired in red velvet tunic and black stockings. Having become used to the daily bathing habits of the Maya, the stink of him, which followed his every movement, crept sickeningly up my nostrils.

His compartment contained a foul collection of soiled undergarments and discarded leggings. Ledger books and papers had escaped his desk and spilled onto the carpeted floor. In a small alcove beneath a gold crucifix was his bed, its embroidered silk coverlet barely visible beneath maps and papers of every description.

As Cortés swept the litter from a pair of brocade chairs and bade me sit down, I felt great humility before him.

"I have come by orders of Diego Velasquez, the new governor of Cuba, to reconnoiter this coast," Cortés told me. "The story of light-skinned men living in the interior has followed us since we landed on Cuzmíl. Frankly, I had not thought it possible. But you have come alone. Where is the other man?"

An urge to pray, such as I have never known before, came over me at that moment, and instead of answering I produced my book of hours, and invited the great captain to kneel with me and say a prayer. He was quite inquisitive as to the writing on this breviary, and I explained to him that I have submitted my thoughts and recounted the details of my sojourn among the Maya in its margins.

"And have you kept your faith, Brother Aguilar?" he asked me, to which I replied that it had been difficult at times, but that I had.

"But where is the other man?" he again asked me. Not willing to kneel next to him in prayer again so soon, I was forced to answer.

"Ah Itzam has gone—" I began, and was interrupted by the startled expression on Cortés's face. "His name is Gonzalo Guerrero, Your Excellency," I explained, "but when we were captured by the Maya of Chichén Itzá, the cacique Nachancán suspected that Guerrero might be a god, since we had escaped death at the hands of the Maya of Cuzmíl. As a test Guerrero was thrown into the cenote—into a great well, and when he reappeared after three days, it was to them as though Christ had risen. They renamed him Ah Itzam, the magician of the water, and made him a lord of the tribe. I would have brought him with me, but he has gone to war with another tribe in order to bring captives to Chichén Itzá for sacrifice. It is the season of drought in Chichén Itzá and if sacrifices are not offered to the rain god Chac, then he will not release water from the heavens."

It was then, by the look of horror on Cortés's face, that I realized that my words were not fully understood and resolved to be more moderate in my recounting of the details of my sojourn with the Maya.

After a while I noticed that Cortés's breathing and color had returned to normal, and he asked, "And what of Don Pedro Valdivia?" Although I now hesitated to speak, I knew that there was no kind way to reveal the truth.

"The cacique of the tribe on Cuzmíl, Ah Balam, killed Captain Valdivia and cut out his heart and then ate him. Nine others were also killed."

At this point the great captain bade me say another prayer, which request I complied with. And then he asked me, "Do you think that these savages will be a formidable enemy in our colonization of these lands?" and, replying as respectfully as I could, I said, "They are fierce warriors, Your Excellency, although their weaponry is primitive."

"But do they have cannons?" he asked, and I replied, "No, but they are expert in the use of the spear and the hul-che, which is a very powerful sling for throwing short spears."

Cortés then showed great interest in the gold that Captain Valdivia's ship had carried. "Where is it kept?" he wanted to know, and I replied that I had no knowledge of that, but that it was certainly not spent, since the Maya use cacao and salt as money and have no use for gold.

This seemed to excite him even more. He rose from his chair and walked around the compartment several times, and then said, "Will Guerrero help us recover this gold for Spain, Brother Aguilar?" which question could not be answered simply, and so I attempted to describe what had become of Gonzalo Guerrero in the eight years that he had spent with the Maya.

"He is a great warrior," I told him, "and has a wife and

three sons," all of which was received well by the great captain. "His appearance is quite altered, Your Excellency. His body is tattooed. Beads and jewels hang from his nose and ears." At this last Cortés cringed as he visualized what I was describing to him. "And his Catholic faith, that too has been damaged. He mixes Catholic rites with pagan ones and participates in the sacrifice of prisoners."

The violence with which my news was received by Cortés altered my impression of him as a tranquil man. His eyes bulged and he pounded one fist into the palm of the other hand angrily. "He is a savage, Brother Aguilar, nothing but a savage" were his words to me, to which I replied with some degree of certainty of my own, "But we are all savages."

On This, the Thirteenth Day of August, in the Year of Our Lord and Savior Jesus Christ, One Thousand Five Hundred and Nineteen

My absence from Chichén Itzá was not noticed. I returned as a great celebration in honor of Ah Itzam's victory in Xel-Ha was in progress. A captured warrior had been sacrificed, and it had so pleased the gods that the following week, during the festival of Uo, the rains came and soaked the fields.

Slaves were not allowed in Ah Itzam's presence except to serve him, but I held a special position, and so was admitted to his house. He appeared weary as we sat opposite each other on the reed mat. Cuzam worked at her loom near the door, humming under her breath, a *tixzula* flower in her braided hair. I had never known her to speak much, but now she spoke hardly at all. I spared Ah Itzam no details of my encounter with Captain Cortés. I told him that the great captain waited for us both. I spoke with great care, fearful that, as with Cortés, my words would be misunderstood.

"Captain Cortés has asked us to help him take these lands and its treasures for Spain," I said to him, to which Ah Itzam responded by asking his wife to bring his three sons to him.

"Look at my children, Brother Aguilar," he said. "Are they not beautiful children? Could it be possible that I would leave children such as these? And my face and body, look how my face is bored and marked and my body is painted." There was sadness in his voice as he spoke and he pulled at his pendulous, jewel-filled earlobes. "Can I go among Spaniards with ears like these?"

I assured him that God saw only his soul, but as I spoke, even I saw the merit of what he was saying.

"The Spaniards are fierce warriors," Ah Itzam said. "Although we defeated them at Chetumal, and I took their gold, they fought bravely. And they have gunpowder and food and will bring more soldiers from Spain. But they have angered me. They killed the babies of the Mexicas and cut off the breasts of their women. I have been alert and vigilant watching for a sign, and last night I saw the shape of the jaguar in the night sky. If Captain Cortés would conquer these lands for Spain, then he must conquer me, too."

I could think of nothing else, and so we prayed together, and before I left, Ah Itzam said, "Send me a gift of beads when you return to Captain Cortés, and I will show them to my sons and tell them that they are from my people in Spain."

On This, the Eighteenth Day of November, in the Year of Our Lord and Savior Jesus Christ, One Thousand Five Hundred and Thirty-Six

I suffer from a stiffening of the joints and so spend my time reading or sitting in my garden. My services to Hernán Cortés have brought me the reward of this house in Seville and servants enough to attend me as I drift into old age. I have few visitors and no desire for any, and so was surprised this afternoon when Father Rodriguez appeared.

"I have news of Gonzalo Guerrero," he began at once, hardly sipping the sherry that I offered him.

I was startled, for I had not had news of Guerrero for the past seventeen years.

"I received a letter from Father Joaquin in Honduras," Father Rodriguez continued. "Gonzalo Guerrero is dead."

I immediately said a prayer, which did not relieve the deep despondency that came over me at the tidings.

"He had won many battles against our Spanish forces," Father Rodriguez said, "and had become a scourge in the Caribbean, stealing gold from Spanish camps. And so Adelantado Montejo was waiting in Honduras with cannons and men to fight him there if he attacked. It was a Sunday morning when he arrived."

"He knew the soldiers would be at mass," I said, shaking my head in anticipation of what would be said next. Father

Rodriguez nodded soberly at my perspicacity, and resumed his narrative.

"Father Joaquin was conducting mass for the soldiers in the garrison church when he heard drums and whistles, and then Guerrero burst in. Father Joaquin said that although he had been warned of an attack, he was so startled by the sight of him, bejeweled and tattooed and with a mighty feathered headdress on his head, that he dropped the wafers as well as the communion cup."

"Did he speak?" I asked, and Father Rodriguez said no, that he had not said a word. "But Father Joaquin noted that his eyes were very melancholy," he continued. "He was about to welcome him to prayer, but before he could utter a word, Guerrero shot an arrow into the soldier who was about to receive holy communion at the rail."

At this point in the recitation I broke into weeping, and Father Rodriguez stopped his narrative long enough for me to recover, after which he continued.

"Guerrero then ran out of the church, and a great battle ensued. Father Joaquin said that the bravery of the savages was astonishing, that they threw stones, they attacked with arrows and spears and swords of flint and obsidian, and that as Spaniards lay dying Guerrero ran among them clubbing and then stabbing them in the chest with his three-pronged claw knife. The falconets of the soldiers, ammunition exhausted, became useless, and they too resorted to swords and crossbows."

"How did he die?" I asked, and Father Rodriguez replied, "It was from the shot of a harquebus mounted on the roof of the barracks."

I could envisage Guerrero's men throwing stones at cannons.

"Was he given last rites?" I asked Father Rodriguez, and he replied, "Father Joaquin ran to him when he was summoned by Adelantado Montejo. Guerrero was still alive and able to comprehend what was said to him. Father Joaquin offered absolution, but Guerrero did not reply."

"Perhaps it was not Guerrero," I said.

"He had fine brown hair and a high-bridged Spanish nose," Father Rodriguez answered, and I nodded, my heart heavy with grief.

"Father Joaquin did not hear Guerrero renounce his faith," Father Rodriguez told me, "but since he had refused the rites, there was nothing to be done but leave the body to the savages. In the evening the Maya came, kicking up plumes of dust to conceal themselves, and they took him away."

"He was once a fine man," I offered by way of explanation, and Father Rodriguez replied, "He was worse than a thousand Indians because he had Christ and turned away from him."

I have written no books of my experiences, nor have I spoken of them overmuch to anyone, since it would contribute nothing to the study of human imperfection. But I could not agree with Father Rodriguez's opinion of Guerrero. He did not live among the Maya as I did. He cannot fathom the soul of another.

When Father Rodriguez departed, I was transported in memory to Chichén Itzá, my head filled with images that lingered through the evening and brought me to my desk. And so I have recounted the final detail of my sojourn among the Maya in the margins of this breviary, and I will place it in the monastery in Seville, as Father Rodriguez has suggested. Perhaps there the Jesuits will find good use for it.

37

"I'm too lazy to paint today." Andre sighed. He put aside his paints and stared idly at the ceiba trees that hung dolorously over the ruins. "Maybe I'll just watch you and Lidia dig."

"He who does nothing gets no lunch," the professor said. He bent to his labors, squatting, dusting, picking, sorting. Lidia brushed clingy earth from the assortment of treasures. Pottery fragments with fanciful markings, copper bells, a ceramic trumpet, a whistle made of the leg bone of a deer, reed flutes, a conch horn, flint knives, polished green stones.

Lidia tooted a mournful wail through the conch shell.

"But can you play 'Cielito Lindo'?" Andre asked.

"You may laugh, Andre," said the professor, "but Dzitnup may yet prove to be profitable, God willing. The Maya were here, drinking the water from the cenote, playing their instruments." He paused and wiped his face with his handkerchief, leaving a dusty streak across one cheek. "Patience is all that's required."

"My patience is boundless," Andre said. "But I think you're digging in the wrong place. You should dig over there, near those two mounds."

The professor glanced at the mounds in question. A stone arch topped the highest rise.

"If I were a Maya," Andre said, "and I had something of importance, I'd put it high up. It's more artistic. And I would put a stone arch over it to give it dignity and—"

"Bring it closer to God," Lidia said.

"Ach! But these objects weren't put here purposely," said the professor. "The stone arches and stelae were incidental to what the Maya were doing, not planned."

"Still," insisted Andre, "Brother Aguilar wrote that the Maya were very orderly. Orderly people don't drop stone arches here and there for no reason."

"You're no archaeologist," the professor said, "but you may be right. We'll explore the arch beginning tomorrow. But now it's time to eat."

Lidia spread a blanket beneath a ceiba tree and then retrieved their lunch from the mule's saddle bag. She removed the banana leaves from around the *cochinita pibil* and sprinkled the meat with black bean paste. Her fingers worked nimbly, and not a drop of the spicy bean paste was dripped as she folded the tortillas and handed one to Andre and one to the professor.

"Juanita's bean paste will be my undoing," said the professor, biting into the meat-filled tortilla. "My stomach has grown three inches in three months."

"Juanita seems to know what you like," said Andre with a smile.

"We're all mature enough not to be ashamed of our sexual urges," said the professor as Lidia's face flushed with embarrassment. "I tell you truthfully I find European culture to be much less satisfying than the Mesoamerican. Tell me where in Europe I would find a woman like Juanita, a modest woman by all standards, but not a prudish one, who welcomes me back without question after a two-year absence. And the life she endures no European woman would endure. Married at ten years of age, and a widow at twelve; since she has no children she is the property of whoever claims her. When I'm here, I claim her, but she isn't mine."

"Our Lord seems very far away in Xan-Xel," Lidia said. "I speak to Juanita of Christ, and she tells me that she accepts him as her Savior. But then she prays to Chac and Itzamná and believes in superstition."

"With all the missionary work of the Spaniards, they were still left with heathens on their hands," Andre said. "It shows you the great resistance we have."

"You're not a heathen, Andre," Lidia said, and she handed him another tortilla. "And I don't think they tried very hard to bring Christ to the Maya. As for Brother Aguilar's breviary, I think he only wrote in it to pass the time."

"No, he was writing to us," said the professor. "He knew that one day I would come here and you would hand me his book, and we would uncover secrets too wondrous to be believed."

Suddenly a moist stillness descended. The leaves did not rustle and the perfume of the jungle became clotted, dank-smelling, and overripe.

"It's going to rain," the professor said. His back was against the trunk of a laurel tree, and as he ate, black bean paste oozed out the sides of the tortilla and dotted his face and fingers and the front of his shirt.

"It looks like it's going to be heavy," Andre said. He and the professor quickly picked up the food while Lidia gathered up the utensils and folded the blanket. The rain had started and the three of them were running toward the mule when the professor stumbled and let out a cry of pain.

"What is it?" asked Andre, turning around.

"The tree," the professor gasped. His face was mottled, his breath wheezing and stertorous. He fell backward on the rain-washed underbrush and pulled at his shirt. Lidia ran to him and knelt in the mud at his side. A scorpion clung to his stomach, the pincer marks visible where it had squeezed the skin with its claws before injecting its venom.

"Don't touch it," he gasped. His fingers trembled as he clutched the scorpion's midsection and dropped it to the ground beside him. Then he fainted.

"I'll hold him by the shoulders if you can lift his legs," said Andre.

"Yes, I can manage." She pulled the professor's booted legs away from the brush. His head bounced against the wet leaves, his face a pale yellow against the glistening green.

When they reached the rim of the cenote, Andre pointed to the shrub-covered mounds. "The stone arch. We'll stay there until the rain stops."

Lidia ran back and got the blanket. She covered the professor with it, and she and Andre half-carried, half-dragged him up the slick slope. Carved Maya faces stared down at them from the stone stelae that stood guard at the top of the ruin.

"Hans, can you speak?" She took the rebozo from around

her shoulders and wiped the rain from his face. Andre held his wrist and felt for a pulse.

"Hans, it's Lidia. Can you answer me?"

"His pulse is weak," Andre said.

"Look in the case he carries," said Lidia. "Maybe there is something in there that we can give him."

Andre went back down the slope and retrieved the emergency kit. He and Lidia looked through the vials, rapidly reading labels and opening bottles to sniff their contents.

"There's nothing that says 'for scorpion bites' on any of these," Andre said.

Lidia wiped the professor's wet face again. "His eyes don't move beneath the eyelids," she said.

"We'll have to get him back to Xan-Xel and send someone for Conrad."

"To put him on the mule would take two men," she said. "I know that I'm not strong enough to help you. Even if I could, the rain is too heavy to walk the mule through the jungle with him on it. It would be hours before we reached Xan-Xel."

Andre hesitated. She looked too frail, too delicate, too helpless to leave.

"Hans might die," she said. "Kiss me before you go."

The professor moaned and turned his head in agitation from side to side.

"*Protégeme, Dios mio, que me refugio en ti,*" prayed Lidia. She crossed herself, and then arranged the blankets more securely around the professor's body. "God is watching over you, Hans. Put your faith in him."

She prayed, and it seemed to her that the professor's breathing became more regular and his thrashing less violent. The rain had also stopped. Boggy spots on the jungle floor had become steaming pools.

"San Ignacio, San Diego, San Pedro—" She recited the saints to him, and when she had named all that she could remember, she started on the festival days.

"Hans, the rain has stopped. Listen to the birds. They're so noisy today, so loud, as though they wanted to wake you up."

She hummed to him and sang all the songs she knew, but the professor's eyes remained closed.

Overhead, large black birds circled and swooped. Lidia

watched them as they dived, reconnoitered, buzzed through the top of the arch where she sat cradling the professor's head. Some of the birds sat like sentinels on heavy tree limbs not too far away, staring, waiting, flapping their wings. *Zopilotes*. Death birds.

"Hans, are you awake yet?"

The birds circled above their heads. She covered the professor's face with the blanket and then rolled him closer to the base of the tallest stela. The stela's carved face looked directly at her, a demon-god, eyes crossed, with jagged teeth in a grotesquely gaping mouth. Kukulcán, the feathered serpent, writhed between its teeth.

She recited five Paternosters and eight Ave Marías. The sky cleared, shafts of sun pierced the trees, the *zopilotes* flew higher in the sky, the sentinels gave up their posts.

"You're safe now, Hans," she said.

The cenote below was swollen with the rain and overflowing. She strained to hear Andre's voice over the sound of rushing water. Finally, exhausted, she fell asleep.

"Oh!" She awoke disoriented, her arm asleep where she had twisted it beneath her. A dazzle of sunlight struck her eyes, and when she looked at the stela, it seemed that the serpent Kukulcán was spinning and twining in a shiver of sun. She rose and walked toward it, touched its head as it turned in a silvery spiral. She felt nothing but the quiet stone beneath her fingers.

Then her eyes fell on the pile of rock behind the stela. There was symmetry in its arrangement. She bent and began pulling rocks away. Then she sat down on the ground and peered into the blackness of the cavern and the staircase they had been hiding.

Brother Aguilar had written in the margins of his breviary, "There are places of burial nearby where the chieftains are laid."

"Hans, a burial chamber." She shook him. "Brother Aguilar's breviary." The professor's eyelids flickered. He breathed evenly now, the rasping gone.

She stood up. "Dear Jesus, I put myself in your hands."

The stairs didn't crumble as she descended, but in the darkness she bumped her head on low-hanging rocks. At each twist of stair it became lighter, the colors on the wall to her right more vivid. Grotesque images pounced on her, threatened her. Paintings of men in feathered headdresses, men on horses, men in armor, men with abnormally large penes, fierce jaguars, fanged serpents, women giving birth to animals, men strung together penis to penis.

"San Pedro, protect me," she cried.

The stairway widened. She was no longer suffocating. Then the stairs ended and she was on a plateau in a grotto. Stalactites verged downward like the steeples of a church. In the center of the grotto, a cenote of purest aquamarine shimmered in a shaft of sunlight. She lifted her head up and a hundred feet above her she could see the sky.

She fell to her knees. "Holy Virgin, Mother of God, I am brought to paradise."

The skeleton sat on a throne of carved jaguars. A feathered headdress perched on its skull, rings of jade and pearls circled the bones of its fingers and toes. Large green emeralds slept in empty eye sockets and fire opals nestled in its ear openings like pigeon eggs in a nest. A *hul-che* stood ready at the side of the throne to repel intruders.

She approached the skeleton. As a child she had visited the Pantheon in Guanajuato and played at the feet of the mummies who lay there. They seemed very peaceful, as though they were resting after their long labors. Her grandmother said that they were to be respected, not feared, because they had been loved in life.

"What do you want to tell me, señor?"

One finger out of all the rest pointed backward. She followed the finger into a dark tunnel filled with hand-hewn crates. In the hazy light she could not be sure what the crates held. They looked like the wood chips the Maya used for their cooking fires. She plucked one up and held it between her fingers. It was cold to the touch. She put it to her mouth. It clicked against her teeth, tasted metallic on her tongue.

"*Gracias a Dios!*"

She slipped the coin into the folds of her rebozo, then skipped through the tunnel like a child.

"*Gracias, señor,*" she said as she genuflected before the skeleton.

Then she scrambled up the steps and into the light.

* * *

"I've found a tomb, with crates of gold and the skeleton of a man seated on a carved throne," Lidia said. She pressed the gold coin against the professor's cheek to startle him into consciousness.

"Gold?" he murmured, his eyelids quivering.

"Gold," she repeated.

He grunted and shook his head to clear the fog and then gave a birdlike screech when he finally realized what she was saying.

38

Conrad held the stethoscope to the professor's chest, listening. "What kind of scorpion was it?"

"The kind that doesn't kill you, or I would be dead," the professor answered. "What's that you're putting on me?"

"Tyrothricin. It'll prevent the bite from becoming infected."

"Luís and I will help load him onto the wagon," Andre said.

"No!" said the professor, pulling himself into a sitting position.

Conrad had been putting his things back in his satchel. He looked up. "No?"

"I am perfectly well. You can send Luís back to Valladolid."

"This is craziness, Hans," Andre said. "Do you intend to walk back to Xan-Xel? You're hardly strong enough to sit up."

"Give me your hands, and I'll show you how strong I am," said the professor, and as Conrad and Andre helped him to his feet, he whispered, "Lidia has found a Maya tomb."

"The stone arch," Andre said.

"Yes." Hans held out the gold coin that Lidia had given him and it shone with a burnished glare in the sunlight. "It must be just the four of us. No one else."

"You can go, Luís," Conrad called out to the muleteer.

"Only once before did I hear of such a tomb, but it had been looted," said the professor as they descended. "There were two skeletons and nothing but cooking utensils remained."

As the narrow shafts of light grew into an incandescent glow that enlarged their vision, the paintings on the walls on either side of the stairway seemed to leap out at them, pulsating and vibrating with life. When they had reached the bottom, the professor collapsed on the cold stones, his brow ridged with perspiration. "I have never seen such a sight as this."

Andre wandered dazedly around the pool, which was now a rainbow of colors in the refracted light. "I never imagined," he said.

"Magnificent!" Conrad said. "To see a specimen such as this, of such age, in these surroundings—" He had already taken a metal calibrator from his satchel and was measuring the skeleton's wrist bone.

"But the gold, you must see that, too," Lidia said, and she ran ahead of them into the tunnel. "Have you ever seen such riches?" She went from crate to crate picking up handfuls of coins and letting them drop through her fingers. "Listen to the friendly sound they make."

Conrad held up one of the coins and studied its markings. "They're Spanish ducats, sixteenth century."

The professor leaned against the limestone scarp muttering, "*Mein Gott, mein Gott.*"

"How much?" asked Andre.

"Oh, I don't know. In pesos?"

"Dollars."

"Probably millions." Conrad grinned. He picked up a few coins and threw them at Andre, who picked up a few and threw them back at him, and then the four of them sat on the floor of the chamber and pelted one another with Spanish ducats and howled with happiness.

They slept in the grotto that night, and in the morning the professor was almost back to himself, except for a draining wound in his stomach, which Conrad kept medicated with the new antibiotic that he had brought. They ate the rock-hard tortillas that remained of the previous day's lunch, and then Conrad began the examination of the skeleton.

"A robust man, probably a European," he said. "A lot of care was taken in preparing the skeleton. It was probably left in the open until the flesh was gone and then gold wire was used to join the bones together so the skeleton could be placed in an upright position on the throne." He had his

satchel open and was measuring bones and checking teeth.
"He's not brachycephalic—the brow is not flattened—so it is
definitely not a Maya."

"But it was certainly someone very important," Andre said.

"His bones are so beautiful," said Lidia, "just like ivory."
She ran her fingers over the smooth bone of the forearm. "Is
he very old?"

"Very old," Conrad said.

A gold breast plate with emeralds and sapphires duplicat-
ing the image of a quetzal bird rested against the throne.
Andre picked it up and placed it against the skeleton's ribs.

"Tell me, Andre," said the professor, "can you draw a
picture of what the skeleton looked like in life?"

"I don't think I can. No, I'd be guessing."

"I'll help you," Conrad said. He waited for Andre to pick
up his sketch pad and pencil. "The arch of the nose is high,
the nostrils thin, the face elongated." He looked over at what
Andre had drawn. "The chin and nose balance the jaw,
Andre."

Andre brushed the soft pencil marks away with a rag and
drew the jaw line again. "Like so?"

"Yes. The cheekbones are flat and slightly sunken. There
are wisps of straight brown hair still clinging to the skull high
on the forehead and falling to the tips of the small ears. The
eyes are round and deep set beneath a delicate brow."

"The lips must be thin, then," Andre said.

"Must be," Conrad replied.

"If he were killed by cannon fire, could you tell it?" the
professor asked.

"The bones are splintered in the pelvis and thorax," said
Conrad. "They're wounds that could have been made by
cannon fire."

The drawing was finished. Andre held it up for everyone to
see.

"It's Gonzalo Guerrero, of course," the professor said.

" 'And he who was so handsome of face and sweet in
temper before he was pierced and tattooed is now turned to
savage,' " Lidia said.

"What a sight he must have been in battle," said Conrad.

"Ach! he was fierce," the professor said. "He fought as a
Maya and was a hero to them. When he was killed in Honduras, the Spaniards left his body on the battlefield, not knowing what to do with a lapsed Catholic of such magnitude. The

Maya retrieved him, and although the breviary stops at that point, we know that they thought Guerrero was a god and that the gold he brought to them were pieces of the sun. Of course they would send him to the next world with his gold. And all the gold he won for them in battle. And any gold they got from the Mexicas in trade. What did the Maya want with gold when they had cacao beans?"

"No matter what they buried him with, all of this belongs to the Mexican government, I'm afraid," Conrad said. "The grotto and everything in it—gold, skeleton, jewels."

"It's bounty of the sea," said Andre, "brought ashore and buried."

"On Mexican soil," Conrad said.

"Does that mean you don't want any?"

Conrad smiled. "I didn't say that."

"The gold would never reach the Mexican people, anyway," said Lidia simply. "Those in government always steal what belongs to us."

"Lidia is right," the professor said. "My conscience is clear. But there is the larger problem of removing the gold and getting it out of Mexico. We can't very well present Spanish ducats to the Bank of Mexico and ask for pesos in exchange."

Conrad sat staring at the skeleton. "I can get it out, get it to the United States."

"How?" asked the professor.

"Through my work. My reports and experiments leave Mexico City for the States via diplomatic courier. No one will know what I'm sending. Of course, it will take some time to get it all out. I won't be able to send too much at once."

"But ducats? Who will buy Spanish ducats in such quantities without wanting to know more?" the professor asked.

"Teddy's brother is a banker in Atlanta," said Conrad. "He'll know what to do, what to melt down, what to sell for numismatic value. That's why I say it will take time."

"He'll want something for his trouble," Andre said.

"Of course," said Conrad. "He's a banker." And then he smiled again. "I told you, it's Teddy's brother. Very honorable, very southern. He can be trusted."

It was raining again when they left the tomb. Lidia showed them how the stones had been placed in the entrance, and when she was sure that stones and leaves and earth were smoothed and arranged so that everything looked as it did before, they set out for the village.

"Wait up, Andre, I have something to tell you," Conrad said as they walked through the downpour, their feet sinking into the boggy path, their clothes hanging wet and heavy on them.

"It sounds ominous," Andre said.

"You be the judge. Trotsky is dead. Someone from Spain, a man named Mercader, said to be a Stalinist agent, murdered him with a hatchet blow to the head."

Andre stopped walking. He stared at Conrad through sheets of rain.

"The police are no longer interested in you as a suspected assassin, but the newspaper made a point of listing you as one of the few associates of Trotsky's who still remains alive. Watch yourself, Andre. Stalin is intent on murdering you all."

39

Four years was not too long when measured in Yucatán time, so that when the man in the large sombrero and drooping mustache came into the village and asked Juanita if there had been any visitors lately, she thought immediately of Andre and Lidia. But something about the man unsettled her, and so she pretended not to understand.

"Do you know anyone named Hans Kobermann?" asked the man. His jodhpurs were new and still had bits of featherlight thread clinging to the sturdy material.

Hans had said that he and Andre would be sent to Germany if the Federales found them in the village. The village *cacique* had said not to speak to strangers, because they might be Federales looking for men to help the Americans fight a war against Germany. Dr. Whitworth had said to take care of Lidia, not to let her do anything strenuous or she might lose the baby, and that if the Federales came asking about him, to tell them that he had returned to the United States.

It was very confusing. Germany was Hans's village. Why would the Mexicans want to fight with it? Why would they want to send Hans back if he didn't want to go? And as for Federales, Juanita didn't know what the Federales looked like, but something told her that they didn't wear floppy sombreros and speak Spanish with an accent that she had never heard before. So she merely smiled at the man.

"I'd like a drink," the man said.

She went into the *choza* and poured a cup of water from the pottery jug. A gnat floated on the surface of the water. She plucked it out with her thumb and forefinger and blew on it until, with glistening wings puffed dry, it squirmed a few times and flew away.

Not too many people stopped in Xan-Xel. Dr. Whitworth and another man came twice a month and took away boxes of little dolls and arrowheads that Hans dug out of the ruins. Somebody once came to deliver more empty boxes to Hans. She couldn't remember when that was. Lidia was pregnant then, and she lost the baby two weeks after that, so it was—Juanita shook her head. Lidia was pregnant now for the fourth time. She had been pregnant every year and hadn't had a baby yet. She looked so healthy when she was pregnant, never complained of sickness or tiredness, but something always happened, and then the goddess Ixchel would kill the baby before it could be born. Lidia went to Valladolid and prayed in the church every time a baby was taken. Juanita had offered to have the *ah-pulyaah* perform his black magic, but Lidia had refused.

Juanita came out of the *choza* and handed the man the cup of water.

"It's very hot here," he said when he had drunk it down. He wiped his forehead with his sleeve. "There are some ruins near here, aren't there?"

Moments went by. "Many," she said.

"Where? To the east of here?" He was looking in the direction of the ruins that Hans always went to.

"My friend is an amateur archaeologist," he said. He pointed to his companion who stood partially hidden by zapote trees at the edge of the jungle.

Juanita stared at him without speaking. Finally he got tired and walked away.

Lidia prepared their lunch on the stone ledge near what remained of Guerrero's toes. Conrad said that the miscarriages that occurred midway through her pregnancy could be prevented if she were in a hospital under close supervision. But she was now well past the midway mark, and although slow in her movements and suffering from occasional dizzy spells, she held tenaciously to this one.

"I think I have made up my mind to go to Guatemala," the professor said. He sat at the edge of the cenote, wriggling his bare toes blissfully in the warm water. "I've explored every inch of this grotto. I know every glyph and carving in it. What more is there to do but grow richer? I'll never spend the money I have now. Perhaps I'll go to Tikal and explore the ruins there. I was there in 1933 with a team of archaeologists. We all fell ill with malaria, and I was sent home. But I remember that it was very impressive, almost as impressive as Chichén Itzá."

He pulled his feet out of the water, wiped them, and then put on his socks and heavy boots. "Ach! Andre, don't you ever have an urge for adventure? Loading gold ducats into boxes doesn't challenge my scientific mind."

"But then you're an explorer and I'm an artist, and that's the difference between us."

They had had this conversation before. For the past two years, while dollars piled high in an American bank, Hans had shown signs of restlessness. He would say over and over again that he was going to go to Guatemala, and Andre would say go ahead. But he never did.

Andre stretched out on his elbow and watched Lidia dice the meat and chiles together. He had begun a series of portraits of her. He liked the mellowness of her body when she was pregnant, the fuller breast, the rise of abdomen. She always appeared so fragile to him, but when she was pregnant he realized that there were muscles banding the rising abdomen, and that they were strong enough to levitate a baby, steady enough to be its fulcrum. She said she was ungainly, but he recognized the subtle maturity in her, the prideful charm that she had never had before. He knew that she was beautiful.

"I think you should certainly go to Guatemala if you want to," Andre said. "Your share will be taken into account. You know that."

"That you should even hint that I don't trust you—"

"Then go."

Lidia wrapped some crisp bits of meat in a tortilla and placed it on Guerrero's lap. She said a few words of prayer and rapidly crossed herself. The first time she had done it, Andre had been dumbstruck, but Hans had laughed and said, "Such a look of horror, Andre. How do we know he's not hungry, just as we are?" Now it was taken as a matter of course, hardly noticed, an eccentricity of Lidia's, as was the small prayer of thanks she recited to the skeleton each time they left the grotto.

"What about you?" said the professor. "You ought to do what Conrad says and take Lidia to Mexico City. There are hospitals there. They can do tests—"

"We'll stay in Xan-Xel," said Lidia firmly.

"You should make her leave, Andre," the professor said. "Stalin's forgotten all about you. You're a rich man. You can afford to get your wife the best medical care in the world."

"Have you spoken to Stalin?" asked Lidia. "How are you so certain that Andre is in no danger?"

"Ach! I think it was all a misunderstanding to begin with. To think that Stalin cares about you enough to hunt you down in the middle of the jungle—"

"Conrad tells me that Stalin's agents murdered two more Trotskyites this past year," Andre said.

"How did they die?" the professor asked. "Did they choke on a lamb chop bone, perhaps?"

"One was axed in his apartment in London. The other one was shot on a New York street by someone in a passing car. Their names were on the same list that mine was. Anyway, there's still gold to be taken away, and it's peaceful here. We have nowhere else to go—nowhere else we want to go."

"I'll say no more about it, then," the professor said.

"And there is nothing wrong with me this time," said Lidia. "This child will be born alive." Then she added quickly, "If God decrees."

When they had finished their lunch, she packed up the remains while the professor napped on the edge of the cenote and Andre prepared another box of gold to be carried back to Xan-Xel.

"Look, Andre," she said, staring up at the wreath of sky above them. "Have you ever seen such a blue?"

He embraced her and felt the baby curling against his stomach. "Are you happy?" she asked.

"I have everything," he said.

Hans heard the sounds first. Andre nailed the wooden top to the box and wrapped it with a blanket. "Animals have ferreted out our garbage," he said.

"I will go up first," said Hans.

"We'll follow in a minute," Andre said.

Lidia knelt before the jaguar throne. "*Gracias, Señor Guerrero, por todo que nos ha dado. Que le vaya bien.*" She rose heavily, holding her stomach with her hands. "I won't be able to do that too many more times," she said, smiling at Andre.

A scream tore through the silence. It ripped through the dark cavern, bounced off limestone walls, hung in the air near their ears. A long, whistling, moaning scream followed by short, staccato ones.

Andre put his hand on her arm to steady her and then ran up the steps. She leaned dizzily against the stone wall, eyes tightly shut, and waited. There was no more sound. Several minutes passed and Andre did not return. She touched her stomach, frightened that the child would come now, but it moved normally within her. There were no contractions, no sharp pains or gush of water. She moved away from the wall and walked with effort to the jaguar throne.

"*Por favor, señor.*" She grunted slightly as she bent forward and picked up the *hul-che* at Guerrero's feet. The men of the village used *hul-ches* to hunt deer. Guns could be bought in Valladolid, but the Maya said that a *hul-che* was a weapon of stealth and not likely to bring a jaguar running toward you as the sound of a gun's explosion would.

She hooked the feathered spear into the grooves of the weapon and started up the stairs. She was breathing rapidly by the time she reached the top. She stepped up into the daylight and looked out from behind the stela. Hans and a strange man lay twisted together beneath the arch. A few feet away Andre lay on the ground, his head covered with blood. A fourth man sat beneath a cedar tree, staring straight ahead, a muddled glaze on his features, his head bobbing as though he were in pain. When he saw Lidia, he yelped in surprise and tried to get to his feet.

"*Dios mío,*" she cried. She stared at the weapon in her hands. It had seemed so simple. The spear hooked into the curved shaft. You pulled it and the spear flew. But where did it fly? How did it fly? How did you aim it? Perspiration ran down her face.

"*Dios mío,*" she whispered.

She and the man stared at each other. She watched while he got slowly to his feet and limped toward her. The baby somersaulted inside of her, oblivious to everything.

She took the steps two at a time now as she descended into the tomb again. Each curve of wall was familiar, each jagged stone. She reached out to support herself with her right hand. In her left she still clutched the *hul-che*.

When she reached Guerrero's throne, she crouched behind it, her body concealed by a lattice of bones wearing a feathered headdress. The man, his shoes scratching along the gritty limestone, entered the chamber and swiveled around, quivering with pleasure at the tomb's beauty.

She saw him very clearly. The club in his hand. The mustache that draped his mouth. The blood-spattered pants. He pivoted on one foot, his mouth open, then dropped the club to the ground and walked, babbling to himself, toward the crates of coins that glinted weightless in a pool of light. He stuffed the pockets of his pants and shirt with gold ducats. When they overflowed his pockets and fell onto the ground, he tried to pick one of the crates up, but as hard as he strained it wouldn't move. He turned frantic, searching the floor for something to put the gold pieces in. And then he saw the emeralds sleeping in Guerrero's eyes.

He took a cautious step toward the skeleton, leaned against its bony knees and reached out his hand. In that moment he looked through the radiating feathers into Lidia's eyes.

"*Dios mío*," she said as they stared at each other.

Then his eyes fluttered. He turned away, searching the floor for the club. When he turned back again, Lidia plunged the *hul-che* spear through Guerrero's rib cage into the man's chest.

At first she felt no pulse in either of Andre's wrists. Then she tore at his shirt and put her lips to his bare chest. It seemed to her that her own heart ceased to beat until she felt the vibrations. Blood had matted on his forehead and upper left temple. She poured water from the canteen over his head, smoothing the clots away with her fingers until she saw the broken edges of skin. He didn't open his eyes or speak to her, but he was alive. She wrapped him in a blanket, then folded her rebozo and propped his wounded head against it.

But Hans lay ashen-faced, growing cold along with the body of the man beside him. There was no heartbeat in him. She tried again and again to hear one. She put her mouth to his to feel for warmth or the soft rush of air, but there was nothing.

"You should have gone to Guatemala, dear Hans." She bowed her head. "Dear Lord, receive Hans Kobermann into your kingdom. He believed, but he did not know that he believed."

She descended the stairs once more into the tomb. The club with Andre's blood on it was on the limestone floor where the man had dropped it. As she bent to pick it up, the corpse looked at her with reproachful eyes. She knelt beside him and closed his open eyes with her fingers. "God forgive me," she said.

When the stones were replaced in the tomb's opening and the club had been set down beneath the arch not far from the fingers of the man who had killed Hans, she came and looked at Andre again. She held his wrist and felt the steadiness of the pulse. No more blood oozed from the wound in his head.

"Andre," she called softly. He should have answered. He looked as though he were merely asleep. She didn't want to leave him there among the dead, but there would be no help if she didn't bring it. And so she looked around her once more to make sure that everything was as it should be, and then she started back to the village.

40

Efforts to reach Conrad in Valladolid brought no response. A messenger was sent to the Mayaland Hotel in Chichén Itzá to look for him there, but the desk clerk said that Mrs. Whitworth and her son had left for Mexico City, and he had no idea where the doctor was. Andre lay unconscious on the reed mat of the *choza* in Xan-Xel. He didn't open his eyes and he didn't utter a sound.

The circumstances of the deaths were so unusual that Nacom Pascual, the *cacique* of the village, sent all the way to Chiapas for a Maya priest to advise him. Baltazar, a renowned *curandero* and *adivino*, arrived with his two assistants.

"You have been wise to send for me," Baltazar said.

"It is said that you have powers equal to the ancient priests'," the Nacom replied.

"My powers are considerable."

Nacom Pascual took him to see the bodies of the professor and the stranger, which had begun to putrefy in the jungle heat.

"How did they die?" Baltazar asked.

"By blows from a club," the Nacom said. "But there was a third man, a painter who lives here in the village with his wife. He was also wounded, but can no longer speak, and so we cannot find out what happened."

"First you must cremate the bodies," said Baltazar, holding his nose against the stench.

After the cremation, Baltazar designated half the ashes as those of the professor and half as the stranger's. The ashes of the professor were placed in a wooden container carved in the shape of the professor's head. As Juanita poured the professor's half into it, Baltazar chanted and sang. "O Lord of the Skies, carry this man's spirit to that place that is shaded by the first tree of the world. Welcome him into the second level of heaven."

Then Juanita put the carved head on a table in her *choza* with lighted candles all around.

"And the ashes of the stranger, what should be done with them?" the Nacom asked.

"Bury them in the jungle," said Baltazar, "but do not mark his grave, and tell no one about his coming here or the people of Xan-Xel will be blamed for his death."

Baltazar swung his censer outside the *choza* to rid it of evil spirits before he entered. Everything was in readiness for him. Inside the *choza* was an altar, a gilt-wood cross, and thirteen bowls of *zaca*, one for each Lord of the Day. One of his assistants held a live chicken and a small doll made of the bark of a rubber tree. Outside the *choza* a long narrow ditch had been dug, and logs now burned and fumed beneath a layer of large stones. Baltazar's assistants had already killed seven chickens, cleaned them, and singed their feathers, and placed them to boil in great vats of water. The women of the village had made tortillas and wrapped them in the leaves of the bob tree. The chickens and tortillas would be placed in the ditch after the ceremony as an offering to Itzamná, Lord of the Skies.

Lidia was sitting on the reed mat when Baltazar entered the *choza*. Andre lay silent beside her, eyes closed.

"I'm a Catholic," Lidia said.

"We are all Catholics," Baltazar replied. "I was baptized, and I confess my sins to a priest twice a year, but there are many gods, and I will ask if one of them would like to cleanse this man. Would you deny him help from all the places in the heavens?"

"But it is sacrilege."

"If he has violated a taboo, then there is no help for him from any god."

He knelt down and touched Andre's head with his dark fingers, then took his wrist in his hand to feel the pulse.

"He has a strong heart," Baltazar said, and took a *zaztún*, a glass ball, from the purse that dangled from his waist. An assistant had brought a cup of *balche*, and Baltazar dipped the *zaztún* in the liquor and then held it to the light for a few seconds before he set it to spinning in his palm.

"What gods has he offended?" Baltazar asked.

"None," Lidia answered.

"Does he have enemies?" When Lidia hesitated, he said, "To cure him, I must know everything."

"Yes, he has enemies."

"They have punished him."

He reached into his purse again and extracted a few dried leaves, which he sprinkled on the wound in Andre's head.

"Oo, Itzamná, Lord of the Skies," he chanted, "if this man has offended you, he repents. Give him life. Exorcise the evil spirits from his head, and he will do penance. I am powerful, a priest. I am a Lord of the Sun who commands the Lord of the Skies to return this man to us. Give him the power to speak to us, O Itzamná. We give you bread and meat as an offering."

Baltazar picked up the glass of *balche* and downed it in one swallow and then took the live chicken from his assistant's hand and touched it to Lidia's cheek, to Andre's cheek, and, then to his own. Then he stabbed the chicken with a knife and let the droplets of blood drip onto the rubber-bark doll until it was saturated.

"The evil has been drawn out of him and taken into the *muñeco*," Baltazar said. "In one week he will speak."

That night after the Lord of the Skies had come down to earth and eaten and drunk his fill, Baltazar and his assistants consumed the remains. By morning they lay on the ground in a stuporous trance. Andre still had not spoken, but Lidia called to Juanita and told her that she would have her baby now.

Lidia's labor was hard. She breathed shallowly and quickly, and when a contraction ended she leaned in heavy exhaustion against Juanita.

Copal burned continuously inside the hut. A pot of thick bean soup and a clay statue of the goddess Ixchel lay next to Lidia's stomach. The women of the village walked in and out. Some came to give advice to Juanita on how to handle the birth. Others just came to gossip. Between pains Lidia listened to their voices. Their stories distracted her. Their presence comforted her.

On the morning of the second day of labor she dreamed that Andre spoke to her. He said the child was a girl and that she was to name her Concepción.

For several weeks after the baby was born, nothing was said to Lidia about the unidentified dead man. Then, one morning, when the air was still cool from the evening's rain, Nacom Pascual came to Andre and Lidia's *choza*. He touched the copper bells that hung at the door, and, since he was the Nacom and could enter any house without permission, he walked in boldly.

Lidia heard the chiming of the bells from the lean-to where she had been braying maize on a milling stone. She looked through the open doorway into the *choza* and saw the Nacom sitting opposite Andre on the reed mat. She wiped the thick corn paste from her hands and went inside.

"He still doesn't speak," the Nacom said. "I do not want to talk of serious matters with a woman." His features were harsh, with an eagle tattooed on his right cheek and a nose that soared upward from his lip, then sank into the ridge between his eyes. His hair hung in a full mane to his shoulders.

"He tries to speak," Lidia said, "but he can't form the words."

She was barefoot and wore her hair in a circular braid at the nape of her neck. The baby was curled against her back, sleeping in the rebozo that hung like a sling from her shoulders. She undid the rebozo and placed the baby on the mat so that the Nacom could see her.

"Her name is Concepción Rosario," Lidia said. "I call her Chayo."

He looked at the child for a few seconds and then waved for Lidia to wrap her up again. "A foreigner was killed," he said.

At the Nacom's words, Andre opened and closed his mouth a few times, then began to tremble. His body became rigid, the arch of his back unnaturally twisted. His eyes curled under his eyelids until only the whites were showing. Lidia took his hands in hers and held them tightly as he struggled against the convulsion. He let out a half sob of relief as his muscles loosened. Then he collapsed against the mat, his shirt wet with perspiration. Lidia spoke soothingly to him as his chest rose and fell rapidly. He nodded weakly, his eyes closed, and finally he fell asleep.

"The gods are punishing him for the deaths," the Nacom said.

"He had nothing to do with the deaths," Lidia replied. She looked into the Nacom's eyes as she spoke instead of averting them as the women of the village did.

"The weapon was there," the Nacom said.

"But it was used against Andre, not by him," she answered.

The Nacom studied the way she spoke. She was forthright and unafraid.

"Juanita said that two men came to Xan-Xel, but only one body was found," he said.

"He must have run away."

"But he is not here now, and so there is no explanation. Baltazar has advised me that the gods must be appeased when blood is shed without explanation." He stared at Andre's sleeping figure. "Or they might send the Federales to Xan-Xel to ask questions."

When the day for appeasing the gods arrived, the feasting and drinking and dancing began early. The women stirred the food in immense cauldrons and watched the men get drunker and their dances grow more frenzied. The men hopped about gracelessly, jumping and hissing and spitting at one another, falling into heaps on the ground, picking themselves up again, and gyrating in greater and greater fury until the zócalo became a sickening spectacle of sotted, drunken men reeling to thumping drums and high-pitched whining flutes.

In the evening the Nacom once again came to the *choza*. Two men half-carried him in, and when they let go of his arms, he staggered, rheumy-eyed, into the dark interior. A heavy red cape clung to his bare shoulders, and he wore a conical hat, beribboned and edged in monkey fur.

He motioned toward Andre. "Come."

"He's sick," Lidia said, moving protectively to Andre's side.

The Nacom ignored her. "Come," he said again, and this time he poked Andre in the chest with his bare foot.

"He's coming," she said. "He'll follow you."

The Nacom turned unsteadily and lurched out of the *choza*.

Lidia changed quickly, throwing her huipil to the ground and pulling on Andre's white cotton trousers and tunic. She shoved her braided hair up into the crown of a wide-brimmed straw hat, which she draped with a dark-brown rebozo that obscured her face. The Nacom was a few steps outside the door. He stopped, turned around, and wobbled from foot to foot while Lidia ran to catch up with him.

The ground of the *zócalo* was a carpet of glittery burning logs, crystalline white and fiery red, fuming, rocketing, shooting flames into the fevered air. Baltazar was already there. He danced drunkenly on the precipice of the fire, chanting in rhythm to the incessant drumming and whistling while the village men, their bodies in white, their heads covered with monkey-fur hats, ran the gauntlet of burning timbers, showers of sparks whooshing between their legs.

"God the Son, God the Father, God the Holy Ghost, First Pahuatun who broke the first rocks," chanted Baltazar, "look how the monkeys, the evil ones, enemies of the sun, Christ's persecutors, purge themselves and appease you in Itzamná's name, in the names of the Yumtzilob who guard the fields and bring the rain and chase away evil spirits. Lovely Lady Madalena, San Miguel, I call on you to see how we appease you and the Lord Zaztunchac in the east. Ekpapatun, Kakalmozonikob, San Miguel Arcangel, may you all be glorified."

The Nacom clutched Lidia's hand and pulled her to the fire rim.

"Dear Jesus, sweet Jesus, Lord protect me, save Chayo, save Andre." Her bare feet hit the flaming wood. "I give myself to you." Her flesh touched the fire. "My Redeemer, I have sinned," she cried. "Accept my atonement for my sins. Chayo will be named in church. I will be thy servant forever and ever. I fear nothing, for thou art with me."

Andre watched her dance through the fire. He held his hand to his head to hold the throbbing back, to keep the fit at bay. He dropped to the ground, bewildered and disoriented as he watched her leap into the fire, saw the soles of her feet grazed by flames. She made no sound, did not cry out in pain. The rebozo that held her hat on her head fell into the flames, began to burn, then turn to ash. Her hat fell and her braids came undone, but the fire did not touch her.

"You see, my son," came Artur's voice in a lull in the

music, "mistakes are always made. Didn't I tell you that I didn't expect perfection? I tried to keep quiet when you ran away to Mexico. I tried to shut my mouth when you said you loved a Catholic girl. I even pretended to myself you weren't living in the jungle among savages. But this, my son, this is something to see."

41

The Nacom's problem was acute. After all, which one would he tell to leave? The man who did not walk on fire or the woman who did? It was an intricate puzzle, one that even Baltazar had difficulty in solving.

"Since a woman walked on fire, then the gods will be offended, not appeased," Baltazar said.

"But I cannot tell a woman to leave," said the Nacom. "It is the man's place to be told to leave."

"Then send a woman to tell her."

Juanita was sent to tell Andre and Lidia to leave the village. She told them as easily as if she had never met them. And all the while she was talking, she stared at Lidia's feet, which were as unblemished as her own.

Conrad examined the scar on Andre's head, made him walk, tapped his back, probed his mouth, gazed into his eyes, listened to his chest.

"You understand everything we've said, don't you, Andre?" Conrad asked when he was through.

Andre nodded.

"You just can't find the words you need, is that it?"

He nodded.

"You have headaches?"

He nodded.

"Can you read writing and understand it?"

He nodded.

"You mustn't worry so much. Blows to the head take time to heal." Then he injected some phenothiazine into Andre's hip and he promptly fell asleep.

Lidia had planted orchids and bright yellow hibiscus next to the door of the lean-to kitchen. She and Conrad sat on the ground among the flowers while Andre slept inside the *choza*.

"There's probably a piece of bone that's pierced the brain tissue," he said.

"*Dios mío,*" she murmured.

"It caused a scar in the part of the brain where he needs to call up words. Expressive aphasia, it's called. They're doing an experimental surgery in the States for head injuries of this type, but I wouldn't advise that he have it. The mortality's too high."

"It won't heal itself?"

"It's unlikely. But a good mental attitude is important with this kind of injury or he'll give up, simply deteriorate. Hope must always be held out to him. As for the seizures, I'll give you a drug that will make them shorter and less violent."

"We have to leave Xan-Xel. Will it hurt him to travel now?"

"Leave?"

"I ran in the flames with the men and it shamed the village."

"What are you talking about?"

"My feet."

He got on his knees and bent to examine her feet, touching the pale olive nails and running his fingers across her smooth instep.

"Well, I've seen men do it," he said finally, "but I've never been able to understand it. You had no pain?"

"Nothing. I have looked at my feet often since then, and I don't understand either why there are no marks, no burns, why they didn't melt away in the fire."

"You did feel the heat, though?"

"I felt nothing. It was like a dream in which you fly overhead, not touching the ground."

"And now Nacom Pascual wants you to leave."

"Yes. But we would leave anyway because of the men that murdered Hans. I heard one of them speak in Russian."

"I can't believe they're still after him."

"Oh, yes, they're still after him. I know they are. I saw

them. I was—" She shook her head. "And now Andre has
seizures and can't talk. I'm frightened for him, but I try not
to let him see that I'm frightened."

"He should be in a hospital."

"They'll find him in a hospital. He can't go to a hospital."

"Okay, okay, then we'll think of something else."

She smiled. "I know you can help us. You're so good and
smart." She touched his arm. "I told Andre right away,
'Conrad will know what to do.' "

Before sunup, Andre and Chayo were in the wagon while
Lidia checked the *choza* to make sure that nothing important
had been left behind. There had been very few things to
take. Brother Aguilar's breviary, Andre's paintings, rolled
and tied with twine. Paints. An easel.

"Is it possible for you to send Hans's possessions to his
sister at the address on these letters?" Lidia asked.

"I'll take care of it," Conrad replied.

He helped her load the last of the food onto the wagon and
the kerosene drum of water and the sacks of maize for the
mules. Then they knelt in front of the *choza*, a map spread
out on the dirt in front of them.

"We're here in Yucatán," he said, "this triangle here. You
go east a hundred miles to the coast. You could do it in an
automobile in several hours easily if there was a highway
through here, but there isn't. There is a road of sorts that the
Maya built to get from the Gulf of Mexico to the Caribbean to
trade with other tribes, but in most places the jungle has
taken over. Try to follow the map where you can and the road
wherever it appears."

He pulled a pistol from a pocket of his jodhpurs and
handed it to her.

"Don't look so upset about the gun," he said. "There are
some tribes who went deep into the jungle after the War of
the Castes. They still think a white person is the enemy."

He pulled a drawstring bag from his other pocket. "Gold
pesos and also some ammunition for the pistol. I don't know
where you'll spend the pesos, but there may be some Indians
who'll trade you provisions for them. Remember, as isolated
as Xan-Xel is, the eastern side of the Yucatán peninsula is
even more isolated. There are tribes there that have been
hiding from the Spanish invaders for four hundred years."

"I understand."

"As for Andre, you have the anticonvulsants, the sedatives, and there are opium pills and kaolin for dysentery. You know my instructions. No medication unless he has a seizure, and then don't be afraid to dose him. Two should knock him out, put him to sleep. Don't forget to take your quinine. If you get sick, then he and the baby are in trouble."

He pointed to the map again. "Just off the coast there's an island called Cozumel. There's not much there, some fishing villages. But the U.S. has an airbase there and a radio." He tore a piece out of the corner of the map, wrote on it and handed it to her. "Give the radio operator this paper and he'll find me, no questions asked. I'll get the rest of the gold out of the tomb myself. When it's all traded, I'll send the rest of Hans's share to his sister, but it will take time. Give me five years."

"We'll meet in five years," she said.

"Yes." He looked up at the sky, which was a cloudless blue, and then back at her. "God, I hope I haven't forgotten anything. You'll use the radio at Cozumel to let me know where you are?"

"I will." Her eyes clouded. Tears darkened the gray.

"Are you all right?"

She hugged him close and whispered, "I killed one of the men. He's in the tomb with Guerrero." He felt a shudder course through her, and then she ran to the wagon and took her seat behind the two mules. The wagon lunged forward heading onto the path into the jungle. Conrad watched until the trees enveloped them, until he only imagined he could see them. When he could no longer hear the lumbering creak of the wagon's wheels, he turned and walked away.

42

They had never traveled this far into the jungle before. For several miles the *sacbe* was visible through the vegetation, the crushed-limestone bed of the road gleaming in the sun as the wagon bumped steadily along. Occasionally a large rock forced the wagon onto the marshy jungle floor, where its wheels whirred helplessly until Lidia could cajole the mules into dragging it up onto the rock path again.

Finally the large rocks became boulders and a curtain of liana vines barred the way. The mules stopped, unable to move forward. Andre pointed away from the road to a place where the vines wound into the zapote trees.

For several hours Lidia chopped at the vines with a machete. Her hands turned black and gummy, and she became breathless from her exertions in the intense heat. Andre guided the mules behind her as she worked a path parallel to the ancient *sacbe*. Every few minutes she stopped and took a sip of water, saving a few drops of it to flick against her face.

Finally the road became visible again, the boulders were behind them, but now the vines tangled tightly over the road, making it impassable.

"I have to rest," she said.

She drank a large cup of water and lay down in the bed of the wagon and nursed the baby, after which they resumed the slow journey along the road, Andre driving the mules and Lidia cutting away the vines that blocked their way. She wore pants and long sleeves, but her feet were bare and her face and hands were exposed. Insects pricked at her, and mosquitoes drew her blood. Her face puffed with itchiness until she thought that the skin would crack. Her light clothing grew heavy with perspiration. Her muscles howled for her to stop.

They passed fields of wild henequen. The remains of a burned-out hacienda rose like an apparition through the jungle screen. A portion of rusted iron grille. A crumbling gateway arch. A manor house with fire char still showing beneath the jungle mold. Spaniards had fled from the Maya here a century before. Now hibiscus flowered and monkeys screeched in the burned remains.

At midday Andre sagged in the seat of the wagon, the reins slack in his hands. Lidia climbed up beside him and laid her head in his lap. "Will we ever forget this time, Andre?" she said, and then she fell asleep.

She nursed the baby, her breast exposed. Andre felt her body strongly here. Desire was not lost. He could feel it rising in him now. He touched the smooth skin of her breast and his temples began to pound, and his pulse vibrated crazily. He stopped, withdrew his hand, but it was too late. His body had already turned on him, was twisting and squeezing him.

She poured the contents of a packet into a cup of water and held it to his chattering lips.

When the seizure had subsided, he lay on the hard boards of the wagon, his face turned away from her, while she sat beside him and stroked his forehead.

"You mustn't feel ashamed to be sick," she said.

Before it grew dark they arrived at a grove of zapote trees and heard the sound of men's voices. Lidia reached into the corner of the wagon for Conrad's pistol. It was heavy and cool in her swollen hand, and didn't frighten her as much as it had when she first touched it. She arranged her rebozo around her so that the pistol was hidden.

When Andre motioned for her not to go, she said, "Christ protects me, Andre. I'll be back."

A few hundred yards from the road there was a cluster of lean-to shelters spread beneath the trees. She looked up through the mesh of leaves at the Maya who were suspended from the top branches of the trees by ropes tied around their waists. They jabbered in Maya as they worked, each man to his tree, hacking horizontal grooves in the trunk, then diagonal ones, alternating, zig-zagging swiftly around the tree, creating an oozing road of latex that dripped into the canvas bag hanging on a peg at its base.

"They race to see whether they can get to the bottom before the chicle does," said a man behind her.

She turned, startled, her rebozo open to reveal the pistol in her hand.

He had freckles and red hair and a pug nose that was crusted from the sun. He spoke Spanish fluently. "They look like monkeys, don't they? The Maya believe that the spider monkey was once a man, younger brother of the sun, who climbed a tree in search of fruit. As he climbed higher, his blanket became hair and his loincloth turned into a tail. And you won't need a gun with me. I don't intend to harm you."

"American?" She shifted the gun to her left hand.

"Sure am. Wrigley Company. Chewing gum. I'm the foreman here. What are you doing in the middle of the jungle?"

"My family and I are on our way to the Caribbean."

"Well, you're lucky you found us. We're leaving this camp at the end of the week. You're welcome to join us. If you go on by yourself, you've got three tough days of chopping through the jungle till you get to Cobá, where the road gets better. The Americans worked on the ruins there in '41. They shoved the jungle back some and improved the road."

The chicleros had stopped their work and were staring down at her from their perches.

"My name's Dale," he said. "What's yours?"

"Lidia."

He walked over to a cooking pot that hung over the fire near a row of bubbling cauldrons of latex. "This one's got stew in it," he said, stirring the pot with a stick. "Go get your family, Lidia. There's plenty for everyone."

They rested in the chicleros' camp all the next day. The Maya talked among themselves in a dialect that was different from that of the villagers of Xan-Xel. And their noses were more beaklike, their bodies more wiry than the stocky Maya of Xan-Xel. The tips of their ears were either missing or ulcerated from the bites of insects that lived in the treetops. Dale spoke to them in Maya and in Spanish as they skittered up and down the tree trunks in their bare feet.

"They look forward to the liquor," Dale said when he handed them their ration of aguardiente after dinner.

"They're very quiet," Lidia said. The men sat huddled together in a silent band at the base of the zapote trees.

"We never have company."

"It makes me uneasy the way they look at the baby."

"It's her blue eyes. They told me that her eyes remind them of the ocean." He motioned toward Andre. "It must be an inconvenience, him not speaking."

That night they slept on a blanket beneath mosquito netting in a corner of one of the lean-tos, the chicleros snoring nearby. Early the next morning, before anyone awakened, Lidia nursed the baby. When she was finished, she shook Andre.

"Hurry," she said, "before they wake up."

When they were in the wagon and on their way again, she said, "They admired Chayo too much."

They reached Cobá on the fifth day. It was tranquil, no sign of archaeologists digging in the partially excavated ruins. Lidia climbed the tallest pyramid, a pillar of stairs to a platform high above the jungle.

"I saw the ocean, Andre," she said excitedly when she had climbed down again. "On the edge of the jungle I could see it. If we travel a little farther now, when we stop to rest we'll be very close."

Marshes and small lakes enveloped the ruins, and when they resumed their journey, the mosquitoes swarmed around them and the road became bumpy with creeping vegetation.

"Chayo is so patient in the heat," Lidia said.

When they emerged from the swamps, Lidia stopped the wagon on the banks of a lagoon where iguanas and crocodiles sunned themselves. She carried Chayo to a sheltered inlet and dipped a cloth in the water and sponged the baby's heat-prickled skin. Then she nursed her again before they continued on.

That night they ate what was left of the food, and when the mosquitoes began to buzz around their heads, Lidia draped netting over the wagon, and they crawled beneath it and went to sleep.

It was the sound of monkeys jabbering to one another that woke her. She reached for the pistol and looked out from beneath the mosquito netting. She couldn't see anything, but she heard a humming sound like bees in a hive, and she smelled the odor of burning tobacco. Then the first hand touched her face. And then another. She didn't move, and the buzzing turned into the clicking singsong of Maya voices. The hands retreated, and she lay back beneath the netting and waited for morning to come.

They were Maya similar in appearance to the chicleros, short and thin, with aquiline noses and dark skin, but they wore sacklike homespun gowns, and their hair bushed out from their heads in tangled masses. They stood around the wagon staring at Chayo and pointing to her eyes.

"Dear Lord," prayed Lidia, "protect Chayo. If you want to take her, she's not baptized in the Church, but she's innocent of sin. She's only six weeks old and hasn't learned wickedness yet. Take her in your arms and carry her to Heaven before she can suffer any pain."

One of the men came forward and motioned for Lidia to give him the baby. When she held fast to the child, he turned and conferred with the others. In a few minutes all the men converged on the wagon and began rocking it from side to side. Andre's eyes were closed now, his hands to his head.

Lidia jumped down from the wagon and held the baby out to the headman, who grasped her ecstatically. The baby's eyes were open, and the men crowded around to look at them. Some covered their faces in terror after a quick peek. Others screamed and cowered beneath the wagon. When they had all recovered their wits and calmed themselves, they came and looked at her again. Each time they repeated the experiment, the reaction was less violent, until finally they were able to stand in a circle around her and touch her face and blow on her hair without collapsing.

"Her name is Chayo," said Lidia in the Maya dialect that was spoken in Xan-Xel.

The headman nodded and began walking into the jungle, the baby still in his arms, the men following close behind.

Lidia picked up the rebozo that held the pistol and ran after them. Brambles tore at her clothes and twigs scratched her face as she ran.

Suddenly trees and bushes and vines were gone and she was in sunlight, the stifling air of the jungle behind her, a brisk breeze buffeting her body, salt spray tickling her nostrils. A low limestone wall encircled a fortress city of temples and pyramids stretching across a treeless, sun-baked plain that ended in a rocky cliff high above the ocean.

"We entered onto a steep path from the shore which led upward to a broad plateau whereat there were towers and temples of stone overlooking the sea."

The headman, Chayo in his arms, climbed the broken steps of a temple at the edge of the cliff while the rest of the men remained below, stamping their feet and chanting.

"Dios mío, give me my baby," cried Lidia when she reached the top of the stairs, but the wind whipping against her face made her voice insubstantial, turned it to a muffled squeak that echoed hollowly in her own ears.

Two Maya in headdresses of red and yellow quetzal feathers climbed the steps. One of them put copal in the stone brazier and lit it while the other one knelt and placed his face into the giant canoe of *balche* that rested on the platform. The headman laid Chayo down on a stone altar and put his face in the canoe also and began lapping at the liquor. Chayo, her face turned to the sun, shrieked until her little body was shaking. Lidia reached toward her, felt the pink skin hot beneath her fingertips.

"Aieee!" screamed the headman, lifting his head from the canoe and pushing Lidia's hand away.

A procession of musicians started up the stone stairway, banging drums and blowing whistles. When they reached the top it was so crowded around the canoe of *balche* that Lidia had to push her way through the crush of bodies to reach Chayo's side. Everyone was singing and chanting and drinking now, even the musicians, who took turns dipping their heads into the trough of liquor, which sloshed in waves over the edges of the wooden container onto the dry stones, turning them as slippery as a slice of buttered bread.

"During festival months the savages make pilgrimages to the city of stone above the sea, where they worship the blue-eyed god Kukulcán. They call this place Tulum."

Lidia grew dizzy from the sun and the incense, and her breasts became engorged with milk that ran in rivulets down her stomach and onto her bare feet and then joined the spilled *balche* that now filled the rocky crevices of the platform. The men skidded over the slick stones as they danced, their heads jiggling and their bodies tilting precariously over the parapet.

Then suddenly women appeared, climbing the steps, arms laden with platters of food. Some of the musicians had already slumped senseless to the platform and the headman and his assistants were no longer paying any attention to Chayo. It was then that Lidia realized that they had not meant to harm the baby, but had only wanted to use her for a while.

"Don't cry, I'm here," Lidia said, lifting Chayo into her arms. The headman turned to look at them, but saw nothing through his alcoholic haze.

"*Con su permiso,*" Lidia said, and she smiled as she picked her way through the bodies of the unconscious musicians to reach the stairs.

"*Con su permiso,*" she said, brushing past the stream of women who, smiling shyly back at her, continued upward.

She clutched Chayo tightly and began to descend the stairs, glancing back only once at the women, some of whom were arranging food on the glistening stones while others were pulling dazed men back from the precipice, propping them upright against the stone altar, and gently wiping the spittle from their mouths.

43

Sandy beaches stretched like a white ribbon up the eastern coast of Yucatán, the fetid jungle to the west of the ribbon, the warm blue-green waters of the Caribbean to the east. In places the beach was concealed by coconut groves, with here and there a reed-and-thatch hut visible through the trees. But there was no sign of a village, and although they traveled for miles paralleling the Caribbean, they saw no people. The coastline began to repeat itself, to look like what they had traveled through several hours before.

"Where should we go, Andre? This is a nice beach. Would this be a good place to stay?"

He scanned the shoreline, and then nodded.

"Then this is where we will go." She turned the wagon off the limestone road and followed the curve of Caribbean to a freshwater lagoon that emptied into the sea. A stone altar and carved stela guarded the lagoon, and blue and yellow motmots flitted through the fronds of the palms.

While the mules drank from the lagoon, Lidia peered into water so limpidly clear that the fish seemed to be swimming through molten glass. She dipped her hand into it, and a school of bright yellow tangs nuzzled her fingers. She giggled at the soft suction of their mouths on her skin. But the sand was rocky and uneven here, not powdery soft as Conrad had described it.

She hopped back up on the seat of the wagon. "I think we should travel a little farther."

When they reached a beach where the ceiba trees dipped their branches in the surf, Lidia stopped the wagon again and looked out at the water. Near the shore it was as blue as Chayo's eyes, and farther offshore, where the herons and pelicans hovered above the coral ridge, was a rim of green. There was no jungle here, and the breeze blew unobstructed.

"This is a protected place," she said. "No one will bother us here."

She wore her huipil now, so that the salt spray could touch her skin. With Chayo swinging from her rebozo, Lidia took Andre's hand and they walked across the sand in their bare feet, the powdered limestone cool and soft between their toes. She glanced at him often.

"You seem so well, Andre. Sometimes I think you'll turn to me and tell me what you're thinking." She put her arm around his waist and leaned her head against his chest. "Your heart beats to mine, so that I can hardly tell it from my own."

They stood in the surf and watched the waves break, turn to foam, and disappear into the sand.

"Look how it passes over our toes, Andre, running away from us as though it were afraid."

She dropped Andre's hand and walked farther into the ocean, her cotton huipil swirling around her like a gauzy jellyfish. She slid Chayo into her arms and dunked her gently in the warm water, and then the two of them bobbed up and down until the soil of the jungle was washed away.

While Chayo and Andre napped beneath the breeze-ruffled ceiba trees, Lidia took inventory of the provisions that were left. There was still a large can of water, and a small, cloth-wrapped ball of masa, but the *pollo pibil* was finished and the dried pork was reduced to a few stringy crumbs. She looked out at the ocean. She would learn to fish. It couldn't require too much skill to catch fish that came up to you and kissed your fingers.

She lay back in the sand and let the sun feed her, let the ocean breeze apply its balm to her battered body, and then she too fell asleep.

The slap-slap of the water jarred her awake. She sat up and glanced back at where Andre and Chayo were still sleeping. There were no mosquitoes to bite them here. She turned toward the sea again, marveling at the shifting colors of the water as the sun moved lower in the sky. It changed from blue to teal and was now deepening to a purple-black. Only one small spot remained unchanged, a speck of white on the horizon, a mote, a dot of chalk drifting on the sea. As she watched, the dot grew larger and became a small white boat. The waves had grasped it now and were hurling it toward shore. A Maya in his mid-twenties, a straw hat on his head, rowed the boat, and two dark-skinned boys clung to its sides.

At the last wave before the surf line, the boys let go and paddled through the water while the man jumped out and towed the boat up onto the sand and secured the wooden paddles. The man was short, his bare upper body muscular, his nose a curved steel blade, like the noses of the Maya in the frescoes in Tulum.

He reached into the boat and pulled out a sisal net filled with fish, then looked in Lidia's direction as the boys ran toward her.

"I don't understand," she said. The boys had skidded onto their knees in the sand in front of her and were chattering in an unfamiliar dialect.

As the man approached, they became quiet. He said a few words to them and they ran back into the ocean to swim.

"I don't understand," she said again as the man spoke to her in the same strange dialect. He lay the net down on the sand, knelt beside it, and picked out two large fish and handed them to her.

"*Gracias*," she said.

"*No hay de qué*," he answered, and sat down beside her on the sand.

His Spanish was polite, but the accent was stilted and archaic.

He looked over her shoulder toward the wagon. "You drove through the jungle in that?"

"*Sí.*"

"Where have you come from?"

"From the jungle. Xan-Xel. But before that I lived in Cuernavaca and in Mexico."

"I know where Mexico is, but I have never heard of Cuernavaca." He glanced intermittently out at the ocean, watching the two boys. "We had Mexicans living here before the war."

"Before the war? You mean the Second World War?"

The man looked puzzled. "The war with the ladinos. The war that began in 1847 and ended in 1901. That's the only war I know of."

Lidia nodded. "I studied that war in school in Cuernavaca. That was a long time ago. There's another war now."

"A Mexican war?"

"Not a Mexican war, but we have been sending men to fight in it since 1943. You haven't heard about it here?"

"We don't hear too many things here. Sometimes Father González tells me things, but mostly they are of no interest. What is of interest is that the government now has given us land to plant our corn again. Before that we were hidden in the jungle, hunting for food. And before that we were like slaves to the Spanish *hacendados* on their henequen plantations."

"There were Maya in the jungle not far from here, but they didn't look like you," she said. "Their hair was long and wild and they wore shapeless dresses like the women."

"You saw these people?"

"*Sí*. We were in a place near the ocean."

"Tulum."

"*Sí*, Tulum. They kept staring at Chayo's blue eyes—Chayo is my baby—and then they took her from me."

"Did they harm her?"

"No."

"It must have frightened them to see her blue eyes. The god Kukulcán also had blue eyes. I've seen such eyes before, so I wouldn't be afraid to look at your baby."

"They put her on a stone altar where they burned incense. Then they drank *balche* until they fell unconscious. I was frightened at first, but then I understood that they meant no harm."

"They were praying to the rain god," he said. "In ancient times, they would have sacrificed her to Nojoch-Yum Chac or Kukulcán, but things have changed. It's very strange that you saw them. Very few people see them. They're Maya, but from an ancient tribe that has never forgotten the time when the Spaniards came. There are only a few hundred of them left, living in small groups with the strongest men keeping the most wives. They're afraid to show themselves to strangers or learn new ways."

She nodded. "Where is your village? Is it far?"

"No. It's in the jungle not far from here. It's very small, maybe twenty *chozas* and a communal *milpa* where we grow maize. When I am not in the fields, I come here to fish."

She looked pensive. "If I knew how to fish, I could be sure that my husband and child would never go hungry."

"Sometimes Mexicans come here to fish. They come in big boats from Cabo Catoche. That way." He pointed toward the north with his finger. "Sometimes I work for them, show them the places where the shrimp beds are on Cozumel. The Mexicans aren't very good fishermen. When they drink they fall into the water. Very stupid. But they pay me with pesos, and the store in Playa del Carmen gives me goods for them, so I don't mind when the Mexicans come here."

"My husband is a German."

"I don't know what that is." Then he added hastily, "But I'm not uneducated. The priest in Playa del Carmen taught me to read Spanish."

"My daughter isn't baptized. We will need a priest."

"He will be happy to baptize her. He has a lot of children to feed."

"A Catholic priest?"

"Of course. Father González came here in 1923. We have no one else. Most of the churches were destroyed during the war and the priests were afraid to come back. Sometimes Father González is Catholic, sometimes he is Maya. It's all the same. But if you are going to stay here, you will need a *choza*. Do you have money? Pesos? Gold?"

"We can pay you."

"Then I can help your husband build a *choza* anywhere you want. Maybe here on the sand, near the water, or if you want to be in the jungle, you can have a *choza* in the jungle."

"Would you help us build a *choza* here beneath the ceiba trees?"

"Of course."

Andre walked toward them, the baby in his arms. At the sight of the child, milk surged into Lidia's breasts, soaking the front of her huipil so that her nipples could be seen clearly. When the Maya stared at the wet spots, Lidia pulled Chayo into her arms and held her close.

"What's your name?" she asked.

"Ignacio in Spanish, but I'm called Keh, which means 'deer' in Maya."

"My name is Lidia. This is my husband, Andre. He had an injury and can't speak." She kissed the baby's cheek. "This is our baby. Her name is Concepción Rosario, but I call her Chayo."

The Maya was silent for a few moments, and then he said, "Well, I will help you build a *choza*, since you are without a man to help you."

A flicker of pain crossed Andre's face. Keh smiled at him, and his teeth were a brilliant white against his copper skin.

"Those are my nephews," he said, pointing to the boys in the water. "One is Miguel for San Miguel, and the other one is Francisco for San Francisco. They work as hard as I do on the *milpa*, and they handle the fishing net like men. Their mother, Rosalia, belonged to my dead brother. When he died, they became my responsibility until they are grown. These are my sons as much as any born to me."

Lidia engaged in her familiar rituals. She scoured the beach looking for stones for a fire ring, then used the last of the masa to make tortillas. Andre watched her busyness and longed to speak to her. His brain had become a pillow of thoughts, words buried deep in its creases. He tried over and over to pluck them out, but the connection was broken; the words would not come, the sentences could not form. He wrestled with his burden: not to be able to make the words roll off the tongue, not to be strong enough to help build a *choza*.

His father spoke to him often now. It had been difficult to know what was happening in Europe when months went by without seeing a newspaper, so Artur brought him the latest news. He told him about the rabbi's lame horse, about the brisket Brina cooked for Sabbath dinner, about the blind artist who could paint only green pictures, about the duck that laid chicken eggs. He refused to talk about Hitler or Warsaw or what was happening to the Jews.

"Andre, now listen carefully." Andre looked around him. His father's voice was so clear. It had never been that clear before. "You've had some bad luck. It's serious, but, thank God, not fatal. And I admit the girl isn't too bad. She takes care of you. A Jewish girl couldn't do better. But if you can't make love to her soon, my son, you'll be in serious trouble. So in the meantime you have to watch out for that Indian."

44

When the cedar poles and roof supports were in place, Keh bundled cedar branches and ceiba twigs together and lashed them to the poles with strips of liana vine, leaving spaces between the bundles so that the interior of the *choza* could receive the ocean breezes. For the roof thatch, he split fronds of the cohune palm and laid them over the roof supports. Then he set hooks opposite each other in the wall poles so that sisal hammocks could be strung between them.

He arrived every morning as the sun was rising and left when the sun had vanished. He brought with him tortillas and *cochinita pibil* and mangos and papayas, which he shared with Andre and Lidia.

"What was the injury that took away his speech?" he asked one day.

"A blow to the head."

"Is he still a man?"

"I don't understand."

"Does he give you what you need?"

That she didn't answer seemed to please him.

While Keh worked on the *choza*, Andre began to paint again. He stuck his easel in the sand near a rotting tree stump a short distance up the beach. His paintings in Xan-Xel had been lush and shadowy, full of primitive images. His paintings at the edge of the ocean were austere and sun-drenched, with blue, barren skies and stark ceiba trees.

During the hottest part of the day, Keh would stop work

on the *choza* and row his boat out to where the ocean was the deepest blue. He would take his spear and disappear beneath the water. When he returned to shore, there would be four or five large fish in the boat, and sometimes a turtle to be boiled into soup.

Keh acted as though Andre didn't exist at all. He hardly spoke to Lidia, since it wasn't the custom, but he glanced at her often. And when he would return from the reef with fish, he would give her half of what he caught and put the rest aside for Rosalia and his nephews.

As the *choza* neared completion and the kitchen lean-to took shape, Keh began to work more slowly, taking more time on the reef each afternoon. There were still gaps in the roof thatch, but instead of gathering more fronds, he would find sticks that were loose in the walls or places that needed to be lashed more securely.

"It takes time," he said. "I have to find the right fronds for the roof. I want your house to be strong. Sometimes there are great storms that come from the ocean, and if the roof is not made well, the *choza* will fly into the sea on the wind god's shoulders."

He dragged out the work as long as possible, but finally it was finished, and he said, "I have neglected the *milpa* too long."

"You won't come back?" she asked.

"Sometimes I come to fish. I might come back. Do you want me to come back?"

"I'll pay you tomorrow, then, for all you've done," she said.

Andre was sketching, not looking in her direction as she walked along the shore. The undertow sucked at the soles of her feet as she stepped into the surf. A few yards from shore the kelp beds began. Slimy grasses and slippery tendrils of seaweed caught her cotton underskirt, tugging at it until it floated free. Her huipil ballooned around her, sheer and lustrous in the ocean wash. Then the kelp was gone, and she could see her feet and hands large against the whisked ocean bottom.

She swam with short untutored strokes. The reef had seemed close when she was standing on shore, but now each time she looked up, it seemed the same distance away. She moved her arms and legs relentlessly, as she had seen Keh do. She became winded with the effort, and longed to stand on the immaculate ocean floor, but it had fallen away, replaced by sharp crags of coral and subterranean caverns.

As she turned to float on her back, she saw how small Andre was on shore. She had swum quite far, but still it was not far enough. She would turn back now. God had made the reef far enough away so that she couldn't reach it, and that was sufficient answer to the mysteries of the ocean.

"The reef is close now," said Keh suddenly at her side. "Hold on to my waist."

He towed her to a furrowed platform of coral. "You can stand here," he said, and he dived beneath the water.

She swayed in the ocean surges, her feet barely holding to the gritty coral.

"What do you have?" she asked when he surfaced beside her again. He pulled the dive net from his belt and opened it for her to see. A steel-gray bonefish, two glossy snooks, and a red-banded snapper thrashed in the net along with a loggerhead turtle.

"He has to grow some more," he said as he plucked the undersized turtle out and set it atop the water. Then he closed the net, tied it around his waist, and vanished again.

She took a deep breath, then followed him, kicking fiercely to keep up. They swam past fingers of jutting reef, over a forest of lacy fan coral. There was movement everywhere. Parrot fish with fleshy mouths spoke to her as they passed. A school of triggerfish, blue tail fins fanning the water, dawdled at crevices, jabbing their snouts into promising holes.

She came to the surface for air.

"Why did you swim out here?" he said, pressing against her.

"I wanted to see what you do when you dive. It's so silent now that you're finished with the *choza*."

"But you don't want to talk to me. You look at me for other reasons. If a man isn't able to satisfy a woman, she should take another man." He swam beneath her, under the flowing huipil, and put his mouth to her breasts. She stared in horror at the water as milk flowed around his head.

"*Dios mío*," she cried, "the milk is for Chayo." And she shoved him away and began the long swim back to shore.

Keh appeared at the *choza* the next morning. His face was set, his eyes lusterless.

"I can take you to Playa del Carmen today to have your

baby baptized," he said. Andre sat at the table that Keh had made and watched them through the doorway.

"I'll find someone else," she replied.

"You won't find anyone else to baptize her. There is no one else but Father González."

She hesitated. "I must pay you for it, then."

"Of course, but you keep the pesos until I need them." He glanced at Andre. "Will he come with us?"

"No. Andre is not a Catholic."

Keh looked up at the sky. "If we take the wagon, we will get there by late afternoon, and we can come back in the morning."

The church in Playa del Carmen was an adobe building painted blue. It had a small bell tower, but no bell. On the beach nearby were a few dilapidated *chozas*, the largest of which belonged to Father González. Its dark interior smelled of mildewed thatch and spilled rum. Father González, a clerical collar circling the neck of his guayabera, was asleep in a hammock, the dirt floor surrounding him littered with pots and pans, lanterns, shovels, enamel chamber pots, axes, machetes, rope, dried deer meat coated with flies, a rusted Gramophone, stacks of sandals and men's shirts, and a box of mammee apples.

"He also runs the store in Playa del Carmen," Keh said.

A young Mayu woman, several children trailing behind her, came in from the kitchen lean-to.

"Do you want to buy something?" she asked in Maya.

"We want to have a baby baptized," Keh replied.

The woman walked over to the hammock, shook the priest awake, and then went back to her kitchen.

Father González looked at them dazedly as he sat up. He was middle-aged and fair-skinned, with stained teeth and a thin, pointed face. There was a colored stone set in one earlobe that sparkled as he touched his bare feet to the dirt floor and walked toward them.

Keh bowed his head and the priest put out his hand to touch his dark hair. "Bless you, my son," he said.

"This is Lidia, Father. She wants you to baptize her baby."

Lidia held out a gold coin.

"For that I can baptize more than one child," the priest said. "Do you have any other children?"

"Just the one."

The church, which had no door, smelled of oily incense and candle wax and dead flowers. The priest picked up the embroidered stole that lay across the altar. He kissed all three crosses, then placed the stole around his neck so that the middle cross rested on his nape and the other two crosses hung down the front of his guayabera.

"The child's name?" he asked as they all stood at the baptismal font.

"Concepción Rosario Frankle y Machado Ramírez," Lidia said.

He looked at Keh, who now held the baby. "You are the father?"

"No."

"He's the godfather," Lidia said.

The priest began to chant in Latin, with Maya and Spanish words thrown in occasionally. Lidia wasn't sure when the exact moment was when Chayo was given to the Church, but the priest finally said, "I do baptize you in the name of the Father, and of the Son, and of the Holy Ghost, and may Itzamná watch over you also from his throne in the heavens."

The news that there had been a baptism of a child spread through Playa del Carmen, and by evening all the families of the village, some forty-five people, had gathered on the beach to celebrate. Keh was greeted by the men with great respect.

"They are peasants," Keh said, "*yalba uinicob*. They are proud to have a descendant of a *halach uinic* visiting them. It has no meaning anymore, but it makes them proud just the same. They believe that the child is mine. That she has blue eyes makes me very admired."

"But she isn't your child," Lidia said. "You should tell them that."

"When a Maya decides the truth of a thing, the facts are no longer important," he said.

A bonfire was lit, and the women prepared the food while the men drank rum and danced to the music of flutes and drums. They executed drunken zarabandas, scraping the sand with their heads, bumping into one another, shouting obscenities and kissing one another on the lips. They danced wantonly, flailing arms and legs, swinging their heads until they collapsed in a heap where they gyrated like a colony of ants, then disengaged, crawled to their feet, and began twirling around one another again. Soon the heaps didn't rise as easily, and when someone set one of the *chozas* on the beach on fire, everyone was too limp to do anything but watch it burn to the ground.

"They would be very disappointed to find out that you are not truly the child's father," said Father González, who was as drunk as the rest. "If you sleep separately, they will know you are not, but if you sleep wrapped together in one rebozo, then they will accept that you, a black-eyed Maya, have performed magic and produced a blue-eyed child."

When Father González and the last of the Maya had passed out on the sand, Lidia said, "By morning no one will remember anything."

"If they see that we are not together, I will be shamed," Keh said.

"I can't have two husbands."

"What if he never recovers and never can be a husband to you again?"

"Then that is the life that God has chosen for me. Marry Rosalia, Keh, and then you'll have a woman of your own."

"It is immoral to marry my brother's widow."

"In the eyes of the Church it would be an act of charity."

"But if you give yourself to me I will help you and Andre. I'm very strong."

"I told you I'll pay you for whatever work you do." She was close to tears.

"But we are happy in each other's company. I can tell by your face, by the way you speak to me."

"I have no one else to talk to but you. Andre is my husband. We have a child. God watches our actions. You are my friend."

"You don't understand anything," he said roughly. "We are not friends any longer. I kissed your nipples yesterday."

Lidia covered her ears with her hands.

"You want to hear only the words that you like," he said, his face twisted in disgust. "Even Father González is not as Catholic as you are."

That night Lidia slept on the floor of the wagon with Chayo. In the morning when the villagers peered down at her to see whether Keh was sleeping beside her, she sat up and rubbed her eyes and pulled her rebozo snugly around her shoulders. "He was here, but he has gone to get water for the mules." She said it confidently, and they had no choice but to believe her.

PART IV

Chayo's Story

45

On November 14, 1951 Lidia wrote a letter to Conrad.

My very dear Conrad,

With much pleasure I write this letter to you, hoping that when you receive it you and your family will be found to be well. Andre and Chayo and I are well, thanks to God.

I promised to contact you in five years. I am one year late. Is it possible that you will forgive me? I think always of you and Teddy and Bix, and pray for you, and send you many messages in my thoughts.

We live beside the ocean in Puerto Morelos. It is very hot, but the breeze pushes the humidity away. There is no doctor. The quinine long ago was used up, but the curanderos have medicines made of plants which work very well for the malaria that sometimes afflicts us.

Andre has grown stronger. He does not have too many seizures now. But still he is unable to speak or write, and so I don't know what he is thinking, but I feel his sadness and know that he must be very lonely. I thank God that when he took away Andre's speech and writing that he left him still able to put what is in his heart into his paintings. Sometimes he makes little sketches for Chayo that tell a story, and I wonder how it is that he cannot put these thoughts into words. When I look at his work, I know that there is a great genius hidden here in Puerto Morelos. I have asked him many times if he wants me to write to the gallery in New York, but

*he always shakes his head no. I don't think he is afraid of
Stalin's agents now. I think he just wants to be left alone.*

*There is a man here in Puerto Morelos who is called Keh
Cocom. He takes people fishing on Cozumel. I prepare the
meals for the fishermen. Keh and Andre and I share in the
money that is made. Several months ago some Americans
came to test for oil on the reef. They used tubes and metal
tanks to breathe under the water. Keh said that it would
bring more people to Puerto Morelos if we had something like
these devices. He said he would teach people how to spear
fish on the reef if he had machines such as these. Keh also
said that more people would come here if we had shelter for
them.*

*Father González is the priest in Playa del Carmen. It is
another village very close to Puerto Morelos. He also runs a
small store where we are able to buy some few things that we
need. Father González told me last week that people from the
government came to him and told him that they want to buy
the land that the church owns on the beach. Of course, my
understanding of most things is imperfect, and in particular
things which deal too much with the world, but do you think
that the government wants to buy empty beaches, where
there are no telephones and no doctors and no newspapers
and very few people, if the land is worthless?*

*It is very possible that we should buy the beaches before
the government does. Although we have money with which to
live, and the fish we eat cost nothing, and Keh provides corn
for us from his milpa, and also picks fruits for us, perhaps
you could come to Puerto Morelos and bring some part of
Guerrero's money with you.*

*There is one other very little thing. Chayo is seven years
old. She is smart and always asks questions and is never
quiet. She should go to school. I do not know where you are,
but if it is in Mexico, is it possible that she can live a part of
the year with you and go to school? Forgive me if my request
gives you hardships or nuisances, because I know you are
always so busy and have so many things to do.*

*In 1950 we discovered that the world war was finished. So
many people died and we knew nothing about it. When
Andre heard what Hitler did to the Jews of Europe, he
became very disturbed and unnatural for a long time. I know
that he was thinking of his parents and his brother. Such*

*news tests our faith, but I must believe that God has a
purpose in all things.*

*I am sending this letter to you through the United States
Air Base on Cozumel. I have only now just begun to wonder
why there is an American base there. I hope it is good for
Mexico.*

*Greetings and a hug to Teddy and Bix, and please receive
from me a special hug and a loving greeting from someone
who will never forget you.*

> *Your devoted friend in Christ,*
> *Lidia*

Like an awkward bird, the Navy PBY swooped low over
the beach, wobbled its wings, teetered on the edge of a stall,
then powered up over the jungle trees again.

"There are a couple of houses on the beach and a Maya and
a kid coming out to meet us in a boat," the pilot shouted over
the roar of the plane's engines.

"That's it," said Conrad, as they circled. "You can let me
out here."

The airplane descended, smacked the water, rebounded a
few times, and then splashed to a stop in a streak of ocean
spray. Conrad opened the door and waited for the boat to
come alongside. When the Maya grabbed hold of one of the
plane's struts, Conrad reached behind the pilot's seat for his
black bag.

"When do you want me to pick you up?" the pilot asked.

"How about Sunday?"

"Sunday it is."

Conrad stepped out of the plane into the boat.

"Are you Keh?"

The Maya nodded and held out his arm to steady Conrad
onto the boat bench. The pilot revved up the engines, skimmed
along the water for a short distance, and then the plane was
airborne.

"I'm Chayo." The little girl leaned with her elbows on the
bench seat and stared up into Conrad's face. She was almost
as brown as the Maya, but her eyes were blue, and there was
a golden sprinkle of freckles across the bridge of her nose.

"*Buenos días*, Chayo. My name is Conrad."

She squirmed and wiggled on the seat. "You came on the
wind god's shoulders, didn't you?"

"Yes."

She stood up and clasped Keh around the neck. "I told you it was the wind god, Keh."

He smiled for the first time. "Your mamá wants a good *huachinango* for lunch, eh? See what you can find." He handed her a net and a spear.

"Will you wait for me, Conrad?" she said.

"I'm here for four days."

She hitched the net to the waist of her cotton huipil, then jumped over the side and disappeared beneath the surface.

"Will she be all right?" said Conrad as he watched for her to reappear.

"She fishes every day," Keh answered. Then he pulled at the oars and carved a smooth path toward shore.

Of course, Lidia had hinted at it in her letter, but it wasn't until Conrad saw her and Keh together that he knew for sure that they were lovers. She didn't try to hide anything, or explain anything away. The situation was as it was. Each night Lidia and Keh helped Andre to his own small adobe house. She and Keh would stay inside with Andre for a few minutes, and then they would emerge, Keh's arm around her, and the two of them would go into the main house together.

That Lidia and Keh were together didn't surprise Conrad as much as the way Keh treated Andre. He was solicitous of his comfort, spoke to him with respect. What Andre thought was impossible to tell, but when Conrad looked at Lidia, barely thirty years old, with the tranquil loveliness in her grown deeper and more mysterious, all he could think was, poor bastard.

"I'll miss Chayo," Lidia said. It was dark on the beach as they walked together. The air was very still, with only a few stars showing. "She has never known any place but this, but a girl should not be raised learning only about ocean and jungle and beach. She has to become civilized, or there will be no life for her later."

"We'll take good care of her, and before you know it she'll be back for the summer," Conrad said. "Teddy has already fixed up a room for her and is talking to the priests at El Carmen about enrolling her there."

They walked for a while without talking, and then Conrad said, "I have a favor to ask of you."

"Anything. Ask me anything, and I'll do it."

"It's the business about buying land along the coast. I'd like to join you in it, pool my money with yours."

"Of course. We'll do it together. There is no favor involved. It is a privilege to be associated with you in that way."

"There's one problem. A day is coming when Mexico is going to throw out all foreign investors. I want you to buy everything you can, from Tulum to Cape Catoche, but all in your name. Will you do it?"

She held out her hand to him and smiled. "¿Cómo no? If you want to, we'll buy the whole Caribbean together."

The pilot held Chayo on his lap and let her hold the controls as they flew over the powder sands of Puerto Morelos. Keh had put a braided string with a jade pendant around her neck before she got in the plane. He said it was to protect her from the bad air of Mexico City.

"Mamá, Mamá," she shouted gleefully at Lidia's figure below.

"Whoa," said the pilot, taking the controls away from her.

"Your work's cut out for you," he said when Chayo finally lay down and went to sleep.

They were over the jungle now, the treetops below them a lovely, unbroken meadow of green. Conrad turned to the pilot. "Have you ever thought of living a simpler life?"

"Nope, I never have. But if you're having doubts, you know what they say. You oughtta go home. Where's that for you?"

"Atlanta."

"No kidding? I grew up in Macon."

"Small world."

"Don't you ever wonder how the hell you ended up working for the CIA in Mexico?"

"I think about it nearly all the time."

He looked down again. There was Xan-Xel, like a dot, a pinprick. He followed it as long as he could.

"It's so hot down there, the steam ripples right up to meet the plane," the pilot said.

Conrad no longer felt like talking. He glanced back to see that Chayo was all right, then he shut his eyes and let the monotonous sound of the engines put him to sleep.

*   *   *

Teddy left Mexico City whenever she could and flew home to Atlanta. "I've longed to hear your southern drawl," she would tell her mother. "And gossip, my Lord, how I do miss gossip." Atlanta, she always said, restored her spirits, made her able to face Mexico City again.

"I do think the problem might be with your attitude," Conrad told her.

"My attitude's fine. I just feel like an outsider here, that's all."

"If you'd try to understand the way Mexicans think—"

"I know the way Juana thinks. She thinks I'm stupid, as if I cared. Lord only knows what she says or does when I'm not around. If the house were falling to pieces around her, she'd never tell me. And how many times have I reprimanded her for breaking another piece of Limoges only to have her blame it on the dish, as if the dish purposely cracked itself to pieces?"

"She doesn't want you to think badly of her. She knows that you're only temporarily here."

"My Lord, people are only temporarily on earth, Connie, that doesn't make them stupid."

But then the letter came from Lidia, and everything changed. Teddy said later that she could pinpoint the exact time and date that she felt at home in Mexico as being a gray day two weeks before Christmas in 1951 when Conrad brought Chayo home to San Ángel.

At the tree-shaded Plaza San Jacinto the taxi driver let Conrad and Chayo off. It was a neighborhood of clipped hedges, cobblestoned streets, mansions hidden behind stone walls and ornate gates.

"Conrad, come see," Chayo called as she skipped ahead. "What is this?"

"A shrine," said Conrad when he caught up with her at the niche in the stone post at the corner of Rincón de Flores.

"*Qué preciosos*," she said, touching the miniature saints and vases of fresh roses.

When they arrived at the cul-de-sac, she jumped on the iron gate and hung there until Juana's husband, Diego, came and unlocked it. Then she swung back and forth for a while before she jumped off and ran up the drive to the house.

Thirteen-year-old Bix, watching for his father from an upstairs window, let out a whoop when he saw him. There was hollering and a clattering of shoes on the tile steps and then the door opened.

"*Buenos días,*" Chayo said.

"*Buenos días,*" said Bix. He was tall like his father, with brown hair and earnest eyes. Only his mouth, wide with full lips, prevented his being handsome.

Chayo walked past him, through the entry, past the stairs, and into a living room full of the Victorian furniture that Teddy had had transplanted from Atlanta.

"My!" said Teddy as Chayo bounded toward the flowered sofa where she sat.

"First time I've seen you not have a thing to say," Conrad said.

Chayo leaned against Teddy's knee and fiddled with her diamond ring, twirling and spinning it around Teddy's finger.

"*Qué precioso,*" Chayo said.

"You are the cutest thing," Teddy said, and pulled her into her lap. "Isn't she cute, Bix?"

"Beeks," Chayo said, her face a grimace of mispronunciation. "Beeks," she said again. Then her face turned serious. "I'll call you Chico."

"You might as well let her," Conrad said. "She pretty much does what she wants."

Chayo had spied the pond and the gray geese through the french doors. She slid off Teddy's lap and pushed the doors open and ran into the rear garden.

"Chico, come here," she called, stepping into the pond with the geese. Bix stood at the door, his hands in his pockets, watching her.

"She'll be good for him," said Conrad, as he saw his son walk closer to the pond and kneel beside it. "He doesn't know how to have fun. She'll give him someone besides himself to think about."

"Well, it's exciting, I can say that," Teddy said. "She has a spunky quality that reminds me of the girls in Atlanta."

"You won't make a Southern belle out of her, I hope."

Bix had removed his shoes and stepped into the pond. Chayo was laughing as the flapping geese exploded the water lilies from their beds.

"Do Mexican girls have coming-outs?" Teddy asked. "Oh, they must have. I'll have to join a few charitable organizations, get myself known around so that Chayo will be invited to parties and such as that."

"She'll be going home once in a while. You know she isn't ours to keep." Conrad watched as Bix stepped into the water, slacks and all, and swam toward Chayo. He had never swum in the pond before, that Conrad could remember.

"Of course she's ours," Teddy said. "And when she visits Lidia and Andre, won't they be astonished to see what we've done with her?"

Teddy put her arm around her husband's waist and leaned her head against his shoulder. Enticing smells came from the kitchen as Juana prepared the evening meal. Bix and Chayo were sitting on the lip of the pond now patting the long-necked geese as they glided past.

"She wears an amulet to ward off evil spirits," Conrad said.

Teddy's eyes, fixed on Chayo, glistened with happiness.

"*Qué preciosa,*" she whispered.

46

Teddy and Conrad, although Episcopalians, saw to Chayo's Catholic upbringing. At seven she was enrolled at Santa Josefina Catholic Girls School in Mexico City. Every morning before school started, there was catechism class with Father Cristóbal, and on Sundays she attended eight-o'clock mass at El Carmen Church. When she was eight she gave her first confession. At nine she took Holy Communion and for the first time tasted the body and blood of Christ. At thirteen she was confirmed, and Father Cristóbal anointed her with oil and prayed that she had received the Holy Spirit. At fifteen she celebrated her *quinceañera*.

Father Cristóbal cautioned Teddy that a *quinceañera* was hardly a Catholic ceremony at all, but merely a custom adopted from the Maya, who believed that when boys and girls turned fifteen they became men and women.

"Don't make a wedding of it, Señora," he said.

"Only a small party, Father," Teddy replied.

A choir sang *"Soy Feliz,"* the altar was banked with white lilies to match Chayo's gown and pink carnations to match the dresses of her fourteen attendants. Caged doves twittered in the naves. Chayo, her pearl-studded gown an unbroken line from her bare shoulders to the carpet, walked down the aisle, Conrad on one side of her, Teddy on the other, with the attendants following. Last down the aisle was the *chamberlan*, twenty-two-year-old Chico, handsome in white pants and white embroidered shirt.

When Chayo reached the altar, she handed the bouquet of pink flowers to the priest.

"Concepción, these flowers represent life and renewal," he said, placing the flowers on the altar. Then he held up the gold ring that Conrad had given Chayo that morning.

"And this ring is a symbol of your spiritual tie to your family, to Mexico, and to God."

He touched the ring of pearls that held the white mantilla to her head.

"May this crown remind you of the victory you have won in a difficult world by coming to the Lord and freely stating your belief in him."

He turned and made the sign of the cross over the congregation. "O Lord, look upon your daughter Concepción Rosario Frankle y Machado Ramírez, who has come to renew her baptismal commitment and to become a disciple of your Son, who lives and reigns with you and the Holy Spirit, one God forever and ever. Amen."

The reception was held in the San Ángel Inn. The french doors opened onto the patio, where blue streamers drifted overhead, mariachis in spangled suits played *zapateados*, and the buffet tables were heaped with food.

Conrad was off in a corner talking to someone he had introduced to Teddy as a school friend from Seattle. Father Cristóbal stood next to the buffet table, a plate of *carnitas* in his hand and Teddy next to him with Chayo's lace mantilla and long kid gloves draped over her arm. The *zapateado* had turned into a waltz.

"Both the waltz and the mariachis are a legacy of Emperor Maximilian," Father Cristóbal said.

"And so is Chayo," said Teddy, as she watched Chayo pull Chico onto the dance floor.

"So I understand," said the priest. "She's a special child. I'm always glad to see her, but I find myself exhausted by the time she leaves."

"She's always had a mischievous side," Teddy said. "But Conrad and I feel that that's because of all the energy she has."

"She puts none of it into her schoolwork," the priest remarked.

"Well, I don't really think that's where Chayo's talents lie, do you, Father?"

"Perhaps not."

Chayo was a head shorter than Chico, and as they twirled around, his arm around her slender waist, it seemed that he held her suspended above the floor.

"She's so pretty, Father," Teddy said. "She just has that special something that warms you up when you see it. I suppose it's in her blue eyes, the steadiest blue I've ever seen. Conrad says when she looks at him and turns her head like she's doing now, he'd give her anything. I've always tried to prevent him from spoiling her. Lord knows, a spoiled child is no fun at all. But we do dote on her, there's no denying that. She just has the ability to charm everyone around her. And Chico, why, if she were his sister, I don't see how he could be more—"

"Theirs seems to be a very close relationship," said Father Cristóbal, frowning as he watched them. "Distance would be beneficial for them both at this time in their lives. She's very young to be stared at in such a fashion."

Teddy looked over at them now. "There's never been anything between them before that I could see. Of course, they *are* close. Chico loves her like we do, but he's been away at school in the United States. He's only here for the *quinceañera*, Father." Her eyes followed them around the room. Chico's lips were brushing Chayo's ear as he whispered to her.

"That's so strange that I never had a hint, but she is so beautiful—" Teddy turned toward the priest. "It wouldn't be wrong for them to fall in love, would it, Father? After all, they're not brother and sister."

"He's not a Catholic."

"But Chayo's father isn't a Catholic either."

"Is that why her parents aren't here?"

"Oh, no, they never leave Yucatán. There's a problem of sorts, a complication that's difficult to explain."

"Are they ill?"

"Yes. No. I mean—"

At the avid interest in the priest's face, Teddy blushed.

"It's not important," she murmured. "It happened long ago."

3 October 1960

Querida *Chayo,*
  It's difficult for me to concentrate on my studies when I remember the night of your quinceañera, *and how sweet your kisses were. You're still very young, but I promise you that*

when I've completed my studies, I'll come back to Mexico and marry you. When I'm with you things lighten for me, the whole world seems less oppressive. My disposition isn't always a happy one, and I'm afraid that one day you'll refuse me because of it. I try every day to remember how you look and sound, and I work hard at changing myself into someone you'll love forever.

My devotion to you,
Chico

4 February 1961

My beloved Chico,
How wonderful it is that we had you here for Christmas. And you mustn't worry that Conrad is angry at you. He knows how hard you work and that sometimes your temper is short. He told me to tell you he will never talk to you about politics again, if you promise not to mention it first! He's very sorry for the argument. Are you sorry? Tell me you are so that I can tell him so and make him happy. He doesn't show his love very well, but he suffers to think that you don't think well of him.

A woman came to hear me sing in the little play that we did at school. She asked Conrad if I can please audition for an orange juice company. They want to do advertisements on the radio, and think my voice would sell a lot of orange juice. Conrad said yes, and I'm very happy.

I cover your face with kisses, and wait to hear from you.

Your Chayo

11 November 1961

Querida,
That you intend to become an actress fills me with pride. You're so beautiful, so delectable, how can a greedy public help but want to smother you with love and kisses, as I do. But don't forget that whatever you do must be done with dignity, and must not bring discredit to you or your country.

My studies go well, and in my free time I've become involved in a student organization that does volunteer work in the East Los Angeles barrio. Some of the people there are as poor as those we see in Mexico.

The bitterness of my last argument with my father still remains with me. He wrote me a letter of explanation about his involvement in the CIA, but there was no note of sorrow for what damage he must have done over the years, no regret that, if anything, Mexico is worse off now than when he and his people began meddling. He calls me a communist. I call him a fascist. Neither of us is right. But how can we communicate with each other when we believe the way we do? How can I not argue with a man like that? How can I not be ashamed of what he has done in Mexico all these years? That you have to hear our constant arguing when I have such little time at home with you breaks my heart. I long to have you here with me, but I know that you must finish school first.

I love you,
Chico

Chico came back to Mexico City in September of 1964. The atmosphere was electric with what was not said between him and his father. They walked around issues, not speaking of what was on their minds. They nipped at each other in small ways. A curt reply, a sarcastic remark.

Chico had begun sleeping with Chayo the summer before, when she was eighteen.

"It's so funny to think that people do this," she said when they first became lovers. "I would laugh all the time, except that when we do it, I forget everything but the pleasure you give me."

Their days were innocent, planned so that Teddy would not see how far the attraction had gone. They went to picnics and movies and rode bicycles in Chapultepec Park. But at night she sat up in bed, waiting anxiously for the sound of him in the hallway, for the small click as her door opened and he got into bed beside her.

"I count the hours until bedtime," he said. "I watch you in the daylight, with the sun on your hair, and all I can think of is the night and the soft pillows on your bed and the smell of your skin."

Some days their need for each other was expressed on the grass in secluded parts of the park or in the back row of darkened movie theaters.

"When I'm in California I dream of you and can't do my work," he told her. "Stay with me while I do my residency, and we can be together all the time."

"But you have me now," she said. "And when I come to do the motion picture you'll have me again. It's good for you to do without me a little, because then you won't get tired of me. And you'll be able to tell everybody that your Chayo is a movie star."

On the evening before Chico was to return to California, he and Conrad had what Teddy later referred to as "their silly argument about politics."

"Los Angeles will be a pleasant place to practice a surgical specialty," said Conrad while Juana served the *café de olla* after dinner.

"Who said I was going to stay in Los Angeles when I finish my residency?" said Chico.

"No one. But why would you want to practice in Mexico? The money is certainly better in the United States."

"Why do you always think in terms of money?"

"I don't always think in terms of money."

"Chico," said Chayo. She whispered in his ear. "Come, let's go to a movie. When we come back, we'll—"

"I just don't understand you, Dad," Chico said. "You've lived in Mexico all these years and you still think like a goddamn American."

"Oh, honey, please," said Teddy, her face pale.

"Maybe that's because I *am* an American," Conrad said.

"Please," said Teddy.

"Let him talk," said Conrad.

"How can you, a doctor, shut your eyes to the poor people in this country?" asked Chico.

"I don't shut my eyes. I do the best work I can at the hospital here."

"For people who pay you."

"For someone who has such contempt for money and Americans, you certainly have taken advantage of both."

Teddy looked helplessly from one to the other as their voices escalated.

"There are poor in every country," Conrad said. "Mexico doesn't have a monopoly on poverty."

"But I don't understand. Explain to me how you justify American involvement on the side of repression instead of revolution."

"Who says I've worked for repression?"

"There's dancing at El Bailar de Méjico tonight, Chico," Chayo murmured to him. She kissed the tip of his ear. "Alicia says that the group at El Bailar is—"

Chico stood up and threw his napkin on the floor. "They've raised you to have an empty head. Is there anything you know except laughing and dancing and going to the movies? Anything at all?"

Conrad was standing now. "Communist sympathizers are not welcome in this house," he said sharply.

"Everyone who disagrees with you is a communist," Chico fired back.

"Chico, wait for me," cried Chayo, but he swept out of the room, upsetting a tray of *dulces* as he went, the door slamming behind him.

Teddy sat on the Victorian sofa and stared at the closed door. "He won't come back to us," she said.

"He left me no options," Conrad replied.

1 May 1965

Muy Querido *Chico,*

I'm here where you are. You will have to see me now, and then how will you resist your Chayo, who still loves you and thinks of you every minute of every day?

We are making a movie here which is called Death of Dreams. *Of course it's in Spanish, but Ramón Mendoza, the director, has made films in English also, and there are many people here who give him money for projects, and so this is where we'll make my Mexican movie career. You wouldn't call me silly anymore if you could see me in this movie. I cry every day, real tears, because my character is so sad. I play Isabel, a Mexican woman who comes to Los Angeles with her little girl to find her husband who has come here to work. She can't find him, and she becomes sick. It's so tragic. Ramón says that in my tears he sees the blood of all Mexico.*

If you would like to see us shoot the last few scenes, come to the merry-go-round in Griffith Park. If you like, I'll take you to see the studios at RKO where we filmed all the inside shots.

Please come. I have missed you and have never forgotten you.

Chayo

"You can stand here next to me, Chico," whispered Ramón, "but don't make a noise because the sound equipment picks up everything, and I don't want anything on the track except Chayo's voice."

Ramón raised his hand and a little girl began to walk toward him from where Chayo lay on a blanket beneath the trees.

"Lift your head, Filomena," Ramón called out to her. "Look at the *tiovivo*."

The little girl looked up at the merry-go-round.

"But sadder, *muchachita*," said Ramón. "Pretend that they have taken all your toys away from you, and you are very sad."

The little girl's lips turned downward.

"Action!" Ramón shouted.

As horses moved up and down on the carousel, the music a faint echo across the dewy morning grass, the sad-faced child walked slowly away from Chayo.

"You see," whispered Ramón, "Isabel is dying and she has sent her daughter away from her, hoping that someone will take pity on her. After all, she is only a child, like the other children who are here riding the merry-go-round."

The camera moved for a close-up of Chayo on the blanket. She coughed softly. "Dear God, take me now before she turns around," she said in a voice that trembled with emotion. "For how will I give her up if she looks in my eyes even one more time?"

Chayo's face glistened with glycerine perspiration, but the tears that filled her eyes were real.

"Ay, what an actress," Ramón murmured.

"I've loved her since she was a child," Chico said.

"I've been an insane man all these months," said Chico.

"But we are together now, *mi amor*," said Chayo, "so what use is there for regrets?"

Chico moved into Chayo's apartment on Edgemont in Hollywood. *Death of Dreams* came out, and no one went to see it.

"No one wants to see pain, no matter how beautiful it is," Ramón said. So he bought five screenplays from a former clown in the Mexican rodeo. They were about Mexican cowboys, and the films were each shot in ten days on a ranch in Chatsworth. When the first one was released it was obvious by the long lines in front of the theaters that people wanted to see Chayo singing and dancing, and if a horse and comedian were thrown in, so much the better. By the time the fifth movie was released, Chayo was a big movie star.

Friction had been building between Chayo and Chico with each film. There were arguments about the inanity of them, about the undignified way that Mexicans were portrayed.

"But we make money, *mi amor*," Chayo said. "We'll make better films later."

The arguments between them grew more frequent and more diffuse. Chico didn't like her friends, he didn't like the way she dressed. He had even begun to dislike the way she talked and acted.

"You remind me of the ridiculous women you play," he said finally.

"You hurt me deeply, *mi amor*," she said. "But if you don't want to be with me, then what can I do to keep you?"

"Nothing," he said, and he moved out of her apartment. The following month he returned to Mexico to work at a hospital run by the Catholic Sisters of Charity. He didn't write to Chayo. He didn't see Teddy or Conrad. The break was complete.

47

Nobody took it seriously at first. Two rival gangs in the Cuidadela district of the city had a fight. One gang was from Vocational 2 School and the other one was from Isaac Ochoterena Preparatory, a school associated with the University of Mexico City. At some undetermined point adolescent feuding changed to political activism, and within days students from the university were stopping people on the streets and asking for donations to promote the six-point proposal for government reform that had been written by student representatives at the School of Economics.

On July 29, 1968, students from Vocational 7 commandeered some public buses and blocked the main streets. On July 30, government troops attacked demonstrators at San Ildefonso Preparatory School, wounding several students and making mass arrests.

"It is the logical extension of the Revolution," some citizens said as they joined the student demonstrators.

"They are nothing but communists," others said.

"It is the deliberate disruption of society by spoiled children," a government spokesman announced.

Conrad watched the events with particular interest. In one of his weekly reports to his superiors in Washington, he wrote: "Perhaps the students are merely testing out ideas and giving themselves a sense of self-importance in the process. But we should think long and hard about the probability that Mexican politics will be unstable for a long time to come.

With the Olympics a few months away, I have advised President Díaz Ordaz to deal firmly with what I think amounts to an insurrection."

There were more demonstrations, more beatings, more arrests. Both sides stiffened in their positions.

President Díaz Ordaz gave a speech in Guadalajara: "Peace and calm must be restored in our country. A hand has been extended; it is up to Mexican citizens to decide whether to grasp this outstretched hand. I have been greatly pained by these deplorable and shameful incidents. Let us not widen the gap between us; let us all refuse to heed the promptings of our false pride—myself, included, naturally."

No one could tell which one was the bull and which one the *torero*.

American and Mexican photographers and reporters lounged against the walls of the Reforma Hotel on Paseo de la Reforma waiting for Chayo Sedano to emerge from her suite in the hotel. A crowd of teenage girls also waited. Every time the doors to the hotel opened, they jumped up and down with anticipation. Finally the doors opened again and Chayo stood at the top of the steps, flanked by security guards. She was twenty-three years old, not much older than the girls who now screamed hysterically at the sight of her. She was in a sweater and skirt and cordovan leather boots. Dark sunglasses covered her blue eyes and a silk scarf was wrapped around her blond bouffant hairdo.

"*Manitas*, little sisters," she said. The girls squealed and ran up the steps, followed by reporters and cameramen.

"You must talk one at a time," she said, laughing. "How can I hear all of you and talk to all of you at once?"

"When is your next picture?" asked a Mexican reporter.

"We start filming in Hollywood in two months. But this is my vacation. I've come to visit my family and to rest and see the Olympics. Are you all going to have a good time at the Olympics?"

"*Sí!*" shouted the girls.

"Did you all see *Mexican Spitfire*?"

"*Sí!*"

An American reporter pushed toward her. "Don't you think you're making a political statement by agreeing to give a welcoming speech at the Olympics?"

"A political statement? Me? Who wants to hear politics

from Chayo Sedano? I'm only proud and happy that President Díaz Ordaz invited me to speak, and that the Olympics will be held here in my beloved Mexico. Who knows? I might even sing a song, and maybe do a little dance, too. But above everything, I'm happy to be home with my friends and to speak Spanish again. Eh, *manitas?*"

"*Sí!*"

The American persisted. "Do you mean to say you're unaware of the problems going on here with the student activists?"

"All I'm aware of are these beautiful girls who love me and my American pictures." She clasped two of the girls to her while the cameras clicked. "I'm a citizen of all the countries of the world. Why do I want politics? I have enough troubles memorizing my lines."

The security guards escorted her down the crowded steps to the waiting Cadillac. Before she stepped into the car, she turned to the girls, some of whom were clutching each other and crying with excitement.

"Go to mass and listen to the teachers, eh, *manitas?* Not everyone who is such a bad student as I was gets to go to Hollywood to make movies."

A young man with long black hair slipped by the security guards and stood in front of the car door.

"Señorita Sedano," he said, his hand on her arm.

She turned toward him, startled. "*Sí.*"

"Hippie, red, get out of the way." One of the guards hit him across the face, knocking him to the sidewalk.

"Are you crazy?" shouted Chayo, pushing the guard away from her. "You *locos,* look at his mouth. His lip is bleeding. *Ay, qué barbaridad.*" She called to the driver of the Cadillac. "Fernando, help me get this *muchacho* in the car."

As the driver got out and came around to where Chayo and the young man were, the crowd of girls grew silent and apprehensive. They edged away from the curb and then began running down the street. The photographers maneuvered closer to the car. The whirring and snapping of cameras was finally interrupted by the shouts of the guards as they scuffled the photographers out of the way.

"I wouldn't take him in the car with you," said one of the guards as Fernando and Chayo helped the young man into the back seat of the Cadillac. "He probably has vermin." He leaned in the open window of the car. "The next time we see your ugly face in front of this hotel, we'll cut your fingers off, and maybe something else, too. Why don't you get your hair cut and take a bath." The car moved forward, and the guard patted the fender admiringly.

They sped away from the hotel, past the Zócalo. Olympic banners hung from the columns of the huge square. All evidence of the last demonstration had been swept from the streets. As they began the turn toward San Ángel they passed several truckloads of soldiers in green field uniform, machine guns in their hands.

"Do you feel better now, *muchacho*?" Chayo asked. She wiped the boy's mouth with her handkerchief.

"*Sí*, better." He looked out the window anxiously. "Where are we going?"

"To San Ángel, but we can let you off wherever you want. What's your name?"

"Gabriel Nuñez," he said hurriedly, "but we can't go to San Ángel."

"What are you saying?" Chayo laughed. "I go wherever I want to go."

"But Chico wants you to bring Señor Whitworth to his apartment in the Colonia Roma and to make sure that he brings his medical bag with him."

"Ay, is this a prank, a trick, *muchacho*? Because if it is, it isn't a funny one."

"No, I'm telling you the truth. Chico said that if he asked Dr. Whitworth to come that he wouldn't do it, but that he'll do anything you ask of him."

"But how do I know where Dr. Whitworth is? He could be at the hospital or the university—"

"Chico said that Fernando would know, that Fernando always knows where Señor Whitworth is. But hurry, we can't waste any more time talking and talking about nothing."

Chayo turned toward the driver. "Do you know where he is, Fernando?"

"*Sí*."

At the Hospital de Pediatría, Fernando parked the car and went to get the doctor. When Conrad emerged from the building, his medical bag in his hand, he was solemn and unsmiling.

"After four years without a word from him, he does this," he said as he got into the car.

"No kisses, no hugs for your Chayo?" she said, holding her arms out to him.

"I missed you," he said.

"That's what I came all this way to see. A smile. Not even a very big one. I'm content with little ones, some wrinkles in the cheeks as the lips go up in pleasure. I don't need the sunrise. A few rays will do."

Soon they were out of the downtown area and weaving in and out of the narrow streets of the Colonia Roma, past the Parque Río de Janeiro, the statue of David on its pedestal in the fountain, and convent girls in middy dresses eating lunch under the watchful eyes of black-garbed nuns. Encircling the park were Moorish-style apartment houses, grillwork balconies clutched tightly to shrouded windows.

"Here, near the pastry shop," Gabriel said. "Park here."

They followed Gabriel through an alley where children splashed in the gutter water and a woman pushed a perambulator full of groceries. At a gray building Gabriel pushed open a screen door and they climbed the wooden stairway to the second floor. He knocked at the door of an apartment at the far end of the corridor.

"*Soy yo*. Gabriel."

The door opened and Chico stood there, bloodstains on his white smock and white shoes.

"*¡Hola!*" Chayo said, pulling off her scarf and sunglasses. She smiled at him. "Yes, it's me," she said. "It's Chayo. Don't be so surprised. I don't want anything. I only came with Conrad to help you, if I can."

Young people lay on the floor of the apartment, the green carpet around them black with blood. Some were moaning, some were lying perfectly still, their faces white with pain. Conrad was already on his knees beside a young girl.

"A fractured spine," he said. "She needs a hospital."

"She'll be arrested if she goes to a hospital," Chico said. "She was at Santo Tomás campus yesterday when the Army occupied it. Many students were arrested after the battle ended, but Gabriel and some others were able to bring a few of the wounded ones here. If I send them to hospitals with injuries like these, the police will know where they were yesterday."

"They have to go to the hospital," Conrad said flatly.

"Let me help," Chayo said. "Just tell me what to do and I'll do it."

"This girl with the spine fracture," Conrad said, "and that boy with the wound in the thigh. Take them to American

Hospital and register them as my patients. I'll have a doctor there take care of them in my name until I arrive. He'll notify their parents, and they can decide what to do from there."

By the fourth trip to American Hospital, the inside of the Cadillac was spattered with blood and vomit.

"I've given her a shot of morphine," Conrad said as the last patient was put in the back of the Cadillac. He had wrapped the girl's hand so that she couldn't see where the fingers were nearly severed.

The girl lay with her head in Chayo's lap. Fernando started the car and they sped through the narrow streets once again.

"You're Chayo Sedano, aren't you?" the girl asked. Her eyes jittered as she strained to focus them on Chayo's face.

"Sí, mana, I'm Chayo Sedano."

The girl sat up and touched Chayo's face with her bandaged hand. "I've seen all your pictures," she said.

48

They faced each other across the restaurant table, oblivious to the music that blared from the balcony, unconscious of the crowded restaurant, the waiters, the jugglers, the vendors selling ices and candied *nopales*.

"You were very helpful with the students," Chico said. It was the first time he had mentioned it since they met that afternoon.

"But I'm yours to command," Chayo replied. "As always." She leaned toward him. "You look at me so hard, Chico, that my face hurts where your eyes land. Can you relax just a little bit with me and tell me that you're glad to see me, too, after such a long and bitter time away from each other?"

He had been wary with her all afternoon, watching her as they strolled through the museum, listening thoughtfully as she spoke. She didn't look like a movie star today. There was no powder on her freckled skin, no mascara rimming her blue eyes. She wore a simple pink cotton dress, with huaraches on her stockingless feet.

"I heard that you were going to marry Ramón and move to New York while he directed a play there," he said.

"You heard that? No, no, he wants to marry me, but for my part it's not possible. Tell me, is there someone here in Mexico who has taken my place with you?"

"No one. I don't have time for things like that."

"But one makes time for such things."

When the waiter brought their food to the table, Chayo

gave a cry of pleasure. "Ay, do you know that I dream of El Arroyo's *carnitas* when I'm in Hollywood? No one in the world makes *carnitas* like they do." She wrapped some pork in a tortilla and handed it to him.

"Like old times, eh, *mi amor?*" she said, smiling at him engagingly. "Did you see my last picture, *The Serpent and the Eagle?*"

"No."

"You should have seen it. It was much better than the other ones. You wouldn't have been ashamed of me in this picture."

He looked down at his food.

"What's the matter, Chico, did I say something that doesn't make sense, like I always do, and you get angry and run away from me?" She touched his cheek and he clasped her fingers in his.

"I'm sorry, Chayo, sorry for everything, sorry for the way I've behaved. I told you once that I would lose you because of the kind of person I am, and I did. None of it was your fault. It was all mine, everything. I have never understood life very well, and when you tried to teach me I turned away."

"Oh, you'll make me cry, and I don't like to cry. You were right about me, *mi amor*. I was silly. Didn't I see the pictures I made? Don't I know how silly I looked? And those American pictures—ay—if I could erase them, with the bananas on my head and the crazy Spanish accent. I did more harm to Mexico than all the dictators we ever had."

A young man passed their table, a tray of meringues in his hand.

"Oh, Chico, *por favor*, bet with the *merenguero*."

"They always win."

"Not today. I feel lucky today, because we're sitting here together and because you're looking at me the way you are. Today I will win, and the *merenguero* will lose."

"*Mozo, ven acá*, come here," called Chico.

The *merenguero* gave a dancer's turn, spun the tray precariously, and returned to their table.

"Heads," Chayo said.

The *merenguero* flipped a coin, and before it landed on the floor, he had slid one of the meringues off the tray and onto the table in front of Chayo.

"You see, I told you," she said.

There was a sudden buzzing in the restaurant. Heads turned in Chayo's direction. The mariachis stopped playing, and the cornet player stepped up to the wooden railing of the balcony.

"*Señores y señoras, sí,* you see her, your eyes are working. It's Chayo Sedano, the star of Mexican and American movies, and one of our own Mexican *muchachas.*"

Chayo stretched out her arms to the crowd. They whistled, screamed, stamped their feet, told her they loved her, told her how beautiful she was, told her how much joy she brought them.

She blew kisses and the people became delirious with excitement.

"I love you, too," she cried. "*¡Viva Méjico!*"

"*¡Viva!*"

"*¡Somos Mejicanos!*" she shouted.

"*¡Somos Mejicanos!*"

The mariachis started to play "Jarochos en el Campo," "Men of the Plains," the Yucatecan song she sang in *Mexican Spitfire.* Chayo began to sing, but her voice could hardly be heard above the clamor. And suddenly, slowly, as though a secret signal had been given, a chanting began. "Chayo, Chayo, Chayo."

Her voice broke, she bowed her head. When she could speak again, she looked out at the faces.

"*Muchísimas gracias, muchísimas gracias,*" she murmured.

When the chanting didn't stop, she leaned toward Chico, her forehead against his.

"Please, we must go," she said, "or I will die of happiness."

They made love in the back of the taxicab. There was an urgency to it, almost a manic frenzy as they held and stroked and caressed each other while the taxi wandered aimlessly through the darkness of Chapultepec Park. Their passion seemed out of control, uncontainable.

"Come back with me to the hotel," she said. "We must be together from now on."

"God, how did I let you go."

"I would have given up the movies if you had asked me. They meant nothing, I loved you so."

"Once more around the park?" asked the driver.

"What? No, no," Chico said, "take us to the Reforma."

The cab circled through the shadows of the cypress trees, then exited the park onto Paseo de la Reforma. At Avenida

Insurgentes Norte the traffic became heavy, the streets crowded with people.

Chico sat up and looked out the front window. "Why are you stopping?" he asked.

"The leftists are having a meeting at the Plaza de las Tres Culturas," the driver said. "They're stopping cars by standing in front of them so they can hand out leaflets."

"Can you go around?"

"I can try, Señor."

The driver crept along in traffic. He kept turning to apologize for not being able to find a way out of the maze of people and cars, and finally Chayo said, "Come, *mi amor*, let's get out and walk to the plaza and see what all the excitement is about. Afterwards we'll go to El Moro's and drink chocolate and eat *churros*."

They got out and joined the crowds on the streets. It had begun to drizzle, and there was a festive air as students ran through the streets with their leaflets. The jam of people and vendors walking toward the plaza grew larger.

Chico bought a *camote* from a vendor, and he and Chayo took turns nibbling at the candied sweet potato as they walked. When they reached the Plaza de las Tres Culturas, thousands of people were milling around or sitting on the ground. Some of them were holding newspapers or umbrellas over their heads, since the drizzle had turned to good-sized drops. Some people sat in front of the sixteenth-century Church of Santiago, while others congregated near the ruins of the Aztec pyramid that had once marked the center of the city. Above them, the lights of the Tlatelolco housing complex burned brightly.

"Gabriel, *qué pasa?*" said Chico, as he and the dark-haired young man embraced.

"We're passing out leaflets, trying to collect a little money for the movement," Gabriel said, "but everyone's having a good time. No complaints, *cuate*." He gestured toward a cluster of photographers near the ruins. "They're taking our picture. They're listening to us now. One of those guys asked me if we were trying to ruin the Olympic Games in order to embarrass Díaz Ordaz. I said sure, if we can, we will."

"There are more than just students here tonight," Chico said. "It looks like your supporters are increasing."

"Well, maybe *sí* and maybe no." Gabriel grinned. "We've got old ladies resting their feet, some families with their kids down from the Tlatelolco project who want some fresh air and entertainment. I even talked to a few who were on their way to the movies. I suppose they think we're going to have a fiesta."

"I like it," said Chayo, and she hugged Chico's arm. "Everyone outside, having a good time."

Gabriel looked up at the sky. "It's going to rain hard."

A student on the balcony of one of the apartments was speaking to the crowd now.

"That's Vega," Gabriel said. "He's from Santo Tomás campus."

"Look, Chico, at that little girl over there, *qué preciosa*," said Chayo. "Would you buy her a *camote*?"

Chico bought another candied sweet potato and Chayo walked over to the little girl and knelt down beside her.

"Would you like a *camote*?" she said. The mother, who was sitting on the ground with her husband, smiled and nudged the little girl to take the sweet.

"Will you let me take her and show her to my friend?" Chayo asked the mother. "He's right over there, see, that tall man."

"*Sí. ¿Cómo no?*" said the young mother.

Chayo picked up the child and started to walk toward Chico. He had moved farther away and was talking to some men who carried a banner that said, Railway Workers Support the Movement.

"You like the *camote*, don't you, *chiquita*?" Chayo tickled the little girl's cheek, and the child looked back apprehensively at her mother, who waved at her encouragingly.

"What fat cheeks you have," Chayo said. She shifted the weight of the child on her right hip to balance the shoulder bag that hung on her left side. Streams of green and red light bounced off the olive planes of the child's cheek as flares burst in the sky above the plaza.

"Look in the sky, little one, fireworks. See?"

There was a sharp noise, cracking and rhythmic, like strings of firecrackers being ignited one after another. The child began to cry as people started to run across the plaza. They ran in every direction, shoving and bumping and pushing at one another to get away. Some fell immediately at the first sound, and were very still. Others attempted to get up or tried to crawl away. There was screaming and shouting and the continuous cracking sounds.

"*Dios mío*," said Chayo as she clutched the child to her. Helicopters appeared overhead. Chayo shouted Chico's name, but she couldn't hear herself over the noise of the helicopters' engines. She began to run, her gait uneven with the weight of the child in her arms. As she ran she saw the men on the roofs of the apartments, their machine guns trained on the crowds below. Little eruptions of light accompanied the bursts of machine gun fire.

The helicopters above them were now shooting at the crowd. Men wearing single white gloves raced through the plaza methodically shooting at everyone in their path. The child was hysterical in her arms. Chayo ran crazily, without purpose. She saw Chico now across the plaza. He called to her, but she couldn't hear what he was saying. A voice on a loudspeaker, amidst the machine gun and rifle fire, repeated over and over, "Don't run. Don't panic."

She held the child tighter, squeezing her, bending over her to protect her from the gunfire. She no longer saw Chico, but she ran in the direction that she had last seen him.

"*Madre de Dios*, pray for us sinners now and at the hour of our death. *Madre de Dios*, pray for us sinners now and at the hour of our death. *Madre de Dios*—"

Soldiers guarded the Church of Santiago de Tlatelolco with bayonets, blocking the crowd's escape. She veered toward the Foreign Ministry building. The Chihuahua building was on fire, but the shooting continued from the roof. Rain mingled with the blood and ran in rivulets down the rutted stones of the esplanade. The men with the single white gloves, some of whom were falling to the stones of the plaza along with everyone else, looked up at the roof and shouted, "Don't shoot. Olympia battalion. Don't shoot."

She passed Gabriel's body, but could not stop. The child was no longer screaming, but made sobbing noises deep in her throat. Then she felt a jolt, as though she had been hit. She stood still, waiting for the pain.

"Oh, no," she said. The child was very still in her arms, the cheek, smudged with candied sweet potato, now also covered with blood. She clasped her tighter and started to run toward the Aztec ruins in front of the church.

Chico caught them both. She felt the child being lifted away from her, saw her laid on the stones, heard Chico say, "She's dead. Run to the church."

"No, I want to stay with you," she said, and as he crept in

the rain and blood tending to the wounded, she knelt down beside him and wouldn't leave.

The shooting had stopped. Only the cries of the wounded could be heard across the plaza. Chico sat down on the ground in the rain and held Chayo without speaking. Soldiers fanned out through the plaza, rounding up those who had managed to hide in the church or in the apartment buildings or behind the Foreign Ministry or in the ruins of the Aztec pyramid. Tanks and trucks moved into the plaza.

A soldier stood above them.

"Up on your feet, *chingón!*"

Chico made no noise as he lunged for the soldier's leg. The bayonet sliced through so smoothly that at first Chayo thought it hadn't touched him at all.

"Chico," she said, crawling toward him. He raised his arm and smiled, and she felt relieved. She put her arms around him and covered his rain-wet face with kisses.

"We'll go home now, Chico, eh? Thank God I still have you with me. When I was in Hollywood I thought of no one but you, but I always knew you were here. I was always sure that when I came home to Mexico things would be wonderful again, that you would love me, that God was good, that he was merciful, that he would not make me go through life without you."

His eyes, open but seeing nothing, caught the raindrops, held them like tears until they overflowed onto his cheeks.

"Chico. *Por favor*, Chico. Don't go. Stay with me."

His lips did not crush against hers when she kissed them. There was no pulse, no warm exhalation of air. She laid her cheek against his and rocked his body in her arms until the soldiers came for her.

Chayo was taken in a truck with some other prisoners to Military Camp 1. From the windows of the building, Chayo watched the garbage trucks pull in and out of the compound all night long with their cargoes of corpses, piling them one on top of the other. Toward morning the bodies were doused with gasoline and set afire. When the ashes had cooled, they were shoveled into wheelbarrows and carted away.

On the third day of her imprisonment an officer came into the barracks where she and the other women were locked up.

"Chayo Sedano? I'm looking for Chayo Sedano."

"*Sí,*" she said.

He took her to an office.

"I'm very sorry," he said. "It was a mistake. There was so much confusion, you must understand that not everyone was clearly identified."

"*Sí.*"

"We were very fortunate, though, that there were so few fatalities, considering the provocation that we encountered from the crowd. No more than sixteen were counted as dead at my last information."

"*Sí.*"

Conrad came for her.

"Thank God you're all right. I had no idea that you were at Tlatelolco. What made you go there?"

She clung to him without answering.

"We're lucky they recognized you. Parents and relatives have been inquiring at the gates of the camp for three days now and haven't been told anything. They don't know whether the people they're looking for are dead or alive."

How could she tell him, she thought, with his face so serene and untouched by grief.

He bundled her into the black Cadillac, and she sat close to him while Fernando drove them home to San Ángel.

49

Lidia and Señor Zamorra each donned a workman's hardhat and stepped into the metal cage. The door clanged shut and the elevator bumped jerkily up through the open shell of the building.

"I have long wanted to meet you, Señora Frankle. I had hoped you would one day come to my office in Mexico City, but since you haven't, I must come here and meet the woman who is most responsible for all of this."

"There have been many others who have participated," said Lidia modestly.

The cage stopped, and they stepped out onto the unfinished top floor of the hotel. The palm-lined coast below jutted fingerlike between the Bajía de Mujeres and the Caribbean. Sure-footed Maya workmen walked the steel girders to the accompaniment of rasping saws and rapping hammers.

"Señor Zamorra has come to see the progress we've made," said Lidia to the construction foreman. Then she walked to the open edge of the platform. "This building that we're standing on, and that one next to us, and that one over there will be finished in a year."

"A year?" said Señor Zamorra.

"Sick people can't work on buildings. But now the mosquitoes are under control."

"Maybe too much time was spent on the workers' city," he said. "At the commission meeting in December all these things will be discussed. Timetables, work schedules, mosquito control, water purification, projected building completion dates, the fifteen-year plan—"

"You talk so fast, Señor Zamorra, that my head aches," she said, smiling. "I only wanted you to see where all of our money is going. Projections and work schedules don't interest me, but seeing Cancún rise from the jungle does."

"It will be clearer when you attend the meeting in December."

"But I won't be at the meeting in December. I never leave Yucatán. Any business I have to conduct is conducted in Puerto Morelos or here. The interests I represent have permitted me to do it that way."

"But all the groups involved, plus the government's people from FONATUR, will be at the meeting."

"Miguel, the young man who drove me here, will attend the meeting."

"But he's very young," protested Señor Zamorra.

"He's the nephew of someone very close to me. I trust Miguel with everything. He'll go to Mexico City for me."

In the afternoon they toured the six hundred block houses in Ciudad Cancún that had been built for the service workers that would one day work in the city. Then they had lunch with a government official at a Yucatecan restaurant on the lagoon at Punta Nizuc.

"The project is going very well," said Lidia when they had finished lunch. "It proves that Mexicans can work together to build something important."

Miguel was waiting at the FONATUR office in Cancún when Lidia and Señor Zamorra returned from one last drive around the island.

"You must come to Puerto Morelos," she said before she got into the truck. "Do you like to fish?"

"Very much."

"*Bueno*. When you come to Puerto Morelos, Miguel will take you diving. You have never seen such fish as are in the waters off this coast."

The drive from Cancún to Puerto Morelos was much easier now that the road had been paved. As Miguel drove, he glanced so often at Lidia that she finally said, "Why are you looking at me instead of the road?"

He reached inside his shirt pocket and handed her a folded envelope.

"It came by telegraph from Mexico City this morning."

Her fingers trembled as she unfolded the paper.

MEXICO CITY OCTOBER 7, 1968
MAMÁ, CHICO IS DEAD. COME TO ME.
CHAYO.

Lidia deplaned in the Mexico City airport, and immediately was swept up into the chaos, the noise, the confusion. Porters and taxi drivers lunged at her trying to grab her suitcase. Frantic-faced people, children and luggage trailing after, scurried to the music of unintelligible instructions shouted through a public address system. Suddenly she remembered the tempo as if it were her own heartbeat, and the weight of her twenty-eight-year exile dropped away.

"You," she said, pointing at one of the cabdrivers, who grinned and plucked her bag neatly out of her hand and then ran ahead of her to the curb and opened the door of his cab.

"San Ángel, *por favor*," she said. "Number eight Rincón de Flores."

She peered out the window as they drove, at the Olympic banners draped on buildings and lampposts, at the armed soldiers on the streets. Chayo had been happy when she came to Puerto Morelos at Easter. She was always happy, always smiling and laughing. Lidia shivered. She felt chilled with only the light rebozo around her. Cotton huipils and bare legs were fine in Puerto Morelos but not in Mexico City in October, when the air was cool and moist and there was the chill of impending rain.

The Plaza de las Tres Culturas was swept and hosed down, all evidence of a massacre erased. The newspapers reported a student disturbance, quickly put down. A few casualties, nothing more. Soldiers patrolled the plaza. When wreaths or bouquets of flowers were placed on the stones, they were quickly collected, tossed in trash bins, and taken away.

Teddy's older sister Delfine, all ruffles and sweet perfume, came from Atlanta to be with her. Lidia decided that Delfine's constant talking was good for Teddy, that it kept her occupied, moved her thoughts away from what was real.

Chayo, in the room she had occupied as a girl, sat in a chair by the bedroom window. At times she got into bed, and Lidia would lie beside her. Sometimes Chayo slept, and when she awoke it was as if someone had slapped her. "Mamá!" she would cry as she sat suddenly upright.

"Sí, Chayo, I'm here."

Conrad stayed in his study. He didn't come out at all, not even when Lidia first arrived.

The priest at the Church of Santiago de Tlatelolco refused to say a mass for Chico.

"Our list of masses is already filled up," he said.

"He'll say no, no matter what day you choose," said Chayo, as she walked away and left Lidia alone with the priest.

"But he died on the plaza in front of this very door, Father," Lidia said. "It's fitting that a mass should be said here."

"But we're filled up."

"Will no mass be said for those who died on the plaza?" she asked.

"It's not on the schedule," he replied.

Lidia knocked on the door to Conrad's study.

"It's Lidia," she said. "Let me talk to you for a little while, Conrad. It's not good for you to be so alone."

The room, cloaked in semi-darkness, smelled of stale cigarettes. Conrad, in a soiled bathrobe, sat behind a desk littered with papers and uneaten food.

"Chayo and I have said a prayer for Chico in El Carmen Church," she said.

"Dear Lidia, your persistent praying enrages me. It's a delusion, all of it. Your prayers and God and Mexico, nothing but delusion."

"We don't own our souls," she said. "We're nothing without God."

"We're nothing *with* God. All is emptiness, all is folly." He rubbed his eyes. "I told Díaz Ordaz to be stricter with them, that small acts of anarchy when accumulated become revolution. Show them what it means to disobey, I told him."

She moved toward him and put her arm around his shoulder. He did not rebuff her. She bent toward him, her cheek on his. "Give your pain away, Conrad, for who among us is not guilty of crimes against those we love?"

50

Very little was written in the Mexican newspapers about the events in the Plaza de las Tres Culturas. A lot was written about the dissension that was growing between competitor nations in the upcoming Olympics.

Thirty-two African nations threatened to boycott the Games because the Olympic Committee had invited South Africa to participate. Black American athletes threatened to boycott the Games to protest racial discrimination in the United States. Some female competitors withdrew when they found out they might be subjected to gender tests. The fear that the drinking water in the capital would cause Montezuma's revenge had some American officials wondering if it might not be better if they housed their athletes north of the Mexican border and flew them down to the Games only when it was their turn to compete. And a Finnish trainer, claiming that the 7,349-foot altitude of Mexico City could prove fatal to competing athletes, caused a number of European athletes to develop a phobia about breathing the thin air.

Avery Brundage, the eighty-one-year-old chairman of the International Olympic Committee, warned all competitors that any country participating in political demonstrations would be expelled. Everyone tried to figure out how much the Mexican government was spending on the Olympics. Mexico City was gripped with Olympic fever, but the events in the Plaza de las Tres Culturas weren't forgotten by the Mexican people, who referred to the night of the massacre as *La Noche Triste*, the Night of Sadness.

* * *

President Gustavo Díaz Ordaz had set aside a block of seats in the Olympic Stadium for Chayo and her friends. At the opening ceremonies eighty thousand spectators watched six thousand doves and forty thousand balloons soar into the drizzly, slate-gray sky. Competing countries marched by in all the colors of the rainbow, flags held aloft, bands playing.

Conrad sat next to Lidia, and in front of them were Chayo and Ramón Mendoza. Ramón, who had flown in from Hollywood the day before, wore dark glasses and an overcoat against the light drizzle, but Chayo wore only a white suit. Drops of rain had made little splats of gray on the material and on the cigarette that smoldered between her fingers. She seemed oblivious to everything but the activities on the field below.

When the blazing torch arrived, carried for the first time by a Mexican woman, twenty-year-old Norma Enriqueta Basilio Sotelo, Chayo stood up and remained standing through the twenty-one-gun salute and the welcoming address by President Díaz Ordaz. Then the president reached for Chayo's hand and she moved toward the microphone.

As the band began to play "Cielito Lindo," a roar went up from the crowd. Chayo closed her eyes and held her arms out as though to embrace everyone. She stood motionless in her rain-spattered white suit as they shouted her name. When the cheers and shouts faded away, and she did not begin to sing, the music trailed off in a whine of percussion instruments.

She dropped her hands to her sides and leaned forward to speak into the microphone.

"Everywhere—" she began, and then paused as her voice reverberated through the loudspeakers in the stadium. "Everywhere in Mexico we hear of the Olympics. On the buildings and hanging from the lampposts we see the words, 'Everything is possible in peace.'"

There was a burst of applause.

"But what about *La Noche Triste* and the simple people who sought nothing but peaceful assembly in a plaza in their own country? What of them? What of their sacrifice? What of their blood? Where are their balloons, their doves? Why do we not see their faces here in the stadium beside us?"

The loudspeakers screeched and squealed and then went dead. A rustle of voices began at one end of the stadium and swept across the field and trilled into the air where the last of the doves and balloons still hovered. One of President Díaz Ordaz's aides got up and said something to Chayo, then took her arm and began to pull her away from the microphone. "No!" she shouted, and shoved him away.

Lidia knelt on the ground in front of her seat, her hand clinging to the back of Chayo's chair for support. *Dios mío, please protect her.*

The aide bellowed into the microphone, but his words could not be heard over the growing swell of "Chayo, Chayo, Chayo."

"They can't touch her, Lidia," said Conrad exultantly. "They can't harm her here."

Chayo lifted one arm in salute. "*¡Viva Méjico!*" she screamed, and the stadium went wild with stamping feet and whistles and the incessant and deafening chant of "Chayo, Chayo, Chayo."

Delfine took Teddy home to Atlanta for a while. The sound of Teddy's sobbing and her sister's incessant talking, both as ever-present as the wallpaper, were suddenly gone.

Lidia lingered in Mexico City. She bought chocolates for Keh and sketch books for Andre. Chayo's photograph was in all the newspapers. The telephone rang endlessly, and there were strange people in the house, coming and going at all hours, talking politics in the living room and then going upstairs and disappearing into Conrad's study.

"I'm going home in a few days," she told Chayo, who kissed her and said, "You go, Mamá, I'm all right now."

On the morning that she was to leave, Lidia brought her packages to the front door. Then she went upstairs.

"Eighty-four million dollars for the Olympics and not a penny for the poor," came a voice through the door.

"Yes, but the government gave free paint to anyone who wanted to paint their house," came another.

She heard Conrad say, "You're acting like school children. School children can't make revolutions."

"Listen to Conrad, *cuates*," Chayo said. "No one here knows as much about how the world works as Conrad does."

Then Conrad's voice again. "We must start slowly. Propaganda at first. Leaflets are fine; you can continue that, but I have access to a few publishers. We'll get out some firsthand accounts of the massacre in the plaza. Then some recruitment—

not too rapid; people tend to become suspicious when actively recruited. But here again the propaganda comes into play."

"If we listen to your advice, we'll be old men like you before Mexico is changed," said the first voice. "I think you're afraid, Conrad. That's what comes with getting old."

"Shut up!" Conrad's voice was a whip cracking. "When you have my experience, then I'll listen to what you have to say. Right now we have to have solidarity or nothing will be accomplished."

"Tell me what I must do, Conrad," Chayo said.

"You must be yourself," Conrad replied. "What you saw in that stadium at the Olympics is a powerful tool. The people love you. You must use that love wherever you can and whenever you're called upon."

Lidia opened the door. The room was hazy with cigarette smoke. Chayo was on the sofa, her arms clasped around her knees. Conrad sat behind his desk, a glass of whiskey in front of him.

"Mamá," said Chayo, startled.

"I want you to come back to Puerto Morelos with me," Lidia said.

Chayo laughed. "Mamá, I'm a movie star. What would I do in Puerto Morelos?"

Lidia turned toward Conrad. "I always thought you would know the right thing to do."

"Mamá, this is politics, what do you know of politics?" Chayo was on her feet and had her arm around Lidia.

"I know that Conrad's politics is not the right politics for Mexico," Lidia said. "He's not a Mexican. One minute he's on one side and then he's on another. He meddles with lives that don't belong to him."

"I left a son dead at Tlatelolco."

"That was Chico's death, not yours."

Chayo's arm fell away from her mother.

Lidia shook her head. "You're not God, Conrad. You can't move the universe."

"Chico's dead, Mamá," Chayo screamed at her. "Doesn't that mean anything to you?"

"Ah, Chayo." Lidia pulled her into her arms. "You're mine," she said. "I'll always love you."

PART V
Children of
Guerrero

51

The call of the chachalaca birds followed them through the jungle. Pepe and Chucho cut swaths in the liana vines with machetes while Bitsy walked behind, prodded along by the dark, squat, gap-toothed man who had clasped his hand over her mouth at the sacred well. He had led them to where the weapons and backpacks were hidden, where they stayed until it grew light. Now he marched beside her, an M16 rifle in his hands.

"You've got the wrong person," said Bitsy for the hundredth time.

"We have the right person," said Chucho, glancing back over his shoulder at her.

"I'm just a housewife from Los Angeles. I'm not political. I don't know anyone political. Most times I don't even vote. I think you've made a mistake, and probably I'll die of the heat before anything else happens. I thought you were a friend, Chucho."

"I am a friend. This has nothing to do with you as a person."

"Thanks a lot. That certainly makes me feel better."

Swarms of butterflies hovered thickly over the springy jungle compost, and as Pepe and Chucho chopped at the vines, a solid carpet of color rose slowly and drifted away.

"Ow!"

"José, help her up," Chucho hollered.

José slung the rifle over his shoulder and pulled her to her feet.

"Something's been eating me," she said, examining the red, swollen knot on her arm.

"Let me see it," Chucho said. He grasped her arm and took a quick look at the swelling. "*Garrapatas.*"

"What's that, for God's sake?"

"A parasite." He took the first-aid kit out of his backpack and cut into the raised portion of skin with a scalpel.

"Ouch! God! Jesus! That hurts."

"I have to get the eggs or little *garrapatas* will burrow into your skin and make you their home."

Bitsy made a face as Chucho showed her the blood-bloated tick he had removed from her arm. He doused the wound with antibiotic powder, put the kit back in his knapsack, and once again began hacking at the vines with a machete.

Toward noon, when they stopped to rest, Bitsy flopped down on the ground and hung her head between her knees.

"Are you sick?" asked Chucho, kneeling beside her.

"Oh, no, nothing like that. Half dead, but not sick. I'm skipping everything in between."

He looked at her eyes and put his hand on the moist skin of her neck.

"Really, Chucho, I'm so hot, I can't breathe. I'm so hot, my teeth ache." She lifted her head up and looked at him. "I might just melt into the ground without a trace."

"Nobody melts," he said. "It's not possible to melt."

Pepe grabbed the end of a hanging vine and slit it with his knife and held it near her face.

"What's that?" she asked.

"It's *bejuco de agua*," Chucho said. "It will quench your thirst better than water."

She opened her mouth and let the liquid flow down her throat, then wiped the drips away with the back of her hand.

"This really has been an exciting time, Chucho, but I think you've scared everyone enough, especially me. And you don't know what you're doing to my sister. She worries about me a lot, and even if things aren't her fault, she thinks they are. If something bad happens to me she'll blame herself for the rest of her life."

"Do you think we're playing games?"

"Well, I don't know. It doesn't feel like a game, but how

do I know? I have no money. Dee's got a little, but not an awful lot— "

"We don't want money. You're the one we want."

"But why me?"

"Your sister has power in the States. She'll make a big commotion over this. Everyone will listen to her. Money is nothing compared to the publicity we'll gain by this."

"You're serious, aren't you?"

"Very serious. The Revolution in Mexico was never completed. You were in Mexico City, you saw the poor. What you saw was but a fraction of the suffering of the Mexican people. We want democratization for Mexico, nothing more than that."

"Kidnapping me won't bring democratization to Mexico."

"It will give us a voice."

He took Bitsy's hand and helped her to her feet. "Do you feel better now?"

"I guess."

As they resumed their trek, the vegetation grew denser. Perspiration ran down Bitsy's legs beneath the huipil. The moist earth seeped into her sandals and loosened the straps so that the leather soles flopped wetly against her feet. When they had been walking about an hour, the heavy growth thinned, and they were on a footpath where the air was less fetid.

"I smell food cooking somewhere," she said.

"Xan-Xel isn't far," Chucho replied.

"Can we stop there for a while?"

"We have no friends there. It's not much farther to the place where we'll stay tonight."

To all sides of them lay mounds of Maya ruins, sleeping mountains beneath blankets of vegetation. They climbed a rocky trail to the top of one of the mounds and Pepe removed some moss-covered stones.

"Come on," said Chucho, giving Bitsy his hand.

"I don't like tight places," she said. "What's down there?"

"Gonzalo Guerrero's tomb."

She stopped walking. "Burial tomb?"

"There's nothing to be afraid of."

José waited until they had all started down, and then he stepped down and pulled the stones in place above them.

Bitsy held her hand to the mildewed wall as they descended.

"Watch your head," said Chucho, and his voice sounded muffled and strange.

"It's so dark," Bitsy said.

"A few more steps and it will be light."

She could see the fabric of his shirt in front of her now. And the paintings on the walls of the stairway. Ferocious animals, men with spears and feathered crowns, women giving birth to serpents. She clutched Chucho's shirt and moved away from the wall.

The stairs grew wider, the light more luminous. It was damper here, but the air smelled sweet and cool.

"Sweet Jesus!" Bitsy exclaimed. Stalactites hung like crystalline spears hundreds of feet above them. The ceiling had an opening to the sky, and the waning rays of the sun shimmered on a turquoise pool before them.

"This is so beautiful," she said. "It's like being in church."

"It's better than a church," said Chucho. He lit a candle and set it down on the rock ledge at the far end of the pool.

"And that is Guerrero," he said.

A skeleton sat on a throne facing the pool, its bony fingers resting on the carved jaguar arms. The gold wire that held the skeleton together glinted in the light.

"Now you've gone too far, Chucho. You wanted to scare me. All right, I'm scared. I'm so petrified I don't know what to do."

"Go ahead, put your hand on his fingers. Feel how smooth they are."

She walked slowly toward the skeleton.

"He won't hurt you."

She touched one bone with her index finger, then withdrew it quickly. Pepe and José began to laugh.

"Guerrero never bites anyone," Pepe said.

"He may have been fearsome once," said Chucho, "but now he's very old. He'd be insulted to think that you're afraid of him."

"Who is he?" She rubbed her index finger against her huipil.

"He was the first Spaniard to come to Mexico," Chucho said. "He's the father of the mestizo, a great warrior of the Maya."

"He should be buried," she said. "It's sacrilegious to leave him sitting there."

Chucho smiled at her. "You're not too afraid, are you?"

"Not too."

Chucho reached toward her and tugged gently at a tangle of blond hair. A jumble of leaves and twigs dropped to the stone floor. "Are you a natural blonde?"

"Yes."

He stared at her until Pepe called to him from somewhere to the rear of the throne.

"We have to find you some clothes," Chucho said. "You can't wear a huipil and those shoes in the jungle. We have a long journey tomorrow. What size are you?"

"Size?" said Bitsy. She followed him into an anteroom stacked with canned food, crates of ammunition, bottled water, and clothing. "I don't know what size in men's pants. Fourteen in women's."

Pepe handed her a pair of pants. She pulled them up partway under the huipil and then shook her head when they got stuck at her hips.

"Try these."

"Maybe I'm a sixteen, but I'll never admit to anything larger than that."

After a few more tries, Chucho found a pair of pants that fit her, and a pair of men's boots, which, with the addition of three pairs of heavy socks, hugged her feet.

José handed her a long-sleeved shirt.

"But it's so hot."

"It will protect you from mosquitoes and *garrapatas*."

She turned her back to them and slipped the huipil over her head, and then pulled the shirt on and buttoned it.

"I have to go to the bathroom," she said, turning around again.

"There is no bathroom in the jungle," Chucho said. "José will take you outside and wait for you. And don't try to run away. The jaguars would be happy to have you for dinner."

A note was handed to Dee by an Indian boy in the parking lot at Chichén Itzá. "Stay at El Mesón del Marquez in Valladolid. Chucho."

Valladolid was twenty minutes from the ruins, a colonial town with a dusty plaza, around which clustered an old church, the chicle workers' union hall, the public market, and El Mesón del Marquez Hotel.

Carlos stopped the car in front of the hotel. The car was a green one, unmarked. A bureaucratic-looking car.

"I'm going to Mexico City in the morning," he said, "but I can stay with you tonight." He had his hand on her arm, his fingers grazing her breast.

"You want to go inside and make love just like nothing happened?" Dee said. She didn't dare look at him, or she would fall inward, disintegrate. She stared out at the pot-holed road in front of the union hall, at the men lounging in front of the whitewashed building. "Maybe you'll recite a love poem to me of Yucatán, and I can write you a thank-you letter when I get back to Los Angeles."

"It was a delicate thing that I was trying to do. I had a department to consider, people who reported to me. I couldn't tell you before that I was working against Chayo and Conrad. I couldn't just—"

"Oh, God," she said. "Conrad Whitworth. I knew there was something strange in the way he looked at me and Bitsy, the way he—"

"He made Chayo the way she is now. She went crazy when Chico died, and then Conrad showed her how she could avenge his death. She was never this way before."

She turned to look at him. "Am I supposed to be happy that she was once a nice person and has only lately taken to guerrilla warfare?"

"It was only by way of explanation."

"Explanations after the fact. What else was too delicate, too secret to tell me about? You let me believe you were a chauffeur. Was lovemaking part of your job?"

"Oh, no, no, no." He pulled her toward him, pressed his lips against hers. "The hotel's a nice one. We'll have a bath and then rest together, comfort each other."

"That's enough," she shouted, and shoved him away. "Enough," she said, her voice lower, but still breathy with anger. "My sister's been kidnapped, and it's your fault. You didn't do it, but you might as well have. There's such a thing as forthrightness and trust when you love somebody. Where was that? Didn't you learn any of that in the seminary?"

His look of distress turned her face hot and made her want to cry. "You didn't warn me. You didn't tell me what you knew. I could have done something to prevent it."

"No, you couldn't have."

"I'm talking about Bitsy. I'm not talking about anyone else. I don't care if Chayo kidnapped someone else. It's Bitsy I

care about. You didn't tell me you were involved in cloak and
dagger operations and I delivered her to Chayo and Conrad
and Chucho—and God knows who else—on a silver platter.
I could have taken her home, taken her somewhere else—"

He started to say something, but she waved his words away
and opened the car door. "You didn't tell me," she said,
when she was out of the car and looking at him through the
safety of the window. "That's all I know. You didn't tell me."

She sat on the balcony of her room alone and listened to
the crickets for a while and then went inside and took a
shower. Then she called Stan in Los Angeles.

"Hi," he said. It sounded like he was yawning.

"Did I wake you up?"

"No, I was watching the news. Are you home?"

"I'm in Valladolid. It's in Mexico, the Yucatán peninsula."

"Oh. Did Sid tell you I dropped in to the courthouse to see
if you were back?"

"No, he didn't."

"You got the reports on your escaped murderer, I suppose?"

"Yes."

"But you're not calling me about that, are you?"

"No. Bitsy's been kidnapped."

There was silence. "Kidnapped as in abducted by party or
parties unknown?"

"We know who did it. A leftist guerrilla group."

"Did they state their aims? Set a price?" He was alert now.

"I think they want the publicity. The whole thing has me
reeling. It just happened this afternoon and I haven't really
assessed it yet. I wanted to tell you, though, see what you
thought I ought to do, how I should play it."

"FBI, State Department. Do you want me to contact some
people I know?"

"That's why I'm calling you."

When she hung up she got the operator on the phone again
and gave her Leon's number. While she waited for the call to
go through, she unpacked her suitcase and put things in
drawers. She avoided looking at Bitsy's suitcase sitting forlornly by the door. Carlos had packed it, but she knew what
was in there. A pink shorty nightgown, cloth slippers, the
kind that fold into a little zipper bag, makeup kit, bras and
panties, Mexican blouses, slacks, trinkets for Leon's family in
San Antonio.

She jumped when the phone rang.

"Leon? It's Dee."

"Hi, how are you?" He was so deferential to her, always so pleasant, it was sometimes difficult to remember that he beat her sister.

"I'm okay."

She couldn't think how to say it.

"What's my wife doing?" he said.

"That's why I'm calling. Look, Leon, something bad's happened to Bitsy."

"What do you mean, 'bad'? An accident? You two been in a car wreck?"

"No. Bitsy's been kidnapped."

"Who? What are you talking about?"

"I don't know who. Terrorists, guerrillas—what difference does it make? All I know is that I'm supposed to stay here in Valladolid until I hear from the people who took her."

"Well, what do you mean—" His voice was high in pitch and as soft and gentle as a girl's.

"I mean she's been kidnapped."

"She told me she was with a movie star, for chrissakes."

"She was—we were—"

"She never does anything right. She fucks everything up." The gentle tone was gone.

"She didn't kidnap anyone, Leon. She *was* kidnapped."

"She's always in the wrong place. If anyone's going to be in the wrong place, it'll be her. I told her to come home. I wanted her to come home. Jesus, Dee, what's going to happen to her? Do you want me to come there? What the hell am I supposed to do?"

"Don't do anything yet."

"I have no money. You'll tell them that, won't you, that it won't do them any good to keep her because I don't have any money?"

"I'll tell them."

Neither phone call relieved her as she had thought they would.

"Chucho thinks I'm beautiful," Bitsy said only two nights ago.

She got a legal pad out of her suitcase and began to write down everything that had occurred since she and Bitsy had been in Mexico, everything she could remember anyone saying, any names Chayo had mentioned.

How did I miss what was happening?

She looked at what she had written. Words on paper had always had the power to reassure her.

Chayo opened a window to the past, and when we marveled at the sight, she mumbled a few words of incantation and we were lost.

She got into bed and put the pad on the blanket beside her in case she woke up and thought of something she had missed. The bed was clean, the room comfortable. Chucho had picked an atmospheric place for her to wait this thing out. The town was quaint, if dilapidated. The hotel was old, but well maintained, its Spanish past still here in the sturdy bricks and quiet garden, in the wooden shutters over windows shaded by laurel trees.

I'm angry at Carlos, because I'm embarrassed at my own gullibility. Chayo, with her little-girl grins and cutesy mannerisms, is smarter than I am. I'm ashamed at how effortlessly she did it, how willingly I followed after her. She was a walking revolution, and I never once thought it had anything to do with Bitsy and me.

Reporters from all the major wire services in the world were in the square in Valladolid clamoring for Dee's attention. She stood on a bench so that they could all see and hear her as she answered their questions.

"Have you heard from the kidnappers?" asked the man from Reuters News Service.

"Yes," Dee said. "A note was handed to me by an Indian boy at Chichén Itzá."

"What did it say?" asked the United Press reporter.

"Just that I was to come to Valladolid and stay at El Mesón del Marquez until they contacted me again, that my sister is all right, and nothing will happen to her if I do as they say."

"Have they asked for money?"

"They didn't mention money."

The Reuters man interrupted. "Do you think they made a mistake, that they really meant to take you?"

"I'm not sure, and I don't think I'd better speculate."

"Do you think your sister's Mexican heritage is a factor in this?"

"I have no idea."

"Is the FBI working with the Mexican government on it?" asked a reporter from Associated Press.

"I'm sorry, I can't tell you anything more than I have. The Mexican government has not been in touch with me. I'm waiting now for a call from the U.S. State Department."

"Are you going to remain here in Mexico like the kidnappers have asked, or are you going to return to the States?"

"I'll stay here as long as I possibly can."

"What about her husband? Is he coming down?"

"No, he isn't."

"Did they get along?"

"I don't think the state of their marriage has any bearing on this."

"Did you know that Chayo Sedano is being sought by the Mexican authorities for questioning in connection with your sister's disappearance?"

"No one told me that."

"Are you familiar with Mexican politics?"

"Only superficially."

"Do you think that your sister is in serious danger?"

She hesitated a moment, and finally said, "Yes, I do."

52

From Guerrero's tomb the real journey began, past abandoned henequen plantations and Maya ruins, through dense jungle that choked the oxygen from the air. The men seemed inexhaustible, but Bitsy, her face a red mosquito-bitten mask, was sapped by the heat.

When Pepe protested that they stopped to rest too often because of her, Chucho snapped, "Since you complain so much, maybe you would like to carry her."

"Don't fight," Bitsy said. "Just leave me here. I'm sure someone will find me. Dee's probably got the Army and Navy and Marine Corps out right now looking for me."

As night fell they entered a village and stopped at an Indian marketplace to buy food. Most of the vendors had packed up their produce and cooking pots and taken down their cotton awnings. Except for a stray dog and a few women who remained at their wood stoves frying strips of pork, the market was a shadowy place that reeked of days-old leavings and rotting fruit.

"I ache all over," Bitsy said. She sat numbly against an adobe wall, Pepe on one side of her, José on the other.

"You lead a soft life," said Chucho, who had returned with a handful of meat-filled tortillas. "You need more exercise." He handed out the food and then sat on his haunches and stared at Bitsy while he ate.

"Is there any news of me in the papers?" she asked.

José laughed.

"There are no newspapers here," Chucho said.

"Oh."

She opened the tortilla and examined its contents, then took a bite and made a face. "It tastes like the meat turned bad yesterday, and it's too tough to chew."

"Eat it," Chucho said. "You'll need the energy."

José and Pepe ate quickly and then stepped behind the adobe wall. There was the sound of zippers being unzipped and two smooth streams of urine hitting the dusty ground. When they were through they sauntered over to the small cantina and disappeared inside.

"You don't seem like a kidnapper to me, Chucho," Bitsy said.

"I'm not. I'm a diplomat."

"You're making fun of me, but I'm serious." She put her hand on his arm. "Let me go. I'll never tell a soul. I'll just consider that we went on an outing. There won't be any hard feelings at all, none."

"There wouldn't be any point to that," he said, his eyes on a young woman in hiking clothes, a backpack strapped to her back. She was drinking a Coke and watching the Indian women at their frypans.

"She doesn't look Mexican," said Bitsy, following his line of sight.

"I heard her speaking German," Chucho said. "Probably just passing through. Germans are great hikers."

The girl bought some tortillas and pork and walked away.

"She may be just a hiker," he said, "but I think it's time for us to leave. I talked to a trucker when I bought the food. He'll take us to the river."

During the long truck ride Bitsy slept and woke and slept again. They stopped in Escárcega, where Chucho got out and went into an adobe building. José and Pepe stood by the truck driver's window and exchanged ribald stories with him in a slangy Spanish that Bitsy only half understood.

"I talked to your sister on the telephone," said Chucho, when they had left Escárcega behind and the truck was once again bouncing down the road.

"Dee? You talked to Dee? Oh, my God, what did she say? Did you tell her not to worry?"

"I told her you were alive, and that made her happy. She said, 'Tell Bitsy to be brave.' Then I told her you would stay alive if she gives President de la Madrid my list of requests. I told them to her and she said she would do it."

Bitsy moved away from him, toward the rear of the truck. "Would you really murder me if you don't get what you want from the government?"

"Don't be frightened."

"How can you say that? It's my *life* you're talking about."

"I'm not going to murder you. You know that."

"According to my calculations, today is December twenty-fifth," said Bitsy, when night fell.

Chucho reclined against his backpack next to her. José and Pepe were asleep, their snores like sharp rocks falling off the back of the truck.

"So?"

"Christ's birthday. Christmas. Don't you even take time off to celebrate Christmas?"

"We celebrate in January."

"We celebrate both. Leon's family is really into Christmas." He sat up and spread his sweater over her. "Go to sleep."

She looked up at the sky. "Same stars, I suppose, as there are in Los Angeles. Do you know anything about astronomy?"

"No."

"I took a class once, but I can't find the Big Dipper. Maybe there's too much moonlight."

"Umm-hmm."

"Leon wanted me to buy Christmas presents for his nieces and nephews. We were going to spend the holidays with his family in San Antonio. I wonder what he's doing now."

"Sleeping."

In the morning they arrived at a camp on the edge of the Usumacinta River. It was a makeshift town of tents and lean-tos. On three sides were the jungle and the lone road, on the fourth was the river. As Chucho helped Bitsy down from the truck, men armed with rifles came running toward them.

"¡Viva los hijos de Guerrero! ¡Viva Chucho!" they shouted.

Aguardiente was passed from hand to hand. Bitsy was jostled and pushed as the men fell on Chucho, hugging him and slapping his back.

"You did it, Chucho," cried one of the men, his rifle raised above his head.

They crowded around Bitsy, shutting off her air, pulling at her blond hair, patting her face with their fingers.

"Chucho," she cried as she fell to her knees in the mud.

"*¡Bastante!* Enough!" Chucho shouted. The men continued to whoop and bellow, pressing more tightly against her. Chucho held his pistol up and pulled the trigger. The blast was an electric streak across the Usumacinta. It exploded the men's frenzy, shocked them, so that they staggered away from Bitsy, confused looks on their faces. Then they began to drift away, slowly, an isolated huzzah and a few frazzled whoops trailing in their wake.

"Did they hurt you?" asked Chucho as he helped her up.

"I don't think so."

Pepe offered Chucho a cigarette, and they stood smoking together while Bitsy waited next to them, ankle deep in mud. Not even the laces of her boots were showing.

"I feel like the prize cow at the Orange County Fair," she said to no one in particular.

They hiked along the path that snaked between the closely spaced tents. From inside the tents came the sounds of family life, and over everything hung the pungent aroma of cilantro and tobacco smoke.

"*Mamá, ya llegamos,*" Chucho called as they entered one of the tents.

"*Ay, mi hijo.*" His mother was barely five feet tall, with wrinkled brown skin. The child in her arms began to cry at the sight of Bitsy.

"Oh, oh, I'm sorry, baby," crooned Bitsy.

"She's afraid of strangers," his mother explained.

"My name is Beatriz Carmen Martínez," Bitsy said, "so now I'm not a stranger."

"My mother's name is Carolina," Chucho said. He took the baby from his mother's arms and sat down at a square wooden table in the middle of the swept dirt floor, while Carolina began to ladle food into dishes.

Bitsy held out a rolled-up tortilla, and the child reached for it and stopped crying.

"Is this your baby, Chucho?"

"Yes. This is Adela. She's two years old."

Bitsy looked around the tent, at the two mattresses on the dirt floor and at Carolina patting out tortillas over a wood-burning stove.

"No, my wife isn't here. She was killed."

"Oh," said Bitsy, and she looked worriedly at the child.

"I was with Lucio Cabañas Barrientos in 1974 when he was killed by the soldiers. Ours was called the Party of the Poor, but some of us were teachers, like Cabañas and me. We're very famous still in Guerrero, but when Cabañas died the *pistoleros* started chasing me around the country. Because of that I'm always a target. In 1980, just after Adela was born, my wife, Eva, took her to Mexico City to visit her mother. The Army took Eva and the baby to jail. Only God was witness to what was done to her there. Later Eva and Adela were returned to her mother, but Eva didn't live long after that. When she died, the doctors told her mother that something had ruptured inside of her and that she had bled to death."

"My God, Chucho, how sad you must have been."

"I was sad, but it was good for me. It made me a harder person, gave me more resolve, enabled me to fight better for Mexico and for what I believe in."

"I don't believe that that's all her death meant to you."

"How do you know so well what I think or feel?"

She looked down at her lap, at the scratched leather handbag that she had carried with her from Chichén Itzá. "I lost a child and I know that I could never say that her death made me a better person. Never."

"Lost? How did you lose her? She ran away?"

Bitsy looked up. "Cancer. Her name was Vickie. Victoria Delfina Martínez."

"But her death wasn't politically connected, so you can't understand what effect a death like my wife's can have on a husband. Chayo understood, because she lost someone in almost the same way."

"Chayo?" The purse slid from her lap onto the floor.

"Even your sister didn't suspect what Chayo had planned."

Bitsy picked up her purse and rummaged around in the bottom of it.

"What are you doing?" he asked.

"Looking for the keys to my Camaro."

His laugh splintered the quiet of the tent.

"Here, Adela," she said, offering the keys to the baby. "All babies love to chew on car keys. It makes their gums feel better when they're teething."

The little girl made satisfied gumming noises as she sucked on the keys.

"None of this impresses you," he said. "Aren't you angry at Chayo for deceiving you?"

"Oh, yes, I'm very angry," she said, her eyes following the baby's movements.

"So we accomplished what we set out to do," Chucho continued, "and now we'll wait until your sister does what she has promised."

Bitsy tickled the baby's chin. "Did you see what she did, Chucho? Adela, do it again for Papá." She tickled Adela's chin again, and the baby reached out to pat Bitsy's cheek.

"If we tell the people about Mexico's problems, about the crisis our country faces, and demonstrate that we are willing to leave our homes, to live like nomads, to fight and die for what we believe in, then the government will surely be shaken to its foundations."

Bitsy put her handbag back on the ground. "Do you think she'll let me hold her on my lap?"

Chucho handed the child over the table to her. "De la Madrid, like López Portillo before him, would like to call us communists and so dispense with us, but we're socialists, and we won't permit the government to hide behind the false mask of institutionalized revolution. Guerrero is the spirit in us, he informs our strength, he lends meaning to our humble lives as we strive toward justice for all Mexicans."

"There, now, I'm not a stranger to you, am I?" Bitsy cuddled Adela in her lap and nuzzled the baby's warm skin with her lips.

Carolina came toward the table. "I'll take her now so you can eat," she said.

"Oh, no, she's fine where she is."

"Since the Second World War there has been no further progress in the Revolution. The Mexican can remain passive for only so long, and then he must act or perish."

"Adela, Adela, what a lovely name," said Bitsy.

53

"Tell the governor it's Dee Sorenson," said Dee when Governor Brown's assistant answered the phone.

"Dee?" came the familiar voice after a few clicks of the international line.

"Yes, Governor. Can you hear me all right?"

"Fine, remarkably well. Ever since I heard the news I've done nothing but make phone calls to everyone who might have some influence with the Mexicans. How are you holding up?"

"Fair. Worried. Also needing to know what's going on at home, that everyone's as concerned as they should be. The newspapermen here make it seem very important, but I know that their interest can wane if there are no developments in a few days."

"Well, don't worry, because no one's going to forget here in California. Besides your friends in the judicial community, lots of Latinos are jumping in now. They think more than one point is being made here, that not only is an American woman being held hostage, but that she's a Mexican-American woman, and that's pretty touchy stuff in California."

"I never thought of it that way," Dee said.

"I've already talked to President de la Madrid and he's instructed his top aides to keep in touch with me. He's very sensitive to the barrage of communiqués he's getting from Washington. He knows that the President wants action."

"I need your reassurance, especially since the Mexicans in

general have gone out of their way not to tell me what's going on or what steps they're taking. I did manage to relay the kidnapper's demands to them through a television program called *Hoy Mismo*. Now I'm waiting again. I feel helpless, powerless to do anything."

"What's happened to you is one of the fears in the back of every public person's mind. Just don't give up. Something'll break soon."

The most private place to talk was in the square across from the Church of San Cervacio. The sun filtered through the dense leaves of the laurel trees, and there was no relief from the heat. Richard Philomen, United States under secretary of state, pulled at his perspiration-stained collar as he sat on the bench next to Dee.

"Should have a Department of Clothing to tell you how to dress in this damned climate," he said.

"Take off your jacket," said Dee. "I'll respect your position in the State Department just as much if you're in shirtsleeves."

"I appreciate it," he said. He removed his wool serge jacket and placing it neatly on the bench beside him. He was a middle-aged man with a bland air and a diplomatic lack of any distinguishing feature.

"Here's the list that Chucho—also known as Jesús—Carrillo gave me over the phone," Dee said. "I don't know whether they're impossible requests or not, but it seemed to me on looking at the seven points he listed that they were no more than a loosening up of the system to allow for more political opposition. I gave a copy of it to *Hoy Mismo*, but I haven't heard anything more about it. I can understand that it's not their number one priority—my sister, after all, isn't an important person—but it's my number one priority. She's very important to me. I want my own country to pay more attention than they have been." She slapped the list down on top of his neatly folded jacket. "I want the State Department to take this damned list and submit it to the Mexican government."

Philomen put on his glasses and read the paper. When he finished, he said, "It's a very ticklish situation interfering in the internal workings of the Mexican government. They have every right to resent our meddling in their affairs." He spoke carefully, his jaw working from side to side between sentences.

"You must understand that the Mexicans absolutely abhor American intervention," he said. "It's a great fear of theirs that somehow if they permit us an opening we'll take over their whole political system. Point of fact, their fears are probably legitimate. We haven't hesitated in the past to jump right into Mexico when our interests were involved so the Mexicans are always glad of an opportunity to embarrass us by keeping us off balance and in the dark as to what they're doing."

"We give them aid," retorted Dee. "Withhold the aid until they produce her."

"Ah, Judge, would that it were as simple as that."

"Then what do you propose to do, just sit here with me on a park bench and debate the finer points of diplomacy?" She took a deep breath. "I'm sorry. I didn't mean to talk to you that way. I never do things like that. It's the strain."

"Perfectly understandable. I park my feelings at the State Department door when I undertake a mission like this. Talk to me any way you want."

"You're very kind. Okay, let's assess where we are." She ran her fingers through her hair. "First, how do we find out what's really going on? President de la Madrid has sent an envoy of Mexican statesmen to see me and they smiled a lot and made a lot of soothing noises, but they said not one concrete thing that made me believe they were actively working to get my sister back. I know evasive tactics when I see them."

"The State Department appreciates that your background and training—"

"A department can't appreciate anything," Dee said. "I want to know that *people* at the State Department are paying attention and trying to do something."

"I can assure you we are. We're not minimizing this thing in the least, but the impact of this incident on American relations with Mexico can be—"

"Have they found Chayo Sedano yet?"

"What? Oh, the actress. No, not yet."

"The Mexicans love her too much to really look for her," Dee said. "It's up to you to find her."

"We have no jurisdiction here."

Dee got up from the bench.

"Where are you going?" asked Philomen.

"I don't know." She took a few steps away from him, then turned around again. "Carlos González, what do you have on him?"

"He's on the Mexican team, a special task force they have to combat subversives. He's their number one man. He's supposedly under civilian control, but there is some connection between his agency and the military. I personally haven't met with him yet."

Dee gazed across the square. "He keeps telling me Bitsy's kidnapping couldn't have been avoided," she said.

"It probably couldn't have been," he replied.

Valladolid was awake after the siesta, and it seemed to Dee that all the inhabitants were on the streets hawking their wares. Since Bitsy's abduction, Dee had gotten into the habit of taking a stroll every afternoon after siesta. The bustle and noise distracted her and the exercise tired her enough so that she was able to sleep at night. At least until five in the morning instead of waking up at three.

"*Con su permiso, con su permiso,*" she said as she bumped shoulders with someone every few feet. The shadow of the market building lay across the narrow street, and the vendors were so thick on the sidewalks that Dee had to step off the curb to get by. A horn honked behind her and she stepped back up on the sidewalk between a pile of red chiles and a coop of yellow songbirds.

A Maya woman pressed a clay figure of an idol into her hand and spoke to her in Maya.

"I don't understand."

The woman switched to Spanish. "*Quinientos pesos. Suerte le traerá, mucha suerte.*"

"*Sí,* I need luck." Dee handed her a five-hundred-peso bill and slipped the figure into her purse.

Suddenly no one was walking in either direction. Automobiles and donkeys pulled as close to the curb as possible. Dee pushed through the throng on the sidewalk to see what was happening. In a few seconds a convoy of military trucks rolled by filled with dark-faced, unsmiling soldiers armed with automatic rifles.

The trucks turned right at the Chicle Workers Syndicate building. When the sixth truck had passed, Dee caught a glimpse of Carlos's face in an unmarked green car. When she got back to El Masón del Marquez, the car was sitting in front. Carlos got out and walked up the steps beside her.

"I've been to Puerto Morelos again," he said. "Lidia says she hasn't seen Chayo, but there was a look on Andre's face that told me she's been there."

Dee stopped at the bar beneath the porte cochere. "A Kahlúa, please. I'll be at a table in the courtyard."

"A *tequila con limón*," said Carlos.

The windows of the eighteenth-century hotel looked down on the potted plants and shaded walks of a secluded courtyard, shut off from the noise and dust of the street. Carlos sat down beside her at a cloth-covered table and watched her warily, as if anticipating the sharp words that he knew waited for him on the back of her tongue.

"What about Ramón Mendoza?" she said.

"We spoke for a long time at his home in Mexico City. He doesn't know anything. It's a big surprise to him what Chayo's done. He says it ruins the show."

"I'm heartbroken for him."

Carlos came to Valladolid every few days. He reported every bit of news to Dee, told her about every lead, no matter how small, related every conversation, no matter how insignificant. They sipped their drinks now, cloaked in the somber shadows of the courtyard, the emotion between them raw and silent.

"Why do you keep coming here, Carlos?" she finally asked.

"If we share this time together, maybe you'll trust me again, believe in my love once more. I know how hard this is for you, and I'm sorry for what I had to do." His dark eyes were on the worn tablecloth, on the band of moisture ringing his glass.

"When did you know what Chayo was up to?"

"Last year. Informants told me she was looking for someone to kidnap. It could have been a Mexican, but she was spending more time at Rancho Mirada than usual, and so I knew it would probably be an American."

"You went to work for her to watch her and she never suspected what you were doing?"

"Chayo plays with danger. She knew. She didn't care."

"What about Conrad?"

"He controls Chayo to a point. I know that he told her to be careful of me. He never wanted me around. He looked at me with such hatred—" He shrugged. "I didn't care."

"But you cared about Chayo."

He looked up at her. "We're like sister and brother. But I can't let her destroy Mexico. She knows that if she misbehaves she'll have to be punished. That's the way it is. It has nothing to do with what we are to each other."

"This whole thing is so crazy. I can't believe how crazy it is. That they took Bitsy, my sister, who's never done a bad thing to anyone, never says anything unkind, goes to church, puts up with an abusive husband—my God, what was Chucho thinking of?"

"This," said Carlos. "Your anger. He knows that you'll do anything you can for her."

"Every time she moves, something bad happens to her. I've always tried to protect her, but nothing I've ever done has ever worked."

"You can't create your sister's life. You can't blame yourself that they took her because of you."

"I know. But I do, and that's what I'm faced with."

They ordered another drink. Dee drank half of hers and then took a deep breath and said, "I've never asked you this before, Carlos. I've been afraid to. But I have to know. Did you want Bitsy to be kidnapped in order to catch Chayo and Conrad in a terrorist act?"

"I would never do anything as cruel as that to you," he said. "I thought we would be there at the moment it occurred, that we would prevent it and—" He looked away. "I'm sorry. It was a miscalculation. It was a terrible mistake."

Guitar music drifted up through the courtyard into the open windows of Dee's room. She turned her head on the pillow and looked at her travel clock. She had been asleep only an hour. She pulled on her robe and stepped out onto the balcony. The guitarists in the courtyard below saw her and strummed more enthusiastically.

Carlos climbed the steps to the balcony. He was in jeans and T-shirt, his face draped in shadow. "Will you keep me away forever because of this?"

He stopped a few feet away from her and waited.

"How much did they cost?" she asked.

"You're smiling."

"It's a silly thing for you to do."

The gentle plucking of guitar strings followed them into the room, and even when the door was closed, Mexican love songs whispered through the open windows and sweetened the air.

They stood against the door, her robe thrown open, his arms around her. "I couldn't live without your forgiveness," he said.

54

New Year's was the hardest, Bitsy decided, being away from home when everyone was getting their hair done, buying new dresses, and trying to figure out whether to serve cheese balls or skewered shrimp with the vin rosé on New Year's Eve. Being away from Leon wasn't too difficult, because he usually started drinking Christmas Day and didn't stop until January 10 or so.

But the holidays came and went, and every day in January Bitsy waited for someone to come and get her, but nobody did. In February refugees poured into the settlement from the Guatemala side of the river. Chucho was gone and Bitsy had no one to ask if she was free to go home except baby Adela, who giggled when Bitsy said anything at all to her.

Every day Bitsy and Carolina walked to the Mexican village of Frontera Corozal to buy tortillas and meat and vegetables for the day. A few times she thought about asking one of the vendors who had a truck to take her to the nearest police station, but either she had Adela in her arms and Carolina had vegetables and tortillas in hers, or the other way around. The timing just never seemed quite right.

When Chucho got back from visiting with the insurgents in Guatemala in March, Bitsy had it in mind to ask him when she could go home, but Adela had learned to say *"¿Cómo estás, Papá?"* and so the first thing Bitsy said when she saw Chucho walking down the muddy path from the river was "Chucho, guess what Adela has learned to say."

In April, Chucho went off on military maneuvers in the jungle and Carolina said, "I'll move my mattress to my sister Leona's tent. It's too crowded in here."

"But I'll be leaving soon," said Bitsy, who now wore her blond hair braided and coiled on top of her head.

When Chucho returned from the military maneuvers, Bitsy thought it was probably the time to ask if she could go home, but he hugged her when he saw her, and she realized how much she had missed him, so she said instead, "I'll heat water for your bath."

She boiled the water with clove leaves and poured it into the tub inside the tent. He took off his clothes and sat in the water while she knelt beside the tub and scrubbed his skin and scoured away the dirt of the jungle. She meant to ask him about going home, but as he leaned back in the tub, his eyes closed, the aromatic water surrounding them, she thought how happy she was, and so she said nothing at all.

"The Army has found our camp," Chucho said. "We're going to Guatemala to get out of their reach." He sat smoking a cigarette, wisps of smoke curling in the golden light of the Coleman lantern.

At first what he had said didn't register.

"Your sister and Carlos and the Army, they all know where you are now," he said. "You'll be happy to go home."

"What about Chayo and the others? Is it all right with them? I mean, they went to a lot of trouble and—"

"Chayo is already busy with other things."

"Well, I'm really sorry that things didn't work out as far as my, you know, the—"

He shrugged. "Oh, they worked out all right. Our demands were read on television and radio for a week. It was as much as I could have hoped for with one kidnapping." He was quiet for a few moments. "Of course, you could stay with me. But only if you want to. I never force my women to do anything they don't want to do. If they like me, they stay with me. If they don't, they don't."

"You have a lot of women?"

"Not now. I don't have time. I used to. Once I had more women than I could use." He shot vulnerable little glances at her.

"I don't know," she said slowly. "More women than you could use—"

"Well, I prefer you. To tell you the truth, I haven't had a woman since my wife was killed. But I could have. But you're here now, and, as I said, I like you." He stubbed out the cigarette. "I like you a lot. But you go if you want to, because you're not a prisoner any longer. You haven't been one for a long time."

She sat on the edge of the mattress and watched him sleep. Nobody was pushing her. He had left it up to her. It was her decision. When was the last time she had made a decision? She couldn't remember. Everyone made them for her. And what about Chucho getting hurt, or even, God forbid, Adela? But *If* she left them and went home, what would happen to them? What would happen to her? How could she live? Who would she be?

Oh, God, what was she thinking of? It was insanity. It was craziness. It couldn't be happening. Leon will die. What will his folks in San Antonio say? Oh, sweet Jesus, what will Dee say?

"Chucho." He turned in his sleep and put his arms around her. "Have you decided to come with me to Guatemala?" he said as he wrapped them both in the blanket.

"I'm a Catholic," she said.

"So am I."

"I believe that the soul will burn in hell for its sins."

"So do I."

"But I can't leave Adela."

"And me?"

She covered his face with kisses. He smelled of the cloves that she had put in his bath water. As they embraced and touched each other, Bitsy knew that no one else had ever shown her such tenderness, such love.

Everyone else had left the camp and headed for Guatemala. A flotilla of wooden rafts had already made the crossing of the Usumacinta, but Chucho and Bitsy and Adela had remained behind, their raft floating close to the Mexican side of the river. Chucho had his binoculars trained on the jungle road.

"They've arrived," he said when the first Mexican Army trucks appeared. "She's in a Jeep with Carlos. She sees us now. She and Carlos are running this way." He let the binoculars drop. "Go ahead," he said. "I'll wait."

The two sisters flew toward each other along the wet bank, waving their arms and shouting.

"Bits, thank God," cried Dee. "Oh, it's so good to hug you. Is it really you? Has it been terrible? I thought I'd never see you again." She held her sister away from her. "Look at you, Bits, you're so thin and gorgeous." Dee stared at her sister's shining blond braid, at the slim figure inside the embroidered huipil.

"I haven't even been trying to lose weight," Bitsy said. "Just think of all the money I could have saved if I had let Chucho kidnap me years ago."

"Thank God you can joke about it. At least he hasn't mistreated you. I worried so that you would be—"

"I feel awful that you had to worry about me."

"What's a sister for? Oh, give me another hug."

"Oh, Dee," said Bitsy, and they both began to cry.

"I know it was awful, Bits, but it's over now. We'll get you back to civilization where you can—"

"But I can't go back now," Bitsy said. She looked nervously over her shoulder at the raft, then back at the troops that had dropped down from the trucks and were lining up along the road.

"Let's not talk about it here," Dee said. "We don't have to go back immediately, if you don't want to. We'll get you back to Valladolid, let you rest for a few days, and then take you back to Los Angeles."

"I can't do it, Dee, oh God, it's so complicated. I don't want you to feel it's your fault, because none of it is, and I don't want you to blame yourself and feel guilty. It's just that—"

"Beatriz, hurry up," shouted Chucho.

Dee looked bewildered. "Why is he waiting? Is he crazy? What are you—'Beatriz'?"

"He calls me that. See, that's what I was trying to tell you, Dee. Chucho has a baby girl. Her name is Adela. She's— God, you make it so hard for me. Don't look at me like that."

"But you can't go crazy over every child you find. What are you saying, that you're going to stay here because of Chucho's child? Leon's waiting at home. You live in California. My God, he's a terrorist, for Christ's sake."

Someone hollered a command, and the troops began to move along the road toward the river.

"Come on, we've got to get out of here before they start shooting," said Carlos, who had run up beside them.

"Shooting?" cried Bitsy. She swiveled around, then raced wildly toward the sandy bank where Chucho and Adela waited on the raft. When she reached it, Chucho extended his arm and pulled her aboard. He shoved at the bank with a cedar pole, and the raft pirouetted on the swells, tilting and dipping with each surge of the current.

"You tell them not to shoot, Carlos, do you hear me?" screamed Dee. "That's my sister. That's Bitsy on that goddamned raft." Then she ran toward the riverbank. She stumbled, fell, got up and continued running.

"Isn't she beautiful?" hollered Bitsy. She held the little girl up for Dee to see. "Her name's Adela."

"I love you, Bits."

"I love you, too," Bitsy shouted back. The raft, churning atop the water rapidly now, gyrated a few times, then found the current and sailed steadily ahead and down the river toward Guatemala.

55

When Dee first got back to Los Angeles from Guatemala in March of 1983, Bitsy's kidnapping, once treated as high drama and potential tragedy, turned into something to make jokes about on the *Tonight Show*. The newspapers now handled it as though it were the plot outline for a Mexican soap opera. *The Los Angeles Times* ran a cartoon showing a blond woman running into the Mexican jungle, a serape wrapped around her shoulders, a Gucci bag hanging from her arm. Jokes circulated in the courthouse corridors about Judge Sorenson's sister falling in love with her Marxist kidnapper. There was whispering when Dee entered the courtroom, and giggles, as though dirty jokes were being told.

But in a few months everyone forgot all about it. Except Dee. She missed her sister. She was also angry at her. For making Mexican women look so dumb. For being such a fool.

At the beginning of 1984, the Valley rapist case over, Dee asked Judge Pelletier to reassign her.

"I'd like a change. I'd rather not hear long, involved cases for a while," she said.

"All right. How about arraignments?"

"I'll take it."

Arraignments were quick. She didn't have to linger over evidence, get involved in lengthy trials. She heard bail motions, decided plea bargains, set trial dates, sentenced people who had already pleaded guilty. It was mindless, rote, automatic pilot.

Sid, who had stayed with her as court clerk when she changed departments, said, "I think you've made a mistake. People were beginning to sit up and take notice of you. I heard you were even being considered for the federal bench. You'll have to climb up all over again."

"My personal life needs attention."

"You're not thinking of marrying that guy in Mexico, are you?"

"Seeing him four times a year isn't enough for me."

"But to give everything up—"

"I just need the time to think," she replied.

April 11, 1985

Dear Dee,

Your letter dated January 3, 1985, arrived yesterday. When I complain to Chucho that I'd like to know how you are now and not how you were four months ago, he reminds me that I'm one of the few people in Florido who receive letters and that no one wants to trudge all day over dirt roads to Panajachel to pick them up. I can't complain. I love your letters whenever they come.

Guess what. I'm pregnant. I never thought I'd ever be again, but I am. Chucho worries about me here with no doctor, but I'm so happy, I can't tell you how happy I am.

I'm glad you got to spend some time with Carlos in December, and no, I won't tell you that you should have stayed in Mexico. Who would take advice from someone who says she's happy living in a sixteenth-century village in Guatemala without telephones or electricity or running water?

The weather continues beautiful after the heavy rains of summer. And thank God, no mosquitoes up here in the highlands. From our hut I look out the door at Lake Atitlán. Three volcanoes line up on the southern shore like the biggest breasts you ever saw. Once in a while the ground shakes and everyone in the village stops what he's doing and looks up at the adobe roofs that didn't collapse in the 1976 earthquake. Living here is a little like living on a fat man's belly and waiting for him to laugh. Socop, the village shaman, told me that the volcanoes watch us and when we misbehave they shake us in punishment.

There's a small school here. The teacher is trying to teach the children to speak Spanish so they can read the few school books he bought in Guatemala City. But there's no paper and no pencils for the children. Don't send any, though. Parcels never arrive.

Adela is so smart. Only three and a half and she speaks a combination of Maya and Spanish and holds the thread for me while I weave. Lucía, Socop's wife, has been teaching me on the backstrap loom. I have a long way to go before I'm even as good as an eight-year-old girl. She has also taught me how to bargain for lime rocks and tomatillos in the market in Chimaltenango and how to prepare Chucho's bath. You light a fire under a pile of smooth stones, then place sweet grasses and water over the stones until the temescal is filled with perfumed steam. Then he sits inside. Sometimes I sit in there with him.

As for food, it's beans, a few vegetables, a bit of meat, but there's lots of tortillas, which I make myself. I soak the corn in lime water, then grind it by hand to make the masa. I cook the tortillas on a hot comal, which is a plain old sandstone slab.

It's nice to have conveniences, and I can't say I wouldn't like to have them, but I'd grind corn with my nose if Chucho asked me to.

Socop is an adivino. He reads the blood and interprets the pulses in the body and claims that when he burns copal on the steps of the church that every step is a different god. On Easter Sunday, when the priest left, Socop and the men of the cofradía marched through the church in their white and purple robes lugging heavy statues of the saints on their shoulders. There are no pews in the church. Everyone sits on the stone floor. Socop put his candles and flowers on the long slab that runs down the center of the church—pink flowers for health, green candles for fertility—and he prayed and lit candles straight out the door.

I don't really believe he speaks to the gods, but you never know. Just in case, I've asked him to say special prayers for Chucho and my baby.

The political situation is terrible. Chucho and his men have joined forces with Manuel, the leader of a guerrilla unit not far from here. Manuel has tried to convince Socop to use his

*influence with the villagers, but Socop refuses to take sides.
Manuel says that the Indians must fight the Army for their
rights. And the Army brings arms to the villagers and tells
them that the guerrillas are against God.*

*Sometimes the soldiers come and take men away, even boys
of eleven or twelve, and no one ever sees them again. They
just disappear. Many Indians who have supported Manuel
have been killed, and so more and more villagers are running
away to refugee camps in Mexico. The Maya believe that
leaving the land where their dead and the umbilical cords of
their children are buried is the same as dying. The whole
thing is a tragedy.*

*I dress like an Indian. Banded skirt, embroidered blouse. I
even cover my hair with a tzute, which is a hand-woven scarf
that you can put on your head like a turban to cushion a
basket, or carry packages in or suspend a child from. All of
this just so the soldiers won't notice me when they come
through the village. If they find me, they'll know that Chucho
and the rest of the rebels aren't too far away.*

A baby, Dee, can you imagine?

I love you,
Bitsy

Dee opened the refrigerator and stared into the empty
interior. A few shriveled plums, a rotted head of lettuce, a
pizza box. She leaned into the moist coolness and retrieved
the box and put it on the sink, then studied the dried pieces
of pizza and tried to remember how old they were. Then with
a shrug she slipped them into the microwave, punched the
time, and waited for the beep.

She ate her solitary dinner in her robe on the deck at the
back of the house. Warm breezes gusted through the color-
washed canyon caressing her face with the licorice scent of
sweet fennel and riffling the papers in the arraignment files
sitting on the table next to her dinner tray. Down the hill the
neighbor's dog welcomed him home, the throaty bark cracking through the still canyon.

She pulled Bitsy's letter out of her robe pocket and read it
again. Then she put it back in her pocket and tried to concentrate on the files in front of her, tried to make sense of the
hundreds of pages of brown, cracked, finger-stained paper.

She reached for a pad of notepaper, intending to jot down
some areas of the law to research, but instead found herself

writing a letter to Bitsy. She wrote in Spanish, and the words spilled out, sprawled onto the note pages, spread their inky splendor over the blank paper, tildes and accents falling into place.

Fourteen pages. They were filled with items of gossip she knew that Bitsy would like plus a list of all the famous people she could remember who had died recently. Bitsy always liked to keep up on that. She didn't tell her, as she wanted to, to come home at once. *What are you doing? Are you crazy? Do you want to get yourself killed?*

She reread the letter, and when she was sure there was nothing else she wanted to add, she took it inside and paper-clipped it to the latest copy of *People* magazine. Tomorrow she would put it all in a manila envelope, take it down to the post office, and send it off to Guatemala.

It was routine August weather in the Valley, windless and warm, a Hollywood moon shining on the swimming pool, a sprawling ranch house ablaze with lights. Bales of hay in the backyard. Chefs in jeans and red-checked shirts barbecuing whole sides of beef over open pits. Two milk cows from Altadena Dairy lounging near the fence for anyone who wanted to try his hand.

Dee and Stan reclined against a haystack, half-eaten plates of ribs and beans on the grass beside them. Their relationship had turned benign, friendly.

"It was nice of you to come," Stan said. "You didn't have to."

"I like your brother's birthday parties," Dee replied.

"The cake has gold leaf and edible Astroturf."

"I'll bet."

"Bernie was named insurance man of the year. Twenty million dollars' worth sold. I personally don't understand all that interest in death. What do you think?"

"Of what?"

"About death."

"Oh. That. Well, I'm against it."

"Did you have a nice time in Mexico?"

"It was very nice. Carlos and I spent the time in Cuernavaca. I almost didn't come back."

"It's the 'almost' that always gets you, Dee. Why don't you just chuck it all and stay down there with him instead of running back and forth?"

"Because I can't toss everything over."

"Can't?"

"I've worked hard. How can I quit? How can I leave?"

"Just sell the house and go. But you don't want to hear that." He leaned closer to her, his jaw jutting, teeth gleaming. "Nobody gives a fuck if you stay or not, Dee. You know that, don't you? The world won't fall if you let go of it. You're so goddamned envious of your sister's freedom that you can't stand it. Why don't you just admit it, instead of giving me all this shit about you can't do this and you can't do that?"

She smiled. "You know me as well as anyone, I suppose."

"How're the ribs?" Stan's brother Bernie stood before them, paunchy in his Levi's, a platter of spareribs in his hands.

"They're wonderful," Dee said.

"Have some more," Bernie said.

"She hasn't eaten what you gave her three minutes ago."

When Bernie walked away, Stan said, "So what are you going to do about all this?"

She leaned back against the hay and gazed up at the lights twinkling on Mulholland Drive. They drove out the stars, blinded you to them, made the night sky as unlike Mexico's as it could be.

"I haven't a clue," she said.

56

To be silent had its advantages. If you made noise you were noticeable. Things were required of you. But if you made no sound, you became invisible, and so could do as you pleased.

Andre stepped back from the easel to see what the colors did to one another. Something in Chayo's eyes displeased him. He had overpainted them several times trying to get the color right. Like people, the paints had separate personalities, but still they had to blend, had to do their part agreeably.

Chayo had come at Easter and sat for him, staring out the window while he studied her face. Although the fuss over the American woman was past, Chayo came to Mexico very seldom, always without notice, and always by private plane, landing on the flat water beyond the reef. Sometimes she came with Conrad, but at Easter she had come alone. Andre had watched from his window as Miguel took the boat out to pick her up.

In the evening they had sat together and listened to a Mozart concerto on the new cassette player that she had brought him, she on the floor, leaning against his knees so that he felt the sorrow in her. She wore a blue blouse, its color zestless next to the true color of her eyes.

"Conrad has decided that we will go to New York for a while," she said when the record was over. "Maybe I'll make a movie. Maybe Ramón will direct it. Who knows? Carlos makes it difficult for us since the troubles began with the

American woman. But I'll write to you and kiss your picture every day."

She had stayed with them for a week, sitting alone under an umbrella on the beach or walking with Lidia. Sometimes she swam out to the reef, taking a spear gun and net bag with her.

"You never forget some things," she said when she would bring back fish for supper.

The day she left she had stood behind his stool, her arms around his neck, and watched him at work on the unfinished portrait.

"You always make me so beautiful, Papá," she said, smoothing the hair above his old scar and letting her lips linger on the red ridges.

He stood back from the easel now to see if he had caught her yet. The easy openness of her glance was there and the lip that was always about to quiver with delight. There was the look of her Jewish grandfather in the questioning way she tilted her head. What a blend of paints she was, this Mexican child of his, this quixotic creature, this reminder of the past.

"The eyes are not right,'" said Lidia, looking over his shoulder at the portrait. "I've brought your coffee. Drink it while it's hot." Since Keh's sickness she no longer lived in the main house, but slept in one of the apartments on the beach. Miguel stayed with Keh and was there to give him his medicine when he awoke at night.

He applied paint to his brush and carefully rimmed the iris of the eye with gold.

"That's much better," Lidia said. She straightened the paint supplies on his worktable and gathered up the newspapers that lay stacked beside his bed.

Sometimes my feelings for her are savage, he thought. I want to harm her so she'll grieve as I've grieved. But then I remind myself of how much I love her, how dear she is, how sad our lives have been, black beyond reasoning for me, guilt-ridden for her.

"I have to go to Cancún again this afternoon," she said. "There is a labor dispute. But I'll be here to make your lunch."

She talked to him like someone thinking out loud. It made him feel like a broken lamp, or a malfunctioning radio. And yet she alone attended to him, would not let servants or employees make his bed or prepare his meals.

"Keh ate part of his breakfast today," she said as she turned toward the bed and bent to smooth the unmussed sheets, "but Miguel said that he hardly slept last night. The doctor is giving him something stronger for the pain."

When Lidia and Keh became lovers, Andre had watched in agony. He had thought of ending his life. He had hoped disaster would befall her and Keh, that her gods would punish them. He had been filled with wild urges, misshapen desires. Then Keh had done the unforgivable: he had become his friend. And so there was nothing to do but acquiesce, to pull inside himself so that only a part of him was visible.

"There will be workmen installing sprinklers on the west lawn," she said. "I've told them your studio is here and that they must work quietly." She straightened up and looked at him. "Your bed isn't even disturbed. Why haven't you slept?"

He touched his fingers to his throat.

"Ay, another cold. I'll bring you a *tisana* to soothe it."

"A *tisana*," he said. "Your favorite remedy."

She gasped at the sound of his voice, and then clutched the arm of the chair and trembled above it moment before she sank onto the cushion.

"I've been as silent as a table for forty years," he said, and her moan sliced through him. "How was I able to do it? I marvel at myself. I wonder at my own cruelty." He walked across the room and gazed out at the whitecaps in the water. "For fifteen years I've been able to speak and yet haven't spoken. My heart's breaking that Keh's going to die soon. He's been my *compadre* all these years, my loyal friend."

"Why have you never told me?" she cried.

"What would have become of the three of us if I had told you?"

She let her head drop down. Her fingers moved over imaginary rosary beads. "I'll do penance for my sins. I'll pray to the Virgin. I'll make a pilgrimage to the Virgin of Guadalupe. I'll—"

"You haven't sinned."

"But I have. You were my husband in God's eyes and I turned away from you."

"Nobody's watching what we do. Nobody cares."

"God cares." She got to her feet, a diminutive, aging woman with youthful defiance in her eyes. "I'll wait until Keh dies. When he's buried beneath the ceiba trees, then I'll go to Mexico City to do my penance. If I don't do it, I won't be able to rest. You can't prevent it. You can't stop me."

Three weeks after Keh's death, Miguel drove Andre and Lidia to the bus depot in Playa del Carmen. Lidia carried Brother Aguilar's breviary and Andre brought his sketch pad and enough money for food and a return bus ticket.

"A bus ride to Mexico City is a fitting way to begin my penance," Lidia said.

The bus, an old one, was crowded with families and animals and packages, and it broke down twice during the three-day journey to Mexico City. When the radiator pipe broke, all the men got out and pushed the bus for ten miles until a new one could be found. When they hit the cow in the road and his horn pierced the radiator, they waited half a day on a dry, dusty road until another bus came by with a soldering iron. On the morning of the second day a woman gave birth to a baby and that afternoon an old man had a heart attack and died.

"The two cancel each other out," Andre said.

When they reached the outskirts of Mexico City, Lidia looked out the window anxiously. At the Palacio de Bellas Artes she stood up. "Come, Andre, we'll get off here."

It was late in the afternoon and they had not eaten since morning. Andre bought tortillas and beans from a vendor, and he and Lidia sat on the steps of the Palacio and ate. She read silently from Brother Aguilar's breviary for a little while, and then she slipped it into the folds of her rebozo, lifted her skirt above her knees and knelt on the hard asphalt surface of Avenida Lázaro Cárdenas. Slowly, with total absorption and concentration, she began to crawl.

"You're too old to do this, Lidia," Andre said, but she ignored him. She was oblivious to the passing traffic, to his pleas, to the stones and bits of glass that dug into her knees and hands.

"Stop and rest, for God's sake," he said when she had been crawling for three hours. The palms of her hands were scuffed and bloody, her knees raw. Blood had run down her legs and drenched her shoes.

"It's for God's sake that I do this," she replied.

At midnight, in front of a movie house, its neon sign blinking on and off above them, she fell forward and lay very still. He knelt beside her and wiped her face with a cloth, then lifted her by her arms and carried her to the side of the building.

"This will kill us both," he said. He ripped the sleeves from his sweater and wrapped them tightly around her knees to stanch the flow of blood. There, resting against the wall of the movie house, they fell asleep.

He awoke to the sound of her whimpering. She had begun to crawl on her sweater-wrapped knees. He ran to her, put his hand on her elbow, but she pushed it away, and continued to crawl down the street, giving little cries of pain each time she moved. It was now fully light, and she dragged herself along in the morning traffic. As cars whizzed past, Andre trailed helplessly behind her. Some motorists honked their horns, a few veered to see how close they could come to her without hitting her, but there were also some who stopped their cars and tossed a few coins into the folds of her rebozo and asked if she would say a prayer for them too.

By seven A.M. she had covered the mile and a half from the Palacio de Bellas Artes to Tlatelolco, across the Plaza de las Tres Culturas, past the Church of Santiago and the ruins of the Aztec pyramid, and arrived at the entrance to the Basilica of the Virgin of Guadalupe. In the bright morning light other penitents could be seen crawling along the street, some having been on their knees for several hours, others only dropping to their knees as they reached the wide plaza in front of the basilica. It was not Easter or Christmas, and so there were fewer penitents, mostly the elderly and sick, not all of them able to crawl, some hobbling along with a relative holding up each arm, others dragging themselves forward on crutches.

As Lidia's scraped hands struck the square in front of the basilica, she touched her lips to the stones. "I've completed my penance, Andre. I've reached the Shrine of our Virgin of Guadalupe."

She sat on a pew inside while Andre washed her legs with water.

"You won't be able to walk if we wait here too long," he said. "The skin will stiffen."

"It doesn't matter."

She turned toward him and it startled him to see the way she looked at him, as though she really saw him, as though she knew he was there.

"Why did you stay with me, Andre? You could have gone

to New York, sold your paintings. Why did you let everyone think you had gone back to Europe and died there? You make me so ashamed that I have taken away your life and given you nothing in return."

"No one has taken away my life. If I had wanted to leave, I would have left. No one kept me prisoner." He took her raw hand in his and kissed the blood-stained palm. "I only wanted to be near you," he said. "Is that so terrible?"

They left the basilica and walked through the plaza, holding hands. At the park next to the basilica Andre bought a cup of sliced watermelon for them to share.

"Watermelon is always very refreshing," she said, and smiled at him. They rested in the park for a while, content in each other's company. And when they had tired of the noise and fumes of the city, they began their long journey back to Puerto Morelos.

Cuernavaca

The summer was unraveling. Dee could feel the cooler air of September overtaking them. Elena moved quietly from stove to table on the open veranda, pouring coffee and wiping away crumbs, while her husband worked in the garden, the *clip-clop* of his gardening shears striking a single metallic note.

"I'll be home for lunch," Carlos said. He put his coffee cup down and covered Dee's hand with his.

"Summer's almost over," she said.

"Yes."

Elena stood patiently beside the table, her dark eyes fixed on a broken fingernail on her right hand.

"Paco says that we can stay and work for you now until February," she said when Dee looked up at her. "February is not a good time to open a store. People have spent all their money for Christmas and don't care if they have holes in their shoes."

Paco had been saving money to open a shoe repair shop since Dee and Carlos rented the house the year before. Paco spun tales of leather soles and shoe polish and silk laces as though he were composing sonnets. But the shop was never ready, the machinery never delivered. Elena and he were always going to leave, but when the time came for leaving, they never managed to.

"I'm sorry about the shop," said Dee, "but Carlos and I are happy you're going to stay with us. I may be going back to Los Angeles myself in February, and if you can stay until then, it would be perfect."

Dee walked Carlos to the gate, past the khaki-clad man who stood on a ladder snipping at the sparse branches of the young coral trees. The garden was Paco's. He had built the shrine to Our Lady of San Juan in the garden wall using Puebla tile and porcelain shards and broken bits of mirror. He had planted hibiscus and dahlias where the sun could warm them and hung cages of canaries on the ivory branches of the rose-flowering morning glory tree. His red oxalis bloomed in pots along the terrazzo walk, and rain lilies, white and pink, nodded heads at the dahlias beside the pond.

"Chayo's new movie is here," Dee said as Carlos kissed her good-bye.

"We'll go tonight and see it if you want to," he said.

She watched him cross the narrow street. She had stretched out this time with him, had justified it by beginning her book on American jurisprudence while he directed the Ministry of Security from an office in the fortress that Cortés once occupied.

Time moved slowly in Cuernavaca. The church bells chimed eight times a day, from matin to compline, calling the faithful to prayer. The young people circled one another in the *zócalo* in the evenings. The hibiscus and poinciana and bougainvillea bloomed all year long.

She walked back to the house. She'd have to call Judge Pelletier soon and let him know what she had decided about next year. But there were so many distractions here. The wild beauty of the Borda gardens. The music in the bandstand in the plaza on gentle evenings. The gardenias that released their scent beneath the bedroom window when she and Carlos made love. The bulbs that Paco said would be sprouting green any day, with flowers, he said, that made you dizzy at the sight. And Concepción and Maximilian. Their presence was like a satin purse against her skin, an insistent moan through the trees, urging her to stay.

Acknowledgments

Every historical fact, date, description, and geographical location in this novel is accurate insofar as I was able to determine. Where the historical record is hazy or nonexistent (Maximilian's love affair with Concepción, the location of Guerrero's remains, the existence of Brother Aguilar's book of hours) I made my own record; I imagined the truth of what I could not know. In those cases where fictional characters and events intersect actual ones, I have dreamed only those dreams that do not distort reality.

Guerrero's transformation into a Maya warrior and his death in battle against the Spaniards in Honduras; Brother Aguilar's rescue by Cortés; Charlotte's madness and disintegration at the Vatican; Maximilian's final brave death; Count Sedano y Leguizano's identification as the "imperial bastard of Emperor Maximilian" and his execution for treason; Frida Kahlo's affair with Trotsky, her fierce love for Diego Rivera, for her friends, for Mexico—they are all true and they are also part of my fictional dream.

In a few instances I have altered the chronology of events to fit the fictional narrative (Father Fischer was not present in the Vatican at the same time that Charlotte was), omitted some of the players in the historical drama (to have used every schemer and conniver involved with Maximilian's tragic story would have served no fictional purpose), and telescoped some incidents (the sequence of events leading up to Maximilian's march to Querétaro).

Finally, both Xan-Xel and Florido are fictionalized names for actual villages.

In the process of writing this book I have incurred debts of gratitude to many:

My husband, who, through his love and support, gives me courage. In his editorial comments, his eye is like an eagle's, his heart unerring.

Señor José Dávila of Mexico City, who treats my husband and me like family when we visit and never tires of discussing Mexican history with us.

Señora María Teresa Ceja de Martínez, of Purépero, Michoacan, a friend for twenty-five years, who has given me whatever insights I possess into the lives of the women of rural Mexico.

Also very helpful were Señor Ernesto Alonso, actor and producer of *telenovelas* in Mexico City; Señor Walter Sanches of Cuernavaca, Director of Tourism for the State of Morelos, who told charming stories about Maximilian and Concepción; and Señor Fernando Cusí, divemaster and raconteur in Puerto Morelos, Quintana Roo, Yucatán.

In Guatemala, my thanks to Señores Rafael Sagastume, Rafael Ramírez, and Edgar Vidaurre CH of Servicios Turísticos del Petén for careful driving and expert narrative.

In the United States, I'd like to thank my nephew, Señor Frank Montero, for correcting my Spanish and being a generally wonderful man; also Deacon Arthur Hiraga, of St. Justin Martyr Church in Anaheim, California, for supplying me with material on the Mexican custom of *quinceañera;* and Carrie Marable, librarian at the University of California, Irvine, for unfailing helpfulness.

And to my agents, Charlotte Sheedy and Faith Hampton Childs, who loved the book and saw it and me through its various incarnations, *mil gracias*.

At Bantam, my editor, Genevieve Young, gave me the benefit of all her years of turning manuscripts into books. Her suggestions were invaluable.

A word of appreciation to the librarians at the National Autonomous University of Mexico and to the curators at the Museum of Anthropology in Mexico City for their help. And I'd especially like to mention the curators who have preserved Frida Kahlo's blue house and Leon Trotsky's house in

Coyoacán. Frida's house, with her dolls and shells and trinkets and artifacts, is so unmistakably hers that you half expect to hear her voice. And Trotsky's house, dark and barren of color, remains as it was when he lived there, even to the bullet holes in the wall.

Nina Vida
Huntington Beach, California

THE UNFORGETTABLE NOVELS
by
CELESTE DE BLASIS

DON'T MISS
THESE CURRENT
Bantam Bestsellers